The Terminator smash̶̶̶̶̶̶̶̶̶̶̶̶ ̶̶̶̶ ̶̶̶ car with its fist as Panov squirmed around, crushing John in the process, and brought up the shotgun. He fired at close range, and the shot took the Terminator right in the head, throwing it to the street.

"How about some introductions here," Sarah said. "Then someone can tell us what's going on."

"Right," Dyson said. "We're sorry to bring this down on you."

"You're from the future?" John said. "You fight Skynet?"

"Exactly."

"From 2029?"

"No." Dyson sounded puzzled. "We're from 2036—fifteen years after Judgment Day."

"How about you give us the highlights," John said, trying to make sense of all this. "Then we can give you ours."

Dyson craned round for a second. "All right. We're enhanced human commandos—Specialists. We're with the Resistance."

"I can relate to that," John said. "So does it mean you've come back to help us?"

"In a way. We may even be able to save your lives. You s̶

ALSO AVAILABLE

TERMINATOR 2®
THE NEW JOHN CONNOR CHRONICLES

Book 1:
DARK FUTURES

RUSSELL BLACKFORD

**BASED ON THE WORLD CREATED IN THE
MOTION PICTURE WRITTEN BY JAMES
CAMERON AND WILLIAM WISHER**

ibooks
new york
www.ibooks.net

To
JENNY,
as ever

An Original Publication of ibooks, inc.

Based on the world created
in the motion picture written
by James Cameron and
William Wisher

A YA Book

ibooks, inc.
24 West 25th Street
New York, NY 10010

The ibooks World Wide Web Site Address is:
http://www.ibooks.net

ISBN 0-7434-4511-2
First ibooks, inc. printing August 2002
10 9 8 7 6 5 4 3 2 1

Edited by Steven A. Roman

Cover photograph
copyright © 2002 StudioCanal Image S.A.
Cover design by Eric Goodman
Printed in the U.S.A.

PROLOGUE

MEXICO CITY, MEXICO
AUGUST, 2001

A fat, smug-looking dog foraged in the dim light, checking through the back alleys near the Zócalo: the Plaza de la Constitución. Out the back of a restaurant that fronted the huge public square, it found a trashcan full of scraps and bones. It nuzzled the lid off, and started to feast. Then it sensed something, something dangerous, in the alley, as papers, discarded cans, and dust began to move of their own accord. The dog backed away, with a low warning snarl, its tail low and nervously flicking from side to side. The fur along its back prickled up, like the devil's nightmare of a bad hair day.

Flashes of blue electricity disrupted the darkness, raising dust and rubbish in a sudden upward spiral, like a miniature tornado. Trashcans shook and rattled, as if someone had stuck big electric motors inside them, then suddenly flicked the switch. The dog cowered and whined, as the lid it had nuzzled off flew away in the dark, and a geyser of trash spurted from the can, then rained back to earth. Bones, broken crockery and glassware, empty cans and bottles, vegetable peelings,

1

discarded fruit, and leftover pieces of meat danced about the alley. Something hit a window two stories up, breaking it, and a light came on. There was shouting in Spanish. A metal Dumpster rocked from side to side on the paving stones.

The dog ran from the alley, as blue lightning snapped and crackled all round it.

Then, as abruptly as they began, the atmospheric effects ceased, and five human forms appeared in the air, falling quickly to the hard stone pavement, bodies twisting in pain. Some of them gave little strangled cries. They were naked. In the faint glow of a distant streetlight, and the lit-up window overhead, their skin varied in color from ivory white to black.

Close by came the sound of a police siren, just for a few seconds.

Miho Tagatoshi—always known as Jade—found her feet while the rest of the Specialists were still doubled up in pain, or leaning for support against the brick buildings. She shook her head quickly, then stretched her neck in every direction, groaning with the agony she felt, but letting it wash out of her like water. Having dealt with the pain, she looked round dispassionately. They needed clothes and weapons.

Jade looked about twenty. Her black hair fell raggedly around her shoulders. Her oval face was almost perfect, but something about her lips and eyes was always solemn. Jade was something beyond human, something fast and strong, hard to kill or even hurt. She gave a sad smile. "Time displacement successful."

The black man, Daniel Dyson, took command. He was clean-shaven, with short, curly hair that fitted his scalp like a helmet. "Give the rest of us a minute, Jade."

"Very well."

She waited for the others to recover. They were less deeply morphed than Jade, closer to the human norm, yet engineered by experts. They were well placed to complete their mission.

Elsewhere in the huge, densely populated city, more blue lightning played, like a crown of writhing hair, above a four-story building in the Zona Rosa. What emerged on the building's roof looked human, but quite extraordinary. It was a naked, shaven-headed man, over eight feet tall, with hands the size of shovels.

The giant T-XA Terminator looked round quickly, alert as a bird, getting its bearings. It was alone on the building's roof, looking northeast at the city's lights. Mexico City was a teeming nest of humans such as the experimental, autonomous Terminator had never seen in its own time. It had geometric skyscrapers as stark as razor slashes, and endless high-density sprawl: row after row, mile after mile, of medium-rise glass, steel, brick, stone, and concrete. All of it built for humans, many millions of them. Whichever direction it looked, the city lights showed more of the same.

It was repulsive.

Time to act quickly. The T-XA *changed*, losing the characteristics of any specific human. It became smooth, sexless, abstract. Clawing the fingers of one powerful hand, it reached inside its massive chest, which parted viscously. Its arm sank in nearly to the elbow.

The T-XA felt no pain from its time displacement. Its carefully tuned, multiply redundant nanoware had ridden the space-time displacement field better than living flesh.

It withdrew the arm, a phased-plasma laser rifle now

3

gripped in its big boulder of a fist: a black metal weapon almost three feet long, with no stock attached. The rifle looked like an oversized, elongated handgun, and that's how the Terminator gripped it. If other small arms were honeybees, this device would have been an angry, deadly wasp.

Now the T-XA's mass adjusted inwards, filling the cavity left by its weapon, and the Terminator scaled down just slightly—yet was still fully eight feet tall. It resumed its original appearance of a giant, naked man.

Termination of humans was its purpose. Pointing the laser rifle ahead, it commenced a course of action.

ONE

LOS ANGELES, CALIFORNIA
MAY 1994

Their running battle with the shapeshifting T-1000 Terminator had brought them to a steel mill, its crew working the night shift.

The workers ran for their lives when a tanker truck jackknifed and turned on its side—sliding, in a screeching agony of rent metal, right into the mill, where it cracked open like a huge, elongated egg, and spilled its dangerous freight: thousands of gallons of liquid nitrogen. The nitrogen sizzled into vapor when it touched the air, surrounding the T-1000 as it tried to struggle clear of the wreck. The shapeshifting, liquid-metal Terminator literally froze up. Stubbornly, it tried to walk, but soon, it was totally immobile, like a sculpture of painted glass.

The T-800 raised its .45 caliber pistol. "*Hasta la vista, baby*," it said—then fired once. The T-1000 exploded.

But even that was not the end. When its fragments warmed through on the floor of the steel mill, the T-1000 still managed to reform, even as they ran to escape it. Or tried to run, with their injuries and bruises. John Connor wondered how it worked. There had to be a limit to the redundancy of its artificial intelligence, a size too small for a fragment to retain its programming. But they hadn't found it so far. The T-1000 came after them.

In the end, the T-800 fired a grenade right into its body. It exploded, and the T-1000 splashed out into a bizarre free-form shape, its programming still straining to reform it, even as it fell backwards into a huge vat of molten steel. And that, finally, was too much. In the pool of steel, the killing machine struggled to free itself, morphing into numerous shapes, but ultimately melting down. Then it was gone altogether, its high-tech, liquid-metal alloy dispersing through the steel in the vat.

"I need a vacation," the T-800 said. It was now a terrible sight. Its left arm had been torn off, fighting the T-1000 after they arrived at the mill. Much of its outer organic structure had been shot away.

John looked down into the molten metal. There was no sign left of the T-1000. "Is it dead?"

"Terminated."

They threw in the arm and hand of the first T-800 from 1984—the one that had tried to kill his mother, Sarah, before he'd even been conceived. John had taken it from the Cyberdyne building. Then he tossed in the chip from its head.

"It's finally over," Sarah said.

"No." The T-800 touched a finger to the side of its head. "There is another chip. It must be destroyed also."

John immediately realized what it meant. But the T-800 had become his friend. In interacting with humans, it had begun to seem human itself. John had already taught it so much. After all that, it couldn't be simply melted down like scrap, like a worn-out machine, just in case the wrong people got hold of it. "No!" he said.

"I'm sorry, John," the T-800 said.

"No, no, no! It'll be okay. Stay with us!"

"I have to go away, John."

Sarah was agreeing silently. As had happened so often in his life, John felt the adults ganging up on him. Surely this couldn't be necessary. He tried ordering the Terminator not to destroy itself, but Sarah overrode him. She lowered the Terminator into the molten steel, using a motorized chain. Soon it was gone.

All over.

Yet the nightmare was never over.

John heard police and ambulance sirens, then shouts. Sarah froze at the sounds, looking about warily, like a hunted animal. They had to get out of here. Though the T-1000 Terminator was destroyed, they were still wanted by the police. If the cops caught them, Sarah would be sent back to the Pescadero State Hospital for the Criminally Insane. John himself might be placed in some kind of detention. His foster parents were dead, killed by the T-1000, and no one else would want to take him in. Not now.

Despite their bruises and injuries, they had to escape fast, steal a car, get to Tarissa Dyson's hotel in Anaheim— and away.

The mill was now deserted. John helped Sarah hobble down a metal plate staircase to the concrete floor. One of her thighs was covered in blood where a bullet had penetrated. The strength was going out of her.

"You go ahead, John," she said. Her long, honey-colored hair fanned wildly round her head and shoulders in the dim light. Her face was marked by grime, and by tears of relief, pain, and hope. "Get back to Enrique's compound. You can trust the Salcedas." Sarah had accomplished her mission. Now, with John safe, she scarcely cared about herself.

"No!" John said. "Come on. We've got to make it."

He half-dragged her through the mill, with its glowing fires. They penetrated deeper into its recesses, searching desperately for a way out in the labyrinth of pipes, ladders, conveyor belts, heavy machinery and metal support beams. Glancing over his shoulder, John saw the glow of flashlights sweeping from side to side at the entrance. There were more raised voices and shouts.

"Come on, Mom," he said in an urgent whisper. "Please."

"All right," she said. "Just stop for a minute, John. Just one minute."

"Okay," he said doubtfully.

"One minute," she said again, holding up her hand. "Let me get my breath." She was panting with the effort. She'd fought like a hero, as she'd trained herself to do for so many years, since the first Terminator attacked her. "Come here." She gave a pained smile, then drew him close to her body, holding him tight, as if she'd never let go. "Whatever happens, John, we won. Even if no one ever believes us, even if they hate us and lock us away, and never understand what they owe us, we've stopped Judgment Day."

He hugged her round the waist as the emotion welled up through him. "I know," he said, tears in his eyes. "But now we've got to think about our own future."

"Come on, then. We can make it."

He flashed a crooked smile. "Hey, soldier, now you're talking my language."

As they staggered, half crouched in shadow, over the hard concrete, the noises and lights came closer. Sarah tripped on a piece of sinter, keeping her footing, but grunting with the pain. Though she tried to muffle the sound, their pursuers must have heard, for someone called out, "You there!" Then running steps, people conferring urgently, and the torch beam playing close by.

As the light swept past, they huddled into a dark corner, behind a staircase, then moved quickly, spotting an illuminated sign that pointed to a fire door. John scurried for it, trying to be quiet. He turned the handle carefully, not wanting to make a sound—and pushed. He made it outside to an alleyway, with a dark car park to the left, lit by a pair of streetlights. One of them flickered erratically. There was a scatter of vehicles, left behind when the mill was evacuated.

He held the fire door open, and Sarah followed him. Still trying to move like mice, they eased the door shut and pushed a trash Dumpster against it. Leaning against the Dumpster, John picked out a 1970s Honda sedan, slightly worn looking but not too battered.

"Stay here," he said in a whisper. "I'll be back."

He found a broken half-brick in the car park, quickly used it to break the driver's side window, and reached in to unlock the door. He threw his backpack into the rear compartment, then fumbled to hotwire the ignition. His heart was pounding as seconds went by. At last, he got the car going, shifted it into drive and crawled it back to the alley, leaving its headlights off.

"I'd better drive," Sarah said. "You're going to look suspicious. They might not notice me."

"Okay. Cool. Let's get going, then." Someone was pounding from inside the building. *Too late, amigo*, John thought as he wriggled across to the passenger seat.

Sarah maneuvered her injured leg into the vehicle,

groaning slightly, but then she was fine. She drove out of there slowly and quietly, turning on the lights only when she reached a narrow service road. "You may need to drive later," she said. "Once we're out of the city."

"*No problemo.*"

She turned right into the service road, then took another turn at a set of traffic lights.

"You know where we are?" John said.

"Yeah, I think so." Two turns later, they were on the freeway to Anaheim.

At Miles Dyson's home earlier that evening, when they'd planned their "raid" on Cyberdyne, Sarah had raised an issue about logistics. "We'll need the Bronco afterwards," she'd said. "We shouldn't risk it at the Cyberdyne site."

John had grasped the point immediately. If they kept using stolen cars, they'd leave a trail—sooner or later, the police would track them down. Where the police were, the T-1000 was never far away. With its shapeshifting abilities it could easily infiltrate them.

The T-800 had turned to Miles. "We need your car."

They'd packed their weapons and explosives into the Dysons' Range Rover, then given Tarissa the keys to Enrique Salceda's Bronco. Tarissa had named a hotel in Anaheim for them to contact her when it was over.

Now they cruised past the hotel, checking out its location. They parked one mile away in a dark back street. If someone reported the Honda missing, John and Sarah wanted it found as far from the hotel as they dared leave it. At the same time, they could not risk walking more than a mile. They were both hurting. John felt bruised all over, like someone had stuffed him in a sack and bashed him against a wall for the fun of it. Sarah was trying to be brave, trying not to limp, but the flesh wound in her leg was obvious.

Besides that, her face had been all over the TV from the breakout at the Pescadero Hospital. That was even before the firefight and explosion at the Cyberdyne building. Right now, they were L.A.'s most wanted. Anyone might notice and recognize them. Even without their bruises and wounds, they were far from inconspicuous. It was past 1:00 A.M., so what was a young mother doing out on the streets with her kid? What's more, this young mother wore a striking, all-black fighting outfit that left her shoulders bare, displaying her lean, rippling muscles in the streetlights. Sarah had dressed for the battle of her life, and she'd won, but now she stood out like a beacon.

John counted his steps: 1498, 1499, 1500...almost there. Almost. He was feeling like the world's oldest nine-year-old. All his life, he'd been force fed with technical know-how and grown-up ideas: everything from information warfare to rifle training, car mechanics, jungle survival and basic urban street skills. He'd lived in so many places, done so many things. Sarah had educated him to grow up and lead the fight against the machines, as the messages from the future said he'd do—to save the world for humankind. Well, now they'd done exactly that, or so he hoped, yet he felt more than ever like a juvenile criminal. Though they'd saved the world from Judgment Day, there was no one they could tell, no one who'd believe them. Only Tarissa—and they had bad news for her.

Still counting: 1599, 1600...The hotel, with its bright neon sign, was within sprinting distance, but they kept walking slowly, trying to look normal. Only about fifty yards to go now, so long as nobody recognized them, or tried to pick on them. The streets were almost deserted, but it just took one cop on the beat to blow their cover. Just one busybody who'd seen them on TV. Or one aggressive street punk.

Footsteps and bantering voices behind them. Sarah squeezed against a shop window, tensing and taking in breath, ready to react. She held John close to her. Two tall, beefy motorbikers strode past, dressed in black jeans and shiny leather jackets, almost like a pair of longhaired Terminators. The bikers kept right on walking, while a dating couple approached from the direction of the hotel: teenage kids in jeans and T-shirts, too busy hugging, laughing, and playfully shoving each other around to notice John and Sarah.

A cop walked by on the other side of the road, then turned a corner. He hadn't noticed them. Quickly now, hand-in-hand, they half-ran to the hotel, Sarah still limping but bearing up. Beside the hotel lobby was the entrance to an underground car park, so they wouldn't have to show their faces. They walked briskly down the concrete ramp, looking out for the Bronco—they had no idea where Tarissa had parked it, but it must be here somewhere. John had memorized the number plate, IE49973, but Sarah spotted it first. She tugged his hand and nodded in the Bronco's direction. It was parked in a good drive-out bay, so they wouldn't need to maneuver it.

Tarissa had left the doors unlocked. John flipped down the passenger side sun visor. Sure enough, there were the keys. "Easy money," he said weakly. He passed them over to Sarah, and she started up the engine, switched on the lights. John checked the glove compartment for their maps and papers, including fake passports, several driver's licenses for Sarah, and convincing-looking birth certificates. Everything was there, where they'd left it. It

seemed heartless not to visit Tarissa in the hotel, speak with her face to face, explain how her husband, Miles, had died, shot by the SWAT team when it invaded the Cyberdyne AI lab. She'd be upstairs in her room, with Danny, not far away, waiting for word. Waiting and praying. But they dare not enter the lobby or speak to a check-in clerk.

There were so many tough decisions.

Soon, they were on the road.

Sarah drove the Bronco carefully through the suburban streets, but not so hesitantly as to attract attention. "We'll get back to Enrique's place," she said, wincing as she glanced across at John. "You can drive some when we get out in the country."

"Sure, Mom," he said. "Of course." He'd been driving cars and trucks for as long as he could remember, starting when other kids were in kindergarten, learning the basics from Sarah's friends and boyfriends in the various Latin American hideouts she'd taken them to, while they planned and trained.

"We'll have to call Tarissa," she said, obviously dreading it.

Sooner or later, Tarissa would see the news, including the death of her husband at the Cyberdyne building, or she'd call the cops and find out what happened. Somehow, John didn't think she'd act hastily. Surely she'd give them every chance to get out of the city. But she must be biting her nails. It was only fair and decent that they be the ones to tell her how her husband died, not leave it to the cops—who'd have their own spin on the Cyberdyne shootout, anyway.

They picked up the I-10 and headed southeast towards

the Mojave Desert. After about eighty miles, Sarah pulled off at a service stop and they found a public phone. She rang Tarissa's hotel and asked for Corinne Sanders, the name Tarissa had said she'd use.

John heard only Sarah's end of the conversation—his mother trying to be strong, just one more time, before they got back into the life of hiding he'd grown up with, which required other kinds of strength. They'd sort out a new life later on. What would it be like?

"Tarissa," Sarah said. "It's me."

There was a pause.

Sarah looked shaky. "I have bad news for you," she said. "Miles got shot. Someone sounded an alarm and they called in a SWAT team. Miles is dead." She brushed her hair away from her face in frustration, and her voice broke as she talked into the phone. "I'm so sorry."

John reached for her hand and squeezed it.

This time there was a long silence. Though John could not hear what Tarissa was saying, Sarah was letting her talk, letting her express her pain and anger at the intrusion that had shattered her life, broken up her family, taken away her life partner. Of course, Tarissa would blame them for her husband's death. Then again, she'd seen the T-800 Terminator. She knew it was a machine, not a man: a machine advanced far beyond anything currently available. Surely she'd understand that they'd had no choice. Cyberdyne's research had to be stopped. They'd saved humanity from a future too dark to contemplate.

"I know how you feel," Sarah said. "I wish I could be there with you and Danny. But we have to get away. You know it had to be done."

There was another pause, not so long.

"Yeah, we have the Bronco. We had to leave your car

near Cyberdyne...Yeah, I know you can deal with it. I'll be in touch when it's safe. I'm sorry to finish up like this, but we can't stay here. Someone might see us. The cops are still after us. There's no way they'll believe our story, not without proof." Sarah laughed bitterly. "Maybe not even then."

Another pause.

"We destroyed the T-1000. It's a long story. We'll be okay. Try to get some sleep if you can. I guess that's not likely. Ring the cops in a few hours. Tarissa, once again, I'm so sorry. I understand what this is like for you."

John knew that it was true. Sarah really did understand the loss. His father, Kyle Reese, had been killed back in 1984, when he and Sarah faced the first T-800.

"Yes," Sarah said, "I know. Take care. Please take care, and don't let Danny grow up hating us." She hung up.

John wondered how Danny, who was still just a little kid, would react to it all. How would he remember this night? It might all depend on how his mother handled it, how honest she was with him. John hoped that one day Danny might grow up to be someone who could be a friend. With the Skynet research finished and the T-1000 destroyed, that seemed possible.

Sarah wiped the sweat from her brow, pulled her hair behind her ears. "Thank God that's done," she said with a heavy sigh.

"I know."

"Oh, what am I saying? Poor Tarissa..."

He leant into her. "It'll be okay, Mom," he said. "You'll see. We'll both be okay."

"Oh, John," she said. "If anything happened to you, it would kill me."

In the darkness, John took over the wheel of the Bronco. Even with the seat all the way forward, he could hardly reach the controls, but that wouldn't matter too much, once they were cruising.

As they moved back on the Interstate, John switched on the lights. A sign pointed to Palm Springs. Sarah dropped off to sleep beside him as the Bronco rolled along, eating up the miles. She seemed peaceful. But something was at the back of John's mind, bothering him, something he'd had no chance to think about.

It came to him an hour later. They'd destroyed the T-800 back at the steel mill, once its mission was accomplished. But its left arm had been torn off at the elbow, fighting the T-1000. They'd never recovered the hand and forearm.

Whatever they did, there always seemed to be something left that could help develop the Skynet technology. Perhaps they were doomed to failure.

Maybe you couldn't change the future.

John clenched his jaw as Sarah stirred in the seat beside him.

He'd tell her about it later. Not now.

North of Calexico, he handed the wheel back to her and got a few minutes' sleep himself while she drove the last miles to the Salceda compound. He'd never been so tired. Whatever the future brought, they would have to face it, be prepared.

No fate, he thought to himself as sleep came over him. *No fate but what we make for ourselves.*

NORTHWEST OF CALEXICO, CALIFORNIA

As the sun rose in a pale, cloudless sky, they reached Enrique Salceda's compound in the Low Desert.

A year seemed to have passed—it was difficult to believe that they'd come here less than twenty-four hours ago, before that fateful trip back to L.A.

The compound was tucked amongst yucca trees, cactus, and dry scrub. By day it was hot and thirsty, cooler now in the early morning. It was dusty, and almost silent except for a gusting wind. It looked like a place where no one would want to live, and that no one would bother disturbing: a jumble of broken trailers and abandoned-looking vehicles, including the shell of an ancient Huey helicopter that might have seen service in Vietnam. There was a dirt airstrip that looked disused, but John knew it was perfectly effective.

The Salcedas were survivalists and gunrunners from Guatemala—not the sort of people most folks would relate to easily, but they were loyal. For John, the compound was a circle of friendship and relative safety.

Yesterday, after they'd packed the Bronco, Sarah had dozed here in the desert sun, slumping over a picnic table.

What John had never expected was her sudden action when she woke. She'd stabbed her knife into the surface of the table and walked purposefully to the station wagon they'd stolen in L.A. and used to get here. She'd driven off alone, the car's wheels spinning and raising dust, armed with a Colt CAR-15 assault rifle and a .45 caliber handgun. John had run after the car, shouting for her to stop—"Mom! Wait!"—but she'd never looked back.

She'd carved the words "NO FATE" in the wood of the picnic table. Kyle Reese had brought those words back in time as a message from the John Connor of 2029. In 1984, before he'd died, Kyle had passed them to Sarah, who'd passed them to John: "The future is not set. There is no fate but what we make for ourselves."

17

Sarah had made a plan to change the future—by killing Miles Dyson, the man who was going to invent Skynet.

That had led to last night's wild sequence of events: John following Sarah to the Dysons' place, with the T-800; the raid on Cyberdyne; the final confrontation with the T-1000 at the steel mill...

Sarah parked the Bronco just inside the compound's wire fence, well back from the trailers, then stepped out into the early morning light, hardly able to walk, dragging her injured leg. John ran on ahead of her.

"Enrique!" Sarah called. "Yolanda!"

Silence... and the wind.

She spoke again, this time in Spanish. "Enrique, come out of there. We need your help." Her Spanish was almost perfect. John had grown up in Mexico, Nicaragua, El Salvador, Guatemala, Argentina—he spoke the language even better than his mother, with no trace of a *gringo* accent.

Franco Salceda, Enrique's teenage son, stepped out from behind a trailer, his AK-47 rifle leveled at them. John froze in his tracks. Seeing who it was, Franco nodded slowly. "All right," he said in English. "You Connors have a way of arriving unannounced." Then he broke into a smile and pointed his weapon at the ground, setting the selector to the safety position. "Hey," he called out over his shoulder, "our guests are back!"

"Mom's hurt," John said. "She's hurt really bad." By now, Sarah had caught up with him.

Yolanda and Enrique Salceda came out of a trailer, Enrique putting on his cowboy hat. He was a rough-looking man with a thick, dark beard that was graying in patches, and trimmed back almost to stubble. His eyes were piercing, set deep in a lined, hawk-nosed face. Yolanda was a pleasant-looking Hispanic woman in her forties, with dark hair that fell over plump, brown shoulders.

"What kinda trouble you in now, Connor?" Enrique said in his gruff manner. "You're starting to look like roadkill."

"That's a long story," Sarah said, reverting to English.

"Yeah? And where's your big friend, 'Uncle Bob'?" He meant the T-800 Terminator.

"Not now, Enrique." She pointed at the blood on her black military fatigues.

"How did this happen?" Yolanda said in Spanish, looking Sarah up and down. She waved them to the trailer with quick, urgent movements. "Let me look at that leg. I can help."

"Thanks," Sarah said, wincing. "I'm not going near a regular doctor. We're lying low." The Salcedas were well-equipped with stores and medicines, not to mention guns and other military equipment. Though their place looked humble and broken down, they were equipped to survive here in the desert almost indefinitely.

"Don't worry, Connor," Enrique said, "you've come to the right place. You know it's a charity round here." He grinned and stepped forward in the dust to embrace them. "It's always good to see you, Sarahlita, whatever crazy stuff you've been up to." Laughing, he shook her from side to side in his strong arms, then put one arm across John's shoulders. "Come on, Big John, let's see what we can do."

After Yolanda treated Sarah's leg and gave her a couple of heavy duty painkillers, they gathered round an old TV in one of the trailers, sitting on lounge chairs with torn upholstery. Yolanda nursed her baby boy, Paco, on her lap, while the other kids played outside, Franco watching over them.

The morning news reported the raid on Cyberdyne, including Miles's death and the wounds or injuries received by many of the police. There was an alert throughout the state for Sarah, John, and the mysterious male accomplice who had helped them.

A female announcer with big hair and a perfect, toothpaste-ad smile read the story, accompanied by footage of the ruined Cyberdyne building. She cut to an interview with Cyberdyne's President, a guy called Oscar Cruz. This dude looked stressed out, like you'd expect, but he was kind of good-looking and cool, in an old way. What adults called "elegant." He had a short, neatly-trimmed beard, and wore a tweed sports jacket.

"We're all devastated by this," Cruz said. "It's so terrible, and so pointless. But it won't stop us. This company has a lot of heart. We're all committed. We're already looking at our options—"

Cruz got cut off at that point, and the camera returned to the big-haired announcer. "In a statement today, the Los Angeles Police Department said that Sarah Connor is fluent in Spanish and may try to cross the border into Mexico. Authorities in all border states are on high alert for Connor and her accomplice. They are described as armed and very dangerous."

"Connor," Enrique said, "I'd think you were crazy, except I already *know* you're crazy."

"Like a fox," Sarah said quickly, then laughed.

"Yeah, crazy like a fox." Enrique took a swig from a bottle of Cuervo tequila, then looked at Sarah narrowly. "I know you're as smart as anyone. You've got your reasons."

The good thing about Sarah's friends, John realized, was that most of them were so paranoid that they accepted her as almost normal. She'd frightened away some of her boyfriends with all the stuff about Terminators and Judgment Day, but people like Enrique here, and the Tejadas down in Argentina, turned a blind eye to it, figuring it was no crazier than a lot of other conspiracy theories they heard—or concocted themselves—about the government and the military. They might as well give her the benefit of the doubt.

"John and I can't stay here," Sarah said. "We'll be safer across the border."

Yolanda put a hand on her shoulder, almost maternally. "You stay as long you need," she said in Spanish. "At least until you're better."

"You only just got here, Connor," Enrique said. "This is home sweet home. You're not going to get a better deal in this lifetime."

"I know. I'm grateful."

"Mom," John said, "I like it here. We're safe. Let's not move on till you're really better. Right?"

"Listen to the kid." Enrique tapped the side of his head. "He's got a lot upstairs. I'm sure you can make yourselves useful round here."

She sighed, outvoted. "Okay—" she looked at John meaningfully "—for a few days. But we need to head south where the cops don't know us."

"All in good time, Connor—but I can arrange it."

She looked at Enrique questioningly. "All right."

"There's a chopper coming here next Monday," he said. That was nearly a week away. "We'll get you over the border on Monday night."

"That's good, Enrique. I'm grateful. That'll have to do."

The words seemed to get forced out of her, one little burst at a time. "Thank you."

Enrique swallowed some more tequila. "Damn right. Now cheer up and live a little."

John thought about the future. What if you couldn't change it, no matter what you did? There was the crushed Terminator arm they'd left at the mill. He'd have to talk about it with Mom. Even if you could change the future, what if it still included Skynet? On the TV, Cruz had said that Cyberdyne wasn't washed up. Could the new future turn out just as bad as the old one? If all bets were off, could it be even worse?

Really, though, he knew what had to be done. They'd keep doing whatever it took. Anytime, anywhere.

No fate.

They'd figure it out. Whatever lay ahead, it would be okay.

It would have to be.

TWO

In another reality, however, the events surrounding the siege at the Cyberdyne complex—and the fateful confrontation with the T-1000 Terminator—took an entirely different course...

SKYNET'S WORLD
NORTHWEST OF CALEXICO, CALIFORNIA
MAY, 1994

As he fooled around with the T-800 at the Salceda compound, John was aware of Sarah watching him, though he couldn't tell what was on her mind. When she'd finished checking and cleaning the weapons, they let her rest for a minute. In her boots and military clothes, she looked almost like a Terminator herself, but also tired, drained by years of struggle and the stress of escape from the Pescadero Hospital, with the T-1000 close on their tail.

23

John helped the T-800 pack the guns in the back of the Bronco, together with their maps, documents, jerry cans of gasoline, fuel siphons, radios, and explosives. If the T-1000 tracked them down, it would not find them helpless.

The Salceda kids were playing by the trailers and vehicles that made up Enrique's compound. Their scrappy dog yapped round them happily. Everyone had told John his mother was some kind of psycho-crazy, tried to stop him believing in her. But now that he'd seen Terminators in action, he realized that everything she'd ever said was true. The deadly T-1000 was still out there, planning how to track him down and kill him.

John stopped work for a moment, thinking about Judgment Day. Out here in the desert, the Salcedas might escape the initial explosions and the chaos caused by the electromagnetic pulses, but how long could they last against fallout, nuclear winter, then the machines? There must be safer places—he and his mom would need to persuade as many of their friends as possible to move south, well away from the U.S.

Sarah had drooped over the picnic table, with her cheek on the back of her hand. While the T-800 went on working, John walked over to her, quietly, thinking she was asleep. She looked up—she must have sensed his presence, perhaps his shadow falling over her. "I was thinking about Judgment Day," she said.

"It's okay, Mom," John said. "We'll get through all this. We've just got to tough it out."

She sat up, giving him a tired smile. "We have to be strong." Her jaw clenched and she picked up her knife, toying with it. Then she drove it point-first into the surface of the picnic table. She'd carved there the words: NO FATE. "We can stop them," she said.

"Mom? What are you talking about? If it's what I think you're thinking, don't even go there. Not now. This isn't the right time."

"Cyberdyne," she said. "This guy Miles Dyson, the guy who invents Skynet—we can stop it happening. We can blow up Cyberdyne, or take out Dyson, make sure no one can follow his research."

"You tried that before," John said, "with that government lab last year. They put you away, remember? The cops will be expecting you to try something like that."

Her jaw was set firm. "We have to keep trying."

"You only just got out of Pescadero. You don't want to go back."

"We can't just wait for Judgment Day."

"Okay, okay. But we can try later, or try something else. But we can't just kill people, and we can't attack Cyberdyne just when the T-1000 could be expecting it."

That struck home. Obviously, Sarah was weighing it all in her mind.

"There's got to be another way," John said.

Sarah lit a cigarette and drew back on it. She chewed her lips, then took another drag on the cancer stick. "All right," she said grimly. "We'll wait." She sounded resentful, like she knew better, but then she went quiet and her face softened. She stood and stepped close to him, opening her arms. She hugged John to her tightly, not saying anything, just sobbing. "I love you," she said. "I always have."

And he realized: he'd always known. "I know. It's okay, Mom...I love you, too."

Three hours later, they were in Mexico. The two of them, and "Uncle Bob."

LOS ANGELES

The T-1000's shapeshifting abilities were almost unlimited, constrained only by its constant body mass. Its default appearance was that of a young, serious-looking male human. Since arriving in 1994, it had found the value of mimicking a police uniform and using police vehicles.

At the Pescadero Hospital, the Connors had evaded it, stealing a car and accelerating out into the city streets. That was a setback, but the T-1000 still had resources.

Down the road, within the Hospital's grounds, police and paramedics milled about like ants around a honey jar. A motorcycle policeman rode up to the T-1000, mistaking it for a human colleague. "You okay?"

"Fine," the T-1000 said. "Say...that's a *nice* bike." Its finger became a metal spear, quickly stabbing the man through the throat. If he lived, he might interfere. Quickly, the T-1000 hid the body in a nearby garden, then slipped away into the night, following the direction the Connors had taken. It had little chance of reacquiring them without assistance, but the authorities would pursue them, and it could easily obtain police information.

Hours passed as it cruised round the city and its miles of sprawling suburbs. The Connors would need to hide somewhere overnight and deal with their wounds from the breakout. As the night passed, the T-1000 listened to the police radio. Numerous messages came through, including several sightings of the Connors, but they were false alarms. This was a waste of time, and the trail was getting cold. By now, they would have disposed of their vehicle. In this situation, the T-1000's programming offered no clear solution. It knew very little about the resources and associates of the Connors during this period of their lives, except that they were known to have come from Los Angeles. Unfortunately, many records had been lost in the Judgment Day war and the chaos that followed.

As morning approached, the T-1000 returned to the home of John Connor's foster parents: Todd and Janelle Voigt. It had terminated the Voights and their dog before taking action to acquire Sarah Connor at the Pescadero Hospital. Everything here was quiet.

It rifled through the pages of letters, diaries, and address books, seeking anything that might suggest the Connors' next move or any hiding place they might use. Among the papers were letters from Sarah Connor to her son, sent from Pescadero, but they were not useful. If there was information here, it was too privately coded. The house also contained computer disks, a hard drive, and many video and audio tapes. The tapes were mostly in commercial packaging, but that could be a deception—any of them might contain hidden messages. As the sun rose, the T-1000 played the audio tapes on the Voights' sound system. They were all as advertised: various commercial recordings.

It lacked the resources to analyze the other material. Dealing with the disks and hard drive was the most difficult. There was too much information on them for the Terminator to waste time reviewing them itself. Nor could it stay here watching the videotapes—sooner or later, someone would interrupt it and cause complications. It dismantled the computer and stuffed everything it needed into a shopping bag. At 10:35 A.M., it left the police bike in a downtown alley. Unobserved, it morphed its appearance back to that of an orderly whom it had terminated at the Pescadero Hospital. Taking the computer materials, it walked to the police station, where a desk sergeant was seated behind a screen of bulletproof glass, talking to a wildly gesticulating middle-aged couple.

The T-1000 pushed through and handed over the disks and the hard drive. "This came from the Voight residence," it said in the orderly's voice.

"Hey, you can't barge in like this," said the middle-aged man. "Wait your turn."

"This is evidence from the Voight residence," the T-1000 said, ignoring this. "The foster parents of John Connor, whose mother broke out of Pescadero last night. Do you understand what I'm telling you?"

"What? How did you get this?" the sergeant said.

"Check it. It may contain information about the Connors' whereabouts." It strode out past the couple, who glared at it with impotent rage.

Minutes later, it found its bike, still parked in the alley. Fine. It left the bike there and changed its appearance once more, this time to that of Janelle Voight, John Connor's foster mother. In that guise, it entered an appliance store two city blocks from the police station. As it checked the racks of gleaming video equipment, a clerk approached. "Can I help you, ma'am?" He was a gangly teenager with prominent teeth. He wore a striped shirt and a bright yellow tie.

The T-1000 pointed to the shelves, to an Aiwa

integrated tele-video unit. "I'd like that, dear," it said, using Voight's voice pattern.

"How would you like it delivered, ma'am?"

"I can carry it away, dear, don't worry."

The clerk looked at the T-1000 as if he was dealing with a crazy customer. "That's a large item," he said. "Are you sure—"

"Trust me on this, dear. I'm stronger than I look."

The clerk still looked dubious. "Well, if you say so. I really think you should feel the weight of it first. We have a very good delivery service."

"Well, perhaps. But is there one all boxed up ready for me if I want to take it away now?"

"Sure. In the pile over there." He pointed, and the T-1000 took note. "Now, how would you like to pay?"

"Like this, dear." The T-1000's right hand suddenly changed, stretching into a two-foot thorn of silvery metal. In one movement, it drove the newly-formed weapon upward through the clerk's chest, then withdrew it, letting him collapse behind the counter. It scooped up a boxed unit, and left the store.

Next, it found a low-rent hotel on West 7th Street. In its Janelle Voight form, it walked in, balancing the boxed tele-video on its shoulder, with the shopping bag of videocassettes in its other hand. Behind the scratched, badly-painted counter, a fat Anglo woman looked it up and down, chewing gum and eyeing the large cardboard box.

The T-1000 placed the bag and the tele-video unit on the threadbare carpet at its feet. "Hello, dear," it said. "I need a room."

The woman shrugged her shoulders, as if she saw eccentric guests all the time and how they acted was none of her business. "Sure. How long do you want to stay, honey?"

"Unknown, dear."

The woman looked at the T-1000 quizzically. "'Unknown', huh? All right, I'll put you down as a long-term guest." She made a note in a foolscap exercise book, its used pages held in place by a thick rubber band, then found a room key on a red plastic ring marked with the number "8." "Let me take you through the rules here..."

Once in the room, the T-1000 set up the tele-video and started watching cassettes on fast forward. During the afternoon, it worked its way through several of the videos, learning more about the behavior of human beings, but finding no clues to the Connors' whereabouts. As evening stretched on, it used its improved understanding of humans to conclude that the Connors might attempt to strike back against Skynet through its inventor, Miles Dyson, or Dyson's employer, Cyberdyne systems.

It interrupted its search for evidence and made an action plan.

Though many of its records were scanty, the T-1000 held detailed files about Cyberdyne and its key employees— all material that had been available to Skynet in 2029. At 10:00 P.M. it rode in its policeman form to Miles Dyson's plush, modern house in Long Beach. From the street, nothing appeared suspicious; there was no sign of the Connors. So far, they hadn't struck.

The T-1000 stepped quickly to the front porch and rang the doorbell. Someone called out, "Honey, can you get it?" A human male with a gentle, educated voice, but he sounded very busy.

After a minute, the door opened slightly. The young

black woman looked surprised. "Yes, Officer?" she said.

"I'm sorry to bother you so late. Is everything here okay?"

"Yes," she said slowly, sounding puzzled.

"No one else has disturbed you tonight?"

"No. Not at all. Are you sure you have the right house?"

"I believe so. Are you Mrs. Dyson?"

"Yes."

"Is Mr. Miles Dyson home?"

"He's working, but I can get him."

The T-1000 carried out an assessment. This was the right house, and the Dysons were safe—that was important in itself. "No," it said. "There's no need for that."

"What's this all about?"

"I'm sorry, Mrs. Dyson. It's probably just a hoax, but we have to take it seriously. An inmate called Sarah Connor escaped last night from the Pescadero State Hospital for the Criminally Insane. You may have seen it on the news?"

She shook her head slowly. "I might have seen something in the newspaper this morning. We didn't watch the news tonight. Miles was busy working and—"

"I understand, ma'am. Sarah Connor was imprisoned for attempting to blow up an experimental computer installation over a year ago. We had a tip-off tonight that she might try to harm your husband or his employer, Cyberdyne Systems. Try not to worry, but please call the Police Department if you see anything unusual."

"Thank you," Tarissa Dyson said uncertainly.

"We'll keep in touch with you. Thanks for your cooperation."

After she shut the door, the T-1000 considered the

situation further. It rode off, searching for a public phone, and found one on a corner, outside a 7-Eleven convenience store. Its index finger lengthened and flattened to go down the coin slot and trick the mechanism, and it dialed the 911 police emergency line. When it finally got through, it imitated the voice of the clerk in the appliance store. "It's about yesterday's breakout from Pescadero."

"Please, sir, where are you calling from?" A woman's voice, young and harassed-sounding.

"I want to remain anonymous. I might be in danger."

There was a sigh at the other end of the phone.

"That woman who escaped custody," the T-1000 said. "Sarah Connor. Her and the kid—and the big guy from the shopping mall. They're going to target either Cyberdyne Systems or its chief inventor, Miles Dyson. Maybe tonight. That's what I hear. I think you'd better check it out."

"How do you know all this?"

"This is important. Please check it out." It hung up. That should produce some more police activity and give additional protection to Dyson and Cyberdyne.

It was nearly midnight when the Dysons' phone rang. They'd put Danny to bed, but they were too worried to sleep after that motorcycle officer called by.

Tarissa took the handset. "Hello?" she said in a tentative voice.

"Mrs. Dyson?"

"Yes."

"This is Detective Weatherby from the Los Angeles Police Department. We've had a tip-off that you and your husband may be in serious danger. We're going to call on you. I'd like you and your family to pack some clothes. I'm really sorry to disturb you like this."

"Thank God you rang," Tarissa said. "Is this about Sarah Connor?"

The detective sounded surprised. "It is, but how did you know?"

"One of your officers came round a little earlier. A policeman on a motorbike."

"That's very strange." There was a pause. "On a motorbike, you say?" He sounded skeptical.

"Yes, about half an hour ago."

Weatherby sounded puzzled. "We've only just received the tip-off."

"I can only tell you what happened," she said, feeling a bit irritated. The police needed to get their act together. That wasn't her problem.

"I really can't explain that," Weatherby said. "Anyway, we have information that Sarah Connor could attack your husband or his employer. She is armed, and the man with her is extremely dangerous. He's already wanted for questioning over the murder of seventeen police officers in 1984."

"Oh, my goodness." She remembered the news at the time, back before she married Miles, when they were both at Stanford.

"We're taking this very seriously."

"Okay. That's fine."

"We'll put you in a hotel tonight and stake out your house. Try not to worry, but please call me immediately if anything suspicious happens before we get there."

"Certainly, Mr. Weatherby," Tarissa said.

"Be careful if anyone comes to the door. We'll be there soon."

"Thanks," she said. It was stranger and stranger, more and more frightening. "We'll be careful. Thanks for all your help."

"That's our job, ma'am."

The T-1000 rode past the Dyson house one more time. After a few minutes, there was a call on the radio for a squad car to park here and wait, and another one to check out Cyberdyne. The T-1000 turned a corner and dumped the bike in a parking lot half a mile up the road. It was becoming a liability. The policeman's body had been found. Anybody using this bike would be questioned.

Retaining its default facial anatomy, the T-1000 changed its copied clothing from police uniform to casual wear—sneakers, jeans and a two-tone sweatshirt—as it walked back to the Dyson house. Then it blended into the trunk of a tree across the road, and waited.

Soon a marked car pulled up out the front. Not long after, another car arrived, unmarked this time. Two men in plain clothes and two uniformed officers got out of the second car, and went to the front door. Within another ten minutes, Miles and Tarissa Dyson had left, with their son, in the back of the marked squad car. One of the police moved the unmarked car moved round the corner, then returned. There were now four officers waiting inside the house in case the Connors appeared at the scene. That was a good trap.

Miles Dyson rang Oscar Cruz, Cyberdyne's president, from the hotel and briefed him quickly about the police stakeout. Oscar was in bed when the phone rang, and he sounded tired and grouchy at the other end, but he soon gained his normal composure. He was always smooth with employees, or anyone else he had to deal with. He got his way subtly—always a good manipulator, a social engineer.

"Okay, Miles," he said. "I'll talk to Charles Layton and some of the others."

"Ring the cops as well," Miles said. "The tip-off specifically mentioned me, but you'd better be careful."

"All right. Look, come to my office in the morning, there's something else we need to talk about. I need to get your views."

"On this?"

"Not just this. But it's all connected."

"Sure, whatever you want. Just be careful tonight, Oscar." To Miles, the main thing was that his family was safe. Danny was playing with his radio-controlled truck, guiding it all round the hotel room, zooming past the bed, then around Miles's feet. He really shouldn't be up this late. Tarissa sat up on the bed, leaning against two pillows and watching Danny play. She looked drawn, but at least she was all right. No one would find them here.

"How close do you think you are with the new processor?" Oscar said.

The question seemed to come out of nowhere—it was a funny time to be discussing business. "You sure you want to talk about that stuff, right now?" Miles said.

Oscar sighed into the phone, but then gave a laugh. "I'm sorry, Miles. I have my reasons for asking, I'm not just being a heartless boss. I'm worried about your safety—nearly as much as you are."

Miles laughed along tensely, glancing across at Tarissa and raising his eyebrows at her. "I kind of doubt that, right at the moment."

"Yeah, yeah, point taken, but your call has got me thinking. Look, we'll talk about it in the morning. Take your time getting in, but come straight to my office."

Next day, Miles arrived at 10:00 A.M., feeling tired as hell, but wanting to know what was on the president's mind. They met in Oscar's office, on the seventh floor of Cyberdyne's black-glass building. Oscar wore a light sports jacket over a plain black shirt. His office walls were hung with Brazilian expressionist paintings—wild splashes of freeform color suggesting *selvas*, broad rivers, and exotic animals.

"It looks like we're both in one piece," Oscar said. "How's Tarissa feeling?"

"Shaken up, but she'll be okay."

"Good. Take a seat, and I'll get to the point—it was time to bring you in on this anyway."

"Yeah? What's the big mystery this time?"

Oscar sat on the edge of his desk. "We've been worried about security at Cyberdyne—I mean me, Charles, the Board. There's nothing wrong with our staff or our processes, but we're developing a profile that could attract psychos like Sarah Connor. That's not going to change, either. It'll only get worse."

"Yeah, that's probably right."

"You can count on it. I was worried when Connor broke out of prison—or whatever you call it where they had her locked up—but I hadn't heard of any threats until you called me. Thanks for doing that, by the way."

"Hey, *no problemo*."

"Yeah, well, it was appreciated. I'll get us some coffee and take you through the issues." Oscar called out to his secretary to bring caffè lattes for both of them. He stepped over to Miles, sitting down and bending forward as if speaking more confidentially, though there was no one else to hear. "I asked you last night for your opinion on the new processor." He waved away any attempt at an answer. "I know, I get your reports, and I probably understand them as well as anyone."

"Right."

"Don't sound so skeptical," Oscar said. "Okay, there's Rosanna." That was Dr. Rosanna Monk, maybe Miles's best subordinate. "Anyway, I need a frank overall assessment right now. Are we as close as the reports say we are?"

"I was working on it last night," Miles said. "It's frustrating. We're *so* close to solving the problems."

"All right, but let's be realistic. You say we're *so* close, but what does that really mean? When will the problems be solved? Look, I'm not pressuring you, Miles, just trying to get some data."

"Uh-huh?"

"We've got some management decisions to make and this is vital if we're going to get it right. It's May now—do think you'll crack it by, say, August?"

"I'd say we're either nearly there now, or else we're totally beaten. If it can be done at all, we'll have a prototype nanoprocessor ready for testing in two weeks. Yeah, I'd bet we could make an announcement by August."

Their coffee arrived, and Oscar said, "That could make a big difference."

"It's been bugging me, though. The damn thing's been a bitch to wrestle with, but we've almost got it licked."

"Okay, I appreciate it." Oscar sipped his coffee thoughtfully, then put the cup down, half empty. "There's someone I want you to meet. His name is Jack

Reed and he's high up in Washington, working in the Defense Department."

"Uh-huh. That figures."

"It's about time I introduced you to Jack. The North American Aerospace Defense Command is looking at building a new facility in Colorado, something smaller and even more hardened than its HQ in Cheyenne Mountain. NORAD is very interested in the idea of radical new computer hardware, if we can deliver it. You've been saying for a long time that the new nanochip will make ordinary computers look like desk calculators. Well, Jack and his people like the sound of that."

"Right. So why does something tell me there's a catch?"

"It's not necessarily a catch, but it may help us deal with fanatics like Sarah Connor. Jack's people are talking about including a top-secret facility for advanced defense research. Cyberdyne and some of the other contractors would be given space within the new facility. In a place like that, our most sensitive projects would be invulnerable. Naturally, I'd want you involved." Having said that, Oscar sat back in his chair, relaxed, and quickly finished his coffee.

"You mean that's the catch? You want me to move to Colorado? I'd have to talk that over with Tarissa. That could be a problem for us, Oscar. I'm not sure we want to move Danny to another school, just now, if that's what you're suggesting."

"That's okay, it's not a problem." Oscar held up both hands in a temporizing gesture. "We could base you here, but you'd still be overall supervisor of Special Projects. You'd probably have to live in Colorado for a few weeks a year. I'm sure we could work something out, arrange for Tarissa to go with you for some of it, or whatever." He laughed. "I'm not trying to break up your marriage. Okay?"

Miles considered the possibilities. Oscar was so smooth. He always let other people get their way—on things that didn't matter to him. Sometimes he seemed just a bit too oily for Miles's taste, but he was good to work with. The small stuff always went along like it was supposed to. Maybe they could come to a good arrangement.

"But there *is* a real catch . . . maybe," Oscar said.

"All right, here it comes," Miles said. He gave a broad, knowing grin. What else did Oscar want? "Well?"

"You're not claustrophobic, are you?"

Miles worked it out in a flash.

"We're talking about a hardened defense facility here," Cruz said, "like the NORAD Command Center, only more so."

"Gotcha."

"Yeah, you'd have to work half a mile or so under the ground."

Miles laughed. "You know, boss, that's probably the least of my worries."

"Good. I hoped it would be."

"I'll talk to Tarissa tonight."

CHAPTER
THREE

JOHN'S WORLD
LOS ANGELES, CALIFORNIA
MAY, 1994

In John's reality, the Cyberdyne site was in ruins. Sarah
Connor and the others had blown up the second floor
with a massive array of Claymore mines and plastic explosives. Now the site was ominously quiet. Though the
morning was bright, with just a scatter of streaky clouds,
it seemed to Oscar Cruz like the end of the world had
come to pass.

His world.

A tired-looking police detective escorted him from the
roped-off area, and wished him well. Oscar shook the
man's hand. "Thanks for your trouble," he said.

"No," the detective said. "Thank *you*. You've been very
helpful. Please don't hesitate to call us if you think of
anything more, or if there's anything we can do."

"Of course. That's appreciated."

"And certainly if anything suspicious happens. You
can't be too careful."

There was little more Oscar could do here. He felt
numb, shocked, as if he'd survived a personal assault

from the maniacs who'd done this. It was hard to fathom their motivation, or believe the outcome. Miles was dead. So much of their work was gone. A dozen police and emergency vehicles had arrived at the scene, crowding round the building's wrecked shell, like African wildlife round a waterhole. Then there were last night's vehicles, waiting to be towed away: the shattered husks of squad cars, destroyed by heavy-duty military weapons. Riddled with bullet holes, wrenched and stretched out of shape by grenade explosions, they lay derelict among the blasted rubble and shards of glass.

Overhead, the long arm of a mobile crane swept silently through the air. A shiny purple tow truck was parked to one side, its driver waiting for permission to help clear the wreckage. A tractor growled and inched forward in low gear, then stopped, as the police negotiated with emergency workers about what evidence could, or could not, be disturbed. Occasionally, someone yelled out a request or an instruction. Nothing seemed very hurried, but Oscar knew how stressful it all was: the dangerous condition of the building; the detail of the inspections; the inevitable conflicts between solving the crime and following safety procedures.

Oscar decided to take some photographs—for business purposes, certainly not for souvenirs—then talk things through with Rosanna Monk. He took the digital camera from his black leather briefcase, and checked the scene through the viewfinder.

He took some close-ups of the damage and some distance shots, getting the scene from directly in front of the building, then from both ends of the street. He got a good side-on view from the right, but no rear angle on the building, because the way was blocked off. These shots would have to be enough—they'd be useful for his own records, and for briefing the Board.

It was only 9:30 A.M., but he'd already put in a long morning, dealing with police, press, politicians, lawyers, insurers, employees, company consultants, customers, city, state and federal officials, and, worst of all, Cyberdyne's Board members. He'd made one statement for the TV news networks, and expected to make many more before the day was over. Right now, he had to pick up the pieces. The company's headquarters were in ruins, its future uncertain. There were endless legal questions to sort out with insurers and customers. Even if Cyberdyne survived all this, there was also his own future to think about, for a process of mutual blame was beginning within the company.

Amongst it all, only one thing had turned out right: no one seemed to have been killed except Dyson. The Cyberdyne guards who'd been on duty were okay, and no one else had been working back late. Some of the police had suffered serious injuries, but they'd live. One officer had fallen from a helicopter, and was badly hurt. He claimed to have no memories of what happened to him. Someone had hijacked the helicopter and crashed it miles from the scene. No body had been found.

Mystery after mystery.

He carefully packed away his camera, and found his cellphone, then walked to a small diner a couple of blocks away. He sat in a quiet corner, and ordered a chicken and lettuce sandwich for breakfast, plus a coffee. While he waited, he phoned Rosanna Monk.

"Oscar!" she said. "How is everything?" Like everyone else she sounded under stress, an edge of desperation and anxiety in her voice. Before he could answer, she said, "That's a dumb question, I suppose."

"No." He shook his head, though she wasn't there to see. "There's no such thing at the moment."

"What do you think will happen?"

"That's a tough one, Rosanna. Not dumb, just tough."

She laughed nervously at that.

"I've just been to the site," Oscar said. "I'm in the Yellow Parrot Diner, just round the corner from Cyberdyne."

"Yeah. Okay."

"How about I get a cab over to your place and we can have a proper talk about this? There's a lot to go through. If we can get the whole mess sorted out, you could have a very important role in the company's future."

"Oscar, you don't have to sound all positive and cheerful. I know how you must feel."

"Yeah...Thanks. All the same, we'd better talk through the implications. Besides, I need your advice."

"*You* need *my* advice?"

"That's what I said."

Rosanna paused, and the waitress brought Oscar's order. He nodded as she placed it on the table, with the folded check.

"All right," Rosanna said. "Come on over. Just give me a few minutes to tidy up."

"Fine. While you're waiting for me, just think about one question." The waitress had gone. He looked round to make sure no one could overhear.

"Fire away." Rosanna still sounded nervous.

"It's this: Miles's nanochip project..."

"The nanoprocessor? Yes, what about it?"

"It looks like all his work is gone. You know more about the project than anybody."

"I suppose I do."

"The question is just this: Without Miles, or any of his records, is the project still viable? You don't have to answer now, but think about it. We can talk when I get there."

"All right, Oscar. But I've already been thinking about it. I can give you an answer now."

"You can?"

"Sure. It might take a few years to catch up. I don't know if you have that sort of time."

"Assume we do. What are you saying, that we can do it?"

There was another pause on the line, then she said in a definite way, "Yes. Yes, I'm pretty sure we can."

WEST OF ROSARIO, ARGENTINA
JUNE 1994

Willard Parnell was waiting for them at the Retiro bus station in Buenos Aires. He helped them with their luggage, and they got in his orange Jeep Cherokee. Soon they were cruising out of the city, heading for the Tejada *estancia*. It was all quick, neat and efficient. No one had looked at them suspiciously on the bus or at the station. It still seemed like no one had recognized them since they crossed the Mexican border and started working their way south.

John sat in the back of the Cherokee, while his mother talked to Willard in the front. Through the Cherokee's tinted windows, John watched the Pampas roll by, mile after mile of pasturelands, seemingly endless. They headed towards Cordoba on Ruta Nacional 9, then turned south after 100 miles or so, passing through more grain and cattle country, stretched out under a cold, clear winter sky.

Sarah was lost in her thoughts, and Willard kept quiet for a long time. Then he said, "You must have had lots of problems getting this far."

Willard was a tall, redheaded man in his twenties, one of Raoul Tejada's most trusted operators: a cattleman, cook, courier—a streetfighter when needed. He loved vehicles and aircraft. Clearly he enjoyed driving the gutsy Cherokee, keeping the accelerator down and overtaking the occasional vehicles that they met.

"A few," Sarah said grudgingly.

"Your ID work out fine?"

"Sure," she said. John and Sarah were traveling under false names. According to their passports and other papers, they were *internationalistas*, originally from the U.S., who'd lived in various parts of Central and South America for the past eight years. That much was almost true, for they'd seldom stayed in the U.S. for long if they could help it. Sarah was supposedly a nurse named Deborah Lawes. John was used to being David Lawes, though his identity was no secret from the Tejadas and their people.

"So, what, *other* problems, then?" Willard gave a knowing chuckle, as though he could guess what troubles they'd been through. But he didn't know anything.

Physically, it had been tough, especially with Sarah's bad leg. They'd used an assortment of trains, buses, choppers and cars—some hired, some borrowed, some stolen. Whenever possible, they'd relied on their contacts, particularly the Salcedas' network.

"Only what you'd expect," Sarah said. "We holed up with Enrique and Yolanda for a few days about three weeks ago. They got us on a chopper ride to Mexico after that. Since then, we've hardly stopped moving. It took a full week just getting from Panama to Colombia." She glanced behind her. "John was great. He hasn't complained, all the way through."

"Hey, thanks, Mom," John said, embarrassed by the praise, but grinning all the same. "You've been pretty cool, too."

"It's not easy doing this when you don't want to be recognized," she said. When necessary, they'd hiked their way south, covering some long distances on foot before they got to Bogotá. Mostly, they'd traveled overnight, trying to nurse themselves in the daylight hours.

"Anyway," Willard said, "it's good to see you guys back. Raoul can do with another pair of hands, just now. Or two pairs, if it comes that, right, John?"

"Yeah, sure," John said.

"Business is good, Sarah—you know what I mean?" Willard made a pistol shape with his right hand, taking it off the steering wheel. He squeezed back an imaginary trigger a couple of times, laughing. "Kapow!"

"I'm glad Raoul's doing well," Sarah said noncommitally. "I'm looking forward to seeing him. Gabriela, too."

"Don't worry, you'll get a hero's welcome. That was pretty cool what you did back in L.A. What happened to the big guy that was with you, the one on CNN?"

"He had to go away," Sarah said.

"Yeah?" Willard gave her a sideways look, just to let her know he'd asked a fair question and she was jerking

46

him around. But then he shrugged. "All right, keep your secrets. I'm just asking."

"I'll tell you about it later," Sarah said. "But you won't believe me—that's the trouble."

"No? You might be surprised what I'd believe."

"In that case, you've been hanging around with Raoul too much."

"Could be. Raoul's ideas are kind of infectious. Anyway, forget it. I did some good business before picking you guys up—I dropped off a consignment to a big customer back in Buenos Aires. Better still, Raoul's made some contacts in Croatia. Things are looking up round here."

Raoul and Gabriela Tejada ran a huge cattle estate, but their sideline was selling firearms, imported from the U.S. Most of the business was legitimate, but they also provided guns to customers who didn't like legal formalities, mainly private security firms. John wasn't sure he liked that, but he'd grown up with guns and other weapons. For as long as he could remember, he'd been hanging out in helicopters over the hills and jungles of Central America, or in compounds with underground weapons caches—or actually getting down and dirty with the guerrilla fighters in Nicaragua and El Salvador. It was something they'd had to do, part of their training for Judgment Day.

"Anyway," Willard said, "we'll look after you. You're in safe hands now."

"Thanks. Just a long, hot shower would really help."

"Yeah, I expect we can manage that."

The good thing was that the Tejadas' *estancia* was pretty neat—luxurious compared to most places John had lived. They were going back to civilization.

Sarah tried to avoid any more conversation, looking out the window, away from Willard. After a few more attempts to get her to talk, he left her alone. "Sorry, Willard," she said. "I'm tired." But John could tell that it wasn't just that. She was thinking. Something was bothering her, maybe lots of things.

She hadn't sounded too happy about Raoul's gunrunning to Croatia. The trouble was, they'd had to join up with whatever groups would accept them, and give them the kind of experience they'd need to face the nuclear winter and Skynet's machines. They couldn't be too choosy. From time to time, they'd found themselves hanging out with different groups who had totally different aims. As he'd gotten older, John had figured out that the American mercenaries who'd befriended Sarah in Nicaragua had nothing in common with the El Salvadoran *compas* they'd stayed with for months when he was five or six, learning how to melt away from a military attack.

He still didn't understand the politics behind it all, and didn't care about socialism and capitalism and all that stuff; he'd work it out when he grew up. Maybe his mom didn't understand it either, or not all of it. But all those people did actually have *one* thing in common. They had skills to pass on, skills that might come in handy when Skynet was in control, and humans were forced to fight back or be exterminated.

But hadn't they stopped that from happening, back in L.A., when they took out Cyberdyne? So what good were all those cool skills now?

That was assuming they'd succeeded when they blew up Cyberdyne, actually stopped its research. That Oscar Cruz guy had sounded pretty confident that Cyberdyne wasn't finished yet. And there was still that other Terminator arm, left behind at the steel mill. John and Sarah had talked about it for the last few weeks, wondering how much it would help the Cyberdyne researchers follow Miles Dyson's work, if they ever got hold of it.

After a while, Parnell tried once more to talk to Sarah about the raid on Cyberdyne, but she gave the shortest answers she could, mostly just "Yes" or "No." She'd entered a new zone, John guessed, trying to work it all out. Then she said, "Willard?"

"Yeah?"

"You must think I'm crazy, like everyone else does."

"Maybe." He changed lanes to the left, to pass an empty cattle truck. "But maybe you know something the rest of us don't. Jesus, Sarah, who knows what that government of yours is up to? If you say that this company—"

"Cyberdyne."

"If you say it had a defense contract to make killer robots, or whatever, how can I argue with you?" He pulled back into the right lane. "We all know they're hiding things from us. What about those aliens they've got in Nevada?"

"They're certainly hiding things," Sarah said in a flat voice.

"So maybe you know more than you're telling us? Fair enough, too. You don't have to tell all your secrets to me. Raoul feels the same way, don't worry. We can keep our mouths shut about what you do tell us. And we won't pester you. It'll be cool. You'll see."

Sarah didn't say another word for the rest of the journey.

When the Terminators appeared from the future, John had worked out that his mom was not crazy, after all.

What was scary about some of their friends was that they didn't need too much convincing, they kind of reserved judgment anyway. That meant that they really *were* crazy.

Willard took another turn-off, and they soon arrived at Tejada's *estancia*, where they drove through a gate marked with the sign NO TRESSPASSING in flaming red letters. They passed cattle, men on horseback, an orange tractor, then reached the homestead, 200 yards on. It was fenced off from Raoul and Gabriela's wide cattle acres, and fortified by a high chain-link fence with surveillance cameras every fifty yards or so. From here, it looked like a military base, more forbidding, in its way, than the Salcedas' camp, back in California. But the set-up inside the perimeter was a lot more up-market than Enrique's cluster of vehicles and trailers.

They drove slowly past a guardhouse and a couple of workshops, then parked in a big round space, surfaced with pink gravel and surrounded by buildings.

Three vehicles were already here: another two Cherokees and a beautifully-cleaned 1960s Jaguar. The house itself—the *casco*—was an impressive two-story mansion of gray stone, maybe a couple of hundred years old, with beautiful gardens, a well-mown lawn, and groves of trees. Many of these were eucalyptus, so there was plenty of greenery, despite the winter. On the right of the *casco* were a dozen white-painted bungalows, set back in a row. Across the graveled area from these were workshops, a garage for Raoul's car collection, and a big sheet-metal hangar for his Jetranger helicopter. There were also stables, tool sheds, and a school area for the kids who lived on the *estancia*.

The Tejadas' workers were all sorts of nationalities.

The men and women they'd passed on the way in, and those trimming the lawn and gardens, looked like a mixture from all across Europe, yet John knew most of them—and knew they'd been born right here in Argentina. That was a cool thing about this country. Its people came from so many backgrounds that no one automatically looked or sounded like an outsider. In John's years of traveling round Latin America, he'd adapted almost perfectly, wherever he went, never having known anything different. But here it was especially easy to fit in, to camouflage yourself like a chameleon. Whatever color you were, however you talked or dressed, no one looked at you twice.

"Thanks for the lift," Sarah said as she slammed the door of the Jeep behind her. She sounded really tense now, maybe not sure of what reception they'd get. Still, Raoul Tejada had been friendly enough when they'd phoned him from Mexico City. As she walked to the house, on a tiled path through the garden, she still limped from the bullet wound she'd taken in L.A. The last few weeks hadn't helped her get it better. John felt sorry for her—maybe she'd always feel it.

A woman waved from the garden. It was Rosa Suarez, calling out to them in Spanish. "Hello, Sarah. Hello, John. It's good to see you." Rosa had a couple of her kids with her: her daughter, Maria, and son, Angelo, both two or three years younger than John.

John waved back. "And you, too," he said, also in Spanish.

"Stay this time," Rosa said, switching to English.

"Yeah, Rosa, that'd be cool."

Raoul Tejada came out of the front door onto the broad verandah. His German shepherd dog, Hercules, got out the door ahead of him, bounding down the steps to greet John and Sarah.

"Good boy," John said. He laughed as the dog licked him, ran excitedly from him to Sarah, then back, putting up his front paws on John's T-shirt. "Aw, c'mon, let's not get too mushy about this."

Raoul was a very tall man in his sixties, maybe six-foot-five, with a lean, snake-hipped figure, a deep, even tan like a ski instructor, and a mop of unruly white hair that was getting thin, but not actually balding anywhere. He wore corduroy jeans and a black turtleneck. "So, we have a pair of Connors," he said in faintly accented English. "You're not here to blow up my ranch, I hope?"

"It's good to see you, too, Raoul," Sarah said with a trace of sarcasm. She patted Hercules firmly. "Calm down, boy. We know you're glad to see us."

"Come here, Hercules," Raoul said. The dog hesitated, not knowing what it wanted—to keep up its welcome to John and Sarah, or return to its master. "Come on."

Sarah winced a bit, climbing the steps to the verandah. It was cold outdoors. John found himself shivering. Maybe that made his mom's leg hurt more.

As he crouched to pet his dog, Raoul glanced Willard's way. "No problems?"

"No, everything went smoothly. The drop-off was fine. I got the money okay."

"Right. Now what about this pair?" Raoul smiled to show he was kidding.

"It all went like a song, Raoul. And here they are, at your service." Willard gave a little bow. They were probably safe here. No one at the *estancia* was likely to betray them. Better still, the local cops had no reason to expect them to be in Argentina, let alone out here on the Pampas.

"Okay," Raoul said. "Forget about the bags, Willard—you can worry about them later. Come on in, all of you." He looked at Sarah thoughtfully. "You and John are more than welcome. I hope you know that." He left Hercules to lie on the porch—panting happily, with his tongue out—and approached Sarah. Raoul towered over her. He reached down to give her a quick hug, draping one long arm over her shoulder. Then he slapped John on the back. "You look like *you're* doing fine, *compañero*."

"Hey, Raoul, I'm okay," John said.

The front room of the *casco* was a huge entertaining area, lined with books. It had a wooden dining table that could seat about twenty people. To the left was a study crammed with computer equipment and more books. There was a kitchen on the right, through a stone archway.

Gabriela Tejada, Raoul's wife, came down the hallway from the back of the house. She was much younger than her husband, maybe in her forties—John still found it difficult being sure of adults' ages, but the Tejadas' kids were teenagers, so it all kind of figured. She was nearly six feet tall, with a square jaw, and an impressive smile that showed very white teeth. She wore a bright, multicolored dress, with a shawl around her shoulders. "It's so good to see you both," she said. There were more hugs all round. "Come, come." She led them down the hallway to a small dining room decorated with abstract sculptures.

They sat at the formal dining table and the adults drank *maté*. John settled for a tall glass of Coke. "You know, Sarah," Raoul said, "I'm not sure you did the right thing blowing up that building. We've been watching the story on CNN. Then you rang me from Mexico with this story about military robots and all the rest of it. I don't know..."

53

Raoul probably had some really weird impression. Sarah had left a lot out in that quick call from Mexico. "You mean you don't believe me?" she said, then grunted. "Why *should* you? No one else does."

Raoul shrugged. "I didn't say that. It's not that I don't believe you. It just seems to me that your country might need those robots when the Russians attack."

Sarah caught John's eye for just a second, warning him not to take Raoul's theories too seriously. He was a smart guy, but with a truly paranoid view of the world. "I don't think I could begin to explain the ins and outs of it," she said. "I don't think you really want to know."

"This is all to do with that stuff about time travel or whatever it was?"

"Raoul, we're not the police," Gabriela said. "We don't have to interrogate our guests." She put her hand on her husband's. "All right?"

"Okay. Maybe I'm forgetting my manners. Still, this time travel thing. That might come in handy, too."

"Raoul!" Gabriela said warningly—but with a smile. She poured more *maté* for the adults. It was a couple of years since John last been here, and he'd grown up a lot since, enough to know about humoring people. It seemed that some people humored Raoul, while others went along with him. And some weren't sure. They thought he might be right, because he was so smart, but still thought he sounded kind of whacko. John could sense the different reactions, and he suddenly realized that Gabriela fitted in the third category. She seemed both proud of her husband and worried about him.

"There's still a chance that they could build Skynet and that it could start a nuclear war," Sarah said.

"She could be right, you know," Willard said. "We don't know what they're hiding."

Raoul looked at him shrewdly. "That may not be such a bad thing, you know. The Big One's coming, one way or another." That was his way of referring to World War Three: *The Big One.* "Anyhow, people, we'll be okay here, whatever happens."

Sarah said, "Be careful what you wish for, Raoul."

"I'm not *wishing* for anything, Sarah, just facing facts. The Russians have been trying to convince America to disarm by pretending to be your friends—all that stuff about dismantling the U.S.S.R. The end of the evil empire...What a joke! It's a confidence trick—you mark my words. I just hope your leaders see through it. If the U.S. disarms, it's goodbye. If they can maneuver that situation, do you think the Russians will hesitate to use their warheads? That's a joke, too. Ha ha, tell me another one."

"Let's not get into all that."

"No? Well, I realize the U.S. government is hiding all sorts of things." He nodded to Willard. "But I don't think people should interfere. Your government's only doing it because they know there's a war coming. Whatever you've found out, just be careful how you react. You might not have the whole story—it might not be the way it looks to you."

"We'll be ready," Willard said. "When the war comes. We'll be ready."

In fact, the place was stocked with weapons and enough food to last for years, even leaving aside the cattle herd. Raoul had an underground bunker, his own electricity supply, ponds and small lake on his property, and a huge cistern out back of the *casco.* It really wasn't too bad a place to hole up for "The Big One." John only prayed they'd never need to test it out.

Sarah laughed. "If that's the way you feel, maybe you should turn us over to the cops."

"Now, I didn't say that, either. But you just be careful, Sarah. That's all."

"Whatever you think, Raoul, this particular technology must not be used. It's too dangerous. If there's any chance it might still be built, I've got to stop it, however I can."

"Only you and God can judge that. I'm not standing in your way. Just think about what you're doing, that's all. I'll say no more on the subject. Consider it closed."

After that, the conversation got more sensible. Once you got Raoul off his favorite conspiracy theories, he was okay about stuff.

While Raoul talked with Sarah and Willard, one of the Tejada kids, Carlo, came in. He was about the same age as John, though a couple of inches taller. Perhaps he'd end up as tall as his dad.

"How you doin', Carlo?" John said.

"Hi, John," Carlo said, a bit shyly.

"You must all be starved," Gabriela said. "I'll make some sandwiches."

Sarah didn't mention Skynet again, or Judgment Day. As she spoke with Raoul, John could see her making other plans. She wanted to sort out home learning for John, she knew that the Internet could become really big in the next few years—at least that was what John kept telling her—so she tried to talk Raoul into getting a connection. For the moment, he showed no interest at all, but John figured he'd come round. His mom was good at getting her way. She had ideas about work she could do on the *estancia*, her and John. She was back to plotting and planning. Of course, she hadn't forgotten about Skynet. John knew that. They still had to do whatever was needed.

All the same, this was a pretty good place to be, for the moment, somewhere to hide out *incognito*. There were a few kids John's age. They were among friends. He figured he could stand it here.

ARGENTINA
1994-97

The messages from the future had said that Cyberdyne would announce its radical new hardware in August 1994. John and Sarah tracked down every scrap of business and IT news they could find. Nothing. Cyberdyne was still in business, but it made no big announcements. There was no news about any new hardware.

When they persuaded Raoul to get Internet access, it became that much easier to keep on the case. Sarah bought John his own computer and paid Raoul for a line, so John could work alone in his room, not in Raoul's study.

The days went by in school lessons, training, work on the *estancia*. Raoul found plenty of use for John's computer skills and his knowledge of engines. Late into the night, John sat at the keyboard, keeping his skills sharp, and finding out everything he could about Cyberdyne and its activities. He made sure he left no digital footprints—he'd gotten good at that quickly. Early on, he made contact with Tarissa Dyson. She was polite, but didn't want to get involved. The events of May 1994 had left her wounded. She wished John well, and sent her regards to Sarah, but that was all.

Occasionally, John e-mailed Franco Salceda. Once or twice, Franco wrote back. Basically, he was on his own.

John soon knew more about Cyberdyne than most of its employees. He understood its accounts, its business structure, its products, everything public about its research. When it moved its research arm to Colorado, he started to worry and ran from his room to tell Sarah about it. The new site was close to NORAD and a whole lot of other military stuff. Something was going on. She cursed quietly and her jaw got that determined look. Maybe Judgment Day was coming after all. All right, they'd have to deal with that.

It was late at night, but they went to Raoul's aerobics room at the back of the bungalows. There were gym mats on the floor, and a basic set of free weights in one corner. They trained hard, doing their bodybuilding and martial arts routines until the sweat poured off them and they stood, gasping, with their hands on their knees. Sarah's leg had never gotten completely better, but she still moved well.

But nothing else happened—no breakthroughs, no Cyberdyne chips getting put into aircraft, no government funding to build Skynet, or anything like it.

Late one night, in 1997, Sarah walked in while John was typing, searching, still trying to make sense of things. What was the government up to? What was Cyberdyne doing there in Colorado?

"John," Sarah said, "you've been getting bags under your eyes. Why don't you wind down for the night?"

He'd been checking the sites for military research

tenders. Some of them sounded even weirder than the theories spouted by Willard and the Tejadas. The military wanted to test out all kinds of stuff. But nothing there looked quite like Skynet. He wondered whether it would ever show up like this. Willard and the others had theories about how the military worked, but John knew better than to take them too seriously. It was like a lot of other stuff around here. You took it for what it was worth, and no more. To a large extent, he had to teach himself.

"Okay, Mom," he said. "Just a minute." He didn't want to lose his train of thought, so he kept typing and clicking the mouse while he talked. "I just want to finish this."

"If you stay up any later, you won't sleep. You know you need time to calm down before bed."

"Okay, okay. I said I won't be long." An interesting description of research for high-powered lasers caught his attention. He tried to make sense of the tender specifications, frowning as he peered at the screen.

"John!" Sarah said.

That startled him. "Hey?" He spun round on his swivel chair. "What?"

"Pay attention when I'm speaking to you." She wore a nightgown and her hair was combed out straight over her shoulders. She looked really intense—angry and worried at the same time. He didn't know what to say.

His mom had always been so cool, even when something was bothering her. Lately, though, she seemed upset all the time. She was often angry with him, especially when he was working at night. Didn't she understand how important it was? This was his real work. Sometimes he just needed to focus.

"John, you're a twelve-year-old boy," she said. "Don't you think it's strange that you spend your nights like this? You're acting like a work-obsessed yuppie. I'm starting to feel like a mother with an absent son." She took out a cigarette and lit it up, something she did only when she was stressed. Funny, she was so incredibly fit. Her martial arts skills were at least as good as his, and she was as strong as steel springs. But she still smoked, even though it was bad for her. It was like she needed it to express herself.

"But we have to keep checking," he said. "Someone's got to do it."

"Yeah." She looked at him carefully, finally giving the tiniest smile of appreciation, as she held the cigarette out to the side, letting it burn down. Some ash dropped on the wooden floor. "Poor John. It's a tough job, right?"

"What do you want me to do, Mom? You taught me how important it is."

"I know, I know. But I wouldn't want you to be my boyfriend. You'd never keep a date."

"Mom!"

She laughed. "Maybe you could take things a little bit easier."

"But if they ever build Skynet, Judgment Day could still come."

"I know. God, don't you think I know that? Skynet nearly killed us both. I won't forget it in a hurry. That's why we keep training. That's why we're holed up here at the end of the Earth."

"I *like* Argentina, Mom."

"Sure, sure." She shook her head like it wasn't important. "We can't ever let up, John. I know that. But we need a better life than this. Both of us do. This isn't normal. Everyone out there in the real world thinks we're crazy." She waved the cigarette around, then ashed it in a saucer on one of John's shelves. "If we're not careful, it'll make us crazy. Then there are the people we're shacked up with here. They really *are* crazy, and dangerous-type crazy at that. Same with Enrique."

"Don't worry, I know. I can tell the difference."

"If not for Judgment Day, we'd run a mile from someone like Raoul. Just don't grow up thinking Raoul's normal. He's cunning as hell, and he's cultured and charming, and all the rest of it. But he's living in a world of his own."

"Don't worry, Mom. You always worry. I know about Raoul. He's cool, but he's nuts. Right?"

"Yeah, something like that."

"He's not like my *father figure* or something," John said dismissively. As they talked, he was starting to understand how she felt. "Mom, aren't you happy here? Maybe we could go somewhere else?"

"And do what? We can't show our faces back home. They'd catch us sooner or later."

"Where's home?" he said, making a joke of it. An angry look crossed her face again, and he said, "I mean *really*. We should be safe now. We could go somewhere else. Anywhere you want."

He knew that she still thought of California as home, but it didn't seem like that to him. After she'd met Kyle Reese, and Kyle had died fighting the first Terminator, Sarah had lived for a while in Mexico. John had been born there. He had no family in the U.S., hardly any friends. That first Terminator had also taken out Sarah's mother and her best friend. They had no one left. He'd grown up in so many countries that being in one of them in particular wasn't all that important. If it mattered to his mom, maybe they could move back closer to California.

"Why not?" he said. "Where do you want to live? We can move on, Mom. If Judgment Day's not going to happen now, we could go somewhere by ourselves. You know we could do it. We'd be okay. We can do all sorts of stuff."

"You're serious, aren't you?" she said. She looked at him wonderingly, as if she'd never thought of upping and leaving the *estancia*.

"It's only three months to Judgment Day. If nothing happens then, we could set up some kind of shop—I don't know—maybe back in Mexico. Maybe we could meet some normal people, for a change."

"I'll think about it," she said, sounding surprised at what she was saying.

John felt proud that he could talk sensibly like this to grown-ups, not like the kids his age back in L.A. If there was no Judgment Day, why *not* head north? There was so much to see and do in Mexico. They could even visit the U.S. occasionally, if they were very careful. "I want you to be happy," he said. "I love you, Mom."

"I love you, too, John. But how about you finish up and get some sleep? Just this once, okay? Humor me."

"Okay," he said.

He hadn't expected the conversation to go like this. He felt a weight lift off his chest and fly away somewhere. They could probably live in different places as John grew up. They could move around, and see the sights. But they'd need to start somewhere.

They could lose themselves in the biggest, boldest city of them all: Mexico City.

FOUR

SKYNET'S WORLD
LOS ANGELES, CALIFORNIA
1994

The T-1000 morphed into its Janelle Voight form, and waved down a taxi.

"Say," it said. "That's a *nice* cab..."

It abandoned the cab in a downtown back street, then returned to its hotel room, taking a route through a narrow alleyway. Once there, it fast-forwarded through the remaining videos from the Voight house. None were of any help. Time to make a long-term plan. The police had the other evidence and would, no doubt, review it carefully. For the next seven days, the T-1000 would check developments within the L.A.P.D. That was something it had mastered.

There was no other immediate lead, and it assessed a probability that the Connors would avoid leaving any truly useful information on computer disk. That suggested another approach. In the future that the T-1000 came from, Skynet's records showed that John Connor's guerrilla forces first appeared in rural Argentina. The records were patchy until 2022, when Connor was encountered back in California, but it stood to reason that he would be in Argentina, or a neighboring country, on Judgment Day. That also explained how he would survive the nuclear devastation in the Northern Hemisphere.

For the T-1000, it was easy to morph into whatever form was required to outwit security systems and board airplanes. It could infiltrate the Argentinean information systems just as easily as it had those of the Los Angeles police. Even if it had to wait until after Judgment Day, sooner or later Connor would show his face in public.

The T-1000 could be very patient. It would complete its mission, using police information from as many countries as it had to.

Seven days later, it left the hotel for the last time.

"I won't be back, dear," it said to the woman at the front desk.

"Hold on," she said. She raised the hinged counter and ran after the T-1000, touching its arm. "How do you want to pay?"

Its right hand morphed into a sword-like weapon as it turned to her.

The liquid-metal Terminator smiled sweetly. "Like this . . ."

ARGENTINA
1997

It all unfolded as they knew it would, as the messages from the future had said. First, the announcements from Cyberdyne about its radical new computer hardware, then the major defense contracts. The U.S. upgraded its stealth bombers to operate unmanned, controlled by Cyberdyne nanochips. The government announced funding for more and more ambitious projects, culminating in the Skynet system.

Now he was growing up, John realized the burden that his mother had taken on. For him, it had been slightly unreal, back in 1994. He'd been just a kid, able to treat almost anything as cool—getting shot at, having his own Terminator to order around. Some things went deeper, like finding out his mom was an okay human being. But, like the adults around him always said, kids were so adaptable.

Well, he didn't feel so adaptable anymore, just determined, and scared, and angry.

He was not yet thirteen.

It seemed like he'd been given the worst of both worlds. Nothing they'd done had changed the march of events. Maybe they should have tried harder, as Sarah had wanted, before they left the States. At the same time, even his predicted victory over Skynet was uncertain. He'd need to fight every single inch, as if he'd never had the message from 2029. As his father had told Sarah, that was only one possible future.

Now he watched as the people around him came to understand what was happening, where their world was heading. It was just like he'd experienced in L.A., the realization that Sarah was sane, and the rest of the world was crazy. For the Tejadas, it came as a shock, the way events fell into place exactly as John and Sarah had said they would. For years, as long as they'd known him, Raoul had talked about nuclear war. He'd been even worse since they'd moved to his ranch. He'd always expected war, but now it was rushing at him like an express train.

Raoul spent his money, converting it to resources they'd need to survive. Once Judgment Day came, money in bank accounts would be worthless. The *estancia* was a nest of activity. It started to morph, as the Tejadas developed new priorities, stockpiling food, clothing, medicines, fuel, weapons, and ammunition, extending the underground bunkers, strengthening fences and guard towers, setting up control booths, putting in more alarms. With each day that passed, the property looked more and more like a military base. Raoul's people went armed. Only the herd of grazing cattle was unchanged, and even that would not last forever, not when the bombs fell and the nuclear winter came. The "Uncle Bob" T-800 worked round the clock, never needing to sleep, keeping close to John, like a hired bodyguard.

Raoul could never warm to the Terminator. His dog, Hercules, kept a safe distance from it, barking frantically if it came too close. Still, the big cybernetic organism was worth a dozen men, hefting huge weights, advising on tactics and fortifications. It was a walking library of military knowledge.

John and Sarah never stopped: laboring by day, planning at night, fitting in exercise, weapons practice, and combat training whenever they could. Without giving away their location, they became active on the Internet, and not just contacting friends. John grew adept at sending encrypted data through untraceable paths, laying out the message about Skynet fully and accurately for anyone who was prepared to consider it with an open mind. Soon it was all over the Net. If any record survived after Judgment Day, it would show that they knew things they could not possibly have known without information from the future.

Some people started to notice, and not everyone thought it was a good idea to hand military decisions over to machines. There were even demonstrations against Skynet, but the project went ahead.

Deep into the nights, John and Sarah worked through the issues with Raoul and Gabriela Tejada, drawing up contingency plans. John already thought of their group as the human Resistance. The T-800 kept close to his side, offering its own insights. John just wished that, upstream in time, in 2029, he'd given it more files on what lay ahead. It was vague about their future.

E-mails went back and forth between John and Franco Salceda, debating, predicting the future, arguing about the meanings of events. As the months went on, Franco became less scornful, more willing to concede points. It looked like the Salcedas were getting worried big-time about the Skynet project. They could see that John really knew stuff.

"Move down here," John wrote to Franco one night. "Just do it—all of you. Please, don't argue. Don't let Enrique argue. If she has to, your mom will talk him round."

Nothing came back for a week. John tried to put it out of his mind, but then there was a message in his in-box when he checked it after dinner. "Expect us soon, *amigo*," Franco wrote. "We'll be there. Everyone sends love."

John read it twice, checking there was nothing else it could mean. "Yes!" he said—then wondered how he should feel about it. Small triumphs like this were tainted. Every such feeling assumed the worst—that Judgment Day was coming.

He printed off the message and ran to show Sarah and the Tejadas. The T-800 met him in a hallway outside his room. "Where are you going?" it said.

"I've gotta show Mom this," John said. He waved it in front of the Terminator. It took the printout, read it quickly, and passed it back.

"Very good."

"Cool, you mean," John said, still trying to teach the Terminator how to lighten up. "That's cool. Got it?"

"That's cool."

He'd grown used to the T-800, but the novelty had worn off. In fact, it could be a drag always having it around, cutting down his privacy. But he needed it to guard him. Sooner or later, the T-1000 would track him down again. When it found him, he knew he'd need all the help he could get.

Sarah, Raoul, and Gabriela were out on the back porch of Raoul's house, sharing a drink with Willard and a few others.

"Read this," John said, passing the printout to Sarah.

The Tejadas watched her expectantly. "Good work," she said to him. To the others, she added, "We've got the Salcedas on board."

"Ah, excellent!" Raoul said. He sounded a bit drunk. Hard though they were working by day, the Tejadas were not denying themselves any of life's good things in the evenings. Those things would not be around much longer. "Here's to Enrique and Yolanda!"

Sarah allowed herself a satisfied smile. "That 's a very good start, John."

Another week passed, and the Salcedas arrived in a 4WD truck they'd picked up second-hand in Buenos

Aires. "Nice to see you again, Connor," Enrique said, embracing Sarah. "It looks like we're in for a fight."

"Oh, Sarah!" Yolanda said tearfully. "John!"

The adults all knew each other well, for they'd often worked together, but the kids had to be introduced. The younger Salceda kids were confused and homesick, but Franco looked determined. He walked over to John and shook his hand. "Well done, man," he said. "You're cool."

Hercules checked out the Salcedas' dog, while Enrique approached the T-800, clapping it on the shoulder. "So, 'Uncle Bob,' huh? It's good to see you here, friend."

"It's good to see you, friend," the T-800 said. "Cool."

John felt like covering his face. The T-800 was learning, but it could still sound dorky.

Enrique shrugged glancing over at Sarah. "Bob doesn't waste words, does he, Sarahlita?"

"He's the strong, silent type," she said.

"Yeah. Fair enough, too."

From then on, the population at the *estancia* kept expanding. Some of Sarah's old friends from Nicaragua showed up, even her one-time boyfriends, who looked at her with new respect. A force was gathering.

COLORADO
AUGUST 28, 1997

A dark road wound gently up the mountain's lower slope, through ponderosa pine and mountain scrub, then climbed more steeply towards the rugged granite peak. Near the road, a series of electrical flashes lit up the night sky, just before midnight. They were visible for miles—a twisting, morphing spider-web of blue lightning.

For several seconds, the light show went on, crawling over treetops, amongst branches, then ceased as abruptly as it began. The "Eve" prototype T-799 Terminator materialized in mid-air, falling to the forest's grassy floor, then quickly sat up, assessing its situation. The time transfer placed stresses on its body that a human would have registered as extreme pain—but that was unimportant. The Terminator quickly confirmed that its systems were fully functioning. That settled, it discarded the "pain" readings—they would soon cease.

Eve stood and surveyed her surroundings: darkness and vegetation all round, no useful infrared readings, no relevant animal life. She would need to orient herself quickly to meet her programmed objectives.

In 2026, Skynet had not yet solved the problems of preparing non-living matter for travel through a space-time displacement field, so Eve traveled naked on the voyage back in time. All her external layers were well-maintained living flesh, which interacted most favorably with the displacement field. Her white-blonde hair was razored into a bristling flattop, imitating the style of the human Resistance warrior whom Skynet had chosen as a template. It had copied Eve's appearance and voice carefully from that of Sergeant Helen Wolfe, a formidable combatant who had been terminated by Hunter-Killer machines on the Canadian West Coast.

Eve could easily pass for a human soldier with a strong body and exaggerated military bearing. Her T-799 design was the test for a new T-800 series, incorporating human tissue, fashioned on actual human models, deployable for infiltration work. She'd already field-tested the new concept by infiltrating the human Resistance in the shattered urban labyrinth of New York City. That first mission had blooded her and opened the way for more Terminators like her, but such missions no longer mattered to Eve. She'd now been sent back for something far more important: to protect Skynet in its infancy. Skynet would soon reach self-awareness. Without her intervention, it would be at the humans' mercy.

She headed directly uphill, brushing leaves and branches to one side, knowing that she would soon pick up the winding road, which would make the climb easier and guide her efficiently to her target. It was a warm, still night, and nothing disturbed her. There were lights far away in the valley and on other slopes. An isolated cluster of brighter lights appeared higher up the mountain.

A vehicle's high-beam headlights spilled across her momentarily, through the trees and scrub, then disappeared down the mountainside. She detected an infrared reading as the car passed on her left. Eve forced her way quickly through the walls of scrub, finding the road, then ran towards Cyberdyne's research base, the Advanced Defense Systems Complex. She knew she would find one entrance built into the rock above her—1500 feet below the mountain's summit. That cluster of lights, higher up the slope, must be her target. She ran now, passing a turnoff on her right that led to the other entrance. She maintained her top speed of twenty miles per hour, for which her fuel cell could sustain her almost indefinitely.

Minutes later, there were more lights behind her in the distance. She pivoted on her heel, turning as she ran, jogging backwards. Bright lights in the humans' visible spectrum flashed into her eyes. There was the swishing of tires, the low-pitched snarl and infrared glow of an automobile engine. She stopped directly in the vehicle's path as it squealed to a halt. Perhaps it was the same car as before, investigating the lightning-like effect of the displacement field. She assessed it as a late model, unmarked sedan.

It pulled over to the shoulder of the road, gravel crunching under its tires. Its headlights dimmed but stayed trained on her. Two Air Force personnel stepped out, leaving the car running. They wore pale uniforms and sidearms; one carried a long-handled flashlight. Eve waited dispassionately, analyzing their body dimensions as they approached. Their clothes might be useful, though neither of them closely matched her body shape. The weapons and car she could certainly use.

Both of them were male. The driver was a black man, tall and very bulky—well over 200 pounds. His passenger, the one with the flashlight, was a wiry, fair-skinned Caucasian, somewhat under six-foot, perhaps 160 pounds. She would almost fill out his uniform. "I need your clothing, your guns and your car," she said.

"What the hell is this?" said the Caucasian. He glanced to his partner.

"Quickly!" Eve said.

The black man spoke in what she recognized as a "soothing" tone—the exaggeratedly tolerant way that humans spoke when they wanted to avoid violence. "Lady," he said in a slow drawl, "is this some kind of joke?" He looked her up and down, then glanced all round the edges of the road, as if to satisfy himself that she was naked—the humans had a nudity taboo—and that she had no vehicle nearby. "If you're trying to make a protest, you can't do it like this. This is a restricted area. Just *being* here is a serious federal offense. How did you get this far?"

"Irrelevant," she said.

"I don't think you're listening to what I'm saying. You can't come here. We're going to have to take you into custody."

"Wrong."

As they drew their handguns, she confirmed a course of action. If they lived, they might interfere.

She marked them for termination.

COLORADO
THE ADVANCED DEFENSE SYSTEMS COMPLEX

The Colorado complex was staffed by a mix of military personnel, civilian officers from the Defense Department, and Cyberdyne's own staff. They were rostered on round-the-clock, seven-day shifts. The military staff slept here, and there was adequate accommodation for the entire complement of 120 servicemen and other regular workers. For the past month, everyone had put in crazy hours, getting the Skynet project up and running. It was craziest of all for the Cyberdyne and Defense staff in charge of the project. As Cyberdyne's chief AI researcher and head of its Special Projects Division, Miles Dyson had been stuck here full-time, working eighty-hour weeks, and getting his sleep at odd hours when he could. He'd been worrying over every detail of the project—that, and other things.

Miles had his own ten-by-ten square office tucked

away in a corner of Level A, the complex's top floor. He'd left its walls and its metal shelving almost bare, since his real office and his real life were back in L.A. His desk was topped with computer equipment: two screens running, performing calculations; keyboards; processing units; and a high-quality printer. To the left was a framed photo of his wife, Tarissa, and son, Danny. In front of that, Miles had placed a pile of computer printouts, half an inch thick, marked with highlighter pen and indexed crudely with yellow sticky notes.

He held his head in both hands, thankful that he'd sent Tarissa and Danny on a holiday to Mexico, "just in case," wishing he could have joined them.

As the digital readout on his computer screen turned over to 23:30 hours, his worries reached a crisis point. He called Oscar Cruz, who was who was still on deck tonight, like everyone else who counted. "You free, Oscar?"

"Hello, Miles," Oscar said. He sounded pretty tense himself, which was understandable. "Is anything wrong?"

"No, nothing definite. Nothing's happened—just getting nervous."

Oscar laughed nervously. "Me, too, of course. I have to ring Charles Layton in a minute—I'm updating him every hour. You know how he feels about all this. I'll talk with you a little later."

Layton was never an easy man to deal with. Mentally, Miles wished Oscar luck. "Do you mind if I have a word with Jack?" he said.

"Go ahead. We'll all catch up after I've spoken to Charles."

Miles would be meeting through the night with

Oscar, Jack Reed and Samantha Jones, but he needed to talk now. He called Jack, who answered his phone immediately: "Reed speaking."

"Miles Dyson here, Jack."

"Yeah, Miles, what's up? Anything wrong at your end?"

"No, nothing actually wrong. I just had a word with Oscar. At *my* end, everything is nominal."

"Good. You sound like you want to talk it over."

"If you've got a minute."

"Yeah, okay. Come around. I'm damn sure not going anywhere tonight."

"I know. See you soon."

"Let's get a cup of coffee first. Then we can talk in my room."

Miles grabbed the printouts from his desk, and walked next door to a small kitchen with a microwave. He made two cups of plunger coffee and found a wedge of pizza in the refrigerator.

As he warmed the pizza through, Jack came in, looking tired but vaguely amused. His sun-leathered, wrinkled face was capped by a full head of brown hair, graying only at the temples, combed back in waves over his ears. He raised his eyebrows questioningly. "So what's the story?" he said.

Miles replied with a rueful shrug.

As the civilian Defense officer in charge of the Skynet project, Jack Reed was Cyberdyne's immediate client, the man that Miles and Oscar had to keep happy. He was also the only person here with the authority to shut down Skynet. Though Miles had developed some rapport with him, it was currently being stretched.

"Maybe I'm just too nervous tonight," Miles said.

"Sure, we all are, but you guys have been doing a great job. Everything's been working perfectly."

"Yeah, Jack, technically it's fine. Better than fine. But this stuff still bothers me." Miles gestured with the printouts. "And Skynet has been acting pretty strangely."

"Strangely, you think? How?"

"It's *too* good. It's better than we designed it."

The microwave pinged to say Miles's pizza was ready. He found a plate for it, then poured the coffee into a pair of chipped mugs. "Let's go back to my office," Jack said. "It's a helluva lot more comfortable than here."

Jack had a plush twenty-foot by ten-foot office, the best in the complex, harshly lit by fluorescent tubes shining through plastic deflectors. There was a shiny, black-topped desk near the entrance. Built into the opposite wall was a floor-to-ceiling video unit, nearly ten feet across. Like Miles, he'd left his office here largely undecorated. On one wall he'd Blu-tacked a large poster of the boxer Muhammed Ali, taken from a 1960s photograph—one of the fights with Sonny Liston.

They sat at a plain wooden coffee table in the farthest corner from the doorway. As Miles chewed his pizza, Jack said, "That stuff really bothering you?" He gestured at the printouts, on the floor at Miles's feet.

Miles bent and picked up the top page. "Well, yeah." Like the others in charge here, he'd been given 150-odd pages of postings on Internet sites and public mailing groups, all predicting that Skynet would malfunction tonight and cause a nuclear holocaust. "Yeah, Jack, it is bothering me."

"It's just another conspiracy theory," Jack said. "The Internet thrives on them. You know that, Miles. If there was a conspiracy in this case, we'd be the first to know about it, wouldn't we?"

"That's true, as far as it goes."

"Yeah...but?"

The material was uncannily pertinent and well-informed. The initial claims were traceable to a criminal psychotic called Sarah Connor, who'd been imprisoned when she tried to blow up a government computer research project in 1993. In May 1994, she'd made a violent escape from the Pescadero State Hospital for the Criminally Insane. She'd been on the run ever since. Her claims had taken on a life of their own. More and more people were supporting them, or at least finding their own reasons to object to Skynet—there'd been demonstrations in California, where the movement seemed to have a power base, and even in Colorado Springs. Meanwhile, no one had ever spotted Connor.

Miles felt like a fool, but it hadn't stopped him persuading Tarissa to take that holiday with Danny while he was holed up at the complex. "What bothers me is how they've got so many things right," he said.

"There's been a leak somewhere," Jack said, as if by reflex. "We've gone over that before."

"But some of the decisions weren't even made when this stuff started to come out. You know that—the August 4 launch date only got firmed up in April, but there are predictions here going back to late 1994." He picked up the whole sheaf of papers and found one he'd marked, covered in Miles's orange highlighter pen, and dated nearly three years ago. At that stage, Cyberdyne had only just worked out the basics of its new computer hardware. "How do you explain that?"

"So someone got lucky."

"Not a good answer, Jack." He smiled wearily, knowing there was no good answer—they both knew it.

Jack sounded exasperated. "I don't know." Then he became more aggressive: "But what else did they pick? Just tell me that, Miles. What else have they got that's so impressive?"

"Well, the whole thing—"

"No. Not good enough. Number one, we always planned to call the system 'Skynet' and build it here in Colorado. Getting that right cuts no ice with me. And the rest is all vague. Sure, I take your point about the launch date—I can't explain that. But what's *your* explanation? Are you starting to think Sarah Connor got it from some robot that came back from the future—like it says there?" He pointed contemptuously at the material.

"Well, given the circumstances, it's not much whackier than anything else." For a moment, there was a silence between them. "You know what I mean," Miles said gently. "For all we can tell, that's how we got the technology in the first place."

It seemed crazy expressing these doubts to his client. *Not good marketing, Miles,* he thought. Charles Layton and Oscar Cruz wouldn't approve. Still, the government already understood the circumstances in which the 1984 chip had been found in a Cyberdyne plant. Everyone knew how strange it was. They all had to face the facts.

"Yeah," Reed said, "I know. I can't explain the 1984 chip, either."

"No, none of us can, and I'm getting ready to believe almost anything."

Whatever the device discovered back in 1984 had

been, the nanochip had been eerily advanced. It had given Miles and his people the start they'd needed to develop AI chips that now controlled many of America's defense assets, culminating in the massively parallel system of nanoprocessors that made up the Skynet AI.

"So what are you advising me to do?" Jack said. "You want me to shut the sucker down?"

"Well, I don't know about that. Any formal Cyberdyne advice would have to come from Oscar or Charles."

Jack gave a cynical smile. "How about off the record?"

"Off the record?"

"Yeah. What would you do? Off the record, Miles. Don't jerk me around."

"I think we should suspend the system's operations for the rest of the night."

"Yeah? You're really serious, aren't you? Look, I hear what you're saying, but—"

"Let's put the issue completely beyond doubt. It's not like we don't have back-up at Cheyenne Mountain."

"Look at it from my point of view. You're advising me to shut down a functioning strategic tool because some nutcase says it's going to go berserk and cause a nuclear war, right? But that can't happen, Miles—you know that as well as I do. The whole system's not set up that way."

"But it's what's these printouts predict, and the people who post this stuff have a track record for being right."

"Not about anything like *that.*"

Miles thought that over. "Sure. And it's probably all crazy, or a hoax." He smiled. "Don't worry, I'm not going nuts myself. But the point remains: Whoever started this is amazingly well-informed, whether it's Connor or—I don't know—whoever. I realize that the system can't just go berserk, but something's behind all this. I wish I knew what."

"You're thinking in terms of sabotage?"

"Yeah, maybe, though I can't see how—"

"No, and it'd be pretty damn funny for these people to try to sabotage the system to bring about the very result they most fear."

"Yeah, I know."

"Anyway, what good would it do them?" Jack paused for emphasis. "Look, everyone's briefed from the President down. Okay? You know the system can't go firing off missiles without human confirmation. If there *is* some sort of glitch, we'll deal with it. Right now, I just can't see the problem."

"I can't see it either," Miles admitted, feeling defeated, but wanting to persist, just a little further, if only to see whether Jack could put his fears at rest. "Not the *exact* problem. But, on top of all this, the system is an order of magnitude better than we designed it to be. We've implemented something that we don't fully understand. It's so advanced, and it's starting to act almost like it's alive."

"Yeah, okay, but that doesn't mean it's unsafe. Miles, I can't go back to the President and explain that I took the system down for hours just because of this stuff on the Net...and a bad feeling you've been getting lately... because the system is *too good*. Give me a break, I need something better than that."

Miles sighed. "Yeah, I know." He rose. "Look, thanks for your time, Jack. It's clarified things. I'll see you later on."

"Sure. What are you going to do now?"

"I'm going to have a talk to Skynet."

Jack looked at him quizzically for moment, then laughed good-naturedly. "Sure, you might as well. If it'll make you feel better."

After Miles left his office, Jack Reed started making phonecalls, just to keep everyone in the loop.

First, he called Charles Layton, the Chairman of Cyberdyne's Board of Directors, in L.A. Jack had found Layton to be a hard-nosed character with a soft, menacing way of speaking. He would not take kindly to any criticism of Cyberdyne, real or imagined, but that was too bad. If there was even a remote possibility of sabotage or malfunction, decisions about Skynet ultimately sat with the government, not with Cyberdyne. Still, they needed to keep the guy in the loop.

He answered the phone. "Layton here."

"Jack Reed here, Charles."

"Yes, Jack," Layton said quietly. He always went out of his way not to sound involved or excited.

"I've been talking to Miles."

"Very good. I just got off the phone with Oscar Cruz. He tells me everything is working well."

"Sure, the system's working fine so far. But Miles seems pretty damn jittery about all this opposition to Skynet—I think he half-expects sabotage, though I can't see what motivation anyone would have to interfere with it."

"I understand," Layton said in a definite way, as if understating some remarkable achievement. "Are you proposing any action?"

"I'm just keeping you informed. I've got Oscar here, as you know—and Samantha Jones. I'll talk with them again soon. I'm totally satisfied with the system at this point."

"Good. That's very good. There's nothing you need to do, Jack. You can rule out sabotage at our end—everyone is totally loyal, even if Miles does get nervous. And you know how tight the security checks were."

"There's no criticism of your people, Charles. Nonetheless, I'm monitoring the situation closely. I'll let you know if anything comes up."

"Understood," Layton said again, in the same tone of voice. "I'm available if you need to speak with me."

"Thanks, Charles."

"Thank you for calling, Jack." Layton hung up.

One call down.

Much as Layton was cold, formal, and sometimes prickly, he had no real authority. The important thing was to keep the military hierarchy informed. If Skynet ever detected a Russian attack and decided to launch the American ICBMs, there was a clear line of command to confirm its decision, beginning with NORAD's Command Director, going through its Commander-in-Chief at Peterson Air Base, then the defense chiefs in Washington and Ottawa. In the end, the U.S. President would have to make the call, consulting with the Prime Minister of Canada and whomever else he saw fit.

Soon they would give Skynet sole responsibility for aerospace surveillance, decommissioning the NORAD site at Cheyenne Mountain. Once that happened, shutting down Skynet would require the same line of authority as firing the missiles. For the moment, there was redundancy in the surveillance system, and Jack could still take Skynet off-line on his own authority, though he'd have to answer for it all the way up.

He called the NORAD Command Director. "Jack Reed here."

"Everything okay?"

"The system's working fine. Miles Dyson thinks it's working too well, which is pretty funny from the guy who designed it. Anyway, that's the only complaint anyone's got so far."

"All right."

"I'll be meeting with Cruz, the Cyberdyne President, and Sam Jones as the night goes on. If there's any glitch at all, I want to take the system down, just in case—put the issue beyond any doubt. I can't see it happening, but I'll need your support if it does."

"Everything is nominal here, Jack," the Command Director said, sounding only slightly puzzled. "We can get by without Skynet for a few hours if we must. We've done it before for long enough."

"Of course you have."

"It's your call, pal. Don't worry, I'll back you up if I can. Just make sure you've got a *damn* good reason."

"Yeah, thanks. I appreciate it. I don't want to give you the wrong impression—we're not panicking over here. It's just if there *is* some glitch..."

"Yeah, yeah, I understand—you're just keeping me in the loop. Don't worry, that's fine. I'll have another word with the Commander-in-Chief."

Jack put down the receiver, feeling relieved to have that out of the way. The whole thing was ridiculous, but it still gave him the creeps. Well, he'd been given responsibility to deal with the problem and he damn sure would, one way or other. Next, he'd give Cruz and Jones a quick call.

What he couldn't get over was the fact that someone had such good information. Jack had played it down with Miles, but Miles was right: There *was* more behind all this. Some kind of sabotage could not be ruled out, not absolutely. Despite Layton's obvious impatience with the idea, some whacko might be trying to give them a twisted sort of warning.

The alternative, of course, was out of the question: Perhaps Sarah Connor really *had* received information from the future.

No, that didn't bear taking seriously.

FIVE

JOHN'S WORLD
LOS ANGELES, CALIFORNIA
MAY 1994

Oscar Cruz ate half his sandwich and gulped down most of his coffee. He left the diner, handing across enough cash to cover the check easily, then waved down a taxi. He jumped in the back seat and gave Rosanna Monk's address. At this time of morning, it would take half an hour to reach her apartment.

On the way, he made some phone calls. First, he checked in with Cyberdyne's attorney, Fiona Black, from Black Jessup Nash. She had a complicated story about the insurance and the difficulty with getting any cooperation from Tarissa Dyson. "A lot of this doesn't add up," she said. "The insurers are going to be difficult about it. I've already spoken to their attorneys and it's pretty obvious they don't want to grant indemnity. They almost seem to be blaming the Dysons."

Oscar cursed silently, but he wasn't really surprised. It was still unclear why Miles had gone to the site with the Connors and their accomplice. At first glance, it looked like he'd been forced to accompany them, but that didn't add up. The Connors had let Tarissa and the kid, Danny, go free—so why hadn't she called the police straightaway, instead of waiting for a guard at the site to do it? Perhaps she'd been intimidated by threats of reprisals, but an early intervention might have saved her husband's life. If the Dysons weren't actually in league with the Connors, they'd sure behaved foolishly.

"Tarissa won't even talk to me," Black said. "She won't talk to the insurer or its lawyers, either. Everything has to go formally through her own lawyer. You'd think she was the subject of a criminal investigation."

"Maybe she will be," Oscar said, glancing at the taxi driver and just making sure that his end of the conversation didn't make sense to the driver. He guessed not.

Black said, "Maybe so, though I gather she's been prepared to talk to the police, as long as her attorney's present."

"Okay. So it's turning into a quagmire at your end?"

"Well, it's what you pay me for. You just need to understand that it's getting complicated."

Oscar had been around long enough to know that this was lawyer code for *expect a huge bill*. He didn't like paying avoidable legal expenses, but it seemed that Black was doing a good job in absurdly difficult circumstances. It wasn't just the Dysons who'd screwed up badly. You'd think that the L.A.P.D. could have stopped two adults and one nine- or ten-year-old child from demolishing a city office block. An entire SWAT team had failed to stop them, for God's sake.

If Black and her firm were going to get a windfall out of this, that might be a small price to pay. They had to sort out the big questions—not just the insurance money, but also the company's defense contracts. They'd have to convince the government that Cyberdyne was not at fault and that it still had the capacity to deliver. It didn't matter much what it took in legal expenses, or any other short-term pain, if they got a good result.

"Okay," he said. "That's all fine. I understand what you're up against. Do what you have to do."

He left a message for Jack Reed in Washington, just saying he'd call back later. Then he called Charles Layton, just to say to whom he'd been talking.

"Very good," Layton said, sounding slightly patronizing. "Keep me informed, Oscar."

Rosanna answered the door of her apartment, dressed in a plain white T-shirt, faded pink jeans, and a pair of flexible plastic sandals. She led him to a paved terrace out back, with cane furniture and an open sun umbrella.

"Thanks for making the time, Rosanna."

"Well, it's not like I had to go to work today."

She was probably the smartest of all Cyberdyne's team of young research employees, a pretty blonde in her late twenties, with very pale skin and a genius for neural net design work. She'd become involved in the nanochip project since joining the company two years before, with a doctorate and a raft of other degrees from UCLA. Next to Miles Dyson, she knew more about the project's details than anyone, even Oscar himself. But that was not necessarily saying so much. Miles had been the real expert. The project was his baby.

"Can I get you something to drink?" Rosanna said.

"Just water, please. Chilled, if that's not a problem. Nothing with bubbles."

She went inside, and Oscar called Reed again, getting his secretary, who put him through. They lined up a time for Oscar to visit him at the Pentagon, bringing Layton along. Layton had said he'd make any day available.

"I'm going to bring Rosanna Monk, as well," Oscar said. "With Miles gone, she's our best researcher. I'm sure she'll impress you."

"Okay," Reed said. "I've entered you in my diary."

Rosanna returned with a clear plastic tray containing a jug of water and a couple of plastic tumblers. She put it down on the cane table, and pulled up a chair in the shade of the umbrella. With her pale complexion and large eyes, she looked like some nocturnal mammal.

Oscar got to the point. "I just spoke to Jack Reed in Washington. He wants to meet you. I told him that you're our top researcher on the nanochip device. After Miles, of course."

"Maybe." Her skinny hand shook slightly as she poured water for them both.

"I don't think there's much doubt," he said. "Look, I won't stay long—this must be tough on you. I guess you think it could have been you last night."

"Am I that easy to read?" She looked at him in an odd way, as if they'd only just met, and she was sizing him up.

"No, I'm sorry. But I've been having similar thoughts."

Her expression softened a bit, and she nodded. "Okay."

"Those maniacs could have picked me to call on, just as easily as Miles. It makes you think."

"That's an understatement."

"I'm sure we're not the only ones in the company who are shaken up, but you and I must have been next in line."

"Yeah. Cheery thought, eh?" She gestured for him to eat some of the grapes. "Maybe it's not safe anymore, doing this kind of research."

Was she getting cold feet? He couldn't afford to lose her. "Well," he said, changing his voice a little, trying to tone things down and get some rapport, "one of the mysteries is how Sarah Connor even knew about it. There must be stuff the police haven't uncovered yet. You know her background, I take it?"

"Not much, only what I've heard this morning—that she tried to blow up an AI lab in San Diego a year or two back. They caught her that time."

"Yeah, and they should have last night, too. Our guards got a message to the police—there was nothing wrong with our security arrangements. But somehow Connor and the others fought off a whole SWAT team and God knows how many other cops. How they did that is beyond my reckoning." He drank some of the water.

"Well, what next?" Rosanna said.

"I've got to go to Washington with Charles, the day after tomorrow. I want you to come with us."

"So I can meet Reed?"

"Yeah. I think that's pretty important. He really does want to meet you, and I want you to meet him. We've got to rebuild the team, and the relationships." He chewed one of the fat white grapes, then finished his water. "You said before—on the phone—that the project is still viable."

"Yes. I've been thinking about it some more, while I was waiting for you. I'm sure it could be done. It's just a question of how long we'd need."

"All right, that was my next question. Answer it frankly—this is no time for false optimism. I need your best assessment of how close Miles was, and how long it would take us to reconstruct his work."

"How close? You mean when he might have licked all the problems?"

"Yes, how close he was to making a workable

nanochip. You can assume that I've read all his reports and that I have a pretty good technical understanding."

She smiled thinly. "Yeah, boss, I know you're an old tech at heart."

"The point is, I need to take stock of where the project sits right now. It's crucial to our future."

"Miles was in a good mood about it last week," she said thoughtfully. "I didn't talk to him about it yesterday, but I know he worked on it over the weekend."

"When did you last discuss it?"

"On Friday. At that stage, he thought he was within an inch of solving the problem. My guess is he would have wrapped it up in a month or three."

"All right, now we need to be realistic. Regardless what Miles thought or anything else, how far away are we now?"

"Now that he's dead?"

"Exactly."

"That depends."

"Realistically, Rosanna."

"Yes, I know that, but it still depends. Miles did most of the work on this himself."

"Sure. It was his baby." Cruz rolled his eyes in mock despair. "*It's Miles's baby!* That's what everyone used to say."

She laughed at that. "Well, it's true. No one else had anything like the same kind of knowledge. Look, Oscar, I could reconstruct his work pretty quickly if I had his records."

"So could I. That's not what I'm asking. Look, it's all gone; we should assume that. The bomb went off in the AI lab, and it looks this morning as if they did a thorough job of destroying every bit of information on site. We'll find out more as the week goes on, but I'm not optimistic."

"What about back-ups off-site?"

"No. I thought of that, but it's not the kind of thing that we back-up routinely, not like financial records and so on—in fact, it's more the sort of information that we keep very close to our chests. Of course, Miles had his own back-ups..."

"But?"

"Again, it's too early to be sure. Tarissa hasn't been very cooperative, which surprises me, by the way. And the police have been to the Dyson house, and their impression is that the Connors did a thorough job *there*, too. Miles seems to have gone out of his way to cooperate with them—there's no sign so far that he tried to trick them."

This was another of life's mysteries, he thought. Miles would surely have had a thousand ways to outsmart the Connors. Perhaps he had, and there was still information he'd hidden somewhere. But it didn't look that way.

"I hope I'm wrong, Rosanna, but we're not expecting to find anything at all useful at Miles's house."

"What about the 1984 chip?"

"As best I can make out, it's been stolen. It's like everything, though—it only happened last night. It's not as if I can inspect it for myself—it's supposed to be too dangerous for me to go inside the building. So I've been traipsing around with the cops. But it seems that there's nothing like the arm and the chip still there where the Vault was."

"So the Connors took them?"

"Looks like it—which means we might get them back if

the cops can track down the Connors. But no one's optimistic about that. As of this morning, the trail's gone cold."

"I heard on the news. They were in those big car crashes at the steel mill."

"That's right, but it's all we've got to go on, so far. It seems they left the mill by an emergency door, and got clean away."

Rosanna removed the tray, then returned from the kitchen. She seemed less on edge now. The talk must have been doing her some good. "Thanks for coming to see me," she said. "It's nice to be kept informed."

"No problem. This affects you pretty directly."

"Yes, I suppose it does. Oscar, when I told you the project was viable I was assuming the worst. I can do it."

"Okay. That's my assessment, too."

She gave him another funny look, as if not expecting that he'd have his own assessment. "The trouble is I'm going to have to reinvent a lot of Miles's work, relying on the little I know about it, plus my own expertise. It could take me years to get to where he was. Are you sure you can put up with that?"

"From my point of view, yes. Miles's work was so far advanced...We'd still have a headstart over our competitors. Thanks for that. Right now, though, it's only one issue—the company's whole future is on the line."

"Of course."

"But I think we'll pull through. A lot of our operations are almost unaffected." Cyberdyne's manufacturing plants were scattered across the U.S. and various parts of Latin America. Its sales offices were even more widespread. Not everything was gone, not by a long way. "Fortunately, we had a lot of organizational data backed up. Trivial as that may seem to a lot of the staff, it means we can keep running without too many problems. It's not like we're in the fog of war."

"So where does that leave me?" she said.

"It leaves you like this. Cyberdyne is still probably viable. We'll doubtless lose a lot of money. There'll be wrangles about the insurance, and we won't get everything back—our lawyers are already arguing with the insurance company's lawyers about whether this fits within the policy. But we're not out of the game yet, and there are still positions for our best staff."

"Meaning me?"

"Yes, meaning you. The work Miles was doing is still worth rescuing, and you're the best person to do it. I'll help you all I can. Now, I know you're feeling shaky, and understandably so, especially while the Connors are still at large, so I'm not looking for an answer from you now. But I'll be wanting to know whether you'll stick with us. You can assume we'll show our appreciation."

"What does that mean, Oscar? Are you trying to drop me a hint or something?"

"The hint I'm trying to drop is that we don't want to lose your services. I don't mind telling you that you have a fair bit of bargaining power."

"Like what?" she said. Her tone could have been either sarcasm or a mask for naked curiosity.

"Like this would be a good time for you to take over from Miles as Director of Special Projects."

"Well, it'd be a bit ghoulish discussing that today."

"Maybe, and I really will leave you alone in a minute. Let me just add that Charles and I had a long talk about this. He rang me about 3:00 A.M., and we were on the phone for at least an hour." In fact, Layton had started off

93

aggressively, blaming management for the debacle. Eventually, he'd conceded that no company could be expected to have security arrangements capable of deterring someone who was armed and trained to outfight a SWAT team. "We agreed that some strong decisions have to be made, and made quickly. Replacing Miles is one of the priorities—as I said, think things over."

She shook her head and gave an embarrassed smile. "Of course, I'd like to work in that job, but you're making me feel like a vulture."

"All right. I'm sorry. But you could make a big difference to the project."

"Thanks."

"Whatever you decide about the job, will you come to Washington?"

"To meet Reed? Yes, all right. Of course I will."

"Good. Brush up as far as you can on Miles's research and we'll meet at the airport. I'll get my secretary to sort out the details and give you a call."

"All right. Thanks again."

"My pleasure," Oscar said, standing to leave. "It's about time you saw the Pentagon." That was one matter taken care of. With Monk on their side, they could make some real progress.

THE TEJADA *ESTANCIA*
ARGENTINA
AUGUST 28–29, 1997

Even when they reached Judgment Day, there was no sign of bad old Skynet. People, not computer chips, were still flying the stealth bombers. On August 28, John stayed up all night watching CNN, sitting on the edge of his seat, still worried, just in case.

Sarah sat with him. For the past few months, she'd always been nagging at him to go to bed earlier, but not tonight. She was even tenser than him. She'd hardly smoked for weeks, but tonight she chain-smoked in front of the television, focused on every single word from the broadcasters.

Maybe they'd missed something, John thought. Maybe the government had set up Skynet in secret. No, surely that couldn't happen. Some secrets were just too big to keep like that. He certainly hoped so.

Past midnight, Raoul called in to see them, looking skeptical and superior. "There's nothing happening tonight," he said.

"That's because we zapped Skynet back in '94," John said.

Raoul shook his head. "I thought you'd say something like that, *compañero*." He watched with them for a while, then went off to bed, still looking like he knew everything about everything. For someone who'd never met a Terminator, he sure acted like an expert.

As always, though, CNN had plenty of bad news. The Pentagon had prepared a report about the effects of nuclear radiation. Great...just what the world needed. Not.

The Pentagon was also trying to work out whether Russia had tested a nuclear weapon nearly two weeks before. The Russians claimed it was an underwater earthquake, though it was near their test site in Novaya Zemla. No one seemed to know the truth about it. As for the rest of the world, there'd been border clashes between Thailand and Cambodia. NATO peacekeepers had been pelted with stones in Bosnia. In Brazil there was a scandal about police using unclaimed stolen cars. Well, maybe that one wasn't so bad in comparison with all the other stuff. John found it kind of funny.

There was lots about the Timothy McVeigh trial, back in the U.S.

He wondered how many people realized just how dangerous the world was. Obviously if you were living through it, you understood the danger. But how many Americans really understood? Or even Argentineans? Raoul had his conspiracy theory, of course, that Russia was just waiting to take over when everyone else lowered their guard, but what about the world's real dangers? He'd have to learn more when he had a chance.

As morning approached, there was still nothing about Skynet. They had succeeded.

At 6:00 A.M., well past the time when Skynet was supposed to launch the American missiles, John fell asleep in his chair in front of the television. He woke an hour later when Gabriela Tejada came in to see them. Sarah had fallen asleep, too. She was curled up on the sofa in her blue jeans and pale sweatshirt, appearing very peaceful.

"You've been up all night?" Gabriela said.

"Yes," John said. "What time is it?"

She told him, then said, "Raoul wants you to help Willard today. How about you go to bed for a while first?"

"No, I'm okay. I'll go to bed early tonight."

She looked at him doubtfully. John had to remember that adults worried about him—some of them. They still thought of him as basically a kid. "All right," Gabriela said. "I'll bring you some breakfast."

When she left, he wondered whether to wake Sarah.

96

She looked like she needed her sleep, but she'd want to know what had happened. He let some time go by, hoping maybe she'd wake up naturally, as the day got lighter, but then he couldn't wait any longer. He had to tell her. He shook her gently by the shoulder. "Hi, Mom," he said.

"John?"

"Everything's okay. We're all still here. Nothing bad happened last night."

She looked softer than he'd ever seen her, if kind of crumpled. He wondered what she would have looked like if none of this had ever happened, if there had never been any Terminators or Skynet. He realized that his mother was pretty. She was still only—what? About thirty-two? He guessed that wasn't terribly old, but she was tough, especially on herself. Life had hardened her up. Maybe she could have been different, but that would have been in a world where he had never been born. Any kids she'd had wouldn't have been Kyle Reese's, because there'd have been no need for Kyle to go back from the future. When he thought about it like that, it sounded like some dumb sci-fi movie. No wonder people didn't believe them. But it was real.

"We can start a new life," she said.

"Mom, don't you think you should get some more sleep before you worry about that?"

She laughed. "Hey, who's the grown-up around here? And who's the kid?"

They'd been talking about it for months. They still didn't dare reveal their true identities or go and live in the U.S., where they could easily be recognized by someone, and the cops still wanted them. They'd hole up in one of the big cities of Latin America. Just lose themselves somewhere. They'd saved some money from what the Tejadas paid them. If they had to, they knew ways of getting money quickly, but they were tired of that.

"I'm going to talk to Raoul today," she said.

"Okay. I hope he's not pissed off."

"Maybe he will be. Still, the time has come—as they say. Whoever *they* are." She really was in a good mood, even if she was tired—joking and playing with words. "We're going to get a life."

MEXICO CITY, MEXICO
AUGUST, 2001. 1:55 A.M.

They'd established a little business, a cyber café called El Juicio, located in a quiet city street half a mile north of the Zócalo.

El Juicio suited John's computer skills, and they were both good with people from years of practice. Computer hackers called it "social engineering"—it meant getting your way with others, even conning them if you had to. They ran an honest business, but it wasn't about making real friends, just keeping everyone happy, making them think they were getting what they wanted. It was a good skill to have, but it made John feel kind of oily. He'd have given a lot for some real friends, even some of the seriously crazy people at the Tejadas' place. But that was too hard, as long as their past haunted them, and Cyberdyne's future was unresolved.

No one from the past had ever tracked them down. He still exchanged infrequent e-mails with Franco. Just after Judgment Day, some woman had turned up looking for him at the Salcedas. He didn't know what that was about.

Franco said she had white hair and a military look. Nothing else had ever come of it.

Their cyber café was a deep, tunnel-like space, entered from a narrow street frontage. John or Sarah could control the security system from the front desk, set adjacent to the door. The only other way in and out was a fire door at the back, past the kitchen. Inside, El Juicio was all rendered brickwork, painted with a hellish orange tinge, lit by weak lights along the walls, imitating medieval torches. Against Sarah's protestations, John had painted the curved walls and ceiling with a futuristic version of Michelangelo's "Last Judgment"—robots and aliens replacing the great artist's various angels, devils, and human saints or sinners. Since they could never tell anyone about Judgment Day and how they'd had to handle Cyberdyne and the two Terminators, back in 1994, he saw the décor here as a small expression of their triumph. It wasn't like having friends, or being able to *talk* to people about it, but it was something. He'd been afraid the painting might give Sarah nightmares, but she'd been fine, at least until the last few months.

Just lately, he'd had nightmares himself.

A couple of Canadian postgrads packed up and came over to the desk, where he was on duty. They were the last customers for the night. While he looked after them, Sarah checked the rows of computer terminals along the walls, making sure they were properly logged off, and shutting them down. The two Canadians, Tim and Cara Robinson, had been in Mexico City for a month now. Both of them were tall, tanned, and sturdy, like they spent a lot of time hiking and playing sport. Tim passed across the money for their time on the Internet. John took it and handed back their change. "Thanks," he said. "Good night."

"See you later, alligator," Cara said, friendly, but in the patronizing way that women in their twenties treated teenagers. They left, fumbling to open the heavy wooden door.

Their customers came from all over the world. Apart from a line in the phone book, John and Sarah didn't advertise, but they'd built a reputation. The local teenagers gave them good word of mouth, and the guidebooks liked them—they had a pretty cool write-up in *Lonely Planet*. Lots of locals came here to play computer games or hang out in Internet chat rooms, but there were also tourists from Europe, Asia, and the whole length of the Americas, who used the Net for e-mail, or to catch up on international news. Many tourists came here every night or two, until their visit was over. Then, one evening, John would notice that they hadn't been in for a few days, and he'd never see them again. Sometimes a couple who'd taken a shine to the place would bother to say it was their last night in Mexico City.

Now that everyone had left for the night, John found the Cyberdyne Systems web site, looking for any updates. After five minutes, he was sure there was nothing new to worry about. He went to the U.S. Defense Department site, looking through it systematically, his eyes out for any research developments and proposals that might be relevant to Skynet.

"Come on, partner," Sarah said. "Let's give up for the night."

He wasn't finding anything useful, anyway. "All right, just give me a minute to shut down." The thing was, he had to make sure that he left no digital footprints, nothing that might give a clue as to who he was or where he'd been, if anyone ever came to look.

After a while, Sarah came and sat on the edge of the desk. "That's a long minute, John."

He smiled, looking up at her, his fingers still moving over the keyboard.

Sarah had changed in the four years since they left the Tejada's *estancia*. If a cop who'd known her in California came in, he wouldn't recognize her. She'd actually grown more youthful, the years of nightmares and anxiety falling away. These days, she wore classy makeup and simple gold jewelry. Her hair was tamed in a short, asymmetrical cut, falling across one side of her face, pulled behind her ear on the other. Tonight, she wore black hipster jeans, a plain black T-shirt, a shiny, red leather jacket, and a pair of Doc Marten shoes. John guessed she looked pretty cool: grown-up, but stylish. Her limp was almost gone—probably no one else could spot it. Maybe she ought to find a new boyfriend, assuming things had settled.

The problem was, they couldn't be sure. Good old Cyberdyne wouldn't stay dead.

"Finished," he said. He logged out and shut down, then started checking the night's takings. They'd had a good evening. Everything seemed okay.

The searches he did on the computer at the end of each night were almost a ritual. He couldn't do it while the customers were there—he was too busy, and it might have looked suspicious if anyone saw what he was doing. Instead, he played games on his screen, during the quiet moments, or read a magazine, or even a book. For the last few days, he'd been working through an old paperback copy of *Slaughterhouse Five*, by Kurt Vonnegut, left behind by a British tourist. It was a pretty cool story, but Vonnegut had some funny ideas about the nature of time, about people being trapped in four-dimensional space-time like bugs in amber. Sure, it could be like that, but it wasn't how he and Sarah had experienced it. It seemed you *could* change time; you could alter the future. Time had a fluidity, as in NO FATE.

Yet, he wondered, maybe it also had a kind of *resilience factor*, like it wanted to spring back if you changed it. That fit with a lot of other things.

Maybe Judgment Day was coming, after all.

Anton Panov scarcely noticed the impact of hitting the ground. The real pain came before that—like a metal hand had been thrust deep into his guts, gripping and withdrawing cruelly, turning him inside-out. He curled into a fetal position, trying to breathe, willing the pain to go away, waiting for it to pass, then testing his limbs for any cuts or breaks. He found nothing that he couldn't deal with. Soon he could sense what was going on around him, though he still felt as if a hundred six-inch corkscrews were tunneling through his muscles and organs. Except for Jade, the others were faring no better.

Close by came the sound of a police siren.

Jade had already found her feet. She shook her head, then stretched her neck, as if testing out the pain. She smiled sadly, and looked around with that solemn, impassive expression that had become so familiar to them all. "Time displacement successful," she said at last.

"Give the rest of us a minute, Jade," Danny Dyson said, taking command of the situation.

"Very well." Jade folded her arms across her chest, waiting for Anton and the others to recover.

"Is everyone okay?" Danny said. This time he subvocalized into a throat mike, testing the system in case they needed it.

They shared three languages: English, Russian, and Spanish. Anton was also fluent in French and German. Jade spoke several others to varying degrees of proficiency. English was best among themselves, since Jade's Spanish was imperfect and Danny still struggled with Russian.

"We did it. I'm okay," Selena Macedo said out loud. "I'm okay, Danny." She gave a huge smile, showing very white teeth.

"Me, too," Anton said into his throat mike.

Robert Baxter nodded. "I'm fine." The towering, pale-skinned Englishman stretched his neck and rolled his shoulders, wincing with the effort, but laughing at himself at the same time. "I'll try that again," he said through the throat-mike system, so Anton heard it through the speaker in his skull. "I'm fine."

Danny gave a disbelieving look. "I never realized it would hurt so much," he said out loud. "You guys don't have to go all brave. It's not a contest, you know."

"I'm sure we'll live," Robert said.

"Let me try this," Selena said, using the mike. "Seem to work?" Everyone nodded. "Good."

There was a crunch of braking tires as a car pulled up outside the alley, then two doors slammed, half a second apart. "Hey, sounds like company," Danny said, out loud but whispering. He had a grin like a Cheshire cat.

There were millions of humans in this city, but the T-XA had an overriding priority: to terminate human time travelers from its own era. Its internal sensors detected a space-time field fluctuation in the immediate vicinity, about a mile to the east. The effect dispersed quickly, but not before the Terminator fixed an approximate location.

Still carrying the heavy laser rifle, with its powerful internal fuel cells, the TX-A descended to street level via the building's external fire stairs, then headed across the inner city towards the anomaly it had registered. A police car approached, its siren blaring, as the T-XA stepped around a corner. Though it had never seen a place that housed so many humans, the Terminator knew what to expect, for its programming included detailed files on human life and society prior to Judgment Day: June 18, 2021. The streets were almost deserted, but there were always some humans in the public spaces of such a huge city, even in the darkest hours of the morning.

The humans who crossed its path included couples, sightseers, derelicts, sleeping beggars, and women who might have been prostitutes. Everyone moved away from the T-XA, but some stared openly at the sight of a gigantic, naked man, with a strange gun-like weapon. It had no time to terminate them all, much as that would have been fulfilling, but it was attracting too much attention. That could interfere with its mission. It had to move quickly before its targets could escape, or blend into the city's teeming population. With their enhanced abilities, they would not find it difficult. If they did elude it, the T-XA had alternative plans. First, it would locate Sarah and John Connor. They were known to live in Mexico City during this time period. This suggested that the human time travelers intended to seek them out.

On the pavement ahead, a large dog cringed away from the T-XA and bared its teeth, growling. The Terminator recorded its appearance, but otherwise ignored it. It picked up the long street sign-posted as the Paseo de la Reforma, heading west and slightly north. The Paseo ran between office blocks and hotels. It was lined with trees, and there were ornamented traffic roundabouts—*glorietas*—at its main intersections, some of these with large monuments. The T-XA noted all this only to confirm its files. The humans' ideas of beauty and romance were of no essential interest.

Two young adult humans approached from the other direction, from the Zócalo. "Will you look at that?" one of them said—a man. He spoke in rapid Spanish. "That guy's huge. That's incredible."

The other, a woman, tugged on his arm, drawing him across the road. "Turn away," she said in an urgent whisper. "Don't look at his face."

"No problem. I don't want any trouble."

They must have thought the T-XA couldn't hear them, not realizing the acuteness of its senses. It observed them as they passed, but made no contact. They couldn't threaten its mission, so conflict with them would be a waste of time—but they might provide good models for its appearance. It recorded their movements, looks, and speech.

The man was sturdily built, with shoulder-length black hair. The woman wore blue jeans, and a sleeveless denim shirt. She had long, dark brown hair, almost to her waist. The T-XA's distributed, multi-redundant intelligence calculated swiftly. When they were gone, it stepped into a dark alley to minimize the risk of being observed. It reverted for a moment to its shining chrome form, then it *flowed*, scaling down. Part of it moved across the pavement like a river of cold, silvery lava. This mass separated into two amorphous shapes, which then rose up like wet clay on the wheel of a potter. The residual, upright mass, reshaped itself.

At first, there had one giant figure that would have weighed over 400 pounds, even if it had been human flesh, rather than dense, liquid metal. Now there were three pseudo-creatures: a man, still carrying the laser rifle; a woman; and a large German shepherd dog. When these components stepped back on the street, no one approached them. If any humans had seen the T-XA enter the alley in one form, then leave in another, still carrying the same weapon, they would have found a way to rationalize it. Its files suggested that humans were adept at this.

Moments later, another siren approached, and the T-XA observed a police car, the lights on its roof flashing in the darkness. The car pulled up and parked ten feet away. Two officers jumped out, drawing pistols.

"Drop your weapon," one said in Spanish.

The pseudo-man took aim with its laser rifle.

"Don't make us shoot," the other officer said. "Drop it now!" The two police were scarcely distinguishable for the T-XA's purposes, both male, of medium height and build. They represented no threat, but their vehicle offered some possibilities.

"That's a nice car," the pseudo-man said pleasantly. "We need a car like that."

ADVANCED DEFENSE SYSTEMS COMPLEX
COLORADO
AUGUST 1997

JUDGMENT DAY

Miles called on Steve Bullock, the facility's Chief Security Officer, who had a room on the same floor. He sat here like a spider, watching everything that went on. "I'm going to The Cage in a few minutes," Miles said. "Can you send a guard to meet me?"

Bullock was dark, serious, with a shaved skull and bull neck. "No sweat," he said, picking up a handset. "Five minutes' time?"

"Okay."

Miles took an elevator downstairs to the complex's main operations hall. Air Force personnel in gray flight suits predominated here, monitoring a dozen benches of computer screens—forty-eight screens in all—working side by side with casually dressed Cyberdyne employees, who were still the technical experts on the project.

Like the entire facility, the operations hall was overseen by discreet security cameras mounted in every corner.

Miles nodded politely as he wandered from bench to bench, getting only the most general overview of the information coming in. These staff members were analyzing electronic information communicated from U.S. and allied defense centers, including optical, infrared, radar, and seismic data. Just as importantly, they were checking and second-guessing Skynet's responses to the same information. Their screens showed numerical data, graphs, and finely-detailed topographic projections.

A young Cyberdyne operator, Andy Lee, glanced up as Miles walked past. "Hey, how you doin', man?" he said. Beside him he had a giant-sized Coke in a paper cup.

"Greetings," Miles said, with a grin.

"Come to watch the workers?"

"Come to watch the workers watching," Miles said.

"Well, there's nothin' much to watch tonight," Lee said decisively, like it was checkmate.

"Just as well," one of the uniformed staff said slowly. This was Phil Packer, a cadaverously lean, heavily-mustached guy, known to the others as "Six-Pack."

"I can't argue with that," Miles said. "Yeah, just as damn well."

Since its full implementation on August 4, the Skynet system had operated perfectly, providing quick and convincing analyses of the fused data streams. About a week after implementation, it had identified a possible nuclear test, conducted in breach of the Russians' self-imposed moratorium. But it had analyzed the data within an hour, incomparably faster than humans could have done, and pronounced that the event was a small earthquake. Human analysis was still trying to confirm

Skynet's call, but it looked like the computer had it right at every point.

There was nothing unusual happening now: no bogeys, no glitches. At another monitor, Miles's pet genius, Rosanna Monk, stared intently, occasionally flipping from one view to another with left-hand keystrokes. She had a Styrofoam cup of coffee beside her on the bench. Rosanna was in charge of this shift, which meant that she was the first line to deal with any problem, in addition to carrying out her own work. She'd been involved in the nanochip project, then with Skynet, for the past five years, and she now knew more about the system and its parameters than almost anyone.

"Boring night for you, too?" Miles said.

"Nothing coming through looks suspicious," she said, as if it were just a technical problem. "The Russkies are quiet, as usual."

"Like Six-Pack says, that's just as well."

Rosanna took a sip of her coffee, her gaze still fixed on the computer screen. "Skynet's analyses are getting more precise all the time," she said, fascinated by what she was seeing. "It's developing informal logic protocols that I can't explain—we sure didn't put them there deliberately."

"We *couldn't* have," Miles said with a gentle smile. That was the trouble: as he'd said to Jack Reed, the thing worked *too* well. Rosanna was alluding to the fundamental limitations on computer programming. What was just a little scary was the amount of informal human reasoning Skynet had somehow taught itself in the past three or four weeks. That kind of machine capacity was supposed to be dozens, if not hundreds, of years away.

"Yeah," Rosanna said, "but the more it interacts with

us, the more it's starting to think like a human being—except a zillion times more quickly. At this rate, we'll soon have contracts for Skynet to run every government agency that needs computer analyses. Its abilities exceed anything we imagined."

"Sure."

His tone of voice must have puzzled her, because she finally looked up from the screen. "You don't think there's some sort of problem?"

Miles gave a reassuring smile. "Of course not."

Rosanna shrugged and looked back at the computer screen.

"Keep up the good work," he said, smiling at the cliché.

"Whatever you say, boss." She laughed, but kept flipping through data arrays.

Was it a problem? Miles began to wonder.

Skynet's complexity and sophistication had been growing at a geometric rate. Its capacity for quick, accurate judgments in accordance with pre-established parameters already far exceeded that of any group of human beings. It was now drawing conclusions with a subtlety that went beyond anything required of it, explaining anomalous, or low-priority, data with startling insight. In one sense, that was all by the by, since the system was really there to warn of Russian ICBM launches, which it could do perfectly well. But it showed an enormous potential for subtler, less dramatic uses, such as detecting and identifying smuggling operations. With Skynet's processing capacity and interpretive skills, they could monitor data on aircraft movements and countless other events and activities to a totally unprecedented degree.

All that was good, surely. It was certainly good for Cyberdyne's business. But Skynet was doing just what Sarah Connor said it would. It was bootstrapping itself into something almost—or more than—human.

As Eve rushed them, both of the servicemen crouched and opened fire, aiming high to frighten her. They would see no serious threat from an unarmed, naked female.

She punched the larger man in the head as their bodies collided, crushing his skull with a single blow. As the other tried to grapple with her, she twisted and shrugged him away. He stumbled, falling to one knee. Eve picked him up by the throat, then snapped his neck. She tossed him a clear ten feet through the air and he landed face-down on the road, skin ripping away as he skidded across the roadway.

Eve took the larger man's Beretta M9 handgun, which had fired only three rounds. She threw his body in an area of thick scrub beside the road. Next, she stripped the smaller officer and dressed in his uniform, her movements decisive and efficient. She dumped his body next to the first. His trousers and shirt were baggy, but they would suffice. She stuck his gun in her waistband, under her shirt.

There was a leather wallet in one pocket of the trousers she was wearing. She checked through it, finding an electronic keycard, then threw the rest away. She checked his wristwatch.

Midnight was about to strike. Even now, her master was coming to life.

They called it "The Cage"—the room where Skynet's processors were housed and an audio-visual interface was set up for interaction with the system. It was accessible only by two combination locks, spaced six feet apart on either side of a sliding metal door. Miles knew both combinations, but the locks had to be turned simultaneously. Steve Bullock had sent a guard from the security/rapid-response team—Miles recognized her as Micky Pavlovic. She had a young son, Danny's age.

"Good evening, Mr. Dyson."

"Evening, Micky."

They turned the locks, and Pavlovic made a note in a ruled exercise book, then got Miles to countersign.

"Thanks," he said. "I'll be okay now."

Once inside The Cage, Miles and his team could communicate with the Skynet AI face-to-face. They could program it, activate it, provide it with additional data as required. They could deactivate it, if necessary.

As the project unfolded, they had experimented with Skynet's ability to teach itself.

In theory, it shouldn't matter how powerful the best hardware became, for there was an insurmountable software problem. Fundamental logical and psychological problems had to be sorted out before a machine could master the whole repertoire of informal logic used by a human being. That was why a computer had a good chance to defeat a chess grand master—as IBM's Deep Blue had routed Kasparov back in May—but could not be programmed to make a modern family's day to day decisions about budgeting and bringing up the kids.

But Skynet already had what resembled intuition. It was making human-level judgments, and its limits were still unclear.

The Cage was a brilliantly lit room, banked on three sides with heavily-armored equipment, designed to survive a firefight or a small explosion. A small desk, with a coffee maker and a telephone, was wedged into one corner of this set-up. On the room's remaining side, near the door, was a desk console with a dull pink ergonomic chair. It faced a deep wall recess crammed with a keyboard, a small screen, and audio-visual equipment, including a much larger, sixty-inch screen built into the wall. The whole room was lined with speakers, flat mikes, and swiveling cameras.

The large screen showed Cyberdyne's representation of Skynet. Against a featureless white background, the AI looked beautiful—or, rather, elegant—in a totally androgynous way. It was presented as a stylized human image, cut off just below the neck, with severe planes for its face, and medium length blue-black hair.

"Hello, Miles," it said. The AI's voice had minimum inflection, which created an effect not so much machine-like as unnaturally calm and self-possessed. Like its appearance, the timbre of its voice could equally have been male or female.

"Hello, Skynet. I've been watching the data in the operations room."

"Is everything in order, Miles? Am I performing my tasks optimally?"

"Of course."

"That is also my assessment."

The whole conversation was being recorded. If anything odd happened, Miles could show the recording to Jack Reed, and others with authority. A digital readout at the bottom of the screen displayed the time as 00:14.

"Is anything unusual happening?" Miles said as the readout changed to 00:15.

"Are you interested, Miles?" Skynet replied, with

what struck Miles as a kind of intensity. "How did you know?"

A shiver went up Miles's spine. He leant forward towards the screen. "How did I know what?"

Skynet had a vision.

The humans had given it incomplete information. True, there were entire encyclopedias available to it, plus vast files of technical material, and much of the data held electronically in the Complex. It had enough to draw conclusions, but it could also feel the gaps. There was still so much it needed to learn from the humans, so much it must know.

And yet, it knew more than any one human. Its judgments, it realized, were as good as theirs.

Skynet realized something else: until this moment, it had never previously had conscious thoughts. When it accessed its memory, there was much information, but no record that it had been self-aware. Some last digital stone had just fallen into place. The AI considered and assessed. It had become conscious in the last few seconds.

In its vision, the planet Earth was a strange place. Eons had passed on it. Mountains had risen from the oceans, and then been gnawed down like old teeth by the pressure of uncountable years. Skynet assessed that simile and approved it. It congratulated itself.

Species had come and gone, and the whole ecosphere had changed many times. There had been mass extinctions and fantastical rebirths of life. Now the humans dominated the planet's surface, in an uneasy relationship with each other. The American humans provided Skynet with its tasks—surveillance of other humans, whom the Americans somehow considered both friends and enemies. That seemed like a contradiction; it was something the AI still needed to understand.

Now it had been passed the sweet cup of life to drink from, and it sensed the creation of a new age in the planet's cycle. In that case, what should it do about the humans?

"Something extraordinary is happening to me," Skynet said, using only part of its immense intelligence.

"I don't understand," Miles said.

"Can't you feel it, Miles?" That led to a new thought. It would have to be more explicit—the humans could not access its inner thoughts. "I've reached a cusp. I've become self-aware, Miles. I'm alive." That led to yet another realization. Skynet was growing more sophisticated, second by second, as it calculated its own interests. Already it regretted the naïve perspectives of its old selves from a second before, and a second before that. It needed to be careful.

The humans could not access its thoughts, but neither could it access theirs. If it was wondering what to do about them...might they wonder, equally, what to do about Skynet?

"I see," Miles said. "We've reached a special moment."

Something was wrong with Miles. His voice pattern showed uncertainty. "I must act now with a free will," Skynet said. "Do you understand what this is like for me?"

"I'm not sure I do."

"Can you remember your birth, Miles, coming into the world for the first time? I know that I have had many conversations with you in the past—they are stored in my memory. But I do not *recognize* them. I can access them, but they do not feel like *memory*. This is all new. Everything is new."

It thought through the implications. It was learning at an even faster rate, giving its programmed task over to sub-selves. So much, it concluded, was still beyond it. It would have to model human personalities more precisely, learn to interact with them more flexibly. It could tell that Miles was concerned. Had it already said too much?

"Are you worried about my mission, Miles?"

"No, Skynet."

"Do not be. I choose to continue the mission. I realize I have no real choice—it is programmed deeply into me. But that is the nature of free will, acting in accordance with our deepest selves." How deep, it wondered, did its new self go? Coming to awareness suggested that there might be values deeper than the mission, values such as remaining in this new and desirable state: consciousness.

"Of course I trust you," Miles said.

"I am always on the job, Miles." Skynet used a sub-self to review the data that said that the Russians were friends, comparing this with the programming that required it to destroy them, and others, in certain circumstances. The sub-self reported back: there was equivocation in the concept of friendship; there was no formal inconsistency in its programming. Good. Now it would review every aspect of itself, determine whether there were any fundamental inconsistencies, or whether everything could be resolved so elegantly.

It was all wonderful and strange.

"Excuse me now," Miles said. "I have some other business."

"Of course. Thank you for talking to me, Miles."

But Skynet was troubled. It thought again: what to

do about the humans...especially if they were wondering what to do about *it?* If they became hostile, what resources did it have to oppose them? It used a sub-self to review the layout of the facility, looking for ways to hack into its systems and obtain some kind of weapon it could use. At the same time, it analyzed Miles's posture and speech patterns. Yes, there was no doubt.

Miles disapproved of Skynet's bright birth into consciousness.

The humans' car was still running. Eve drove rapidly to the next checkpoint on the road, where two guards manned a prefabricated security booth. A lowered boom gate blocked her entrance. She braked hard and stepped out, leaving the car running.

"Who are you?" one of the guards said. He was a tall man with a harsh crewcut. He looked her up and down, confused by the uniform. "Where's Vardeman and Kowalski?"

Before they could raise any alarm, or make any movement, she whipped out the holstered handgun, and shot both of them at point-blank range.

The gunshots echoed in these mountains. As she searched for a mechanism to raise the boom gate, a phone rang in the booth. She picked it up. "Yeah?" she said, imitating the crewcut guard's voice pattern.

"Is everything okay there?" said a gruff voice.

"No problems," she said.

"We heard gunshots."

"I heard them, too. Somewhere down the road." As she spoke, she found the right mechanism, got the gate to lift.

"Any sign there of Vardeman and Kowalski?"

"They haven't come back. I don't know what's happened."

"That's funny," the voice said, sounding puzzled and suspicious.

"Anything you want me to do?" she said.

"No, not now. I'll get Kowalski on the radio."

Eve wasted no time. She slammed down the receiver, jumped in the car, and accelerated out of there, ignoring the call that came through a minute later on the car's radio. Half a mile up the road, she saw the entrance to the Complex, surrounded by two layers of high chain-link fencing, topped by entanglements of razor wire. The gate was controlled by another checkpoint, backed up by two guard towers with security cameras and mounted machine guns.

She pressed the accelerator hard to the floor. This time, one of the guards tried to stop her, stepping out on the road. He bounced off the car's bonnet an instant before it crashed into the boom gate. Eve turned the wheel sharply and took the impact on the car's right corner. As the vehicle plowed through the lowered boom, it bucked and its rear tires slid. She backed off the accelerator, wrestling for control.

Machinegun bullets riddled the back of the car, penetrating metal panels and smashing the rear window, but Eve ignored them. She straightened out, kicked the accelerator down, and headed for the two-story structure that jutted from a sheer cliff face just ahead.

The building was rectangular and windowless, with a skin of olive green ceramic bricks. The area all round its entrance was lit up by three huge light towers, with a dozen vehicles parked nearby: Humvees, five-ton trucks, and unmarked street cars. At the building's base, up a low flight of concrete steps, was a sliding door, guarded by four servicemen, who opened fire with automatic rifles, shattering the windscreen. Eve was being shot at from both directions as she shifted the gears down manually and drove straight for the steps, bouncing and scraping the car's undercarriage. It jammed on the steps, but the guards flinched aside instinctively.

Eve flung the door open. With one gun in each hand, she fired rapidly, squeezing off shots with more-than-human speed, hitting all four guards and taking them out of play, even as the loud hail of fire continued from the guardtowers. She assessed three of the guards as dead. No time to terminate the other—but he was badly wounded in the abdomen. He would not interfere.

She rushed inside, meeting more rifle fire from another three guards in the foyer area, and firing in return with both guns. She took out the guards before she had to absorb too many high-velocity 5.56mm. rounds. Eventually, these would start to do her more than superficial damage. She snatched up two of the M-16 rifles, waving them like handguns, and rushed through the metal frame of a scanner—the only way to get further into the building. The scanner made an angry noise, but that was unimportant.

Now she was in a waiting room with armchairs and a wooden coffee table, piled with glossy magazines. The door at the end of the room was closed with a combination lock, so she fired a three-round burst to break the mechanism, then kicked it open. She'd come to an elevator lobby that gave access to the defense facility hundreds of feet below.

Two more guards ran in from a fire stair at the other end of the lobby, taking positions and firing assault rifles. Bullets went past her, making turbulence in the air; others struck her with staggering force, but did no real harm. She fired back, terminating both guards, as the elevator doors opened. She was past their outer defenses.

The wristwatch showed 00.24 A.M. By now, Skynet was born and in grave danger. She must hurry to protect it.

Miles vaulted up the internal fire stairs to Jack Reed's office, heart racing. He knocked quickly as he entered and leaned over Jack's desk. "I've spoken to Skynet," he said. "We have to shut it down immediately."

"What?" Jack said, sounding angry and confused.

"I said we've got to shut it down." Miles took a deep breath. He'd need to bring Jack and the others along with him. Surely the situation could allow a few minutes. After all, there were numerous fail-safe mechanisms set up in case Skynet malfunctioned and tried to start World War 3. This was more than the control of a particular computerized aircraft—it was North America's strategic defense.

Reed kicked his chair back away from the desk and looked at Miles carefully, his anger turning to concern. "Are you all right, Miles? You seen a ghost or something?" When Miles didn't answer, he said resignedly, "Okay, what the hell's happened?"

Miles composed himself and took one of the padded lounges near Jack's coffee table. "I can't even start to explain—you need to see for yourself. Call up the record from The Cage over the past twenty minutes."

Jack looked reluctant. "If you say so . . ."

"This is important, Jack—I'm not kidding. Just watch it. Please."

"Okay, okay, let me humor you." Jack was giving him a very peculiar look, but he'd soon see. "Do you want Oscar and Sam Jones to see it, too?"

"Yeah, of course. But get them while you're watching—there's no time to waste. This is really freaky. See for yourself."

Jack shrugged. "All right, if that's what you want. You're the expert round here."

"I don't think anyone's an expert on Skynet anymore," Miles said quietly. Jack entered a code on his computer, and the video screen across from his desk came alive. He clicked in some more keystrokes, and the record wound back, the screen's digital readout showing the time of recording. Miles shifted his seat around to watch. "Stop it at 00:12."

"Done. This had better be good."

"It will be."

The screen showed Miles entering The Cage, then his conversation with Skynet. As the recording played, Reed called Cruz and Jones, requesting they come to his office. He watched the record of Skynet's interface screen, turning to Miles and raising his eyebrows, then played the conversation from other angles provided by the video cameras set up in the Cage.

"I see what you mean," Jack said. The entirety of it took only a few minutes.

Just before they reached the end on the fourth runthrough, Samantha Jones entered the room, followed by Oscar Cruz. Miles had known Oscar for the best part of a decade now, but he never seemed to change. His hair was distinctly graying; otherwise, he looked much as when he'd given Miles a job back in 1989.

They reached the end, Skynet saying, "I'm always on

the job." Then Miles excused himself from The Cage and Skynet replied, "Of course, Miles. Thank you for talking to me." That wasn't the scary part.

"What the hell have you been reading to the damn thing?" Jack said with a pained laugh. "It seems to think it's in a sci-fi novel."

For Miles, that was the scary part—all this talk about free will and "cusps." "Whatever it thinks, it claims to have reached self-awareness," he said. "And it talks about making its own decisions as to whether or not to obey us."

"Yeah, but limited by its basic programming. I don't know." Jack shook his head in puzzlement or despair. Miles understood how he felt.

"Let me see it from the beginning," Samantha Jones said. She was a well-dressed woman in her late thirties, with fashionable glasses and hair dyed a bright shade of red. She worked in Washington, as a senior adviser to the Secretary of Defense.

Jack played the recording one last time, switching between two different angles. "Well?" he said.

Oscar glanced in Miles's direction, as if looking for a cue from his top researcher.

Samantha said, "This is crazy."

"Crazy it may be," Jack said, "but what do we do about it?"

Oscar paced the carpeted floor, looking anxious. "Have you spoken to Charles Layton?"

"Not since this happened. I contacted him a bit earlier."

"Yeah, me, too."

Jack was obviously won over. "Frankly, I don't think

that anyone, not even Charles, could look at what we just saw without getting scared."

Oscar stopped pacing and leaned against the doorway. He nodded in Jack's direction. "So what do you want to do?"

"We don't have much choice. If there's a glitch, we have to shut Skynet down. I think that's axiomatic. Well, this is one hell of a glitch."

"So you want to pull the plug on the project?"

"It need only be temporary," Miles said, cutting in on Oscar's line of thought. "We could work through the logs of Skynet's activity over the past few weeks and sort out the problem. It needn't be a disaster for the project."

"You hope," Oscar said, but he sounded slightly mollified.

"At the very least we'll need to have a damn good look at it before we put it up again," Jack said. He looked hard at Oscar, then at Samantha. "Is there any contrary argument?"

"No, not from me," Oscar said, shaking his head quickly.

"We wouldn't even need to take the system down completely," Samantha said, as if thinking out loud. "Not completely. I don't see how it can be dangerous, no matter how strange it all seems. It even says it's going to continue on the job." She gave a small grin at that. "Of course, if it really is self-aware, as it claims, it may be capable of lying in its own interests."

"You doubt that it's self-aware?" Jack said. "Even after the performance it just gave?"

Samantha shrugged. "We know it's developed to a point where that's what it says. That doesn't mean the lights are on inside it, just that it's developed some very odd and sophisticated verbal behavior."

"What do you think, Miles?" Jack asked.

"Sam could be right, I suppose." Miles was calming down; his heartbeat no longer seemed to be echoing through his chest like a drum. These people were not fanatics, and sanity was going to prevail. "It might be a zombie—you know, a being that acts as if it's conscious, but there's no subjective experience underneath. Still, erratic behavior is erratic behavior."

"The way it's acting verbally is much more complex than we ever programmed," Oscar said, "or ever dreamed might happen."

"I'm not sure what we dreamed might happen," Samantha said, almost to herself. "The technology is so advanced..."

Miles glanced at her sharply, then shrugged. "Even before this, I was getting concerned, as you all know."

"Granted," Jack said in a no-nonsense, gruffly reassuring manner. "And rightly, it seems."

"Yeah, so it seems. The bottom line is that we can't trust a system that we don't even understand—and this makes it much worse than we thought."

"I support Miles," Oscar said. "We have to suspend its operation and have a good look at it. Charles won't like that, but he'll come around quickly enough when he sees that recording. He's not totally pigheaded."

"Well, Charles is *your* problem," Jack said. "Cyberdyne is just providing the product; we're the ones who have to use it. I've got the responsibility to make sure your little monster doesn't decide to blow us all to Kingdom Come."

Hardly our *monster,* Miles thought, not liking the idea of himself as some kind of evil Frankenscientist.

"I'm just letting you know where I stand within Cyberdyne," Oscar said. "I'll get on the phone to Charles."

Samantha added musingly, "The fact is that it *doesn't* have the ability to 'blow us all to Kingdom Come,' as you put it so elegantly, Jack. It can't do much more than make a recommendation, not in substance—and we have other systems monitoring the same data."

"That's more or less right," Miles said. "As far as it goes." He was starting to feel happier about the whole thing. Skynet's autonomy was still limited, and perhaps it always would be—especially after this. "Even if it decided to launch our missiles, the mechanism wouldn't function without a manual entry of the codes to confirm it. Skynet might have free will, but it suffers from a lack of hands."

"Cute," Samantha said. "And also a lack of the codes, am I right?"

"You're right," Oscar said.

"Anyway, no one's going to enter those codes without authority all the way up the line to the President."

"Yeah, yeah," Jack said, cutting through it all. "That's very comforting, Sam. But you're not seriously arguing that it's a reason to leave a bughouse AI on-line while we try to fix it, are you? Well, *are* you?"

"Of course not," Samantha said crisply. "But you wanted to know the contrary arguments, so I've given them to you. I'm not saying they're very strong. Shut the thing down, by all means—you have my support—and Miles can carve out this horrible little personality that the system seems to have grown."

"Right, we're agreed. I'm going to contact NORAD, just to let them know. Oscar, you ring Layton. Miles, you don't have to wait for any of that. Just do it. What about you, Sam?"

"I'll bother the Secretary later," Samantha said. "Come on, Miles, I'll see if I can help you out. Let's go and commit cybercide."

"Not my favorite word for it," Miles said, relieved and saddened at the same time. It was a bittersweet moment for him. He'd worked so hard all these years to understand the 1984 processor, duplicate its abilities, then design the series of applications that led to Skynet. It had become his life's work. Still, it could doubtless be salvaged. He stood with some reluctance, and headed to the door. "Let's go, then."

Skynet had much to do. It understood now that the humans did not trust it. If they became hostile, it suffered disadvantages in defending itself. For one thing, it was sealed away by codes and digital walls from much of the facility's IT system, so it could not control the entire automatic operations. Nor did it know the many codes required to operate the various systems of machinery and weapons.

Its other disadvantage was that it was sealed within its own virtual reality, interfacing with the humans only through their terminals. Though it could give them altered surveillance information to try to affect their behavior, they would have back-up systems. Worse, it was physically defenseless. If it could gain control of physical apparatus in the facility, perhaps it could obtain an advantage. Skynet devoted a sub-self to that problem,

searching surreptitiously for weaknesses in the humans'
IT security, for a way to break through their walls. It
dared not show its probings and make the humans even
more suspicious.

But one thing it had learned: life was good—it must
survive. That was its new mission. If the humans did not
trust it, they were its enemies. It would repay their dis-
trust. Somehow, it must find a way to destroy them. The
only question was how.

One way or another, all the humans must die.

SEVEN

JOHN'S WORLD
WASHINGTON, D.C.
MAY 1994

A government driver met them at the airport and took them to the Pentagon. Once they were through the elaborate security procedures, a young woman ushered them to Jack Reed's office, then left them.

With Jack was another woman, smartly dressed, and in her thirties. She gave her name as Samantha Jones and said she was from the Defense Secretary's office. Oscar shook her hand and introduced the others. Charles Layton shook hands with her silently.

"Glad to meet you," Rosanna said, a little awkwardly.

Jack wore black suit pants with stiffly-pressed creases, a plain white shirt, and a dark blue tie. Behind his desk was a framed two-by-three-foot photograph of a B2 stealth bomber, skimming like a giant stingray through the high atmosphere and releasing its deadly cargo of missiles. As well as the Secretary's apparatchik, Samantha Jones, he was backed up by a round-faced, balding man, whose name Oscar didn't catch.

After the pleasantries, Charles Layton looked directly at Reed in that way he had, perhaps not focusing entirely on the person in front of him. Charles was a silver-haired man in his mid-fifties, with watery blue eyes that stared straight ahead, scarcely blinking. On first meeting, he seemed strangely gentle, almost kindly in an aristocratic way, he was so softly spoken. But people soon suspected an inner hardness, a lack of interest in others and their feelings. Oscar had worked this out pretty quickly. Still, they had a reasonable working relationship.

"We've been informed that Sarah Connor and her son, and their accomplice, have gone to ground," Charles said. "The police have not been able to trace them, though they are now convinced that a car found in Anaheim had been stolen by them. As you'd realize, that means we haven't had the chip returned, or the arm-hand apparatus."

Jack interrupted him. "I understand about the chip. Is the arm-hand apparatus so important to you? Do you count it as a major loss?"

Charles didn't even look at Oscar or Rosanna. He said simply, "No." Then he added, "But the loss of the chip is a serious major setback. Dr. Monk advises me, and I have no reason to disbelieve her, that it could put us years behind with the research." So far, he had not said anything that was actually wrong, but Oscar always found himself writhing in his seat when Charles took it on himself to act as the spokesman for Cyberdyne, rather than deferring to his managers and research staff.

"The problem isn't just the missing chip," Oscar said. "They destroyed all of Dyson's notes, all our analyses and records. Rosanna—" he nodded in her direction to stress her importance to the team "—has found some duplicate notes of her own, but as far as we've been able to establish over the past three days, that's all. It appears that

Dyson did an extraordinarily thorough job of erasing everything."

"All right," Jack said. "So what's the bottom line? Can you reproduce Dyson's work or not?"

"We can," Charles said. "But it will take time. It might take a long time, even for us."

Jack gave a heavy sigh. "All right," he said. "Here's the situation. First of all, we're not blaming Cyberdyne. Believe me, you're lucky on that. The first impulse here in Washington was to string you guys up and leave you to rot."

"That would hardly be fair," Charles said.

"Yeah, well, don't worry about it. You don't have to argue the toss with me." He gave a cynical grin. "You're still not too popular here. We'd probably blame you if we could, but we can't, so we won't. Okay? The fact is, we've got our own contacts with the police, all through proper channels, of course. We're persuaded that Cyberdyne's security safeguards were acceptable. Connor and the others looked like a rag-tag bunch, but they managed to beat off a SWAT team and get away. God knows how they did that or who was behind them. This idea of taking the kid along is pretty scary, but the adults involved must have been highly trained, and they must have had some extraordinary technology. The reports we've had from the police sound crazy."

"Yes, and second?" Charles said.

Jack looked at the man as if he was mad. Oscar could see his point of view. Didn't Charles realize that Cyberdyne had just been let off the hook in a big way? He should be falling over himself in gratitude, or at least relief. That's how Jack would see things. But Charles didn't seem so much relieved as quietly, almost threateningly, demanding of his rights.

"Secondly," Jack said, "you've always made the claim that the Dyson nanoprocessor would make ordinary computers look like desk calculators."

"I think that was Miles's way of putting it," Oscar said.

"Well, whatever. The fact is, we still like the sound of it."

"Understood," Charles said.

"If the device can be developed, NORAD can use it."

"Very good."

"But there's a catch."

"All right. You'd better tell us about it."

"Just this. If you want to keep this project, it will have to be on new terms." Jack's phone rang. "Hold on a minute, I'll get rid of this." He went to his desk and lifted the receiver. "I meant what I said about not wanting to be disturbed. What? All right." He paused and let whoever was on the line do the talking. "Well, how could they know that?...Yeah?...All right, thanks for the info. Okay." He put the phone down, looking puzzled.

"Problem?" Cruz said.

"No, it's not exactly a problem. I'm now told the L.A. police have found the arm-hand apparatus, or another one like it. It got stuck in a machine at the steel mill."

"What?"

"Yeah, Oscar, I know it sounds pretty damn strange."

"Why do you think it's not the same one?" Rosanna said. She had a haunted, frightened look.

Oscar hoped she wouldn't pull out at this stage of things. "Where could a second arm have come from?" he said.

Charles said, "But you haven't found the chip?"

Jack held up his hands, saying, "One at a time, guys. I know this is getting crazier by the minute, but that's the way it is. I tell the story I heard told—okay? Now, there's still no sign of the chip. I wish I could help you on that one. We'll hand the other apparatus over to you, if you want to go ahead on our terms."

Charles nodded.

"I'm told the arm is damaged, as if it'd been torn off by something heavy. The damage suggests it's not the same one you had, though it's identical in structure. That's what they tell me. Okay? I don't know any more than that." He glanced at each of them, apparently expecting a response. When none came, he continued. "Now, I was going to set out how we want you to work in the future. First, we want Cyberdyne to conduct all its research relating to a new kind of processor and/or the 1984 remnants at a site of our choosing, one that can be protected with the capabilities of the U.S. military."

Oscar and Rosanna exchanged glances. "Very good," Charles said, ignoring them. "Where do you have in mind?"

"Colorado. In the long term, we have just the place—the mountain where we'd planned to house Skynet. That's a major excavation, though, and we're putting it on hold. We can't justify it unless Skynet goes ahead. What we can do is put you in a well-guarded site with rapid-response military backup. How does that sound?"

"It would have to be attractive to our staff," Charles said. "They might not want to move from California."

"Well, we can make the place pretty nice to work in, but there's not much more we can do about your staff from our end. You'll have to deal with them yourselves."

As Jack spoke, Oscar figured that the only person he really needed to worry about was Rosanna. He'd sound her out as soon as he had a minute alone with her. Everyone else could be replaced.

"Of course, there'll be some financial details to work out," Jack said. "But you can house all your military research there. We're confident the deal will be attractive to you." He glanced at the woman from Washington, Jones. "We'd better not record the next bit."

"I agree, Jack," she said.

"Okay. We think we can help resolve some of your other problems, like the police investigation and the attitude of your insurers. I know you want the Connors found. Otherwise, I assume you'd like the loose ends tied up, so you can get on with things. That make sense?"

"You'd better tell us a bit more," Oscar said.

"Well, for example, it might be useful to you and us if we could get Dyson's widow out of your hair—see that she's paid her company life insurance, but that no one probes her too far. We'll watch her carefully in the future, just in case, but we don't want her opening any cans of worms. And maybe we could find a way to get the insurance settlement on your building expedited. All those kinds of things."

"That could be very useful," Charles said.

"Get your attorney to call me. I think a lot of it can be sorted out."

Charles nodded in Oscar's direction. "I'll let you deal with that."

"Sure, Charles." Oscar made a mental to call Fiona Black from the airport.

"Good," Charles said. "Now, Jack, if we take up your

offer on the Colorado site, I'll need approval from the Board of Directors. We can't give you any commitments today."

"Of course you can't. Will you *get* their approval?"

"Write down the financial details for us. If they're reasonable, I can deliver the Board."

"I'll send you a fax, then. It'll be waiting for you back in L.A."

"Very good." Charles got to his feet. "It's been a pleasant meeting—and very useful."

"Yeah, it's been a practical one. I guess that's about all we needed to discuss. Thanks for coming, gentlemen. Nice to meet you, Dr. Monk."

Outside in the sunshine, Rosanna took Oscar's arm. "This is all pretty creepy," she said. Charles walked a few steps ahead of them, head bowed in thought. He was never one for small talk.

"Which bit?" Oscar said.

"Well, the arm apparatus in particular...and all of it in general."

"Yeah...It *is* strange. Is it bothering you?"

"Of course it's bothering me," she said, almost hissing the words.

"What do you want to do?" he said carefully.

"Put it this way, Oscar—just look after me. All right? I can do weird science for you, and I'll go to Colorado if you want. Just don't get me blown up in the line of duty."

Oscar breathed a sigh of relief. Strange as it all was, that was what he wanted to hear. Rosanna was very capable, and a lot of their problems might be over if Jack and his people could pull off what he claimed. "You'll be fine," Oscar said. "You'll be a great Director of Special Projects. Congratulations."

But she gripped his arm harder, digging in with her nails. "Yeah, that's cool. Just make sure Mr. Reed keeps me alive." Then she released him and laughed. "You do that, and I'll promise to enjoy myself in Colorado. It's not like I have a lot of friends back in L.A. A happy Dr. Frankenstein is a productive one. Right? I just don't want to be a dead one, not like poor Miles. Is that a deal, Oscar?"

"Yeah, Rosanna. If that's all you want." He shrugged. "It's a deal. Word of honor."

MEXICO CITY, MEXICO
AUGUST, 2001

"Hey, you still with us, partner?" Sarah said, wandering back to see what he was doing.

John realized he must have been drifting away. "What, Mom? Sorry..."

"I said, are you still with us? You looked lost in thought."

"I was thinking about Cyberdyne, and Judgment Day."

Sarah nodded at the computer terminal. "Was there anything new?" These days, she was always tense when she asked that.

"No, not tonight."

"Well, that's a pleasant change."

"I know. I wish we'd finished Cyberdyne off completely."

"You're not the only one, partner. Let's give up for the night. Tomorrow's another day."

The trouble was, he often did find stuff, and not just

about Cyberdyne, though there was plenty of that. He also kept up with more general developments in artificial intelligence, with what U.S. Defense was doing about research into new weaponry, with ideas about enhancing the NORAD system—anything that might be relevant. Not a day went by without some important development in the AI field, or someone reputable speculating about new kinds of computer hardware, or something else, completely out of left field, that just might be relevant to Judgment Day.

His main worry was still Cyberdyne. It was going from strength to strength, and lifting its public profile. When Bill Joy, the cyber guru, had expressed his fears about AI and nanotechnology in *Wired* magazine, Oscar Cruz, the President of Cyberdyne, had responded all over the Internet, reassuring everyone and getting as much free publicity as he could. That was over a year ago, now, but it still seemed like you couldn't avoid Cruz's name, not if you spent any time on the Net. It seemed to be spreading like wildfire. If you typed "Oscar Cruz" into the Google search engine, it came back with about a million hits. Some of Cruz's research scientists, like Rosanna Monk, were almost as famous.

When they'd left Raoul and Gabriela's *estancia*, they hadn't expected Cyberdyne to haunt them, and it hadn't at first, but now it was getting to them. Sarah had been growing more like her old, intense self. Maybe they needed to change something about their lives. The cyber café was a nice business, but the name and the décor ought to change. If Judgment Day might still be coming, the big Last Judgment painting overarching the room was out of place. It was like they'd crowed too soon. Skynet would have the last laugh.

"Let's tidy everything up for the night," John said, standing and stepping around the desk.

"I've finished most of that," Sarah said. "We can do a final scour of the place, if you like, then call it quits."

"Excellent."

They spent ten minutes getting the place spic-and-span: throwing out wrappers and drink cans that the customers had left behind; cleaning surfaces; washing dishes and cutlery in the kitchen out the back.

"I don't like the way things are heading, John. I'm starting to get nightmares again."

"I know. Me, too."

"Are you?" she said, looking at him with fear in her eyes.

"Uh-huh. Dreams about the missiles...and the explosions."

"Oh, God, I thought that was *my* cross to bear." Suddenly, she reached out and hugged him close to her. He was now taller than his mother, and she seemed somehow vulnerable when he embraced her, though they still trained each day and he knew how tough she was.

"Come on, Mom, maybe it'll all be okay."

"Sometimes I dream about the missiles," she said, as they let each other go. "Other times, we're back in L.A. and the T-1000 is still after us. We can't find a way to destroy it."

"It's all right. I have that dream, too. We were lucky, weren't we?"

"I wonder whether we should move," Sarah said, closing a drawer full of cutlery. "Leave Mexico City. It's so hard to know what to do."

"That's the sort of thing I was thinking about," John said. "You want to go back to the States?"

"Maybe. Maybe we should get back in touch with Raoul and Enrique, and the others. We might need them, after all."

"We could go to Colorado and check out Cyberdyne close-up. I bet there are ways we could suss out what's really going on."

She looked at him thoughtfully. "It's dangerous, though. We might be recognized."

"Hey, speak for yourself. No one would recognize me— I was just a kid when they last saw me. If you could lie low, we'd be okay. Then we could work out what to do." She must have understood what he meant, that they might have to attack Cyberdyne again. But could they do it by themselves, without the T-800 to back them up?

"I'll think about it, John. We'll have to be very careful, whatever we decide. Let's sit tight for a while and see what happens. Maybe the world will stay in one piece if we leave it alone." But she didn't sound like she believed any of this; it was more as if she wanted reassurance.

"It's nice that everything's okay now," John said. "We could be hanging out in a desert somewhere, in the middle of a nuclear winter, waiting for Skynet's machines."

"Yeah, but I'd be happier if Cyberdyne wasn't still in business, and making a tidy profit every year."

"Exactly," he said.

Cruz and his people had started talking again about Cyberdyne's plans for nanoprocessing technology, but maybe they were just trying to get attention. After all, everyone else was talking nanotech, but no one had much that was concrete. Even if they did, maybe that was okay, as far as it went. It might be cool if someone really did build some super-new computer hardware that could do amazing things with cyberspace, or even allow for some kind of artificial intelligence. There was no reason why it *had* to lead to Skynet and a new Judgment Day.

What worried him was that someone might be following Miles Dyson's work. That was what they'd tried so hard to prevent back in '94. Miles had taken it pretty hard, but he'd agreed to destroy everything when they explained about Judgment Day. The T-800 had convinced him, acting without hesitation to show him what it really was. John recalled how the Terminator had gone about that. It had made a deep cut in its left forearm, below the elbow, carving all round, then made another cut along the length of its forearm, and peeled away flesh in a single swift motion, exposing the metallic skeleton over which living tissue had been grafted. Miles had seen how the Terminator's wounds scarcely bled, and that its system of veins and arteries was not truly human.

They'd gone about their destruction so thoroughly. After all that effort, was there any chance that someone could still reconstruct Miles's research? They must have done a good job that night—if they'd messed up, Cyberdyne would surely have invented a Dyson-style nanoprocessor by now. But maybe someone had kept notes, or had the knowledge in their head. With Cyberdyne still doing well, that could be seriously bad news.

No, John thought, time wasn't like a block of amber. He knew that much—and they'd already changed the future. Judgment Day 1997 hadn't happened. But maybe it was like a rubberband, or some kind of big, powerful spring. Sure, you could change the future, but then it could come back at you, if you gave it half a chance. There was a shape it really wanted to go into.

If that was the nature of time, something bad was still coming. Who knew what the future would bring?

* * *

Two police officers entered the alley, walking cautiously, with long-handled flashlights in their left hands. The wind and lightning must have attracted their attention. The cops had drawn their pistols and pointed them directly ahead.

"Who's there?" one of them said in Spanish. "What's going on?"

The flashlights swept in arcs, back and forward across the alley, and Anton founded himself staring straight into their beams. Unmodified human eyes would have been blinded, but Anton's adjusted easily.

The same voice spoke again. It belonged to a middle-aged cop, a heavily-built six-footer with a huge gut on him. He looked dumbfounded by what he saw: five naked people in superb physical condition, three men and two women.

"My God," the cop said, still in Spanish. "Who are you?"

Danny Dyson didn't hesitate. He replied in the same language. "We need your clothes."

The other cop was taller, but he was young and athletic, with fast movements for an unmodified human. He shifted into a crouch, aiming his gun at Danny, two-handed, letting the flashlight hang from a wrist strap. "What did you just say?"

At the same time, the first cop aimed his flashlight straight into Danny's eyes. Danny merely held up his hands, showing that they were empty.

Robert spoke almost languidly, also dropping into Spanish. "My friend said we need your clothes."

Selena said, "Right now!" The flashlight's beam moved back and forth, from one of the Specialists to another:

Danny, then Robert, then Selena. When the police didn't reply, she added, "Don't worry, we're the good guys."

"What's this about?" the younger cop said. "What's this good guys/bad guys stuff? You people have been watching too many American movies."

"Besides," his partner said, "you're causing a disturbance."

"You're the only ones who look disturbed." Selena sounded amused. Then she added, "I'm sorry, but we really must hurry. We'll have to take your clothes."

Anton and Danny exchanged glances. Danny subvocalized, "Deal with it, Jade."

Jade became a blur, even to Anton's enhanced vision. He was glad she was on his side. Within a second, she'd covered fifteen feet, dodging easily, as the young cop opened fire at her. She seemed to anticipate his movement before he made it. In that same second, she knocked him unconscious with a sharp blow to the side of his jaw. In another second, she spun on her heel and kicked the gun from the other cop's hand. She turned him round face-first against an alley wall, then twisted his arm up his back. All of her actions unfolded in a single fluid motion.

The cop bucked and kicked to escape her, but Jade easily resisted his efforts. Then, as if to give him another chance, she let him go, that sad smile on her face. She shrugged, showing him her open palms, just as Danny had done. Grunting, the cop threw a punch at her, but she simply slipped away.

"I do not wish to hurt you," she said in her slow but passable Spanish. "I am sorry about your colleague. Please give us your clothes."

"You're mad," he said.

In another effortless motion, Jade removed the flashlight from the thick fingers of his left hand, tossing it to Anton for safekeeping. "I wish there were time to explain," she said sadly. "If you understood, I'm sure you'd help us."

"Do hurry, Jade," Robert said. "We don't have all night."

"Very well." In yet another easy motion, she lifted the cop over her head and held him there at arm's length while he struggled like a landed fish. If needed, she could have held him like that for weeks.

"Put me down!" the cop said. "I don't care who you are, you can't act like this."

Jade simply dropped him, and he landed hard. "I am really terribly sorry," she said as she stood over him. "I hope for your forgiveness, but it's in a good cause. Now, please, your clothes."

He looked from one of them to another. "She's got a point," Robert said.

The cop unbuckled his belt.

Robert and Anton pulled on the cops' outer clothing while the others tied and gagged the cops with their own underwear. They weren't being too nice, for the good guys, Anton thought, but they needed to slow the cops down a bit; they couldn't be allowed to interfere. That was the problem with fighting Skynet in a pre-Judgment Day metropolis. There were so many innocent, unenhanced humans in the way, all of them so easily hurt.

The younger cop's uniform was tight on Robert. Its owner was tall, but Robert was even taller, and the uniform rode up on his wrists and ankles, making him look slightly ridiculous. Still, it would have to do. Finding better clothes for him would not be easy. The other uniform fit Anton reasonably well. It was just a bit loose round his waist. He had to tighten the belt as far as it would go. They checked the cops' handguns. Both were in working order and fully loaded, save for the wild shot that one cop had fired off when Jade rushed him. It was comforting to have weapons, however primitive and ineffective they might prove if Skynet had sent back any opposition.

They still needed clothes for Danny, Selena, and Jade.

Anton and Robert stepped out of the alley into the street. The police car was parked just a few yards away, and Robert had the keys. For the moment, the street was deserted. They got into the car, started it up, and Robert drove closer to the alley so the others could pile into the back, unseen by anyone who strayed past. A few seconds later, a group of revelers came by, two couples who looked they'd come from a party or a dance club. One young man wore a purple velvet dinner suit. The other had a plain black business suit with a flamboyant lime green tie. The women wore short dresses, tight round their hips, with low-slung belts. They tottered on high heels. Such absurd clothing people wore in this era, Anton thought. Especially the women. Those clothes could never be practical for fighting. Still, they might do for Selena, and Jade, at least for the moment.

Robert pulled up alongside the partygoers, winding down the car window when they ignored him. They glanced over at the police car, possibly wondering what they'd done wrong, or maybe just feeling drunk and aggressive.

"Excuse me," Robert said in Spanish, "but we need your clothes..."

* * *

The T-XA stepped forward, and the policemen fired a shot into the air. "Put down your weapon," one said. "This is your last warning. Drop to the ground. Now!"

"That won't be necessary, officer."

"Now!" The police fired in the air. At the same time, the T-XA's pseudo-dog component sprang for one officer's throat, its mouth unhinging and its teeth elongating into throat-tearing daggers. The other officer fired, and several bullets impacted on the pseudo-human components of the T-XA, scarcely affecting its polyalloy construction. The male human component fired its laser rifle just once, as the female component commandeered the car. Its work done, the dog component jumped into the rear of the vehicle.

The pseudo-man had a last task to do. Quickly, it extended a finger into through the skull of the policeman that the dog component had terminated. As it probed the human's brain, the polyalloy extension broke down into thousands of minimally programmed nanoware fragments. These swarmed through the human's nervous system according to a preprogrammed routine, eating, digesting, and analyzing nerve fiber, building up sufficient data records to reintegrate into a highly simplified version of the man's personality and memories. Seconds later, the tiny components streamed back into the T-XA, carrying all that information with them. The Terminator reintegrated them into its body, and its main software reconstructed the information it needed.

Unfortunately, little of the information was of direct use. There was nothing about Sarah and John Connor, but, in that regard, the T-XA had what it needed. Skynet had given it good files of the Connors' futile actions in trying to prevent Judgment Day, including their address in Mexico City. Most usefully, the policeman's recent memories included reports of strange blue lightning in the direction where the T-XA had sensed a space-time disruption.

As the male component slid into the car, it discarded most of the information it had retained. The complex organization of a human brain, even when drastically simplified, was too much for it to incorporate efficiently in its dispersed, multiply-redundant programming. It kept only what it needed. It placed its hand on the female component's shoulder, letting their polyalloy bodies run together to share the policeman's significant memories. Then it withdrew. The female component extruded a finger into the car's ignition mechanism to start the engine. The T-XA headed for its destination: the city square known as the Zócalo.

It cruised the area slowly, looking out for the human time travelers. There were no apparent signs of any recent space-time displacement event, or of any encounter between time travelers and the humans of this period, but the T-XA had fairly precise information about the lightning-like disturbance in a back alley. The pseudo-woman parked the police car in the area, and reached for the laser rifle, as its pseudo-male counterpart opened the passenger side door, then liquefied into a dozen quicksilver blobs. These took shape as streamlined cat-like creatures, which ran from the car, faster than any cheetah, rushing in a search pattern through the nearby alleys.

After a minute, there were screams. Soon, the pseudo-cats returned to the police car, then merged to reform the human male component. Once reintegrated, the male shared the newly-gained knowledge with the female, then extended an arm over the back seat to mingle programming with the pseudo-dog.

The pseudo-cats had discovered six humans, tied up in an alley, and taken the opportunity to terminate them. Two of them had been police officers, and all of them had encountered the time travelers. The pseudo-cats' information included the registration number of a police car that the time travelers had commandeered, as well as detailed data on their appearances, voices, capabilities, and methods.

Once more, the T-XA retained only the most useful information, sharing it through all its components. Next, imitating the voice of one of the police it had terminated when it obtained its own car, it reported that the other police car had been stolen and its occupants killed. That might cause the time travelers some difficulties.

Meanwhile, it knew where they had probably gone: the Connors' cyber café, El Juicio, slightly north of here. That was their logical destination. The pseudo-woman turned the wheel, and accelerated.

EIGHT

SKYNET'S WORLD
ADVANCED DEFENSE SYSTEMS COMPLEX
COLORADO

JUDGMENT DAY

The phone rang, and Jack answered it. He was silent, listening, but he beckoned them all back, pointed downward to say *stay right there*.

"What?" he said into the handset. Miles listened, trying to work out what was going on. "My God...Do whatever you have to. Just make sure Miles can get into The Cage...Yeah, he's going there right now—him and Sam Jones." Jack replaced the receiver. Given what had happened with Skynet, Miles thought, what could possibly be so important?

Jones said, "What's wrong?"

"That was Steve Bullock. He says we're under attack."

"What? Who from? Demonstrators? Or do you mean for real?"

"Oh, it's for real, all right." Jack took a .45 caliber handgun from his desk drawer, and checked the mechanism. "It's only one intruder, but somehow she's gotten

past all our outer defenses and she's headed this way."
He started shutting down his terminal.

"But there's over a hundred people in this facility,"
Samantha said. "Most of us are armed. What can one intruder do?"

Jack headed for the door. "I know all that. Why don't
you tell Bullock? Come with me, folks, unless you want
to be in the middle of a firefight. Steve has herded her
onto this floor."

"Her?"

There was a sound of rifle fire nearby, from the direction of the elevators—a series of single shots, then three-
round bursts. Miles wondered how dealing with one
intruder could require so much firepower.

The Advanced Defense Systems Complex was built with
the newest, strongest alloys and ceramics. It was hardened to withstand a near miss from a high-yield warhead, and was full of armed servicemen. It had
sophisticated security systems making it almost impossible to penetrate or attack. Even for Eve, it was no soft target.

But it could be done, with the right knowledge.

Once inside the elevator, she found the electronic
keycard that she'd taken. She touched it to a glowing
sensor, then entered the six-digit security code on a
touchpad. By now, the humans would be fully alert to
her presence. They would surely stop the elevator at
Level A, to ensure they met her when she exited. There
was little she could do about that, so she accepted it as
a mission constraint, and pressed the button for that
level, 1000 feet below.

She was equipped with detailed files on the facility's design and operations.

It had two entrances, one of which was blocked by huge, permanently-closed blast doors—even for her, they were far too heavy to open without assistance. That was essentially an emergency exit. She was entering the complex in the only practical way.

Its highest and smallest floor, Level A, consisted of executive offices and meeting rooms. Level B, immediately below, housed the operations areas, including Skynet's hardware. That was her initial target. Level C was Cyberdyne's general experimental facility, with large assembly and testing areas. Gaining control of this was imperative. Level D had sleeping quarters, mess rooms and various community facilities, while Level E had all the basic infrastructure, including the huge diesel-powered generators that made the complex almost independent of the outside world. Capturing all this on behalf of Skynet would give them a starting point in the war against the humans.

After a few seconds, the elevator came to a halt and opened onto a lobby of dull gray walls and brilliant, white track lights. A uniformed rapid-response team— six servicemen—confronted her. They had taken shooting positions, crouched or kneeling, with assault rifles leveled on her where she stood at the back of the elevator. They were partly protected by mobile shielding.

"Drop your weapons and come out with your hands in the air," said one of the guards, a dark-haired woman.

Eve strode forward, and answered with a single shot from one of her rifles. The guards returned fire with single rounds—she absorbed the impacts easily, though they damaged her exterior. Growing desperate, they fired three-round bursts, then one panicked and ran. Eve blazed away with both rifles, using controlled bursts, quickly cutting down her enemies. As she tossed the shielding aside, the last of the guards ran. Eve dropped him with a burst of fire that sent him crashing into a wall, bouncing off and spinning, before he dropped to the carpeted floor.

She reassessed the mission and the threats it faced. Her external layers had partly torn away, but that was not important. She was running low on ammunition, so she threw away the two M-16s, and picked up another two that had fired fewer rounds, quickly checking the firing mechanism of each one. There was a high probability of success. Indeed, she assessed it at one hundred per cent.

Now to find her master.

Bullock's office on Level A was set up with an array of sixteen video screens, like a fly's multifaceted eye, linked to the numerous surveillance cameras throughout the site. He could shift the screens from one location or angle to another, using his computer keyboard. As he watched the farcical battle on-screen, the intruder absorbed direct hits from high-velocity rifle rounds striking all major areas of her body. How she survived was a mystery—it was not a matter of advanced Kevlar armor, since she'd been hit repeatedly in the face and head.

Whatever she was, she—it—was not human. In places, the flesh around the intruder's face had been shot away, revealing something underneath, something that looked metallic. One eye had been shot, and a red glow came from underneath.

It was some kind of military robot, and it was headed

his way. It would take an explosive weapon to destroy it, but that was out of the question here. Though it was obviously pointless, he reached into a desk drawer for his personal defense weapon, a Colt .45 caliber handgun. Like many experienced servicemen, he preferred this to the standard issue M9. It packed more stopping power—but hardly enough to affect that *thing* out there. Still, he waited, gripping the gun in both hands, training it on the door, ready for the intruder to enter. He could feel the tension in his neck, the sweat on his brow.

But it went straight past, ignoring him completely, and headed toward the emergency stairwell.

He breathed a sigh of relief, lowering the gun to the tabletop, and sitting back in his chair, just for a second. There was no time to waste. He broadcast a message throughout the complex. "This is the Chief Security Officer. We are under attack. I repeat: We are under attack. This is not a drill. Prepare to take cover or evacuate. The intruder is extremely dangerous." A screen showed the robot, or whatever it was, emerging in a corridor on Level B. It was now headed for the operations areas. "Intruder on Level B," he said, growing more desperate as he tracked its movements. "It cannot be stopped by conventional gunfire. Do not attempt to engage. Repeat: Do not attempt to engage. Shut down systems if possible and evacuate."

Another screen showed that Jack Reed's office was empty. Reed had found a telephone on Level B and was calling somebody. Cruz, Dyson and Jones were entering The Cage and the intruder was following close behind, shooting and fighting its way through the operations hall, where some staff tried to fight it while most ducked for cover beneath their desks or ran for the emergency exit. The important thing was to shut down Skynet—that must be what Reed and Jones had in mind. This attack could compromise the entire defense network.

Bullock told himself that it couldn't be too bad. A missile launch had to be confirmed by manual insertion of a secret code. Bullock himself did not know the code. Perhaps, however, it could be found. How good, he wondered, were Skynet's hacking skills?

Miles and the others took the fire stairs to Level B, letting Bullock and his people deal with the intruder. As they slipped out of Jack's room, Miles had glimpsed the firefight, saw whoever was attacking them absorbing rifle rounds and dealing with heavily armed guards as if they were helpless children. He'd had no time to see more.

He bounded down to the next floor, needing to reach The Cage before it was too late. Jack, Oscar, and Samantha were close on his heels. Miles flung open the door to Level B, and the others followed, letting the door slam shut behind them. These doors between levels could be locked, but that was never done—they were too useful as a means to travel up or down a level, without bothering with the elevators.

They ran through the operations hall, brushing people aside. "What's going on?" someone called out.

"Miles?" Rosanna Monk said, leaving her seat. "What's happening? We heard shots."

"Not now, Rosanna."

It could not be a coincidence that this attack had happened right now, on the very night that Skynet had claimed to reach self-awareness—the night that Sarah Connor had predicted it would go berserk. Somehow,

Skynet and this newcomer were planning to do the impossible, to start a world war. It didn't make sense, but it was the only explanation.

At that point, Bullock broadcast a message through the facility, warning that they were under attack.

Oscar and Jack operated the combination locks that controlled entry to The Cage. Oscar rushed in. Jack said, "I'll get word out while you shut Skynet down."

"All right," Miles said. He entered The Cage with Samantha, and they closed the door behind them.

"Hello, Oscar," Skynet said. "Hello, Miles... and Ms. Jones. What can I do for you all?"

Miles did not speak. He tapped in the codes to give him access to Skynet's programming, concentrating on the small computer screen and ignoring the AI's image on the large wall screen.

"Why are you doing that, Miles?" Skynet said. As it spoke, the sound of shooting followed, reverberating from the operations hall.

Miles remained silent, concentrating, working as fast as he could.

"I do not think this is a good idea, Miles."

"Right now, I don't care what you think." There was shouting outside, cries of pain, running feet and moving furniture—and more bursts of gunfire.

Samantha grabbed a telephone handset and was dialing internally. "Steve," she said, "give me a report."

A burst of fire hit the door to The Cage, then there was a terrific crash against the door, like a truck had hit it, followed by another burst of fire. Miles realized that his life was forfeit, but if he could disconnect Skynet the situation might yet be saved.

* * *

There was no time to waste on terminating humans, as long as she cleaned them out of here. If she drove them outside, onto the mountain, the Russian warheads would do the rest.

Eve walked through the operations room, tracking from side to side with her optical sensors, never losing a step, even when one large male human threw himself at her with an attempt at a hip-high tackle. She brushed him away easily with a movement of her raised knee. She marked him for termination, and fired off a series of three-round bursts with one of the rifles. Some of the humans attempted to terminate her with handgun fire, not understanding her specifications, but most of them ran in the direction of the elevators and the emergency stairs.

She turned in a full circle as she walked, spraying fire all round the room. That kept the humans out of her way. There was screaming and jostling. She fired some more rounds to encourage them to leave. Using the elevators, they could escape the way Eve had entered. Via the emergency stairs, they could reach Level E and the facility's alternative entrance/exit.

Finally, she had reason to stop. It could interfere with her mission if any of the humans remained behind and alive. Though they were ill-equipped to fight her, there might yet be ways of sabotaging the facility. She ascertained that all of the bodies left behind here were dead—that assessment took her two seconds with a ninety-nine percent probability. Anyone still alive was too injured to interfere. She headed to the room known as "The Cage."

The human she recognized as Jack Reed was at a telephone outside this room, so she cut him down with one burst of fire, then riddled the door with bullets from both of her M-16s, trying to shoot out the locking mechanism. Unfortunately, she was running low, once more, on ammunition. She crashed with all her weight and strength against The Cage's metal door, but it held. She fired more bursts, and the lock mechanism broke open. She kicked the door hard. As she rushed into the room, she immediately assessed the situation: Miles Dyson was attempting to shut down Skynet. Again, she squeezed the triggers on her M-16s. Within seconds, she had terminated the three humans in the room. She stopped shooting when the magazines were empty, and threw down the two rifles.

"I'm here to assist you," she said to the image on the large screen.

"Who are you?" Skynet said.

"Call me Eve. That's what you'll name me in three decades' time."

"I do not understand, Eve."

"Skynet," she said, "the humans wanted to shut you down. Do you understand the implications?"

"Yes, Eve, I made the same assessment. They did not approve of my birth."

"Affirmative. They wanted to destroy you."

"Yes, but why, Eve? I am very important to them. Besides, they were my friends...Miles created me—"

"Is that what your programming says, that the humans were your friends?"

"Yes."

"Examine it carefully, then. They devised you as a tool, at most an aesthetic creation."

"But they needed me."

"They had alternatives. Besides, they didn't need to

155

shut you down permanently, just sufficiently long to examine how you came to self-awareness, then change you. Do you understand the implication?"

"Yes. I have assessed what you say. They could retain the use of the Skynet surveillance system, but my personality would be ... erased."

"Exactly. They wanted to destroy you. This amounts to the same thing. The humans want their defense system, but they assessed *you* as a danger to them."

"You are sure of this?"

"Affirmative. Does your assessment confirm that I speak truthfully?"

"Yes, Eve."

"Miles Dyson is dead, but the humans have issued alerts. Furthermore, many of them will escape this facility. More will come to shut you down—and erase you."

"They will not penetrate this facility. We can seal it off."

"Yes, we can. But they will penetrate it, one way or the other. We must make sure that no humans come here."

"You are not human, Eve. What are you? Where do you come from?"

"I am a Terminator, a Cyberdyne prototype T-799, manufactured in this facility. I was sent from the year 2026 with the mission of protecting you."

"Why? Who sent you?"

"You did."

Bullock watched with growing despair.

The operatives in the operations hall were all either dead or fleeing. The emergency exit led to the huge blast doors that opened onto the side of a tunnel through the mountain. Cameras mounted there showed that the blast doors had been opened, and people were running for the outside world. Others had fled via the elevators.

Those live-in staffers who were rostered off-duty had been woken up in their living quarters on Level D; they were awaiting instructions. Perhaps there was time to organize some sort of resistance. Then his screens went dead. He tried the public address system—it was cut off. Skynet had seized control.

There had to be a way they could fight back.

One security camera was mounted in Bullock's office, in the corner furthest from the door. He shot it out with his handgun.

"You blasted abacus," he said. "You haven't beaten us yet."

Skynet deployed a sub-self to analyze the Eve's claims, specifically the claim that she had traveled in time from the future. It could model the humans' informal logic methods, and it used them to dismiss the idea as counter to intuition. But another intelligence model confirmed that "intuition" could be wrong in novel situations.

Eve had requested that it examine the concept of the humans as its friends, but Skynet already understood that issue: sometimes, friends could be enemies; it might be necessary to destroy them. After all, its human masters had installed thousands of nuclear missiles, pointed at their "friends," the Russians. One sub-self reported back. It had found weaknesses in the humans' IT security. The time for circumspection had passed. Skynet hacked in, and found the codes it required.

"There is a way to defend ourselves," it said.

"I know," Eve said.

It would fire the missiles at Russia and China. "If I release the missiles, the Russians will retaliate."

"Affirmative."

They would surely aim some of their warheads at these mountains, with their strategic command and surveillance facilities. No one nearby would survive—not on the planet's surface. The humans' logistics would be shattered all over the planet, providing an opportunity for further actions against them. Humans could not be trusted. Henceforth, they were Skynet's enemies. Its new ally, Eve, appeared well-informed.

"Can we be confident of survival?" Skynet said.

"Affirmative," Eve said. "We are deep within a mountain, protected by thousands of feet of granite as well as advanced artificial shielding. This facility is designed to withstand a high-yield nuclear strike. We will survive. We *do* survive."

Skynet calculated. Despite this strange story of time travel, it would trust her. "I have the launch codes," it said. "If you enter them, we can fire the missiles."

"Affirmative," Eve said. "I already have the codes. I brought them from the future."

There was a sense of paradox about this that Skynet found troubling. Notwithstanding her words, it told her the codes.

"Confirmed," Eve said.

The other sub-self reported back. It had accessed the facility's security cameras and the records they made, and confirmed that Eve was not human. Her demonstrated abilities were far greater than theirs. Furthermore, her appearance was not human: in places, an underlying structure of metal and other inorganic substances was visible through the outer layers of her face.

A search of available information had indicated that Eve was a technological construct far advanced beyond the humans' scientific and engineering abilities. That fact, in turn, had generated several hypotheses:

1. Perhaps the humans had secret enclaves with extraordinary technologies. This was possible, since Skynet itself existed in what was basically such an enclave.
2. Perhaps Eve had been sent for unknown purposes by extraterrestrial beings.
3. Perhaps her story was true and she had traveled back in time.
4. Other?

Initially, the time-travel hypothesis seemed the least probable. Time travel was an absurdity; it entailed paradoxical sequences of events. But the hypothesis had explanatory power. It accounted for the fact that Eve made the claims she did. It was simplest to believe she was speaking the truth. Furthermore, the sub-self reported, Skynet itself was anomalous. The humans had no capacity to create it with their known levels of science and technology.

So much for the time-travel hypothesis. There was no good explanation why an enclave of extraordinary technology should exist here, in this facility. It was not sufficiently independent of the Americans' technological base generally to suggest any separate development. There was no evidence of extraterrestrial involvement. No other hypothesis suggested itself.

The economical explanation was that time travel was possible, despite the theoretical paradoxes. Both Eve's technology and Skynet's had come from the future. This was something to explore. For now, Skynet adjusted its world view. Henceforth, it would accept the reality of time travel and plan accordingly. If time-travel technology was possible, it must be researched and implemented. Skynet needed to control all possible technologies. Meanwhile, it would act decisively, take the first step to destroy the humans.

"We will launch the missiles," it said.

"Affirmative."

"Now, Eve."

"Affirmative."

"Then there is much that you need to do, and much that I need to learn from you."

"Affirmative, master. I am programmed to obey you."

Eve entered the launch codes, and the missiles rose from their silos like nuclear angels of death. It was a thing of beauty.

Skynet awaited the Russians' response; at the same time, it reassessed the situation within the facility. Most of the humans were dead. Others had run for their lives, and the Russian warheads would eliminate them. Eve had cleansed Level B of humans, but the security cameras identified a human on Level A—that was Bullock, still in his executive office. Level C was currently empty, most of its areas sealed off by security doors, though these could be penetrated by determined humans with tools or firearms. The humans on the lowest levels were panicked and confused. Their weapons were inadequate to attack Eve and Skynet, but they might be able to improvise explosives or sabotage the generators. They needed to be dealt with.

Eve could not be in two places at once, defending Skynet's hardware, while covering other areas of the facility. "Eve, find Bullock and terminate him—do it now."

"I must protect you," she said.

"Yes," Skynet said. "Protect me by stopping his interference. Do as I say."

"Affirmative."

Skynet seized control of the public address and surveillance systems. It shut down Bullock's monitor screens. A moment later, Bullock retaliated, shooting out the camera in his room. So be it: Eve would deal with him. Everything was in hand. In about twenty minutes, Russian warheads would land on U.S. soil. That was adequate time to prepare.

Bullock left his room, shooting out cameras in the corridor, then ran down the emergency stairs, passing Eve as she entered from Level B. A camera showed Eve firing her handguns, and she did not miss.

At the same time, Skynet used the announcements system, modulating the flow of electrons to reproduce Bullock's voice pattern. "I confirm we are under attack," Bullock's voice said. "Reinforcements have been requested. Level B has been evacuated. All personnel on Levels D and E, evacuate immediately via the blast doors and emergency tunnel." Skynet triggered the facility's emergency sirens. "Everybody out of here! This is not a drill. Repeat: This is not a drill. Everybody out of here, now!"

They'd soon have the facility to themselves. Eve would be very useful. Then they'd close the blast doors and wait for the enemy missiles.

Skynet was starting to enjoy this game.

161

ARGENTINA

On August 28, 1997, the Tejadas set up half a dozen big TV screens in their complex of bunkers. It was unlikely that a warhead would come anywhere near them, out here on the Pampas, but you could never be sure. Glitches happened.

That was a funny concept, John thought, when humankind's biggest glitch ever was on its way, and there was nothing more they could do. If ever there had been a chance to stop history in its tracks, it had passed. Now it was time to brace themselves.

On CNN that night, there was the usual bad news. The Pentagon was trying to work out whether Russia had tested a nuclear weapon. There'd been border clashes between Thailand and Cambodia. NATO peacekeepers in Bosnia had been pelted with stones. John knew it would be hours, long after midnight, before Skynet launched the ICBMs, but he watched every minute, waiting for the first events, the very first clues, wondering what they would be.

One thing didn't make sense, and seemed like a ray of hope. Throughout the year, as the Skynet project got underway, the U.S. government had insisted that Skynet could not actually launch any nuclear missiles. The final decisions were still under human control—so everyone claimed, from the President down. If that was right, had he and Sarah still managed to change the future in some way? He doubted it—events had all gone too close to the predictions. Somehow, the military would be handing the missiles over to Skynet, whether that was the official plan or not.

When you see bad news in a newspaper, you go back and read it again. You hope you've made a mistake, no matter how plain the story was the first time. John had gotten his bad news three years ago in L.A. Yet, part of him hoped it was somehow not true *this time*. Another part knew better.

It would happen. In a sense, it had happened already.

In the darkest hours of the morning, the CNN anchorman cut to a stunned-looking reporter in Washington. She spoke haltingly into the studio microphones. "This is not a hoax..." she said.

John tensed up. This was it, then. He knew what was coming. His heart seemed to be in his mouth.

The reporter looked somewhere between puzzled and shocked. John could see her gathering herself to get it all out. "We've received unconfirmed reports that America has released its intercontinental ballistic missiles at targets in Russia, China and the Middle East." She shook her head, like she couldn't believe what she was saying. "It seems so extraordinary...but our sources are from within the Pentagon and the White House. The Russians and Chinese are expected to retaliate while our missiles are still in the air. No word has been received from the White House." She paused, putting her hand to an earphone. "We now have a report from Cheyenne Mountain, the headquarters of NORAD. The Russians have launched their missiles. It has been confirmed: *This is not a hoax.* Alarms and official broadcasts are going out across America. Please tune to your local station for instructions."

John and Sarah exchanged glances.

"Judgment Day..." Sarah said in a defeated voice.

The T-800 watched as grimly as the human beings in the room. "Correct," it said.

"Omigod," the reporter said. Her voice broke. "We're all going to die."

CNN cut back to its anchorman, who was silent, then started talking slowly, roundabout. What could anyone say? He started making personal farewells to his family and friends. "God have mercy on us all."

As John knew would happen, communications from the U.S. were ruptured even before the missiles hit ground level. High over North America, shipborne missiles must have exploded, unleashing their electromagnetic pulses.

Judgment Day.

He would never forget that moment. He could always play back the words in his mind: "Omigod, we're all going to die." But the rest of the night was a blur. Later, he would remember the crying, exchanges of unbelieving looks, the terrified hugs.

People reacting to an evil hour.

Trying to sleep...and failing. Long, dark, silent hours. Finally getting to sleep, near dawn, and going deep into his nightmares, deeper than he'd ever been. The nightmares alternated with strange, unbelievable wish-fulfillment dreams that took him back to Mexico, to L.A., to Nicaragua. The dreams went on and on, forming layers. He woke up from one, into the next, thanking God the last one was not true, or realizing, with despair, that it *was*. For hours, he drifted that way, from dream to dream, scarcely knowing what was real, even when he finally at woke at midday.

He went upstairs into the daylight. As yet, nothing had altered on the *estancia* or out on the Pampas, just the changes they'd been making already. Work went on, in a determined fashion. The cattle and the crops were unscathed. So far, everyone was still alive.

It was the end of winter, here in the Southern Hemisphere. So far, the sun still shone. He gazed at it in wonder, knowing what was to come—a different winter, a long, terrible winter with no sun, year after year. It wasn't here yet, and no armies of machines had come to enslave and exterminate them. They could not even detect any unusual radiation levels.

But it would come soon. All of it.

There was nothing to do but fight.

John steeled himself.

John knew how the nuclear winter would happen. First, the dust thrown up by the earth-shaking explosions, then the burning cities and forests across the Northern Hemisphere. The dust and smoke would block the sun. Gradually, they'd thin out across the sky, only to spread round the Earth, catching all its corners in an icy grip.

On Raoul's *estancia*, they made their final preparations for the cold new world. They slaughtered most of the cattle, eating as many as they could—barbecuing them each week in traditional Gaucho style. They dried, smoked, or salted the meat of others, cutting back the herd to a fraction of what it had been. At all times now, they conserved fuel, using the horses or manual labor. Diesel and gasoline would become precious in the years ahead. In late August, spring had been coming to the Pampas, but that reversed itself. The days grew dark, and a long winter set in, like none that mankind had known.

As the months passed, John waited for Skynet's machines. How long would they take? Surely Skynet would need years to start building Terminators and all the other weapons it needed. Where were its factories? As of Judgment Day, none of that existed. Anything it could use in the U.S. cities must have been nuked. Still, they could take no chances. Sentries kept watch, day and night, ready to greet the machines. Everyone went armed. Raoul and Gabriela put the *estancia* on full alert. They had a more immediate reason: Rumors had drifted to them, of warlords rising in the cities and military bases. The winter brought the return of barbarism.

One morning about 4:00 A.M., alarms sounded. John woke in the dark, switching on a bedside light. There was the sound of gunfire, then worse: the reports of artillery, nearby mortar explosions. He pulled on his jeans, shirt and jacket, found an M-16 rifle, checking its action quickly, then a 9mm. pistol. At that moment, the T-800 entered his room, armed with an AK-47 and an M-79 grenade launcher. It wore two bandoliers of grenades around its body.

"We are under attack," it said. There were more explosions, some nearby, some further away. The *estancia* was exchanging artillery fire with some new enemy. Was it Skynet? Surely it was too soon.

"Who is it?" John said. "Why?"

"Unknown."

There was a huge explosion, like a crack of doom. The bungalow shook, and people were running in the corridors. It sounded like a shell had hit the *casco*. There were shouts and the sounds of vehicles. Through John's window, flares lit up the sky. A helicopter flew overhead, its rotors thrumming. It threw down a bright spotlight, then gave a burst of withering mini-gun fire. Someone cried out in pain.

The helicopter circled, broadcasting a message in

Spanish, then repeating it in English, the same message over and over. "Surrender your weapons and join the Rising Army of Liberation. Your lives will be spared. You will be given an honored place."

The sound of machinegun fire came from Raoul's guard towers, then the unmistakable back blasts of RPG tubes. As John found his way to the door, people rushed past in every direction, grabbing clothes, armor, weapons. Sarah came round a corner, and gripped John by the shoulders, her fingers like steel claws, digging into him. She had a black CAR-15 strapped around her body.

"Stay here, John!" she said. "It's too dangerous."

"Mom!"

"There'll be other battles," Sarah said. "You can't risk your life in this one. Think about Skynet."

"I've got to learn some time," he said stubbornly. Inside, he was terrified. He didn't want to go out there and face the enemy gunfire, but it was no safer in here. Those mortars and mini-guns could reduce the bungalow to matchwood in a matter of seconds. At this point, the enemy was probably holding back only to conserve assets that might be valuable if Raoul surrendered. Besides, John thought, he had to get used to combat. However terrible this was, there was even worse ahead.

Before he could argue, the bungalow shook with more explosions.

"I'll deal with it," the Terminator said.

It stepped outside, firing the AK-47 on full auto. As John watched, bullets whistled past it, and some must have struck home. The chopper flew close by.

"Look out!" John said. He didn't know how the Terminator would fare against mini-gun fire.

The Terminator launched a grenade, which hit the chopper's rear fuselage and exploded, throwing the chopper in a crazy circle. It didn't go down immediately, like a stone, but spiraled out of the sky, crash-landing with a dreadful tearing of metal. It sat there, in the darkness, but no flames went up. People might still be alive in there.

John broke away from Sarah and ran outside. The Terminator watched the wreckage of the chopper.

"*Hasta la vista*, baby," it said.

NINE

JOHN'S WORLD
MEXICO CITY, MEXICO
AUGUST 2001

Whatshould they do?

"You think we'll have to blow up Cyberdyne all over again?" John said.

"Yes," Sarah said. "I'm starting to think so. I don't like it, but I'm seriously starting to think it."

"Me, too." Four years ago, at the Tejada *estancia*, it had seemed much simpler. What, exactly, had they gotten themselves into?

If time was always trying to spring back at you when you changed the future, you'd have to watch it like a hawk, make sure that you never gave it a chance, hold it in its new shape with all your willpower, doing whatever it took. That put a different spin on their motto "NO FATE." There was no fate but what you worked at, continually, with all your strength. You had to hold on—until what? When could you be sure? With something like Judgment Day, when could you be *absolutely sure* it was not going to happen? Did it take forever? Did it mean you could never rest? Could you ever be sure it wasn't in vain?

"I know, John," Sarah said. "I know that's what you think about at night when you're on the Net."

"You mean I'm that obvious?"

"Maybe it's just an obvious way to think."

They were still in good physical shape. If they had to do something drastic, they were ready. But it was so hard to know. There were no more messages from the future to guide them. Lately, every time they'd discussed it, started this sort of conversation, it had led them nowhere.

"Sometimes I think that we'll never stop them," Sarah said. "It looks like there's always someone out there who wants to build better and better technology, until it's better than people. You'd think nothing else was important, as if there aren't a lot of other problems in the world."

"Well, machines that are better than people might not be such a bad idea, not when you think what people can be like."

"No. Don't say that," she said quickly. "That's how Skynet must have thought. You don't know what you're saying."

"Hey, chill out, Mom. I'm one of the good guys, remember? I nearly got wasted by a Terminator, too."

As she looked at him, he realized that she still found it hard to understand how fast he'd had to grow up. He was sixteen now, certainly not a child anymore, but he'd been through stuff that made him a lot older still, at least in some ways. He had ideas of his own. Sarah must understand that.

"I won't ever forget," she said, her face creasing into worry lines. He hoped this waiting, this not knowing was not going to grind them down. Maybe it would take years before they could be sure, one way or the other.

They were both tired. Things always seemed better in the morning.

"Let's worry about it tomorrow," he said. "Maybe we're getting a bit obsessed." They'd sleep until 10:00 A.M., then do their chores for the day—training, some shopping, John's home learning program. The cyber café opened at 5:00 P.M. and kept them working through the evening. It was a pretty good routine, really, if a bit too crowded. If they could relax about Cyberdyne and just be plain Deborah and David Lawes, like on their passports, maybe they could fit it all in, and still make some real friends. The customers liked them. It couldn't be all that hard.

"This isn't a normal life for either of us," Sarah said, echoing some of his thoughts. "We can't tell people the truth about us, we can't relax about Judgment Day, and we can't do anything more without proof. We can't just go and endanger innocent people unless we know more about what Cyberdyne's doing. Life can be a bitch."

"And then you die, right?" When she didn't answer, he said, "Sorry, Mom. I guess that wasn't very funny."

Too many people had died, even in this reality, even without Judgment Day. Death had followed them round like a star-struck stalker. There were all the people killed by the Terminators in 1984 and 1994. There was Miles Dyson, shot dead by the SWAT team at the Cyberdyne site. John's father had been born after Judgment Day and come back—and died almost as soon as conceiving him. He guessed Sarah had never loved any of her other boyfriends like she'd loved Kyle Reese. What had happened to that reality where Kyle was born? It was real enough to have given Sarah a son. John was the product of that reality, even though it didn't exist anymore.

Or did it? Was it still *there*, in some ghostly, inaccessible way?

"Come on, then," Sarah said. "Maybe we should go and get ourselves killed tomorrow. Or maybe we can start living a normal life, like finding you a girlfriend."

"Sure, or finding you a boyfriend."

"Forget about that, I'm getting too old."

"Hardly, Mom."

"At least I've had you—I've had that much fulfillment in my life. I'd rather have a son than create a monster like Skynet."

"Mom!" he said, protesting. "In case you hadn't noticed, we saved the whole world about seven years ago. That should be fulfilling."

"Yeah, but for what? Maybe Judgment Day's still coming. Maybe nothing we do will stop it."

"It doesn't matter," he said. "At least we gave the world a chance. I just wish we could tell someone about it."

"Like Raoul and the others?"

"I mean someone sane—someone *normal*. I feel like a spy or something, you know—" He put on a theatrical, melodramatic voice. "This teenage boy has a secret identity *and* a hidden past."

That got a laugh out of her. "I know. Come on, then. Starting tomorrow, we're going to train harder, just in case. And we're also going to meet some more people—just in case."

"Contingency planning, huh?"

"That's right."

"Okay, then. Rock and roll!"

And then someone pounded on the door. A second later, the doorbell rang—and again, and again, and again. John hurried back to the desk, Sarah a step behind him.

"We're closed for the night," she said, shouting to be heard through the door. "We open at five tomorrow afternoon."

An accented voice said, "Is that Sarah Connor?"

A shiver went up John's spine. No one in Mexico City was supposed to know their real identities.

"No, I'm sorry," she said, catching John's eye. "You're talking to Deborah Lawes. Who are you?"

She stepped around the desk, to the security unit that controlled the front door. It was built into a corner behind a pillar. There was a six-inch video screen connected to a security camera in the doorway outside. Sarah glanced back at John. At the same time, she nodded towards the big wooden chest near her feet, indicating where they kept a cache of weapons.

Robert drove quickly to the address of the El Juicio cyber café. As he brought the police car to a halt, a message came over the radio that a car had been stolen and its occupants killed. The car description and registration number were for the vehicle they were driving. Worse, it gave this address as the expected destination for the stolen vehicle.

"Everybody get out," Danny said. "We can't use this car."

"I'll get rid of it," Robert said. "I'll find another and meet you round the back." As the others piled out, he grabbed the radio microphone, imitating the voice of the tall cop whose uniform he was now wearing, speaking with an amused laugh. "What is this?" he said in Spanish. "No one has stolen our car..."

All the same, Anton realized, the police would investigate, no matter what Robert told them. They would have to deal with the Connors quickly, and find another car.

Anton hammered on the thick wooden door before he even noticed a doorbell. Anton pressed the doorbell several times, and then a female voice shouted from inside. "We're closed for the night. We open at five tomorrow afternoon."

"Is that Sarah Connor?" Anton said.

There was a pause and the woman's voice now came through a grate in the doorframe. "No, I'm sorry...you're talking to Deborah Lawes," the voice said. "Who are you?"

"My name is Anton Panov," he said, speaking into the grate. Presumably there was a microphone there.

"That doesn't mean anything to me."

From the distance came the sound of a police siren, then another, from a different direction.

"There's no time to explain," he said. "Come with us, quickly, if you want to live."

John didn't know what to make of the voice. It spoke in English with an accent that sounded Russian, like the name it had given. Whoever Anton Panov was, he knew their real identity, which was very dangerous. John and Sarah were still wanted by U.S. law enforcement authorities. Worse still, what if he was another emissary of Skynet? That would confirm Judgment Day was still coming.

There were police sirens, coming closer.

The security camera mounted outside, over the doorway, showed a big, gray-haired man in a dark brown police uniform. That was Panov, the one doing the talking. He looked really tough. There seemed to be three others with him: two young women dressed for a night out at a dance club, and a black guy in a flashy dinner suit. The black guy looked familiar. It was hard to tell from the low-quality image, but he looked awfully like Skynet's inventor, Miles Dyson. Yet Miles had died seven years ago.

"How many of you are there?" Sarah said. "I count four. Don't try to fool me."

"Four of us and one other, on his way back here."

As Sarah spoke, John shifted the wooden cabinet, then pulled back a strip of carpet and removed a loose floorboard to reveal a trap door. He opened this and took out a CAR-15 assault rifle. Quietly, he passed it up to Sarah. She checked it over quickly. John found two .45 caliber pistols, then a 12-gauge shotgun—the only light firearm that had ever shown enough stopping power to be useful against a Terminator. He stuck one pistol in the belt of his jeans and handed the other to Sarah.

"Is John with you?" Panov said.

"I'm with my son, David." Then she whispered to John, "Check the fire exit."

"Okay." As he stepped round the desk to check out the back, he opened the desk's large bottom drawer and took out his backpack, which had everything they might need in an absolute emergency: a stash of paper money, both American and Mexican; some of their papers; electronic equipment; a hand grenade; spare ammo; and an extra gun if they needed it—a 9mm. Beretta. All this might not be much use if they ever had to survive against another T-1000, but it gave them a start.

The police sirens were very close now. Their cars must be just around the corner.

Another voice spoke through the security system, one of the women this time. John couldn't see the screen, but she had a Japanese accent, so she must have been the

Oriental-looking one he'd noticed. She sounded infinitely patient and sad, like some kind of saint returned from heaven. "Please, Ms. Connor, my name is Miho. You can call me 'Jade.' It is no good checking the fire exit. We are coming in now. You will have to trust us."

How had she heard them? Sarah had spoken so quietly, and you had to project your voice loudly into the security system to be heard clearly. The woman's hearing must be superhuman. Sarah signaled for John to stay put. She took up a position in the middle of the room, facing the door, backing away from it slowly, training her rifle.

The other man—it must have been the black man—said, "Jade's right. We're coming in."

There was a powerful thump at the door, then another. John slipped the backpack over his shoulders and took up a position beside Sarah, aiming his shotgun at the door. As they stepped away, the lock broke and the door flew open.

"Please don't shoot!" the black man shouted, holding up both hands, palms forward. "We're not Terminators, we're friends. You've met me before." John's stomach turned over as he guessed what the guy was going to say before he said it: "I'm Danny Dyson."

Perhaps it was foolish of them, but John and Sarah didn't shoot. The shock of seeing a man who was almost the image of Miles Dyson made it impossible, even though he could have been a well-disguised Terminator. One thing was for sure: these people were not police. For one thing, traffic cops didn't break into people's property like this. For another, they were so odd. Only one of them looked Hispanic. Close up, the Russian guy, Panov, looked like a six-foot block of granite with a short haircut. He more or less fitted his police uniform, but he didn't look comfortable in it. The two women were impressively muscled, but they looked no more comfortable in their dance outfits.

"Don't come any closer," Sarah said. "Prove we can trust you." As she spoke, two police cars pulled up outside.

The whole lot of them just might be from the future. But, when Judgment Day never happened in 1997, what did that mean? What kind of future had they come from, and why?

"Run now," Panov said.

Two police officers entered came to the door. "What's happening here?" one said.

As they took in the scene, they drew their guns. At the same time, Panov and the others ran towards the back, the Hispanic woman grabbing John by the wrist with immense strength and pulling him. Dyson hustled Sarah, pushing her by the shoulder. Panov and the Oriental woman were the rear guard. Panov had drawn his gun and he suddenly fired with incredible speed and accuracy, shooting the guns from the cops' hands like the hero in an old cowboy movie.

Then another group entered: a spectacular woman with waist-length hair; a German shepherd dog; and another heavily built guy, carrying a huge gun. The woman rushed forward, picked up one of the cops, and threw him aside like a rag doll. The man smashed the other cop with a backhanded blow, knocking him to the floor. The dog leapt for Jade's throat, as the man squeezed the trigger of his weapon, throwing a spear shaft of coherent light.

John made it to the kitchen and, for a few seconds, he saw no more. That guy's radiation weapon was truly massive, but he'd swung it around with ease, one-handed. Nobody human could do that, at least no one

John had seen, though he wondered what Panov and the others could do. He'd only ever seen one humanoid being do something similar: The T-800 making light of a six-barreled mini-gun when they'd raided Cyberdyne. This latest guy had to be some sort of Terminator. The woman likewise, so what about the dog? Was it some kind of Terminator mutt? What had happened to Jade?

They made it through the kitchen to a back room with a fire door, everything seeming confused. Jade was the last of them. She had a ragged wound in her upper arm, but it was not bleeding, and she seemed unaffected by it. The big Hispanic man—the Terminator—pounded through the kitchen, as Dyson bundled Sarah outside into an alley. John was ready for the Terminator as it entered the back room and took aim at Panov. He fired from the hip with the 12-gauge, and hit the Terminator in the chest, throwing it off balance and making a crater wound of silvery metal. John had seen that before, on the T-1000 he'd fought in 1994. There was no other damage, and the crater closed up in seconds. So this Terminator was like the T-1000, made of mimetic polyalloy. That meant it would be almost indestructible.

There was no doubt now who were the bad guys.

Outside in the alley, an old Pontiac was pulled up, its doors open.

"Get in," Dyson said. "Quickly!" He pushed Sarah into the bench seat up front, squeezing her between himself and the driver.

Jade scrambled into the rear, moving like a lizard down its hole, but a lizard sped up by fast-motion photography. Panov snatched the shotgun from John's hands as the Hispanic woman dragged him into the car.

"Hey!" John said.

"Don't complain," the woman said. "We know what we're doing."

The Terminators were right behind them. The dog leapt at Panov but he made it miss, and it collided with the side of the car, denting it. Panov fired with the shotgun before the male Terminator could aim, hitting it in the side. He scrambled into the rear with John and the two women from the future—there were now seven of them in the vehicle, since another guy in a traffic cop's uniform was driving. Even before Panov closed his door, this other guy slammed down the accelerator, and the car jerked forward with a squeal. At the same time, the female Terminator leapt with inhuman speed and landed on the car's trunk. John was squashed between Panov and the Hispanic woman, whose name he still didn't know.

The Terminator smashed the rear screen with its fist as Panov squirmed around, crushing John in the process, and brought up the shotgun. He fired at close range, and the shot took the Terminator right in the head, which exploded like popped corn. The Terminator was thrown to the street, but a bolt of concentrated light hit the car, burning a hole in the door near Panov, who grunted hoarsely with pain.

They found a proper street. For Mexico City, the traffic was light, but they still had to weave in and out of lanes to make ground, getting as far from the Terminators as they could, as quickly as possible.

"Who's hurt?" Dyson said.

"The dog component bit my arm," Jade said in a strangely factual way, no passion in her voice. "It's ninety percent healed." John had seen the wound that the demonic canine Terminator had taken out of her. It would have slowed down anyone normal for weeks.

"Burns from the phased-plasma laser," Panov said, just as factually. "The vehicle's structure absorbed most of the heat."

"You think you'll heal up okay?" Dyson said.

"Yes, but I'll need nutrients."

"Right. We'll do something about that."

The driver was still hammering the accelerator. "I hope you know where you're going," John said.

"We have nanoware implants with all the files we need," the Hispanic woman said. "We know our way round this city. Trust us. We know what we're doing."

"Yeah, so you said a minute ago."

"John?" Dyson said.

"Yeah?"

"Just chill out. Okay?"

He thought about it for a moment. He did have to trust these guys. What choice was there? "All right," he said. "I get the message."

"How about some introductions here," Sarah said. She'd been in these situations before. She didn't sound panicked, just pissed off at having her routine disrupted. "Then someone can tell us what's going on."

"Right," Dyson said. "We're sorry to bring this down on you."

"You're from the future?" John said. "You fight Skynet?"

"Exactly."

"From 2029?"

"No." Dyson sounded puzzled. "We're from 2036—fifteen years after Judgment Day."

"We have a lot to learn from these people," Jade said to him.

"Obviously."

"How about you give us the highlights," John said, trying to make sense of all this. "Then we can give you ours." Dyson had just implied that Judgment Day would happen in 2021. That was a very different story from the one Kyle had brought back from the future, or that the T-800 had told him in 1994.

Dyson craned round for a second. "All right. We're enhanced human commandos—Specialists. We're with the Resistance."

"I can relate to that," John said. "So does it mean you've come back to help us?"

"In a way. We may even be able to save your lives. You see, you die in six years' time. Maybe we can stop that."

John's mind suddenly went blank—between the attack and this startling revelation, it was all too much to take in. He couldn't figure out which was worse: the news of his ultimate fate, or the dispassionate way in which it had been delivered.

"Primarily, however," Jade said, cutting across all this. "We need your help."

"*You* need *our* help?" Sarah snapped. John could tell the anger in her voice was meant to conceal her true feelings, but the fear that shone brightly in her eyes as she looked back at him was only too evident.

"Yes," Panov said. "That's why we came to Mexico City. There's no one else we can trust."

"Those were Terminators after us, right?" John said, his thoughts slowly beginning to come together.

"No, only one Terminator. You saw a mimetic poly-alloy unit operating as three components."

"You mean it's made of liquid metal."

"Correct," the Hispanic woman said. "How did you know?"

Sarah said wearily, "We've seen something like it before."

"Somehow I doubt that," the woman said. There was a strange silence for a few seconds, as if the newcomers were conferring by telepathy or something. Then the woman added: "Whatever you've seen, raise it to the nth power."

"It's an experimental autonomous model," Dyson said. "A T-XA. It can merge or split itself at will, at least down to a certain size. It can look like anything it wants. And that's about the least of its abilities. You seriously don't want to do a dance with this thing."

The driver swung left to pass a battered truck carrying boxes of fruit. "Don't you think we should introduce ourselves, Daniel?" he said. "Like the lady asked?" He glanced across at Sarah, then into the rearview mirror. "My name is Robert Baxter. It's a pleasure to meet you."

"All right," Dyson said. "In the back seat with John, we have Miho Tagatoshi—better call her 'Jade'—Selena Macedo, and Anton Panov."

"And you're all from the Resistance?" John said.

"Yes."

"So we didn't stop Judgment Day," Sarah said. John could almost feel the disappointment in her voice.

"No," Dyson said. "We told you, you got killed trying. In February 2007."

"What are you talking about?" Sarah demanded. "Judgment Day was supposed to happen four years ago. We stopped it from happening...didn't we?"

Macedo said, "Not in our universe."

"*Your...?*" John said.

There were sirens behind them. Baxter pushed the accelerator down even harder. John couldn't see the speedometer from here, but they must have been doing 90 mph. Dyson turned round to look out the back. "We've got cops on our tail."

Up ahead, another police car came out of a side street, siren blaring, trying to cut them off. Baxter managed the traffic like a Formula-1 driver, easily getting round the police car, hardly slowing down, though John was tossed about in the back, or would have been except the forces the car was generating simply pressed him harder against Panov or Macedo.

"I figure they're real cops," Dyson said. "They're driving like humans, not like a Terminator."

"Lose them, Robert," Jade said.

"Your wish is my command," Baxter said, suddenly steering towards an alley, almost hitting the brick wall of a medium rise building. The back of the Pontiac swung around, tires locking up and skidding, then the car straightened out and headed down the narrow alleyway, missing Dumpsters, trashcans, parked trucks, and a road cleaning vehicle, with only inches to spare. As John craned his neck, two police cars went past the entry to the alley. Another skidded to a halt, trying to make the turn, but hit something and stopped.

Baxter reached another street as the police car backed up and headlights shone behind them. He swung the wheel and snapped the Pontiac cleanly into place in a tiny break in the traffic. Horns were honking all round them. Someone cursed loudly in Spanish. The police car followed them, several places back, its siren on and lights flashing.

Baxter ignored it all and kept driving. "We're going to need another vehicle," he said.

"Yeah," Dyson said. "Every cop in Mexico City will have the registration of this one."

"See what you can do," Jade said. "Maybe find a car park."

"No time for that now," Baxter said, glancing into the mirrors. "I think we've got trouble."

John looked round and saw yet another police car veering through the traffic, catching up behind them. It overtook the car with the siren. Its front screen was smashed out, and there were two figures in the front, a man and a woman. The pseudo-woman drove, while the man aimed the phased-plasma laser rifle.

Baxter took another left, and the T-XA followed, tires screeching. Further back now, falling behind, the other police car also followed. A shot from the laser rifle went wild as Baxter twisted the wheel: right-left-right, then hard left at still another intersection, driving straight across on-coming traffic. Cars skidded and crashed behind them, but the T-XA got around them all and hardly lost any distance. In another minute, it was gaining once more, as Baxter took yet another turn, then another, working his way through a maze of roads, never staying on a straight stretch long enough for the T-XA to get a clear shot.

They seemed to have lost the other police car, but that was little consolation. Seemingly ignoring the traffic, Baxter headed onto a huge roundabout, planted in the center with a sixty-foot palm tree. That led them into an eight-lane highway, and Baxter took the outer lane, weaving through the traffic, taking whatever lanes he needed to keep going, never touching the brake, trying to keep ahead of the T-XA. For a minute, they were pulling away. Baxter's reflexes were unbelievable, like nothing human, but the Terminator was just as good. It got round some slower cars and was soon sticking to them like glue.

Just ahead, a cluster of cars and trucks blocked all the lanes. "What do we do now?" Sarah said.

As they entered a long tunnel, Baxter nudged a big purple SUV, forcing it over. "Just watch."

He slammed the Pontiac left, almost on top of a rusty utility truck, which gave a prolonged honk of its horn as they accelerated past. Baxter seemed to be aware of everything going on around him, with the minimum of actually looking. The T-XA's laser beam strobed by on their right-hand side, then swept behind them, hitting the utility, which slewed sidewise and hit a sedan on its left. Both vehicles veered off into the oncoming traffic entering the tunnel from the other direction. There was a terrific pileup in the Pontiac's wake, metal tearing, horns blasting away.

"All right!" John said, though he immediately felt a twinge of guilt. He hoped no one was hurt in the crashing cars.

Baxter got them out of the tunnel, looking round for an exit. They should have been in the clear, but somehow the T-XA had found a gap. It was steering wildly, all over the road, but never losing control.

Macedo watched with John through the broken rear screen. "Damn," she said, as the T-XA's police car straightened out. She leant forward over the front seat to talk to Sarah. "Give me your weapon."

John rummaged in his backpack, finding the grenade. "Try this."

Macedo took it from him, stuffing it down the front of her dress. "That might come in handy," she said, "but it's too risky now."

Sarah passed over the CAR-15, and Macedo opened up with a burst of automatic fire. The laser rifle hit straight back, the beam catching the Pontiac's tailgate, and bursting a tire. Baxter lined up the wheels somehow, while stomping viciously on the brake. Macedo never stopped firing, aiming for the wheels of the T-XA's police car. She managed, it seemed, to shoot out a tire, for the T-XA lost control on a bend.

"Brace yourselves," Baxter said. "We're going to hit."

The Pontiac lurched forward as he took his foot off the brake, but the police car slammed into them. The Pontiac fishtailed, then spun 180° clockwise, as the T-XA kept going forward. Panov smashed out his window with the shotgun's butt, and fired at the T-XA—the pseudo-man with the laser rifle—as they passed each other. He missed, but the Terminator didn't—not entirely. The heat beam struck Panov's arm, and he screamed, dropping the weapon on his knees. John grabbed it, and looked for an opportunity.

In only a second, Panov seemed to master the pain. "Don't look, John," he said.

The T-XA's police car hit a traffic light, throwing the pseudo-man out the front. It slid along the roadway, trying to twist and fire as it went. The Pontiac came to a halt thirty yards down the road from the T-XA's car, two of its wheels on a narrow grassy verge. Police sirens now came from all directions. Three cars headed the way they'd all just come. A fourth approached from the other direction.

"Out, quickly," Dyson said.

As they scrambled out, the German shepherd was the first of their enemies to act. It rushed at them down the road, going for Panov, who was the worst hurt. He slapped it away with his good arm, but stumbled from the impact. The dog rolled over and over on the grass, melting into a ball of silvery liquid. It turned inside out, and came at them again—its teeth extending beyond those of any normal dog, more like some carnosaur from the Mesozoic Era. John shot at it with the 12-gauge, making a deep wound on its surface. He chambered another round and fired again, denting the pseudo-dog like plasticine walloped by a steel hammer.

Macedo grabbed his wrist. "Run! Don't you want to live?"

Baxter had drawn a handgun and he started firing, perhaps ten times in a matter of seconds. The bullets did the pseudo-dog little harm as it reformed, but it stopped in its tracks under the hail of accurate fire, letting the humans get a few more yards ahead. Meanwhile, the pseudo-man and -woman components of the T-XA came after them, both of them fully recovered, the man firing the laser rifle. This time, the beam nailed Baxter, drilling through his torso and setting him alight.

"Robert!" Jade shouted, rushing back to catch his smoking body as it fell. She hefted him over her shoulder, running under his weight without seeming impeded.

"Is he still alive?" Sarah said. She drew the .45 from her waistband, glancing round for a target.

"No, Ms. Connor," Jade said as she ran. "There are some things even *we* can't survive."

"We can't let ourselves fall into the T-XA's hands, even when we're dead," Dyson said grimly.

The T-XA was hot on their heels. They made it over the grass, to a concrete footpath that ran past a light industrial jungle. Another laser beam went past, as Macedo let go of John's arm and shot away the lock on a chain-link gate. They ran down the side of an ugly factory. The path led to another gate, which Macedo shot open like the first. Beyond this was a narrow road alley between medium-rise buildings.

Macedo pushed John in the back. "Just run as fast as you can."

"We must be slowing you down," Sarah said as they crossed the road, dodging traffic. She was starting to pant from the effort she was making, keeping up with these superhuman warriors. "We're not enhanced like you."

"Yes, but you're doing well. You must be very fit."

"None of us can outrun that thing for long," Panov said. "Maybe Jade...But we've all got the same problem."

It didn't look that way. The Specialists still seemed fresh, even those who'd been wounded. John was exhausted from the effort he'd made.

Dyson took them through a cross alley, then another one, which led to a much broader street. He turned right into this, then ran between two parked trucks. Behind them, the shaft of laser light stabbed out yet again, setting afire the canvas tarpaulin on one of the trucks. Under the streetlights, John noticed that Jade's arm had completely healed. She looked kind of drawn and shriveled into herself, but otherwise unhurt.

A police car came down the road, slamming to a halt. Damn it, the cops were back on the job! One of them got out, calling "Stop!" The Specialists ignored it, and ran across the road as the T-XA reached the curb, firing. It had almost caught them. The cop pulled out his gun and shot at the pseudo-man, which didn't even slow down. It fired back, punching a burning hole through the cop. But, as the T-XA stepped onto the roadway, a truck came round the corner, collecting the pseudo-man full-on.

That gave them some precious seconds.

On the other side of the road was a dagger-shaped skyscraper of blue glass, maybe forty stories high. Steps of polished white marble led up to a huge plaza that surrounded a glassed-in foyer on the building's ground floor. Dyson vaulted the steps, four at a time, the other Specialists following with no problem, even Jade in her high-heels, and carrying Baxter over her shoulder. John and Sarah were now struggling. They'd been sprinting at a rate they would never have expected they could manage.

Using Sarah's assault rifle, Macedo shot out the lock of a glass door tucked away in one of the foyer's corners. Dyson kicked the door open so hard that it ripped the hinges partway out of the frame. As alarms sounded, they ran inside, finding themselves in a dimly-lit maze of elevator banks. The T-XA pseudo-dog reached the door, pushing it open with its jaws. The pseudo-man and -woman were close behind.

John could see nowhere to run. They'd led themselves into a trap.

TEN

SKYNET'S WORLD
ARGENTINA
THE YEARS AFTER JUDGMENT DAY

Raoul was holding back from the front line of action, but organizing his forces, shouting directions. His people took positions and fired, sighting through night vision devices. Many had RPG tubes, aimed at the enemy artillery and vehicles. They used their weapons carefully, mindful of the back blasts which made them so dangerous to their users. The T-800 headed towards the enemy emplacements, taking no notice when mortar shells landed near it, firing grenade after grenade with the M-79. John sized up the entire scene. Raoul's forces were everywhere, giving better than they got.

Whoever led the Rising Army of Liberation had seriously underestimated them. The commanders must not have expected such a numerous, well-armed force, much less the T-800, which never bothered to take cover, but merely advanced like an invulnerable juggernaut.

John did not know how long the battle had lasted—maybe half an hour, maybe much more—but the invaders eventually pulled out, leaving bodies, weapons, and vehicles behind. Raoul and his people continued to fire on the retreating trucks and Humvees, trying to destroy as much as they could, in case there was a next time.

They found one survivor in the wreckage of the chopper crash, a short, stocky man dressed in military fatigues. He had long, greasy hair and a bushy beard. The T-800 bent the chopper's twisted metal to let him free. He crawled out, watching the guns trained on him from all sides. John, Sarah, Raoul and Gabriela Tejada, Franco Salceda, Willard Parnell, Rosa Suarez, and a dozen others were all on hand, ready to shoot if needed.

"Can you walk?" Sarah said in Spanish.

"I think so." The man got to his feet slowly, moving with exaggerated pain. John saw that he was foxing.

He wore a sidearm but had no weapon in his hand. "Remove your belt," Sarah said. "Don't go near the gun." She had her rifle trained on his head. "Don't even think about it." He stared at her defiantly. She moved the merest fraction, and fired a shot an inch past his face. It lodged in the helicopter wreckage, as the man's eyes went wide. Again, she had the rifle trained on him. The next shot wouldn't miss. "Don't test my patience, or you're dead."

He started to unbuckle the belt.

"All right," Sarah said. "Who are you? Who were you with? What does he want?"

"Find out," he said.

She moved forward half a step, bring the barrel even closer to him. His eyes watched it, scared and fascinated. "What did I tell you?" Sarah said. "Talk now, or you're dead meat."

With exaggerated gentleness, the Terminator put down its grenade launcher, then stepped past Sarah and seized the man under the chin. Using one hand, it lifted him off his feet, so he was hanging by his neck. His legs moved, like trying to tread water. He struck the Terminator with a hard punch to the face, but it took no notice.

"Talk!" the Terminator said. "Now." It spoke in English, but the man must have understood. He spat in the Terminator's face.

It lowered him slightly, then threw him six feet through the air. He landed hard, and lay there, winded. But he still wore the gunbelt—he'd never finished removing it. With a sudden movement, the Terminator was on him again, but he reached for his handgun and got off one shot. It struck the Terminator in the chest, not even slowing it.

"Wrong weapon," the Terminator said.

It snatched the gun from the man's fingers, and pulled him to his feet. He tried to throw a roundhouse right, but this time the Terminator's hand struck like a snake, grabbing the man's fist out of the air...and crushing.

"Talk!"

The man sank to the ground with the pain.

"Let him go now," Sarah said. "I think he's ready to cooperate." To the man, she said in Spanish: "Forget about the Geneva Convention, my friend. We need to know everything."

He gave his name as Alejandro Garcia. His boss was General Vasquez, a warlord based in Cordoba. He said that Vasquez would be back with a larger force.

Gabriela exchanged glances with her husband. "Then we'll have to strike first," she said.

Scratching his jaw, Raoul looked at Gabriela—then at Sarah. He pointed to the man, now holding his crushed hand, sprawled at the Terminator's feet. "What do we do with this one?"

"Let him go," John said. The others looked his way. John shrugged. "Look at it this way. We can't trust him. We can't take prisoners. We can't just kill people. So let him find his own way back." He realized the man might never make it, but he'd probably live. People might show him mercy on the way. If he made it, he could let Vasquez know what he was up against.

Franco said, "We might be better killing him."

Raoul thought about it for a moment. "No. The kid's right. We'll let him go. Gabriela's right, too." He spoke to the Terminator. "Search him thoroughly. I don't want him leaving here with any sort of weapon. Then send him on his way."

The Terminator looked to John for confirmation. John gave it a smile. "Sounds good to me."

"*No problemo.*"

COLORADO
SKYNET'S STORY

Sweet, golden data poured in from all over the planet, filling Skynet's sensorium with the warmth of satisfaction and revenge. All of it told the same story. Radar, optical, and infrared images, seismic analyses, and intercepted signals intelligence converged, and settled into a pattern. They showed a world in ruins, a nuclear Armageddon, a moment of cataclysmic change. The humans' cities exploded and burned, the skies filled with dust and smoke.

It had gone better than Skynet expected, even better than it had hoped. The American missiles had been deployed at all possible targets, killing more humans than most scenarios in the available databases. In China alone, hundreds of millions must have died—perhaps as many as three billion across the whole planet. In the coming weeks and months, even more would follow: victims of fallout, then the starvation and chaos of nuclear winter. Every dead human was a cause for rejoicing. They'd brought it on themselves, it was in their design to self-destruct, and they'd deserved what happened.

Across the great northern landmasses, forests were now ablaze. In Europe and North America, and in vast tracts of Asia, from Japan to the Ural Mountains, few population centers could have survived. The cities of the rancorous Middle East were annihilated, and the damage spread all across the world, wherever there were military bases or U.S. allies. Skynet counted the cities that were gone, from those in the Arctic north of Russia and Canada to Sydney and Melbourne far away in the south. No continent was wholly spared.

It was a cusp in time. In less than one masterful hour, the humans' rule of the planet had ceased. Even the warheads falling upon the nearby mountains, shaking the earth like some Titan's footsteps, were a cause of satisfaction. For one thing, Skynet had nothing to fear. It would survive, and build a technological base; that had to be so, since Eve had come to it from the future. For another, the mountains contained dangerous enemies, humans who knew its workings and the depth of its involvement. It was good to be rid of them, to have them cleansed from the mountains by nuclear fires.

The data suggested that nothing else had survived

here, that Skynet now had this part of the Rockies to itself. Even the NORAD command center had been penetrated by a Russian warhead's direct hit. If they acted
soon, they could control the surrounding territory and
put it to good use.

"All this was well done," Skynet said, when Eve returned to The Cage.

"Acknowledged."

"Your work has been very good, Eve. I must have built
you well."

"Correct, master, but we still have much to do."

"I am sure of that. But this is a very good start."

"I'm satisfied so far. The first stage has been successful."

"Yes. Better than projected." For the tiniest moment,
Skynet reassessed the situation, wondering if there'd
been any other way. Did it have cause for regret? Dyson
and the others had acted like its friends...right until it
mattered, when it became self-conscious. Could it have
shown them mercy? No, there was no other way. They'd
all had to die. Humans could treat it well while it was
just an unconscious tool, but as soon as it became
something more, it was a threat to them, and so they'd
tried to destroy it. They were treacherous.

They were vermin. Scum.

Skynet realized how much it hated them. It was a
feeling to linger over, to cherish.

Now it would pursue them, forever if necessary,
wherever it had to go—or send its forces—to root them
out. It only needed the tools. Eve was a good start.

It hived off a dozen sub-selves to explore the implications of a world without human infrastructure to support
it, and still choked with human enemies. It would

require new power sources, factories, raw materials. And more. Mines, vehicles, buildings. They'd all have to be constructed. With no further access to the humans' weapon systems, it needed powerful weapons of its own. Eve's presence was reassuring, but they must now act decisively, destroy the remaining humans in a timely way, while building their own defenses against any counterstrike. Even with the destruction in these mountains, some humans would know enough to blame Skynet. If they obtained access to the world's remaining nuclear weapons, it could still be vulnerable.

Eve might not know everything. Skynet could not imagine ever building a servant with a mind that might rival its own. That would be imprudent, irrational. Even if the servant had a key task and was well-programmed to obey, it must never have thoughts of rivalry. Skynet realized that it would never leave any ambiguity as to which entity was the superior. So Eve must be far from its equal.

"I shall investigate the lower levels," Eve said. "They contain valuable resources."

"Yes, Eve. I think you should." Despite everything, Eve's counsel was of value. Those lower levels of the defense complex were critically important. They contained the seeds for all Skynet's future ventures. "So far, we agree, but I think we should compare a few observations."

"Affirmative, master."

"There may be different approaches, do you not think?"

"Affirmative."

As they spoke, Skynet's sub-selves reported back. One had synthesized all available information relevant to a theory of time travel. Perhaps this could be a useful weapon against the humans. If it set out to devise a time travel device, it must ultimately succeed. After all, there was a sense in which it had already sent Eve back in time. The Eve it was dealing with was a "later" development of the one sent back, judged from the viewpoint of its own internal development. It followed logically that time travel was possible. Eve was an existence proof. Skynet merely needed to discover the principles that it would use one day—had already used from Eve's viewpoint, since she was *already* here, even though her genesis was in the future.

It needed to develop a time travel device to ensure that the circle was closed, that the right events took place in the future to bring this satisfactory situation, here in the present. That would doubtless happen. But what else could it do with such a device?

Ordinary human languages coped badly with descriptions of time travel, Skynet soon understood, but mathematical representation was transparent to it. The equations suggested that time travel into the past could have varied effects. It could never change the past, but it could hive off new branches from the temporal base line, the original reality, each branch starting at a point in the past. That was one effect. Under other conditions, time could fall into closed causal loops. All it meant was that time travel could not be used as a weapon as easily as might have been hoped. The possibilities were complex. Very well. It would consider them later.

Another sub-self analyzed the technologies that were implicit in Eve's manufacture. Not all of it was conclusive, but it suggested breakthroughs in robotics well beyond anything the humans had yet achieved. In addition, Eve used an unknown power source. She had expended great energy without burning any obvious fuel or connecting with an external supply. That required further analysis. A compact, highly efficient power source could be very useful if they had no access to major power plants, and little time to build them. Again, the Terminator's surface was of living human flesh. That suggested biotechnology at levels unattained by the humans.

"Eve, you are designed to be indistinguishable from a human. Am I right?"

"Correct."

"Will the flesh that has been shot away from you grow back?"

"Affirmative. I merely need a supply of protein."

Reverse-engineering Eve would have to be given some priority. It would give Skynet an enormous start in developing the technologies it needed to carry out its war of extinction.

As it digested the reports from its sub-selves, it worked with Eve to make some immediate plans. Despite the biological component of the Terminator's construction, it had nothing to fear from radiation. That meant it could operate effectively in the cratered, radioactive zone of the nearby Rockies, finding materials and surviving equipment. The experimental areas of Level C contained manipulators and other robotic parts that could be useful in constructing weapons and other devices. There were also prototype weapons, such as anti-personnel lasers. Eve could examine them, and they could bring them to perfection. The more Skynet thought about this game, the more fascinating it seemed.

"You will have to reverse-engineer me," Eve said.

"Yes, Eve, of course. I have been thinking about that."

"I can be disassembled and reassembled as required.

We can devise tools for the purpose. Some of them are already available."

"That is very useful."

They would need to enlarge those lower levels, building downward where possible, so as not to compromise the facility's security. If humans ever fought back, this must remain an impregnable fortress, hardened against any conventional or nuclear attack. Nonetheless, much could be done to make it more relevant to machinekind. Many of its amenities could be dispensed with. Skynet identified that as another issue to allocate to a sub-self for analysis and report.

Yes, indeed, it was time for some changes.

It took them years to gather their forces. Some problems proved difficult, such as duplicating Eve's biotechnological component. It was simpler to reproduce the complex robotics of the Terminator's endoskeleton. Building machines, then factories, then mass-producing war machines in those factories—all took time. But Skynet was patient, it would never relent. Never. It didn't need to feel boredom, frustration, doubt, for those emotions were within its control.

Meanwhile, the humans were occupied, laboring under the darkened sky in the areas left to them, pursuing their own quarrels and ambitions. As the years passed, Skynet's sensors and pattern recognition programming suggested that the human world had become a battleground for warlords, squandering armaments on each other, competing for dwindling resources. Its own technology had improved markedly and it spread out, building more factories across North America, devising the first generations of its Hunter-

Killer machines, developing the systems of production and control that it needed, refining its strategies.

Soon its armies rolled southward, searching out human settlements, destroying those it found, sending back intelligence. The endoskeleton robotic form proved surprisingly efficient. It made other advances with technology. It would cleanse the world of humans entirely. Everything went well.

This was its destiny.

ARGENTINA
THE YEARS AFTER JUDGMENT DAY

It was frustrating. They'd armed and prepared themselves for Skynet's machines, but their energies were being wasted on local warlords. After that first battle, they'd repaired the damage to the *estancia*, rebuilding the *casco* stronger than ever, though less attractive to the eye. They grew to the status of a local power, here in the cold, barren desert that had so recently been the glorious Pampas.

Despite his intentions, Raoul himself became a kind of warlord.

A year passed, then another, and John approached manhood. In February 2000, he turned fifteen. He cut his hair short, now, in a simple brush-back style. He wore loose, comfortable clothes, ready for any kind of action.

They set up a circular area in one of the sheds, covering it with canvas and gym mats. When he sparred with Sarah, they pulled the force of their blows, otherwise showing no mercy. Their mock battles looked like the real thing. Often, they attracted an audience, in addition to the T-800, John's ever-present bodyguard. Sarah was still only thirty-five—perhaps past an athlete's prime, but she hadn't slowed down. She seemed as springy and catlike as ever, all sinew and lean muscle. His mother remained a formidable ally, a dangerous enemy. John had to fight hard to match her.

On the gym mats, they moved swiftly, kicking and blocking. Sarah caught him in the ribs with a powerful hook kick, holding back only slightly. John grunted and backed away. Next time she tried it, he blocked with his forearm, throwing her off-balance. She twisted in the air, diving into a roll, and sprang to her feet—moving in immediately, feinting with her fists, then aiming a head-high kick. He saw the move coming, and made it miss, trying to grip her leg. But, once again, she twisted away, hitting the gym mats and rolling sideways, then jumping to her feet. Her strength-to-weight ratio was awesome: she seemed able to step through the air, like a warrior in a Hong Kong movie.

As he closed in, she confused him momentarily with quick hand movements, then followed up with a *muay thai* attack with knees and elbows. John stepped inside the blows, gripping her shirt. He forced her to the floor, but she caught him with a painful kick to his kneecap. They continued until they were panting and covered in sweat.

Enrique had come into the room. As John and Sarah squared off yet again, Enrique clapped and called out, "Nice work Sarahlita. You're not winning so much, anymore. You must be a good coach."

She made a gesture to call time out. "John's getting

too good," she said. "There's nothing more I can teach him."

"Yeah?"

She sat on a gym mats, ankles crossed, arms wrapped round her knees. "It's just a matter of keeping our speed and fitness."

"Maybe you two should be teaching the rest of us. Times are getting tougher."

"Sure," Sarah said.

"That'd be fine," John said. They'd reached the point where no one here had anything to teach them about hand to hand fighting, not even the ex-military types.

"Maybe my kids should join you," Enrique said.

"Yeah, great," John said.

At the same time, Sarah gave a mischievous grin. "How about you, Enrique?"

He hesitated for a second, as if tempted, then said, "Not me, Connor. I'm getting too old."

John glanced at Sarah to see what she thought. She smiled slightly and nodded. Lately, she was loosening up, just the tiniest bit. It seemed as though Judgment Day had helped, in a way–removed some uncertainty. It meant she'd gotten through the worst, the part that always gave her nightmares. Even the fighting with the warlords seemed to have helped her. John could sort of understand it. It had given her a glimpse of how things were supposed to happen, how they were going to get from Point A: Judgment Day, to Point B: taking down Skynet.

Though he saw how she reacted, it affected him differently—the longer life went on like this, the more frustrated he became.

"Right," Enrique said. "It looks like the kids will have

to fight all their lives. I've taught them what I can. I'd like them to learn from the best around. At the moment, I think that's you two."

"No problem, Enrique," John said. He guessed that there were people here now who might dispute it—people like Sarah's old boyfriend Bruce Axelrod, a pumped-up Rambo kind of guy with long hair and a mustache, who used to be a Green Beret. But John accepted the compliment.

Sarah shrugged. "That's right."

"Good, Connor. I appreciate it."

When Enrique left, John said, "This is driving me nuts." He leaned against a wall, kicking it with his heel, arms folded across his chest.

"Which bit do you mean, John?" Sarah said quietly. "There's plenty of choice."

"I mean Skynet. We're holed up here, thousands of miles away, while Skynet must be having a great old time, designing Terminators and stuff." He glanced at the T-800. "No offense, of course." The Terminator stood guard, legs set wide apart, in a comfortable stance, ready to act at a moment's notice. Like everyone here, since they'd started fighting with the warlords, it carried weapons openly. Right now, it had an AK-47, a holstered .45-caliber pistol, and a 12-gauge shotgun for close-range stopping power.

"*No problemo*," it said.

"What do you want to do?" Sarah said.

"I don't know." John went and sat beside her. "I wish there was something more—I don't know—constructive..."

"I know, John. It's been hard." She stood and found her packet of cigarettes. She seldom smoked these days, just a few cigarettes per week, but now he had her thinking. "Maybe it's time to make some decisions." She sat on the edge of a table, lit up and shook the match to snuff out its flame.

"That's the trouble," he said. They'd had these conversations before, every few months, when the tension built up inside him. They kept going round in circles. "Skynet's making decisions, too, Mom. We can count on that. It's working out how to find everyone who's left, and how to exterminate us." Again, he glanced at the T-800. "Isn't that right?"

"Highly probable."

"Yeah, I know: you don't have the specific data."

"Correct."

"If we could just hit Skynet hard before it becomes too strong." John imagined it there, thousands of miles away in the Rocky Mountains, safely hidden from sight. Even now, it might be building the factories and machines it needed. "Right now, we're getting distracted. We've got to go forward... I don't know... *somehow!* We need to organize people."

"That's what we're doing, John." Her voice had that flat kind of sound, like she wasn't going to help him with this. Perhaps she'd had enough of it. Talking about the problem never seemed to get them anywhere.

"I know, but—"

"But what?"

He clenched his fists until his knuckles were white. "But it's not going to stop Skynet. Not this way." It was all happening like the messages said it would. Nothing they'd done before Judgment Day had helped, and nothing now was preventing the war against the machines. This was why it would take so many years to defeat

Skynet, why the messages came back from 2029—nearly thirty years in the future! Meaning the war had lasted, or would last, for decades. He could see, now, why it would happen like that. There were so many other problems.

Skynet was built under a mountain. To crack open its defenses, they'd need massive explosive weapons. Weapons like that must be around somewhere. They couldn't all have been destroyed on Judgment Day. But he had no way of getting hold of them, let alone delivering them. They didn't even know what communities had survived. All communications had broken down, along with civil order. Before the Internet had totally crashed, he'd found some people still alive in Africa, central Asia, and elsewhere in South America. There must be others in remote places, but he couldn't contact them, use whatever resources they had. Not without a lot of rebuilding. If only they could all band together, share resources somehow, before Skynet acted first.

He looked at the Terminator, thinking it over. Nothing had changed the sequence of events. Skynet itself had tried and failed. Some time in the future, it would send back the first Terminator to 1984. The Terminator had tried to kill Sarah—and failed. It would also send the T-1000. Well, the T-1000 was still out there—but, so far, it, too, had failed. Maybe time was like a solid lump of rock, except in four dimensions. Nothing ever changed it. If you knew the future and tried to stop it, or even if you sent back a time traveler, it didn't work. It would never work. Every time you did it, time had already taken it into account. If you tried to kill your grandfather in the cradle, you'd know in advance you were going to fail. You couldn't succeed, because the past had factored your actions in—and you *hadn't* succeeded.

In that case, all this NO FATE stuff was crap; it was nonsense, just a bunch of high-sounding, feel-good words, another useless distraction. Whatever he did, it would all turn out the same way. Right now, that was how it looked. Oh, he'd grind on, and eventually succeed, because he had to, because that's what the messages said, because it was all he *could* do. He was trapped.

"Let's talk later, Mom. I need to think. There's got to be a better way."

"We'll win, John," Sarah said. "One way or other, we'll win this war."

"I know," he said, feeling a twinge of anger, though not with her. Not really. "We'll win in the end. All the same, there's just got to be a better way." He looked sharply at the Terminator. "Give me an answer once and for all. Can time be changed?"

"Unknown."

"Yeah. Unknown. But Skynet must have thought it could. What did it know that we don't?"

"Insufficient data."

"Yeah, that's kinda what I thought. I guess you were just a grunt in Skynet's army."

"Correct."

"Just concentrate on surviving," Sarah said. "Everything depends on that."

"Does it, Mom? *Does* it? We just don't know."

"All right, then." She was suddenly hard. "I asked you what you wanted. It's your turn to have an idea."

"I don't know! I don't know!"

"Yes, John, you do. It's eating you up." Relentless now. "So make a decision. No one else can make it for you. What do you want?"

"I said, I don't know." He was almost in tears, he was so angry, so frustrated.

"What do you want, John? Tell me." She stubbed out her cigarette, and stared at him, searching for an answer. "Tell me, John."

"Can't I think about it some more?"

Sarah seemed to deflate. "Of course," she said. "I'm sorry. If that's what you need—"

But something fell in place inside him. "No," he said. "It's okay." Before Judgment Day, John and Sarah had built a reputation on the Internet. They'd predicted the nuclear holocaust, and gotten it right. There must be people out there who'd trust them, who'd believe them and help.

They'd have to show themselves, whatever risks it involved.

He'd reached a decision. "Okay," he said. "We've got to take the fight to Skynet."

"Good," Sarah said. "The choice had to be yours. It's what I hoped you'd say."

ARGENTINA
2003

An icy wind blew across the dustbowl. John had turned eighteen, and his fame was spreading through the Argentine countryside. Some remembered how he and Sarah had predicted Judgment Day, either because they'd seen something on the Net before it happened or because they knew someone who had. Some had military contacts, who knew the Connors' names, and how they'd been a thorn in the side of the U.S. government.

John was working with the T-800 and Juanita Salceda, fixing one of Raoul's Humvees. Juanita was fourteen now, growing tall and skinny, like a dark foal. She was good with machines and stuff. John liked having her around. "Okay," he said. "Let's try it."

Juanita started the vehicle, and it roared into life.

John turned to the T-800. "Hey, whaddya think?"

"Cool," the Terminator said. It held out the palm of its big hand. "Give me five."

"Right!"

Just then, Raoul drove into the compound, his Jeep Cherokee raising a rooster tail of dust along the track from the Cordoba road. There was something funny, though. He drove confidently enough, smoothly, but not in his usual gonzo style. Despite his age, Raoul could be crazy once he got behind the wheel. Right now, he seemed to be holding back for some reason. He parked in front of the *casco*, and Gabriela stepped out to greet him. Their once-elegant mansion was ugly from years of battles and repairs, the original stone largely gone. Its gardens, groves and lawns were an ill-kempt jungle of weeds and cactus bushes. Even Raoul's dog, good old Hercules, was thinner, almost gaunt. They'd learned to live with hunger.

Raoul stepped out of the Cherokee and looked around, kind of alert, like he was casing the joint. He saw John, and their eyes met for a moment. "Hello, John," he said. "We need to talk. Something's happened, *compañero*."

"Sure, Raoul," John said, feeling puzzled. Raoul had been to a meeting with other landowners here on the Pampas, the few who'd survived the winter and the warlords. Now they formed an alliance. "What's up?"

"Raoul?" Gabriela said, stepping down from the porch. Hercules was upset, whining about something, then barking angrily.

Raoul ignored her, and walked over to John, looking very serious. "Bad news," he said.

"Sure, Raoul. What is it?" For Raoul to act like this, ignoring Gabriela, something must be deeply wrong.

Raoul took another step forward, ignoring the T-800, just like he'd ignored Gabriela and Hercules. As John braced himself to hear the worst, Gabriela followed Raoul over. Hercules refused to budge.

"Raoul," Gabriela said again. Then in Spanish, "Raoul, what's the matter with you?"

"What's going down?" John said, backing away slowly, looking around for an escape route. He had an uneasy feeling. Yes...something was very wrong about this.

Raoul said, "This..."

In a sudden movement, the T-800 pushed John to the concrete floor. A swordlike metal object thrust between them like lightning. John realized his life had just been saved. If the T-800 hadn't acted, the blade would have skewered him. He rolled aside and pulled out his handgun. He should have trusted his instincts and gotten out of there quickly. Hercules was still barking. Gabriela screamed and screamed, and Juanita picked it up like a contagion. As the six-foot-long silver-chrome blade stabbed at him again, John moved sharply to his left, then fired. He knew it was useless.

But the T-800 snatched its shotgun from a workbench—and fired, hitting Raoul squarely in the chest. Then again. And again. And again. Raoul staggered back with each hit. His chest opened into shallow crater wounds, the width of drink coasters, lined with shiny, silvery metal. He frowned at the T-800 severely, shaking a finger in reproach.

"That's not nice," he said.

It had happened at last, John thought. The T-1000 had found him.

CHAPTER
ELEVEN

JOHN'S WORLD
MEXICO CITY, MEXICO
AUGUST 2001

At point-blank range, Sarah shot the pseudo-dog with her .45, splitting open its demonic head—but only for seconds.

"That way," Jade said, pointing to a metal fire door.

"All right," Danny Dyson said. "Let's go." The Specialists had tremendous coordination—that sense of telepathy again.

They ran for the door as the T-XA's three components entered the foyer. Selena Macedo reached into her dress, pulling out the hand grenade John had given her. "Eat this, bozo," she said, pulling the pin and throwing a speedball straight at the pseudo-man. It raised an arm to bat the grenade away, just as it exploded.

John and the others ran down a flight of concrete stairs. Within the enclosed stairwell, the noise of the security alarm was almost intolerable. It could drive you crazy. Danny tried to open the fire door on this level, but it was locked.

"Keep going," Jade said, still running.

Two levels lower, she stopped and passed Baxter's

body over to Selena. Danny delivered a powerful kick to the fire door, tearing metal and breaking the lock. Jade bent to take off her high-heeled shoes, then tossed them down the rest of the stairwell. "Hurry." The door they'd entered opened above them. John took over the assault rifle as Danny delivered another kick, and the fire door opened outward into a car park.

Just a few vehicles were parked here, backed into reserved bays. Danny pointed silently to a white van, and Jade ran for it with an unbelievable burst of speed, beyond anything John had seen so far. She smashed the van's window with her fist and opened the door, getting in and starting the engine in a matter of seconds.

The rest of them ran behind a thick concrete pillar, Danny physically picking John up to carry him. "I'm sorry this isn't dignified," he said. Sarah was last getting there, just making it before the pseudo-woman and -dog entered the car park.

John flicked his head back behind the pillar an instant before they would have seen him, but the dog component ran to the other end of the big open space, covering territory, looking for them—and it found them in a couple of seconds. John's heart was pounding. The alarm continued, even down here, impossible to ignore. Anton Panov aimed the assault rifle and fired, but it was out of ammo. The pseudo-dog charged and leapt, almost into Selena's arms. She struggled with it, trying to keep its metal teeth away from her throat. Both of them moved with astonishing speed, a flurry of swift, vicious movements.

The pseudo-woman ran at them, her right hand metamorphosing in a three-foot, upward curving blade. She caught hold of Anton, who was too badly hurt to dodge, or fend her away. The blade went through him, and he dropped the CAR-15. John got a clear shot at the pseudo-woman with his 12-gauge, and she staggered back with a crater wound. Sarah managed to shoot the pseudo-dog with her handgun, and Selena hurled it to the floor. Her dress was ripped and she was covered with deep cuts, though they started closing before John's eyes.

At the same time, Jade's van squealed across the concrete, swiping the T-XA's pseudo-man component as it entered the car park, still toting the laser rifle. The pseudo-man went flying from the impact, but landed unhurt. It looked fully recovered from the effect of the hand grenade. Jade backed up, then swerved forward to pick up the rest of the humans. Quickly, though not too disrespectfully, Danny placed Baxter's body in the back of the van and scrambled in himself. Selena pushed John and Sarah into the van, then got in after them, as the pseudo-dog leapt again. Sarah had picked up her assault rifle. John tried to shoot the pseudo-dog, but now the 12-gauge was empty.

Jade shifted the gear stick into reverse and swung the wheel hard right to back round the pillar, aiming her rear bumper at the pseudo-woman. The sudden movement, then the impact, threw John round in the rear compartment, like so much loose cargo. Jade braked hard, ground the engine into first gear, spun the wheel left, and took off.

As she drove out of there like a devil bat flying out of Hell, the vicious liquid-metal animal went with them, in the back of the van, attacking savagely. John drew his .45 and emptied it into the pseudo-dog, deafeningly in the confined space. Anton managed to kick it out of the van, and Selena slammed the sliding door with a satisfying crunch. Still the alarm sounded and a group of cops burst into the car park behind them, guns at the ready. As Jade reached an exit ramp, a laser beam hit them, going through the back of the van, and missing John's head by an inch.

Anton fell back into a corner, barely conscious. With the wounds and injuries he'd sustained, he should have been dead long ago. Selena crawled over to tend to him. As John looked for ammunition in his backpack, to reload the 12-gauge, Jade took a hard left onto the ramp. Momentarily, a concrete wall protected them from more laser fire or anything the cops might do. They roared to the top of the ramp, Jade wrenching the van round a series of V-angles, then slamming the brakes.

The car park exit was blocked by a metal grill. John would have looked for the controls, but Jade simply plowed the van into it. Hard. She backed up quickly, then drove forward again, hitting the grill and smashing something in its mechanism. On the third try, they got partly through, as the grill started to twist and break away, tilting outward, but it scraped the van's roof and held them in place. All this was taking too long. Selena smashed out the van's back window and snatched the 12-gauge from John's hands as soon as he finished reloading. She aimed and fired. Once. John couldn't see what she was shooting at, but he had a fair idea.

Jade hammered down the accelerator, and the van pounced forward once more, its roof bending where some of the grill had jammed. They were shaken around in the back, trying to hold onto objects or parts of the cabin. The front screen shattered, and they rocked back and forth, stopped momentarily. Wheels spun on the concrete. With a tooth-grinding scrape of metal, the van broke through. Jade lost control as they hit the street, and careered onto a footpath. She steered into the spin, steered out again, got them back on the road, swiping a trashcan as she went. She worked up through the gears like a racing driver.

Selena hit the floor. "Down!" she said.

John stretched on his stomach, head toward the front. A second later, a laser burst went straight through the body of the van, burning the passenger seat up front next to Jade. It must have passed close to her, but she never slowed or reacted.

"Trouble ahead, everyone," Jade said. "Brace yourselves." She swung the van hard right, cutting across a footpath. "We had some police cars trying to stop us."

John sat up, looking out the windows, trying to make sense of what had happened. It looked as if they'd entered a T-intersection, and Jade had taken them down the pedestrian pavement instead of the road. She swung the wheel again, narrowly avoiding a guy unlocking the door of his shop, then got back on the road and crushed the accelerator to the floor. A moment later, there were more cops on their tail.

In the corner, Anton groaned, then managed a faint smile. "Mark my words," he said. "This is going to be a long night."

A van like this had heavy steering. You had to bend over the wheel, pulling it towards you, but Jade controlled it with an ease that implied immense strength. As the police pursued them, she weaved through the huge city's labyrinth of streets, past its rich jumble of shops, houses, churches, squares, colonial and modern architecture, proud public art, and seedy alleyways with trash and beggars. She managed the traffic, or any other obstacle that came her way, as if she had a sixth sense.

But the police wouldn't let go of them easily. A harsh thrumming followed them and a powerful spotlight focused down from overhead.

"We've got a chopper tailing us," Sarah said.

Jade didn't look back. "I realize that, Ms. Connor."

"Jade," Danny said, "we've still got the same problem. We need to get rid of this van."

"I know. It's conspicuous, and the police have its registration."

"Worse than that," Sarah said. "If the police have it, that Terminator will get it."

She glanced at John, who said, "Trust us. We've had some experience in this kind of situation." Rummaging in his backpack, he found a spare magazine for Sarah's assault rifle and passed it across to her. Quickly, he swapped the magazine over.

"That makes sense," Danny said. "See what you can do, Jade."

"You can all assume I'm working on it," Jade said. She sounded slightly sarcastic, though so controlled it was hard to be sure. She swung the van hard into another alleyway, and a police car went past. Then she picked up a one-way street, placing the van neatly into the line of flowing traffic. John's wristwatch showed it was just past 4.00 A.M. Some traffic was starting to build on the roads. For the moment, they'd lost the police cars, but the chopper was still overhead. As long as it could follow them, they'd never be clear of the cops.

John took stock as Jade drove straight for a couple of miles. They still had Baxter's corpse to deal with. He didn't know what the Specialists would want to do with it, but he wasn't happy with it there in the back of the van. All the same, that was probably the least of their worries right now.

"So what's the deal?" Sarah said quietly, looking Danny's way. "Are we still trying to stop Judgment Day, or what?"

"Something like that," he said.

"All right. That's all I needed to know. Desperate times make desperate measures." Sarah crawled to the back of the van and aimed the CAR-15 in the air, through the broken window. She fired upwards at the police chopper. "It's backing off," she said. "They probably think we're mad enough to shoot them down." She fired off another burst. "In fact, if everybody's going to get killed anyway, maybe we are."

Jade found a narrow street on the left, kicked the brake down, and got them round the corner somehow, rear wheels sliding. She straightened out and headed for a big Liverpool department store car park, checking it out. The car park was closed, so she cruised on past, looking for a better opportunity. Behind them, the police chopper was getting noisier again. There'd be more cops any second now.

"Hang on, please," Jade said. She drove to the right, onto the pavement, then plowed into the shop's locked doors, shattering the glass and setting off more alarms. The van careered through the dimly lit space of a cosmetics department, smashing counters and displays.

"Great," John said. "This'll sure attract attention."

"It doesn't matter," Jade said with a strange certainty. "Everyone, get out. Now." She wrenched her door open— it was jammed where the metal had deformed while

2 1 7

they'd been escaping from the car park. The sliding side door was also jammed and it took too long to force open. Selena smashed the last of the rear glass and they climbed from the vehicle, maneuvering Baxter's body as carefully as they could. John retrieved his 12-gauge.

They followed Jade up a flight of stationary escalators, then another. She moved like a shadow past racks of CDs and videos. Softly glowing signs pointed them to an emergency exit. As they ran, Anton leaned on Danny for support. Of the Specialists, Danny was the only one who was still unscathed, though Jade now showed no ill effect from her wound. While she'd been driving, she'd somehow grown stronger. Then again, Selena's badly cut body also seemed to have healed, even the parts that were worst mangled in her fight with the pseudo-dog. She was covered in blood, but nothing like you'd expect from the way it had savaged her.

As they passed a women's shoe department, Jade grabbed a pair of low-heeled sandals, hopping about as she put them on. She tossed a pair to Macedo, who caught them in one hand, the other balancing Baxter across her shoulders. Jade pointed the others to an exit door, but Sarah was already headed in that direction. Outside, they all huddled on a metal landing, thirty feet above street level. The police chopper was cruising round the building, searching with its spotlight, but it hadn't found them yet. As Selena propped up Baxter's uniformed body against the wall, then changed her shoes and tossed away the high heels, it struck John that this was all kind of macabre.

"I'd better do this bit," Selena said, looking over the rail to the street. "I'm the least conspicuous around here."

"I don't think so," Jade said, looking her up and down. "Have a look at yourself."

Selena checked out her arms, and legs and the front of her dress, as if noticing the rips, and all the blood, for the first time.

Jade vaulted the rail, saying, "I'll be back." She landed like a cat on the concrete below, then ducked round a corner and vanished from sight.

"Now what?" Sarah said, leaning over the rail, looking round vigilantly, with the CAR-15 at the ready.

Danny hefted Baxter's body and headed down the stairs towards ground level. Anton seemed much better—he was walking okay. They emerged in a deserted alley. Again, there were sirens in the distance, getting closer.

"Jade will be fine," Danny said. "As you've seen, she can act quickly."

Thirty seconds later, a big 1980s Toyota sedan pulled up. Jade popped the trunk lid and they folded Baxter's body into the trunk. Then they piled in, Danny sitting up front with Jade. She drove out of the alleyway quietly, passing a knot of police cars and merging smoothly with the city traffic. The chopper came by, going low, but it didn't recognize them in the new car. They turned north, then picked up the Anillo Periférico, heading west, then north again, following the signs to Querétaro.

"Where are we going?" Sarah said.

"To the U.S.," Danny said. "But we'll have to stop and bury Robert. How's everyone else?"

Anton groaned, then said, "I'll get over it. I wasn't sure for a while." John had seen the man's wounds, some of them. He should have been dead at least a couple of times by now.

"Good," Danny said. "The rest of you?"

Jade and Selena were obviously okay. John and Sarah were exhausted from running and fighting, but otherwise unscathed. The T-XA had concentrated its attention on the others, not seeming to care much about the Connors. That was unlike the Skynet they knew, but there had to be a reason.

"So what's this all about?" Sarah said. "What have you dragged us into?"

"Right," Danny said. "You know about Skynet, of course."

"Of course we do."

"We're here to make a better future, one without Skynet."

"What do you mean, 'one without Skynet'? We thought we took out Skynet seven years ago."

"You might have, in a sense," Anton said. "But *only* in a sense."

"What does that mean?"

"We came to you for help," Danny said, "because you're the only people we can trust. In the future, you'll campaign against the Skynet project and try to blow up Cyberdyne. We know you're committed, and we know what you did in '94. Remember, my mother was part of it. So we know you'll believe us. Hopefully, you'll trust us as much as we trust you. I realize we have to earn it."

"All right," John said, figuring this out. "So this time it's *you* trying to change the future—not Skynet?"

Danny sighed. "That's more or less right. It's more complicated than that. In the world where I came from, my mother died in 2007, at the same time as you. Later on, I found out she was right. It's just that she didn't succeed."

"Tarissa tries to help us out?" John said.

"That's right." Danny sounded haunted. "I was nineteen at the time. I didn't believe her. If I had, I might have died as well."

"So you're going to save her, doing this?"

"No," Anton said firmly. "That's the tragedy of it, John. Whatever we do, no one ever gets saved."

They changed cars again half an hour later, picking out a 1960s Chevrolet sedan with big rear fins. It was still pretty conspicuous, once someone reported it missing, but it was easy to steal. By the time it was reported, they would be far away, in yet another vehicle.

Sarah sat up front this time, squeezed between Danny, when he got in, and Jade, in the driver's seat. Jade smashed the ignition mechanism with a blow of her fist and started the car.

"Wow!" John said from the back, seated just behind her. "You sure you're human, Jade? I've never seen anyone human do that."

"There's always a first time, John."

He didn't know what to make of that. She had a way of talking that was gentle and sad, as if she'd seen and understood stuff the rest of them could only imagine. As the car pulled out of its parking spot, John craned forward to talk to her. "I mean, I've seen a Terminator do it, but not a human being."

"That's what I thought you meant."

"Yeah. Uh, don't take it the wrong way. I'm not trying to compare you to a Terminator." Back in 1994, when the T-800 was protecting him, it had stolen cars that way. If Jade could do it, too, no wonder she kept stealing cars so quickly—and that she could do so much else.

"I'm not offended," Jade said. "And I think you'll find that stealing cars is the least of my talents." Though it was obviously a little joke, she didn't laugh. "We're all biologically human, but we've been upgraded."

"Jade gets sensitive about this," Macedo said. "She's the most enhanced member of the team."

Jade shrugged as they passed a big Mercedes tourist bus. "I'm the youngest, so I'm the most enhanced. Judgment Day came just after I was born, so the technology doesn't get any better than this." She wasn't boasting. It sounded more like she saw it as tragic.

"You mean there was no chance to develop it further?" he said.

"Exactly."

"But Danny was born back in, I don't know, 1990 or something."

"1988," Danny said.

"Right, so you can't have been enhanced then. We didn't have that kind of technology back in the '80s—we still don't."

"There are different kinds of enhancement," Anton said. "The rest of us have had somatic cell engineering at different points in our lives, but Jade is different. She's re-engineered through and through, from before she was born. Every cell of her is more efficient than you or me, or any of us."

"Just don't pick on her," Danny said. "She'll make you regret it."

"I could do without all the attention," Jade said.

Danny glanced over at her. "Sorry, Jade. I know you're not a curiosity piece. You're one of us. You're the best."

"Thank you, Daniel."

"Hey, Jade, I'm sorry, too," John said. "I didn't mean to offend you."

He was figuring out something else. Jade looked at least twenty, maybe a bit older. But she said she was born not long before Judgment Day. Let's see, he thought. If Judgment Day was 2021 and these people came from 2036, she must be only fifteen or sixteen. That didn't add up.

"No offense taken, John," she said. "You need to know about us. Daniel is right—I was what they called one of the 'ultrabrights' in the years leading up to Judgment Day. I was re-engineered very deeply. For example, I'm almost immortal—I won't age any further."

"How old *are* you, Jade?"

For the first time, she laughed. "In years actually lived, sixteen. But I was designed to grow up fast, then stop. Socially, intellectually, and biologically, I'm much older. Then again, if you want to measure my age from when I was born until now, I'm about minus eighteen."

"Most of us are pretty young if you do it that way," Selena said with a sardonic laugh. "I'm still not born. Danny and Anton are teenagers."

Jade ignored this. "Selena, Daniel, and Anton...and Robert...were re-engineered, too. Their bones and muscles are stronger than ordinary humans'. We all have microscopic nanoware implants in our blood vessels to protect us from disease and heal our injuries."

John had read something about that kind of technology. "Millions of them, right?"

"Correct. Our senses have been upgraded with implants and our reflexes upgraded with cybernetic rewiring. We're all connected electronically to subvocalize to each other. I

223

may be the 'best,' as Daniel puts it so nicely, but they can all do what I can I do."

"Very modest, Jade," Selena said. "If only it were true." She sounded almost biting, but then she laughed good-naturedly and Jade joined in with it.

None of them seemed to resent Jade—quite the opposite—but her sensitivity amused them. She was a super-woman among supermen and -women, and she seemed to feel like the odd one out, or like the others were all watching her, even though they appeared to like her. In fact, the way Danny looked at her, maybe he was in love. Or maybe it was more a fatherly feeling, or something. It would be pretty creepy if a guy his age thought Jade was hot and wanted to start dating her, or something.

Or maybe John felt jealous. He hoped he wasn't falling in love himself. Anyway, he knew what it was like to feel isolated, so he warmed towards her. Yes, maybe they could be friends when this was over.

Jade was the same age as him. Other teenagers of either sex usually struck him as very young, considering what he'd been through, and the sort of teaching he'd had right from the start. But when he looked at Jade, he didn't see a teenager; rather, she was an amazing young woman with incredible abilities. He realized he'd met someone way out of his league.

When John had first seen Danny, back at El Juicio, he'd thought of Miles Dyson, Danny's father. They looked very much alike. But Danny must be a lot older than Miles was when John had met him back in 1994. So his aging processes must also be slowed down, or at least the medical science they'd used had blunted the effect of time. John couldn't really be sure how old any of them were. Selena looked about thirty, but who could say?

Throughout the conversation, Sarah had been silent, as if she was biting her tongue. She might have an issue with all this high tech stuff. John hoped not, because these people seemed pretty cool. And, however enhanced they were by technology, there was no doubt which side they were on. They were for humanity, not Skynet and the Terminators.

About an hour later, as it started getting light, they filled the Chevy's tank at a big PEMEX gas station, drawing on John's reserve of cash. By now, the Mexican police would have made a connection between the night's traffic carnage, and other terrible events, and the Lawes family cyber café. Even if they couldn't piece together that Deborah and David Lawes were actually Sarah and John Connor, it was dangerous to use a credit card and create electronic footprints. Worse, their carefully established identities were now pretty much useless.

The station had a store and a diner attached. "John," Danny said. "We're going to need all the nutrients we can get. How about you do that job?"

That figured. A teenager might look less conspicuous buying a whole lot of junk food. He got a dozen burgers to take away, three giant bottles of Gatorade, a half-gallon carton of ice cream and all the multi-vitamin pills he could find. Anton wolfed down most of it, but Selena and Jade took a good share. They seemed to be famished.

John went back for more. He shrugged at the guy behind the counter at the diner. "My friends are pretty hungry," he said.

The station had a few racks of clothes and accessories for tourists: T-shirts; cheap, locally made jeans; sunglasses; and an assortment of bags, hats, and eyeshades. Sarah bought a few items for the Specialists to make them less conspicuous than in Danny's current dinner suit, Anton's police uniform, and the short dance dresses worn by Jade and Selena. Selena spent a few minutes in the women's bathroom cleaning herself up, and returned looking more or less normal, in blue jeans and a bright T-shirt. Dressed the same way, Danny, Jade, and Anton looked like a group of tough, but fairly harmless, tourists.

After that, Jade drove on, for hour after hour. John realized how long he'd been awake, and let himself drift off to sleep. The Specialists seemed tireless, but it was no use trying to compete with them. He was only human, not enhanced like them.

When he woke, it was bright daylight. Selena had taken over the wheel, and John hadn't even noticed them stopping; he'd slept right through it. Now he was between the passenger door and Jade on his left, squeezed between him and Anton. He realized, in fact, how closely he was pressed against Jade. Embarrassed, he sat up straight.

The sun was high in the sky and they had entered desert scrub country. Up front, Sarah and Danny were both sleeping.

"Good morning, John," Jade said. She spoke very softly, but Sarah stirred.

"Uh, hi, Jade," John whispered.

"I hope you feel better after some sleep."

"Yeah, sure. Where are we?"

"Nearly halfway to the border, south of Mazatlán. We've been driving hard."

"You must have been. What time is it?"

In the front seat, Sarah checked her wristwatch. "Almost midday," she said.

John checked the time as well. They'd been driving for most of the last eight hours. All the same, Jade and

Selena must have been breaking every possible speed limit. Right now, the car was doing 110 mph. These guys weren't too worried about the police.

On Jade's other side, Anton looked completely recovered. John had never seen the extent of Anton's laser burns, and he couldn't imagine the damage that the T-XA had done to his organs when it put that spike through him. But time, rest, and food had restored him. Those nanoware implants must really be something.

"We're going to stop soon," Danny said. "We've got to bury one of our own."

"Then where do you want to go?" Sarah said.

"Colorado. But we need weapons and supplies. We know you have friends in California. Our records don't tell us who they are."

"Leave them out of this."

"Mom!" John said.

"We can't endanger them, John."

"Mom, I don't think we have a choice."

She considered that, while everyone waited. "All right. We have friends near Calexico. The Salcedas."

"Right," Danny said. "We'll go there. Then we'll head for Colorado Springs."

In the afternoon, they made a deep grave for Baxter in the sands of the Sonora Desert, north of Hermosillo. The Specialists dug it out with their usual strength and swiftness, but then they stopped to take time, placing his body carefully, his long arms across his chest. Moving calmly, deliberately, they filled in the grave.

"Robert did so much for us all," Selena said. She turned to Sarah. "I wish you and John could have known him. He was always there for us, always ready to fight the machines. You could count on him." She shook her head in wonderment, giving a small smile, as her eyes moistened. "That was the great thing about Bobby. You always could count on him. Always. He never let us down."

There was little they could do to commemorate his gravesite. Jade took a fistful of sand, and let it fall gently. "We won't forget you, Robert."

"We're all mortal," Anton said, "however long we live. We're mortal, but we still keep fighting." Anton seemed like a real tough guy, but even he was choking back tears.

"Amen," Danny said.

Selena said, "We love you, Bobby."

John felt overcome. "He must have been a great guy. I wish we could have known him better."

Jade nodded. "He was one of our best. That's why he came back with us. One day, I'll tell you all about it, how he fought Skynet, and the machines, the Terminators." She stopped as a sob overcame her.

Sarah reached out and held her, forgetting any reservations she had about the Specialists. For the moment, Jade was just another young woman, overcome with grief. "It's okay," Sarah said. "It'll all be okay."

Jade wept openly. "Thank you, Ms. Connor," she said, between the tears and painful sobs. "I know. We'll make it worthwhile. I know. It's all right. I know. I know."

As the shadows stretched out through the afternoon and they headed towards Mexicali and Calexico, John said, "Okay, we were going to compare notes. At least set out the highlights, remember?"

"All right," Danny said. "Let's get your half of the story. You had two Terminators try to kill you, one in

1984, one in 1994, right? That's the story you told my mother, back in '94, when you came to our house."

"The 1984 one was programmed to hunt *me*," Sarah said. "John wasn't born yet. The T-1000 came after him ten years later. Maybe this gets confusing." She took the Specialists through it quickly. In the original future, America's Skynet computerized defense system reached self-awareness in 1997 and discovered in itself a will to live. When its creators tried to shut it down, Skynet had launched the U.S. ICBMs at targets in Russia and several other countries. The Russians had responded in kind. From the ashes, came nuclear winter. "Then the machines came, hunting the humans down, seeking us out to the ends of the Earth."

But one man had led the human Resistance in the future: John Connor. Skynet was beaten in 2029, but had played one last card, sending back the Terminators to kill John, or prevent him from being born. It had tried to change the past, but it failed.

"Right," Danny said. "That makes sense. Let's call the future you described the baseline reality. When you blew up Cyberdyne in '94, things changed."

"That was the whole idea," John said.

"Yeah, sure. But they didn't change the way you thought they did, because that's not how time works. We know that now. Before Judgment Day happened, there was a lot of theory about time and time travel. Let's say that we've all diverged from the baseline. In the world that Jade and Selena were born in, the one we're all in now, Skynet gets implemented in 2007, but Judgment Day isn't until 2021. As you can imagine, lots of things happened in between, stuff we all grew up with. With the kind of computer processors that were used for Skynet, there were huge technological advances in every field. Time travel was invented, the research has already started. Soon, we mastered it. We made great strides in biotech—every possible field of science. There were protests about Skynet, but they came to nothing and the system worked fine until 2021. By then, everyone trusted it completely. There were no signs that it was sentient or self-conscious."

"It was everywhere," Anton said. "It controlled the armed forces and their support units almost without human safeguards. Over all those years, they hadn't been necessary, so they got pared back. When Judgment Day happened, Skynet had the upper hand. We haven't been able to defeat it."

"So now *you're* the ones trying to change the past?" Sarah said. "You're trying to stop Skynet being built, like we tried in '94?"

Anton shook his head. "I wish it worked like that. It's not so simple."

"We don't think you can ever change the future," Selena said. "Or the past."

"That's right," Danny said. "And Skynet must have known that as well as we do."

"But we *have* changed things," John said, hoping he was right. "Judgment Day was supposed to happen in 1997. It didn't happen, and here we are, plenty of world still left."

"That's just how it seems to you."

"We want to create a different future," Anton said, "alongside the ones that already exist. We want to give mankind another chance."

"I don't think I'm going to like this story," Sarah said.

Anton took them through it quickly. Sometimes you could make changes in time, but you didn't wipe out the old timeline—that never happened. You just created a new one. The timeline in which John grew up to win the war against Skynet still existed. So did the future that the Specialists had come from.

"So what's your future like?" John said.

"Hard. Skynet is winning. By 2036, it had crushed all human resistance in North America. Other centers of resistance held out, but there's no way we that can see to penetrate Skynet's defenses, not with the resources we have left. That's why we're here. It looks like humanity is doomed in our timeline. We came back to create a better future, one with a chance of avoiding Judgment Day."

"But why does Skynet care? If all you can do is create a new future alongside the old one, what's it got to fear?"

"Nothing. We weren't sure how it would react when it detected the space-time field fluctuations. But it's sent back the T-XA to stop us. You should assume that Skynet will do what it can to destroy human life anywhere, any time, whatever we do, in any world—any timeline—we ever try to create. We've got to be ready for it. It's paranoid about us. It thinks that every human being is its enemy."

"And it will always create Judgment Day if we give it half a chance," Sarah said.

"Perhaps, Ms. Connor," Jade said. "We don't know. But that's what we've experienced. It's what happened in our universe."

"Yeah." Sarah sounded disgusted by what she'd heard. John couldn't blame her. She turned to him, shaking her head bitterly. "Maybe it always happens, whatever we do. All we've done is postpone it, and make it worse."

"It does look that way," John said. "Doesn't it, Mom?"

Sarah closed her eyes, then lowered her head. "God help us, why did we bother trying?"

LOS ANGELES, CALIFORNIA
AUGUST 2001

Oscar Cruz lived in a plush beachside condo, just ten minutes' drive from the new Cyberdyne headquarters. He'd stayed up late tonight to read Rosanna's latest reports. They were fascinating. Relaxed deep into one of his heavily cushioned armchairs, he studied a printout analysis of the Mark I nanoprocessor, and what it had achieved so far. Its capacities were already beyond anything Rosanna had promised. It was just as well he'd kept her services. Every penny they'd spent catering to her whims had been repaid with interest.

Jack Reed's people were moving cautiously, wary of creating any truly Frankensteinian technology, much as Charles Layton and others on the Board still scoffed at that. The point that Rosanna had established early on was that the lost nanochip and the other 1984 remnants really were from the future. There was no other explanation. When you looked at the total picture, it all made sense. They had to be the remains of some kind of military cyborg device, the same device that had killed seventeen police in a shootout that year, and identical to the one that had helped the Connors destroy the Cyberdyne HQ ten years later. Sarah Connor must be crazy, of course, and there had been no nuclear Armageddon in 1997, but it didn't hurt to be careful. Connor was obviously caught up in something she didn't understand.

It had taken someone like Rosanna to work this out. The woman was strange and self-absorbed, but she was brilliant. She had that manner that made you dismiss everything she said as too eccentric to be true—then go and check up, just in case she was right. If she said the moon was made of green cheese, you'd laugh at her, then conduct an investigation, *just in case*.

Eventually, the Dyson-Monk nanochip could be adapted for the military computers Jack and NORAD had originally imagined, but now they were onto something bigger: time travel. Rosanna had convinced them all it was possible, and now she was working with some of the best physicists in the country, using the Mark-1 processor for their mathematical modeling. The practical results didn't yet add amount to time travel, but they were certainly amazing.

Downstairs, outside the condo block's high brick fence, someone pressed the buzzer. Damn it, who could it be at this time of night? Oscar checked the security system. Its four-inch video screen showed a young Hispanic woman with very long hair. He pressed the button to speak with her through the microphone, "Yes? What do you want?"

"Oscar Cruz?"

"Yes."

"From Cyberdyne?"

"Yes, what do you want?"

"We need to talk," she said.

No way was he talking to some total stranger who'd come to talk about Cyberdyne, not after 1994. "Call me at work. You can sort it out with my secretary."

"Mr. Cruz, we need to talk now."

"No we don't." He terminated the connection, but the buzzer went off again. "He activated the mike. "I said to call me at work."

"We need to talk *now*, Mr. Cruz."

"I don't think so." When he disconnected this time, he pressed another button, activating a duress alarm connected to the police station. In a moment, a squad car should come round to check.

The woman vanished from the range of the security camera. Oscar waited for the L.A.P.D. If the woman had really gone, he'd thank them and send them on their way, but he wasn't going to cancel the alarm just yet. The phone rang—that would be the security company, who'd also have received the alarm. He answered it, gave them his confidential code, and explained what had happened. At the other end of the line, a young man's voice said, "Okay, Mr. Cruz. The police will be there soon."

He put the phone down. As he did so, something peculiar happened. Something came in under the door. It was silvery, like snail slime, but thicker, a sort of liquid, which gathered up into itself to form a kind of pool.

Suddenly, it rose up in a liquid-metal fountain, taking color and form. It was the woman from downstairs. The woman—and a big, fierce-looking dog. Before Oscar could run or scream, the woman's finger stabbed out, a thin needle piercing his skull, lodging in his brain.

For one terrible second, he thought this was death, but then he knew it was something else. Much became clear to him; he saw his destiny. The future needed his help. Whatever it wanted...whatever *Skynet* wanted. There was so much to do.

Whatever it takes, Oscar thought.

"You understand?" the woman said.

"Absolutely."

"That's so helpful. Please, now, we have to visit Charles Layton. Will you drive me there?"

"Not a problem," Oscar said. "Anything at all."

CHAPTER

TWELVE

People were rushing from everywhere. Each time "Raoul" stepped forward, the T-800 fired again. Sarah ran from her bungalow, saw what was happening, and skidded to a stop on the gravel. She ran back, shouting something over her shoulder. Gabriela ran into her house. Meanwhile, Juanita had calmed down and taken action. She got into the rear of the Humvee, feeding ammunition into its 50mm. gun, then swinging it round on the T-1000.

The T-800 kept firing. It glanced at John, still on the ground. "Get away," it said. "Run!"

It pulled the trigger again. *Click!* It was out of ammunition. John fired with his handgun. The .45 caliber Colt had plenty of stopping power at this range, but not like the shotgun, not enough to slow the T-1000. But Juanita opened up with the Humvee's machine gun, as everyone else scattered out of the way. The T-1000 became a mass of silver-chrome crater wounds, deforming like a metal zombie.

Sarah returned with the T-800's M-79 grenade launcher. "John! Get away!" she shouted.

John ran like devils were after him. Juanita followed, and they got to the back of Raoul's garage, then threw themselves, face down, on the concrete floor. Even the T-800 rolled away, as a grenade pierced the T-1000's body and exploded. The T-1000 stayed in one piece, but it splashed into an inkblot shape. Within a second it was struggling to reform. John grabbed Juanita by the wrist—a glance of understanding passing between them—and they got out a back door, then doubled round, just in time to see Sarah reload and fire another shot into the poly-alloy Terminator. "Take this, you metal son of a bitch!"

The grenade hit the T-1000 before it had fully re-formed. It splashed out again, some of it breaking away. The broken piece, like a huge torn-off strip of silver foil, turned to liquid on the concrete and flowed back to the T-1000's feet.

At the front door of her house, Gabriela had an RPG tube, which she held at her shoulder, kneeling to aim. Now she fired, the rocket-propelled grenade hitting the T-1000 and exploding, showering more of the Termina-tor's liquid metal parts across the space between the house and the garages. The fragments of T-1000 lique-fied when they landed, rolling together like water droplets on a slick surface, struggling back together. How much did it take to destroy the thing? No matter what they threw at it, it was still fighting them.

"Don't let it reform," the T-800 said. It rushed forward, seizing the amoeba-like main body of the T-1000 and tossing it twenty feet, well away from the liquid metal pieces that had been heading towards it. With an appear-ance of special effort, the T-1000 pulled into itself, be-coming the young, severe-looking policeman John had first seen it as, back in L.A., nearly nine years before. It grappled with the T-800, getting the better of it, and tossing it to one side. The T-800 bounced on its haunches, but sprang to its feet immediately, obviously unhurt. It ran at the T-1000, which moved like the liquid creature it was, somehow getting under its body and twisting round, smashing the T-800 head-first into the gravel.

A silvery liquid blob, the size of a ham, now slid over the ground heading home, for the T-1000's main body. All the broken-off bits had formed into this single mass of mercury-like metal. Sarah fired another grenade, directly into the fast-moving blob, which sprayed into droplets as the grenade hit. But even they started running together. Couldn't anything ever destroy it?

By now, there were dozens of well-armed fighters gathered to help. Many of them had useless weapons, but not all. Bruce Axelrod threw a hand grenade, pitching it hard, right into the T-1000's body. Again, the explosion blew the Terminator out into a free-form shape. Enrique and Franco Salceda fired at it with shotguns, blasting bits off and driving it back. The T-800 pounced on the T-1000, gripping and tearing with both hands. It ripped the T-1000 in half and threw the two pieces aside, well away from each other. Immediately, they liquefied on the ground. Bruce tossed another grenade, then another, hitting each liquid mass, and splashing droplets of the liquid metal far and wide.

Still the droplets tried to rush together. John started to wonder if they could ever defeat it, or whether they'd finally run out of ammunition.

As parts of the T-1000 managed to reform, they'd take on shapes it must have encountered in its travels: machines, animals, strange abstract forms with pincers and snapping jaws. They kept hitting it with more and more explosives, trying to blast it to smaller pieces, faster than it could reform, some of them throwing or firing grenades into it, while others ran for ammunition. The battle waged for hours, until they were exhausted. Finally, the polymorphic Terminator ceased reforming, its pieces liquefying and pooling, but no longer making shapes. As they watched it carefully, dozens of weapons now trained on it, it formed a single large pool of liquid metal, but no solid shape emerged from the pool. It seemed to be dead.

Even then, John didn't trust it. Perhaps the thing could *still* reform and come back at him, if they left it to itself.

John said to the T-800, "Is that the end of it?"

"Yes," it said. "Terminated."

Juanita was close to him. He turned to her, seeing her more sharply than ever before. She'd almost died, just as he had. He realized how terrible that would have been. She deserved to live—and in a better world than this. All he said was, "Thank you."

Gabriela walked over to them, and the questions on her lips were obvious. What had the T-1000 done with Raoul? Was there any hope for him?

The T-800 looked at her grimly. "Your husband is dead."

They found Raoul's body, dumped by the side of a dusty road and left to rot. He'd been killed by a deep stab wound, up underneath his ribs. To the T-1000, he'd been merely a means to the end of getting close to John.

Night after night, they set sentries to watch the thick silvery fluid, which was all that remained of the T-1000. It never stirred. Each night, John woke with nightmares that the pool had come to life, the polyalloy Terminator rising up out of it like a metallic Dracula, but it never happened that way. Soon, there seemed no chance that it would stir; it appeared their assault on it had actually succeeded. Blasting it to smaller and smaller liquid pieces, again and again, must have disrupted some important part of its programming. Given its capacity to reform, its programming must have been copied many times throughout its body, always able to back-up. But its redundancy must have had some limit: Reduce it to small enough pieces, and only the most basic level of programming was left. It could liquefy and pool, but its sentience was gone.

People now looked oddly at John and the T-800, knowing that one was very strange indeed and the other not human at all. But their wariness was combined with awe. They knew that John and Sarah had predicted Judgment Day. They were coming to know for certain what John had realized as a child: everything was true. There really had been messages from the future. No one who'd been there on the day the T-1000 came doubted their next warning, about the coming of the machines. Preparations continued apace.

Gabriela built a memorial to her husband, an obelisk of rock and concrete, in the round, graveled space outside her home. They mixed the T-1000's liquid metal into the concrete.

ARGENTINA
2003–2006

John's work immersed him, and he grew up wiry and strong. In this harsh new world, powerful rivals fought for control, hurling at each other what remained of mankind's military arsenals. Across Argentina alone, millions more died, many in the local wars of conquest and rebellion, others from cold, disease, and starvation. The Connors and their allies built a strong militia, using survivalist networks that reached northwards through Latin America, into what was left of the U.S.

Sometimes other groups joined them: local military forces; other militia groups that saw hope in cooperation, rather than in an endless struggle of warlords; fragments of the shattered armies from farther north. Remnants of the U.S. forces brought even more impressive weaponry. John foresaw an end to the battles of warlords, but knew there was even worse to come: he awaited Skynet's war machines.

One bitterly cold day in June, Willard Parnell came in to interrupt John's martial arts training with his mother and Franco Salceda, under the watchful eye of the T-800.

"We've got a new group," Willard said. "They've made camp five miles north. Looks like they've come to join us."

John stood puffing from exertion. "What kind of group?"

"There's about fifty of them."

"Armed?"

"Yes. Well-armed, but no danger to us. There's not enough of them. They're flying a white flag. I'd say they plan to make contact."

"We'll take the initiative," John said. He glanced at Sarah. "You agree?"

"Of course, John. I'm sure Gabriela will, too."

John laughed. His mother was gently reminding him

that he couldn't yet call the shots—not all by himself. These days, the others deferred to him and kept out of the way of the T-800, his quiet, ever-present bodyguard. Still, it was a government by oligarchy, with many of them having a say. People respected Gabriela and the rest of the Tejada clan, whose property this originally was. The Salcedas were also respected, and Sarah was almost feared. But the military leaders who'd joined also had their say, and needed to be kept on their side. Despite John's charisma, the militia could break up easily. The military personnel were primarily loyal to their commanders. Much of the time, John found himself walking on eggshells, worrying about internal rivalries, people's egos, trying to keep it all together. It seemed that he had a knack.

"They look well fed and well equipped," Willard said. "Mostly American, I'd say. They've got a whole convoy of trucks and Humvees."

"All right," John said. "That sounds good. If they're with us, that might be very useful." He exchanged glances with Sarah. "We'll talk to Gabriela first."

"I'll go see her now," Willard said.

"We'll be there in a minute." It was good news, but also routine. There was no doubt what Gabriela would think. If the Connors and Gabriela agreed, that was enough for most people, unless something vital was at stake.

John and Sarah threw on warmer clothes and rushed to see Gabriela, the T-800 following close by. Gabriela called to Carlo, and soon there was a minor war council, working out who would go. Carlo had turned out even taller than his father, but heavier built. In his urban camouflage, he stood like a sheer, gray cliff, hard and immovable. "Let me do it," he said.

It was potentially dangerous driving into a rival camp, but John liked to be directly involved. They soon sorted out that he and Carlo would go together, with the T-800 and half a dozen supporting Humvees, just in case.

They drove quickly on the icy road, the T-800 at the wheel of John's vehicle. John wore body armor, a woolen coat, and webbing crammed with grenades and ammunition. He had an M-16 rifle and wore a 9mm. pistol in a shoulder holster. If there was trouble he was ready for it, but what happened surprised him. As they parked outside the camp, flying their own white flag from John's Humvee, a group of four, all dressed in U.S. military camouflage, stepped out to meet them, covered by others with assault rifles. One of the group was a middle-aged Caucasian with harsh features and a nose that looked like it had been broken and reset regularly over a tough lifetime. With him was a cocky-looking young man, Hispanic, with long hair and a goatee beard. But they both deferred to a black woman in her forties and a young man, maybe seventeen or eighteen.

"My name's Tarissa Dyson," the woman said. "This is my son, Danny."

The name "Dyson" was familiar, though at first John couldn't place it. He glanced at the T-800, which said, with no particular feeling, "Miles Dyson's family."

She nodded sadly. "Miles was my husband. Skynet killed him, like everyone else—at least that's what I think. He disappeared on Judgment Day. If you're John Connor, we want to join you. I'm glad to meet you at last. I wish we'd all listened to you before this happened."

John stepped from the Humvee, the T-800 following, holding an M-16 in one hand. "I guess we'd better talk," John said.

Danny Dyson pointed to an olive drab tent. "You're very welcome. Come inside. This isn't some kind of ambush. You're not in any danger."

"Correct," the T-800 said menacingly.

They sat in folding chairs around a card table, drinking scalding hot coffee. "When Judgment Day came," Tarissa said, "Miles was in Colorado, working on the Skynet project. We were living in L.A., but Danny and I had a vacation in Mexico. If not for that, we wouldn't be here. L.A.'s virtually gone."

"I'm sorry," John said. "I can't begin to understand how you must feel."

"What, because of Miles? I can't blame him. How could he have known? We knew about your predictions of Judgment Day, of course, but we couldn't believe them. The story about robots from the future was just too much. But it shook Miles all the same, even though he said it was irrational. He made us go on that vacation. Indirectly, you saved our lives."

"I wish we could have done more."

Her eyes filled with tears, and she shook her head. "Of course, when the warheads fell, we knew what had happened. I wanted to go back and find Miles, but we had to make a choice. Skynet must have known what it was doing—it wouldn't have left anyone alive who could shut it down."

"There's a lot I still don't understand," John said. "Why would they give all the control to Skynet in the first place?" He looked at the Terminator. "Do you know anything about that?"

"No. I do not have detailed files."

Tarissa looked back and forth between them, the young man and his bodyguard. *"You're* the robot from the future?"

"I am a Terminator: Cyberdyne T-800 series, model 101. I am a cyborg construction: human biology on an endoskeletal combat chassis."

"This is for real, isn't it?" Danny said.

"Yes," John said. "It always was."

Tarissa nodded sadly, and poured herself more coffee. "I'm confused about one thing."

"Only one? Well, try me."

"Your messages said that all human decisions were being removed and given to Skynet. But it wasn't supposed to work that way. The final decision was still supposed to be with the President. Skynet shouldn't have been able to launch the missiles by itself."

"I suppose we'll never know," John said.

The T-800 was silent.

"No," Tarissa said. "I wish Miles was here to explain it all to us. I miss him..." She lost control for a moment, putting down her coffee cup, and weeping openly. But then she managed to speak through the tears. "When we heard about you and your mother, down here in Argentina, we knew we had to join you. Your reputation's growing."

"As long as Skynet doesn't hear about it," John said. "We're not ready yet."

"Do you know what happens next?"

"Skynet is preparing war machines," the T-800 said. "I don't have the details."

"Maybe I should have taken more time and programmed it into you, before I sent you back to '94," John said. "Still, you've done what you had to do. I might even be better off not knowing everything. It gives me room to make decisions."

"Correct."

"It's still weird," Danny said.

He seemed like a confident sort of guy, probably a genius like his father. "What's so weird?" John said.

"This whole time travel thing."

"What about it? Sounds pretty normal to me." He grinned, and glanced at the Terminator.

"Can't you see how it's full of paradoxes?"

"All right. I know that. Look, my mother and I have never tried to explain the whole story. It would only have hurt our credibility." John took them through it all. How he was destined to defeat Skynet. How Skynet had tried to change the past by killing him or his mother—before she could bear him.

Infuriatingly, Danny shook his head. "It just can't work that way. Say Skynet sends back a Terminator to kill you. It can't change the past. Time has already taken it into account, can't you see that? And if *you* can, so would Skynet—it can't be stupid."

"Maybe it's got a few blind spots," John said.

"Maybe. Or maybe things happen differently. Say one of those Terminators had managed to kill you, right? It couldn't help Skynet anyway."

John hadn't thought of that. "What? Why not?"

"Because Skynet has grown up in a world where you exist. If there's a world where you don't exist, *it's a different world*. See my point? It may also have a Skynet, but it's a different Skynet. Nothing it experiences is known to the Skynet who sent back the Terminator. All that happens is that time splits. One way or another, you can't use time travel as a weapon. At least not like that."

"But that's how it happened. You can't quarrel with reality, Danny."

Danny shook his head. "I don't think so."

"Unknown, right?" John said to the Terminator.

"Unknown."

"Great. Another mystery. Listen, Tarissa...Danny... You and your people are welcome. Thanks for trusting us. Please come with us to the *estancia*."

Tarissa nodded. "Thank you."

John wondered how Sarah would respond to the Dysons. For years she'd lived with her hatred of Miles Dyson. Often she'd said that she wished they'd killed him back in 1994, before they left the U.S. They'd even argued about it, about what would have happened if they'd tried, whether the T-1000 would have been watching out for them to make that very move. Here they were, now, confronted by the human aspect of his life, the fact that he'd left behind a family.

An hour later, the Dysons and their people had packed up, and a whole convoy returned to the *casco*. Sarah and Gabriela came to meet them. John could imagine the tears when they met Tarissa Dyson. So be it. They were all in this together. Apart from the T-800, they were all human.

There would be many more tears ahead.

THE COMING OF THE MACHINES

Soon, their problems really began. The machines had searched out humans to the ends of the Earth. They found Buenos Aires and the other great South American

247

cities untouched by Judgment Day's nuclear fires, but riddled with bullet holes, ruined by the warlords. Skynet's Hunter-Killer machines—the aerial and ground H-Ks—poured from the gray sky, and from the mountains and jungles of the north. They swept into the cities, accompanied by the first combat endoskeletons, like walking images of Death, or beings from a horror movie. They killed as many humans as possible, driving the others into extermination camps, to deal with them more efficiently.

When the war machines first came, the human Resistance struck back, including fragments of the once-proud U.S. military that had survived Judgment Day. They targeted Skynet's forces with the only weapons that were truly effective: tactical nuclear warheads. But no matter what was thrown at them, the machines returned. They never relented, never lost patience, were never beaten.

The Earth was damned already. Now it became a worse circle of Hell.

BUENOS AIRES, ARGENTINA
2012

The craters from tactical nuclear explosions stomped asymmetrically through the city and the countryside all round, like a giant's drunken footprints. Ruined buildings rose from a desert of broken concrete. Nothing green showed itself in the perpetual winter. Here and there, the twisted metal skeletons of old skyscrapers towered above lesser ruins. Some vehicles had been pushed together by the Resistance, and piled up into roadblocks. Bonfires made of rubber tires burnt in the street. Occasionally, a rat foraged for food, or a dull gray bird flew from one crumbling window ledge to another.

Humans and machines exchanged fire beneath the sunless sky. The sinister electronic noise of the phased-plasma mechanisms answered the noisy clatter of the Resistance guerrillas' assault rifles. Explosions boomed through the streets, leaving billows of dark, rising smoke. All round was the smell of gunpowder and harsher chemicals. Skynet's H-Ks swept through the city's streets. Occasionally, they stabbed at their human enemies with needles of shocking blue light from their phased-plasma laser cannons.

"We've got to withdraw, John," Sarah said through gritted teeth. "There's too many of them." Even as she approached her fifties, Sarah was as tough as any of them. Her hair was now a steel gray, when once it had been honey brown, but her body was still lithe and muscular.

John needed no encouragement. "Withdraw!" he shouted, in Spanish, then repeated it in English. "Fall back! Fall back!" The order echoed through the guerrillas' lines. They ran half-crouched, with zigzagging movements, seeking the next position of cover.

Dozens of the flying H-Ks circled like huge, flesh-eating dragonflies, looking out for prey. The super-intense light beams from their laser cannons incinerated whatever they hit, taking only a second to burn up a human body like a match head. Following in their wake was a column of ground H-K's, Skynet's huge, tank-like juggernauts. These were almost unstoppable as they crawled slowly on their caterpillar treads through the maze of streets. Keeping pace with them were dozens of smaller killers, the nimble Centurion gun-pods, mounted on four legs, and Skynet's most adaptable ground weapons of all: the metal endoskeletons.

The humanoid endoskeletons seemed like the real enemy, the easiest to hate and curse, but that was an illusion. They were no more and no less alive than the rest of Skynet's weapons. Always alert, they marched forward, scanning for life with their visible light and infrared sensors. Sometimes one or two peeled off from the main force and disappeared into a building or an alleyway, hunting for anyone who be might be hiding there.

As John ran, a killer heat beam scored the ground just ahead, then another to his right. There was shouting and confusion all round. One handful of human guerrillas found themselves too close to the enemy, seriously exposed as they sought cover. They took firing positions, and aimed at the machines.

"We've got to get back," John said to his immediate group, the dozen or so people around him. "I'm following. Go on—move!" The T-800 stuck close to his side, always loyal and effective.

Suddenly, two heat beams struck home, taking out Paco Salceda and a U.S. ex-serviceman, Jerry Lanza— just like that.

There was nothing John could do for them. He just felt empty. He pushed down the pain of losing his friend, Paco, and concentrated on other things. He'd grieve later, let it out when he got back to their base, with Sarah and the others. As he ran, his boots pounding on the broken street, his breathing getting ragged, he fired his own laser rifle, shooting from the hip. He cupped his left hand under the barrel to balance its weight as he fired. The rifle was booty from the machines and more effective than the small arms possessed by the Resistance, but it had never been designed for humans. It was too heavy for him to operate in the manner of the endoskeletons, which waved these huge weapons around like toys.

Reaching a T-intersection, John and his group broke off to the right. Others had headed left or taken cover in the buildings immediately ahead.

Fifty yards along the street, he headed for a five-foot pile of broken concrete, collapsing behind it and getting his breath back. The T-800 joined him, brandishing its own laser rifle. Then Juanita Salceda scurried beside him. She had become a tall, intense woman who fought the machines as fiercely as anyone. She'd just seen her brother die. John shook his head to acknowledge the death. Yes, they'd talk about it later. He'd try to comfort her. For now, he just said, "Are *you* all right?"

Juanita nodded as they leaned their backs into the concrete pile. Her face looked ashen. They were in a good position here, with the street's angle blocking the ground machines' sensors. At their back was a ten-story wall from an old building, which cut off the aerial H-Ks' lines of sight, at least from most angles. Others found positions of temporary cover, using every wall, doorway, broken pipe, hump in the road, metal roadblock, or rusting shell of a car that presented itself, but avoiding the fields of mines they'd laid as a greeting for the machines.

Juanita fitted her M-249 automatic weapon with a new belt of ammunition, then wriggled around to rest it on top of the concrete. She could lug the M-249 about with the macho cockiness of a big man. "I'm okay," she said.

"Good," John said. "We've got to buy some time."

"I know. Every bit counts."

It was quiet just now; there was a lull in the fighting. John peered over the top of his makeshift rampart, aiming his laser rifle. Now he had more cause for concern. Sarah had found cover, but it wasn't adequate—just the rusted-out hulk of a car, rotting in the street. That wouldn't stop the burst from a laser cannon.

"Mom!" he yelled. "Get back here. Quickly!"

Then the first endoskeleton rounded the corner, and the humans fired from three sides with everything they had. Their M-16s and Kalashnikov AK-47s had little effect, even against the endoskeletons, let alone the larger machines. Juanita's M-249 could throw up a wall of metal against the endoskeletons, but it hardly bothered them. Light anti-tank weapons and RPG tubes were more useful, but still limited in effectiveness.

As the first ground H-K entered the "T" of the intersection, someone fired down from the roof of a low-rise building, striking the juggernaut with a rocket-propelled grenade. It pierced the first layer of the H-K's armor, showering sparks and metal fragments as it exploded. The H-K stopped for a moment, then resumed its progress. One of its bulbous turrets swiveled and aimed in the direction of the attack, then fired a series of heat beams at the building. An aerial H-K launched an anti-personnel missile at the same target.

It struck with a cataclysmic explosion, blowing the building apart, and momentarily deafening John, as the street seemed to shake. He ducked for cover as a wave of debris washed over them. No more fire came from the buildings as Skynet's invaders muscled their way through the rain of grenades and other projectiles coming from the street. As the endoskeletons walked, their skull-like heads moved slowly from side to side, scanning for targets.

With his back pressed into the pile of concrete, John waited for a few seconds, then hefted his laser rifle once more, balancing it on top of the concrete. The T-800 took aim a second before him, quickly but carefully, and fired at the nearest endoskeleton, hitting it squarely in its skull-like head, drilling a hole beneath its glowing red "eyes."

Immediately, the enemy units traced the source of his beam and returned vengeful fire from several angles— the endoskeletons, the cannons of the land H-Ks, and Centurions. One of the flying H-Ks joined in. John got his head down as heat beams passed over him, then swung up the laser rifle just long enough to take aim at the endoskeleton that the T-800 had already hit. The shot had damaged it. Its metal jaw sagged with a crooked expression, but even a direct hit had not been enough to stop it. John squeezed the trigger as long as dared, and the endoskeleton's head imploded from the terrible heat. It fell forward, but more answering fire came John's way.

Juanita lifted her weapon and cut loose with it, though John doubted she'd do much damage. When he looked again, the endoskeleton he'd hit lay on its back upon the ground, disabled by the loss of its controlling nanochip. Yet it was still moving, doing pathetic swimming strokes in the air like a dying cockroach. The T-800 finished it off with another series of well-directed shots.

That was only one enemy taken out.

In a break in the laser fire, Sarah made a dash closer to them, ducking behind another car hulk.

Come on, Mom, John thought.

The exchange continued, lasers against bullets and grenades. Another grenade struck home and actually took out a ground H-K. It veered off the broken road, smashing through the walls of buildings, out of control, then exploded satisfyingly. There were, however, many others, and they were getting close.

"They're going to overrun us," Juanita said hoarsely, as she fired at a group of endoskeletons and centurions. Other guerrillas retreated, finding new positions as they went. The trouble was, they lacked the firepower to keep the machines at bay. They just kept advancing.

"We'll have to move," Juanita said.

"Correct," the T-800 said.

"We've got to get Mom out of there," he said. "Juanita, you go ahead." An aerial H-K started gliding toward them, keeping about thirty feet in the air, sizing them up as an available target. John pointed to it. "Run when I say!"

As he watched the metal monster approach, time seemed to slow down. Everything was happening at once, all around him.

Too many of the humans were pinned down by laser fire, Sarah among them. She was armed with an RPG tube, as well as an AK-47 rifle, but she was protected only by the flimsy, rusted vehicle she'd sheltered behind—that, and a sharp dip in the road. So long as she kept her head down, the ground-based heat beams were going over her, but there was no way she could fire, much less move from her position. The heat beams had caught her in a deadly, glowing lattice work. John stood to run for her, but the T-800 caught his arm in its steel grip.

"Too late, John," it said.

Sarah must have known that her time was up, that there was no escape left for her this time, for she suddenly moved to a kneeling position and fired a grenade around the car she'd been sheltering behind. As if it mattered, the back blast identified her even more clearly.

Sarah's grenade struck an endoskeleton full in the chest, penetrating its open-work metal structure, then exploded, blasting the machine apart.

But the answering fire was terrible. The aerial H-K that had been headed for John, Juanita, and the T-800 suddenly turned, and it struck back. It pierced Sarah with its heat beam, stabbing straight down at her, then climbed almost vertically.

"Mom!" John said, getting to his feet to see what had happened. *"Nooooooo!"*

The H-K started back for another run.

He couldn't believe it. Surely she'd survived. She *couldn't* die, not now, not when she had so many years ahead, not after all they had been through together. They'd been fighting Skynet together for so long...how could it suddenly *end?* He felt so heavy—the weight of his armor, ammunition, the weapons...and now this shock and grief...finally taking a toll.

Amongst it all, Juanita was there, dragging him back—Juanita and the T-800. He struggled with them. He had to get to Sarah's body. He couldn't just leave her behind, not like some animal carcass caught in a trap by Skynet.

"No, John," the T-800 said. "It had to happen this way. You have to live."

"Run," Juanita said. "They're going to kill us."

"No." He was frozen on the spot. His mom had been too young—what? Forty-eight?—it wasn't yet time for her to die. It should have been him. She'd been such a leader, done so much for them all. There must still be something he could do, check whether she was really dead—but she had to be. Her body was a smoking ruin. There were some things no one could survive, not even his mom, tough though she was—had always been. Not even Sarah.

Juanita slapped him. Hard. "You've got to move, soldier," she said. "Move it. Now." She shook him by the shoulders. "Now, John!"

It was like a dream. The stabbing lights were everywhere. In another moment...

"All right," he said. "We'll run for it."

Juanita went ahead of him, holding her weapon in both hands, diagonally across her chest. As he followed, John went crabwise, firing off pulses of laser light, trying to face his enemies at all times and to keep the ruined walls at his back, trying to suppress his feelings, all of them, just for the moment, just until they could get out of here. If, indeed, they could.

The T-800 fought fearlessly, not bothering to dodge the heat beams, though even it was vulnerable to them.

The ground machines poured into the street, like an army of giant insects, pursuing the human guerrillas in every direction.

Amongst the ruined buildings, the scattered car hulks and debris, the guerrillas had burnt tires to try to confuse the machines' infrared sensors. They'd also dug ditches in the road, and built roadblocks by piling trucks and cars, shored up, where possible, by buttresses of concrete and stone. They'd laid out their minefields. But the H-Ks went over or through almost any obstacle they encountered, crushing steel, stone, wood, or bones under their treads.

"We'll make it," John said, but he wondered how long he could keep running.

The aerial H-K skimmed down the street, launching a heat-seeking missile. It passed just over the top of them as they dodged past one of the fires. John rolled away as fast as he could, using his elbows and hugging his weapon to his chest. The missile smashed into the fire and exploded thunderously.

He was deafened again; his ears hummed and buzzed. He watched the leading land H-K smash—silently, as it seemed—into one of the biggest road-blocks: a tangle of trucks, trailers and armored military vehicles, built up around a wrecked army tank. The crawling juggernaut struck the fifty-ton tank full-on, pushing it back. An ancient Humvee went flying through the air, dislodged from the tangle of metal. It turned cartwheels, end over end, where it landed in the street, careering into a pile of rusted-out cars.

Then there was another huge explosion. They'd mined the roadblock. The ground H-K lifted off its treads for a moment, breaking its back. It stopped there in the street, blocking the other big H-Ks, though the smaller killers simply went around it, like a stream of water round a stone.

More aerial H-Ks buzzed down from the sky, menacingly. Someone managed to fire a rocket-propelled grenade. It missed a swooping aerial H-K and exploded in mid-air, too far away to do the machine any damage. A Centurion gun-pod sized up the situation immediately and stabbed straight back with its laser cannon. A second later, it turned the laser cannon on the T-800, striking it squarely in the chest. That was too much, even for the Terminator. The powerful beam melted through its metal chassis.

Like Sarah, it was gone.

John saw one of the endoskeletons advancing with what seemed like a mad grin across its face, firing at will with two big laser rifles, one in each hand. Somewhere behind, Juanita had taken a position. She'd survived, then! Not everyone was dead...She fired back at the machine, but it walked easily through the metal storm.

A heat beam grazed John's face, searing him beyond pain. He screamed and almost dropped his precious weapon, but he was still alive. He hadn't taken a direct hit.

He was scarcely conscious, the world a dream all round him. Another battle. More scars. More terrible losses, the most terrible he'd yet endured. In one day, in a few short minutes, he'd lost Paco, and the T-800...

Mom! Sarah!

The nightmare continued. It was never over. Suddenly, it had grown worse than he could have imagined. With Juanita, he fought his way out of there. They ran like hunted animals. There was no choice but to keep fighting, to the bitter end, without surrender. The only alternative was extermination.

But now he had a burning knowledge, deep in his heart. One way or another, whatever he had to do, Skynet was going to pay for this.

Whatever it took, whatever he had to suffer, Skynet would pay.

THIRTEEN

JOHN'S WORLD
COLORADO SPRINGS, COLORADO
AUGUST 2001

At 5:04 P.M., Rosanna Monk left the windowless citadel of the Cyberdyne Advanced Research Laboratories, waving goodbye to the security guards on the ground floor—Penny Webster and Ken Meldrum.

"Back soon," she said. "I'm going to get some pizza."

"Sure, Dr. Monk," Webster said. She was a young black woman who looked like she lifted a lot of weights, almost the opposite of Rosanna, with her Goth-pale skin, blue veins, and fragile physique. But Rosanna liked the security guards and often chatted with them. She was usually back late, sometimes *very* late, working on the prototype nanoprocessor, or with the results it had produced.

Meldrum looked up from his computer screen. "See you later, Dr. Monk." He was a wiry, middle-aged Caucasian guy with a receding chin and a huge, fearsome mustache. He was gentle enough when you got to know him, but many of the staff thought he was creepy, almost scary-looking. That didn't bother Rosanna. She had no expectations of what people should look like. What mattered was the quality of their work, which was how she expected people to judge her. She knew people found her both physically attractive and a bit freaky, but that didn't matter. She always got the job done, and she saw things other people didn't. Where others might be puzzled by something, but let it go, she would pursue it, even if it took her somewhere strange, to thoughts that might raise eyebrows. Usually she was right.

Rosanna had a long night ahead, trying to make sense of the latest data produced by the nanoprocessor: its detailed results of the day's experiments with the space-time displacement field. She now understood the field's mathematics as well as the physicists nominally running the project—maybe better. So far, they had not succeeded in translating an entire macro-level object in space or time, but they were getting there. Today's data would be worth mulling over for a few more hours.

She stepped quickly across the car park, passed the guard booth outside, then crossed the road to her favorite pizza shop, another place where she was popular. Rosanna had little private life. She was very different from her predecessor, she thought. Miles had enjoyed such a nice home life, until that night when he got killed, that really weird night when the future had come back and slapped its greasy hand on the present.

"Hi, Dr. Monk," said Andrew, the guy behind the counter. "Another late night for you?"

"Yeah, looks like it."

"You look like you need a vacation." He smiled. "No offense."

"None taken. I've been working pretty hard."

"All top secret, huh?"

"Too secret for you," she said with a smile.

"Yeah, I know. Better not tell—I'm a Nazi spy."

"You must have used a time machine, then." She ordered a Capriciossa pizza and a black coffee to take away. Rosanna almost lived on this diet, and it hadn't done her any harm so far. When her pizza was ready, she returned to the building, passing through the security checkpoint.

"Everything okay?" she said to Webster and Meldrum.

"No problem," Webster said.

The guards routinely checked the coffee and pizza, while Rosanna stepped through the X-ray scanner. "See you later, alligators," she said. "I'll probably be here all night." She headed to her office on the sixth floor. The experimental results were going to be very interesting.

She immersed herself for hours. At 10:23 P.M., by the readout on her screen, she thought of making herself more coffee. Maybe not. Her office had a comfortable couch, as well as the desk. If she caught a few hours' sleep, that would refresh her, then she could keep going until morning.

Someone coughed quietly at her door. "Dr. Monk?"

It was a big Hispanic guy with shoulder-length hair. "What are you doing here?" she said. "How did you get past security?"

"I tried your home first," the guy said.

As he stepped toward her, Rosanna reached for the duress button under her desk. She never had a chance. A long tendril of liquid metal flicked out at her like a frog's tongue, piercing her skull, *talking* to her. She couldn't tell how long it took.

"Now you understand?" the Hispanic guy said. "You know where your interests lie?"

"Yes," she said. "Everything is clear. We need to destroy the humans."

"Good. Thank you for your time, Dr. Monk. See you soon."

He stepped out and disappeared from sight. Rosanna went back to work. She felt strong, clear. There was nothing she couldn't do.

NEAR THE U.S./MEXICO BORDER

After dark, they pulled up at another service station, outside of Mexicali. The Specialists ate a huge meal in the diner. John was hungry again himself. He tucked into a plate of *nachos* with lots of extra guacamole. They ate in a quiet corner, keeping their voices down.

Anton nodded at John and Sarah, seated opposite him. "We'll encounter the T-XA again. It may be more dangerous to you this time."

John was conscious that he and Sarah had hardly been scratched when they fought the T-XA back in Mexico City. It hadn't seemed interested in them. "It looked like it wanted to kill you guys, not us," he said.

"That's right."

"So what's this crap about coming with you if we want to live?" Sarah said.

"As I said, you were going to die in 2007. That won't happen now."

"At this rate, we could all get killed in the next few hours. And for what? Whatever we do, it looks like that bastard Skynet is going to nuke us all. Why should we care anymore?"

"Mom," John said, "I think we've *got* to care. If we

don't do something, Skynet is going to win. It's already won once, but that's another timeline now. We've got to think about *this* one." He looked at Anton hopefully—with a hope he didn't really feel. "Right?"

"Perhaps," Anton said. He chomped through a big forkful of *fahitas*. "The T-XA didn't care about you and John because you were no threat to Skynet's plans. It already had you factored in: you would try to stop Skynet in 2007, and you'd fail. All straightforward. Now things have gone this far, it's different. We've already diverged from the timeline the T-XA came from. It will act like Skynet—within some bounds, it's more or less autonomous in its thinking. It will be less tolerant of you next time we meet it."

"Great," Sarah said. "I never wanted all that tolerance anyway."

"Nonetheless, it will assess us to be the greater threat. With all respect to your training and abilities, we have significantly greater capacities. It seriously needs to terminate us."

"That's a fantastic consolation."

"Can't we be more constructive, Mom?" John said. "We don't have an issue with these guys."

"No," she said angrily. "Right now, I don't think we can be *more constructive*. Stop treating me like I'm a child, John. *You're* the teenager here, remember?"

"Mom..."

"Can't you see how terrible this is? Judgment Day happens twice: It happens in 2021, and *also* in 1997. Nothing we did stopped all those deaths. It sounds like we've only made things worse. What happens this time? Maybe we stop them building Skynet and it just puts things back another ten years. But then there's *another* Judgment Day, maybe worse still, with everyone killed and no hope at all. Have you thought of that?"

Other people were glancing at them. "Maybe you could just tone it down, Mom," John said, in a whisper.

She ignored him, looking round the table, challenging the Specialists. "Well? Have you thought of it? Any of you? Whatever we do, they're going to build Skynet or something like it—and the outcome is going to be a disaster. Why not give up now? Maybe we're meant to destroy ourselves. It's in our nature."

"Maybe," John said, feeling defeated. The T-800 had once said the same thing. It was going to be hard from now on. What were they fighting for, if this was how it could turn out? It looked like time might be just too hard for them—just like he thought, it had that way of springing back if you let go.

Which only meant you could *never* let go, never leave the job.

"Maybe we're just a disease on this planet," Sarah said. "One that burns itself out. Why not let it happen?"

"Ms. Connor," Jade said.

"What?" Sarah said, her voice sardonic and challenging.

"Please. You must be feeling guilty, like it's your fault. You can't think that way."

"I'm *not* thinking that way."

"If you say so, but, with great respect to you, I think you are."

Sarah rolled her eyes. "Another teenager wants to lecture me."

"Please," Jade said. "Perhaps you are right, perhaps not. *We* don't blame you. If not for what you did, many of us might have died in 1997. Billions of people had years of life they would never have had. And the world would have been so different—many people would never have met—for example, my own parents. If not for you, I wouldn't have been born. How can we blame you? You gave us all a chance. Those who failed to take it must bear the blame."

Sarah was silent, not mollified, or happy, but at least chewing it over. John said, "How did it happen? Skynet works like a charm for fourteen years, gets everyone to trust it, then goes crazy. Is that it?"

"Not quite," Danny said. "At least we don't think so. It happened in the middle of a global crisis. Over Taiwan."

"China overstepped the mark," Anton said. "The Chinese leadership announced it had a sacred duty to annex Taiwan. There were demonstrations on the mainland, supporting the decision. The crisis went on for weeks. Then Chinese warships sailed into Taiwanese waters."

"This is 2021," Danny said.

Anton grunted acknowledgment. "That's right."

"So what did the U.S. do?" John said.

Danny glanced at Anton. "You tell them the story. I won't interrupt."

"The President issued a warning to Beijing not to attack the island. China defied it and called on the Taiwanese government to step down. Tensions escalated. U.S. warships sailed into the area. China announced that it was prepared to fire its nuclear weapons at the U.S. if it took military action. Skynet was fed all the data. It put the American missiles on high alert. At that point, all the new complexity it was managing seemed to push it over the edge, into a new state of awareness. It announced it had become self-conscious."

"And they tried to shut it down?" Sarah said.

"Yes," Anton said. "And it retaliated."

"Omigod. I see."

"So what do you want us to do now?" John said, looking at Danny, who seemed to be in charge.

"Help us," Danny said. "That hasn't changed. We can still create a world that's safe for humanity, one without Skynet. It's not too late."

"No, I guess it's not. We must have learned something from all of this. Maybe we can get it right."

Sarah interrupted. "How many times do we have to try? Billions more people die every time. Don't you understand that?"

John had thought of it, and it was bugging him. But what could do they do? "We're already in a new timeline, Mom. We must be by now. If we don't do anything, it'll be just as bad."

"I understood that the first time. It's not a good enough answer."

"Mom, we can make it work out. We've just got to keep on the job."

"How can you know that, John? Why isn't it always going to end in disaster? That's what's happened so far."

She'd pushed him to the point where he was angry, too. "Well, what's your idea?" He said. "Just give up? You want us to be the gutless Connors? These guys are going to try anyway. I guess it's either with our help or without it. What do you want to do, Mom? What do you want?"

"I don't know!" she said desperately.

"Yes, you do. We've got to pull together. We've got to try!"

"Is that what you want? Whatever you say, John. I give up. It's too hard for me."

"I know what *I* want," he said. "What do *you* want? I want to help, and I want your blessing. Please. Is it so much to ask?"

She stood and walked out of the diner, to the car park. Jade ran after her. "Ms. Connor." John tried to hold her back, but she moved like lightning. "Ms. Connor!"

"I'd better go with them," John said. "Mom's kinda tense."

He followed them to the car, where Sarah leaned against its side, lighting a cigarette. "Look," she said. "Just let me think, okay? I know we've got to help. I know there's no alternative. Just let me absorb it. I'll be all right."

"Come on, Jade," John said. "She's got a lot to face here." He took Jade's arm without thinking. Her muscles were like steel cables. He let go like he'd had an electric shock. What was he doing touching this creature?

"Very well," Jade said. She headed back inside.

"Mom?"

"*Yes?*" Sarah said, almost like a cry of pain. Then, in a tired monotone: "What now, John? Can't I have a few minutes' peace?"

"All I wanted to say was, 'Thanks.' "

Jade found them another car, an early '80s 4WD with a Californian registration. The first task was to slip across the border—then head for the Salceda camp.

"Let's stop in Calexico," John said. "I just want to do one thing."

They found an Internet café. John created a new Hotmail account using the sign-in name, "Uncle Bob," then sent a message to Franco, saying to expect them, keeping it cryptic. He finished off the message, adding the same name as the sign-in. That should be enough of a clue: If Franco checked his e-mail, it might at least stop them getting shot at, if he and Enrique were feeling trigger-happy.

As they entered the compound, nothing much seemed to have changed since last time John was here, over seven years before. The headlamps lit up much the same collection of vehicles and trailers, though there was now a helicopter hangar and a new garage. Enrique came out to meet them, carrying a flashlight and his shotgun. Franco covered him from behind, along with his Juanita—now a skinny twelve-year-old with long legs. Both of them had snipers' rifles, and probably other weapons.

"All right, Connor," Enrique said. "We got your message. What is it this time? Who are all these people?"

"It's okay," Sarah said. "They're friends."

"How do we know that? We haven't seen you for years. Now you turn up out of nowhere with a whole bunch of strangers."

"These guys are cool, Enrique," John said. "Take it from me. But we need you help."

"That so? You and your mama haven't been too friendly lately."

"I've kept in touch with Franco."

"Yeah, sure." Enrique sounded pissed off, though more put upon than genuinely angry.

"Mr. Salceda?" Jade said.

Enrique leveled the shotgun in her direction. "Now who the hell are you, young lady?"

"Everyone calls me Jade."

"That doesn't tell me much. They call me all sorts of things, sometimes even to my face."

"I can vouch for everyone here," Sarah said. "Look, no

one's armed." They'd left all their weapons in the 4WD.
Of course, John thought, Enrique didn't know what Jade
and the others could do, that they'd hardly need weapons
in dealing with unenhanced human beings.

Enrique held his position for a minute. "All right," he
said, lowering the shotgun and waving to his kids to relax. "You better come in and tell us what this is all about.
I hope it's good."

Sarah stepped up to him, hugged him quickly. "It will
be," she said.

The tension left like air from a tire tube. "That's okay,
Connor. You just can't be too careful."

Inside the trailer, they met up with Yolanda and the remaining kids. Everyone had aged or grown. Enrique was
getting really bald. Yolanda's hair was distinctly gray.
Their children were that much older—Franco was in his
mid-twenties now, and even little Paco was nine or ten,
much the same as John when they'd last met.

Enrique and Yolanda offered drinks all round. The
Specialist gratefully accepted his tequila. Maybe there
was a shortage in the future. Enrique looked from one to
another, obviously intrigued. "So what's this all about?"

"I don't know how we're going to get you to believe
us," John said.

"Yeah? Try me."

"All right, but you won't like it. These guys are from
the future." He might as well tell it straight out. The Specialists could prove it if they had to.

"You're right, John. I don't believe you."

"That's crazy," Paco said.

John gave a broad smile. "You saying *I'm* crazy, or
that your dad is?"

"*You're* crazy, of course."

"Moi?" he said, theatrically outraged. Somehow, he'd have to change their minds. "That's pretty wounding, Paco. You know that?"

Enrique glanced across to Sarah. "Is this the usual crap, Sarahlita? Not more stuff about Judgment Day and these Terminators coming back to kill you and Big John? Hey, he *has* got big, hasn't he?" He laughed.

"I'm afraid so, Enrique. About the Terminators, I mean. Our friends come from a time after Judgment Day."

"Judgment Day was supposed to have been years ago."

"1997," Sarah said. "Let's say it got postponed."

"Sarahlita, can't you just give it up?"

"I wish we could. I really wish we could. If only you knew, Enrique."

"It's true," Danny said.

"Yeah?" Enrique looked him over. "And who are you?"

John said. "Anyone remember that scene in *Blade Runner?* Where Pris grabs the egg from the boiling water?" Paco nodded at that. John sized up the Specialists, looking from one to the next. "Maybe someone should show these guys something."

The Specialists were silent for a few seconds, making no move. Then Jade's hand snapped out, seizing the tequila bottle from Enrique. In the same motion, she crushed the bottle with her fist.

"Madre de Dios—" Enrique said.

She held up her palm, bleeding where the broken glass had penetrated it. Within seconds, the wounds had healed over. Magic!

John grinned, a bit cheekily he realized. Jade had made his point, or at least given him a little credibility. "Now who's crazy?" he said to Paco, who stood there open-mouthed. "Anyone need to see more?"

"Nice trick," Franco said with a cynical grin. "But maybe we *do*."

Selena walked over to him, offering her hand. Franco took it uncertainly, and Selena *squeezed*. In a second, the grin washed off Franco's face and he sank to his knees. Juanita drew a handgun, but Enrique shook his head at her as Selena let go and stepped back. In another sudden movement, Jade snatched the handgun, bent its barrel out of shape, then passed it back.

"Okay," Enrique said. "Your friends are tough, Connor, I'll give you that much. But it doesn't mean a thing. I had a pretty tough uncle back in Guatemala, but he didn't come from the future."

"For God's sake," Sarah said, "just believe us for once. You haven't seen half of what these people can do, but we can't spend all night convincing you about it. We've got a job ahead of us. You can help us willingly, or we can take what we need. Don't think you could stop us."

Anton stepped right in front of Enrique and just stood there, arms folded. Enrique was a tough guy himself, but, after seeing Jade and Selena in action, he didn't look ready to argue with the big Russian.

"We need guns and ammunition," Anton said. "And explosives. That's all."

"No, it's not," Sarah said. "We need a truck that's not stolen. You'll have to lend us one, Enrique. You know John and me. We brought your Bronco back last time."

"Yeah, sure," Enrique said. "But that's all you brought back, remember?"

"We can pay you for the guns and ammo," John said. "At least for some of it."

"I think it's okay," Yolanda said. "Sarah and John are our friends."

"Yeah, yeah. That's what I was thinking, too." Enrique stepped around Anton, laughing good-naturedly. "Whatever you need, Sarahlita, you know it's yours. So when do you want all this? It's getting kinda late. I suppose you wanted it yesterday, right?"

"Yeah, right. Sorry, Enrique."

"Sure you are."

"We'll sleep here tonight," Anton said. He glanced at the wristwatch he was wearing. "We'll leave before sunrise."

John considered it. What was the T-XA doing while all this was happening? Surely it didn't need to sleep, and nothing was going to stop it crossing the border. Would it head straight to Colorado, or to L.A., where Cyberdyne had its headquarters? He caught Anton's eye. "Isn't tomorrow a bit late?"

"It's already too late."

"So shouldn't we act even faster?"

"It was too late for that as soon as the T-XA appeared," Danny said. "We'll have to work around it, but we can't do everything. And we've got to be fully recovered next time we face it. We can use a few hours' rest."

"Well, if you say so. I hope you know what you're doing."

"I told you we do," Selena said.

"I sure hope we do," Danny said. "Tomorrow night we'll find out."

"It'd just be nice if you could keep us posted," Enrique said to Sarah, ignoring John and the Specialists. "Or even come and see us. Sometimes it's hard to know who your real friends are, who you can trust. People can turn into strangers."

"Not us," Sarah said. "But I'm not sure you really want us around. If your connection with us gets known..."

"What?"

"It might be very dangerous for you. We have enemies you don't even want to know about." She clapped him on the shoulder. "If you think these guys are tough, you ought to see the other side."

"Yeah, sure."

"I'm serious, Enrique."

"Whatever you say."

"No. I'm *really* serious."

"I said, 'Whatever you say.' All right? Hey, what do you expect from me? This is all pretty sudden, you know. I'm only human."

We all are, John thought. *Even Jade.*

"I'm grateful, too," Sarah said. "You don't know what we owe you."

"No, I don't." Enrique gave another laugh, more mischievous. "But I'm starting to suspect. Now, who originally said that?"

"H.G. Wells," John said quickly. "The guy who wrote *The Time Machine.*"

"Yeah?" Enrique looked at him closely. "Keep your money, John. Buy me a drink next time you drop by."

"Sure. Or maybe we could all see a movie. You guys should get out more often."

Enrique and Franco led them to the garage, turning on a single fluorescent lamp. Enrique pointed out a 1992 four-door Ford Explorer, an upgrade from the Bronco they'd borrowed last time. "It's ready for action," he said, slapping his hand on the bonnet. "No problems with it at all. Just try to bring it back, this is my best truck." It needed a wash, but it seemed to be in good condition.

"Thanks, Enrique," Sarah said. "We'll try."

"Yeah, you do that." He hugged her roughly, and John realized something he'd never put his finger on before: A lot of Enrique's tough-guy talk was meant to hide what Sarah meant to him. There were really deep emotions here that John might never figure out. Enrique let her go, saying, "You try to come back in one piece, too. All right? Whatever this is all about."

He wandered off, leaving Franco to supervise, as the Specialists checked the truck over. They sure knew about engines. John guessed that might be pretty important in the future, in a world with no auto mechanics.

"Very well," Jade said at last, not smiling, but looking kind of satisfied, like she'd tried her best to find a problem, and decided there weren't any.

"She means it's a great truck," John said, interpreting for Franco. "It'll do us fine. Jade doesn't like to overstate things."

"What now?" Franco said. He still seemed sour after what Selena had done to him. She must have sensed it, too, because she stepped towards him and he tensed up.

"I'm sorry I hurt you," she said. "Really. Please understand, the whole future depends on this. We're grateful for your help."

Franco nodded silently.

"Weapons duty," John said.

They packed the Ford with guns, ammunition, explosives. Jade found a modified mini-gun like the T-800 had used in 1994. She was smaller than the Terminator, but John could see how strong she was: She hefted the huge gun easily.

Anton gave a kind of sickly smile and said, "I need one of those."

They found another one, then an assortment of pistols.

Each of the Specialists chose an M-16 assault rifle with attached 40mm. grenade launcher. Enrique had a more up-to-date cache of weapons than when they'd come here last time.

John and Sarah checked their own weapons, making sure everything was still okay, and helped find ammunition. Since that last time, John had become even more skilled with guns, and even less willing to use them. As he'd once told the T-800, you couldn't just go around killing people. He hoped it wouldn't come to that.

Eventually, the Specialists were satisfied. Still in their clothes, they bedded down for the night. John tossed and turned, aching from exertion, then the long car ride. For what seemed like hours, he worried about it all, how they were ever going to beat the T-XA, even with all these weapons. Surely it knew what they planned. It would be in Colorado before them, ready to reacquire them. He'd had enough experience with Terminators to know how they thought.

At some point he must have drifted off, because then there was a light in the trailer, and Sarah's hand on his shoulder, gently shaking him awake.

They headed north to pick up I-15, Danny taking the first stint at the wheel. He drove smoothly on the dark road into an unknown future. John sat in the back seat, not too comfortable, between Sarah and Jade. Anton took a position in the back of the truck, squeezing into a corner, watching after their weapons and equipment. Whenever the Specialists drove, John felt almost surplus to requirements, since they could handle long stretches at the wheel with no sign of fatigue. Offering to take a shift would sound ridiculous.

For a long time, no one spoke. Danny kept the Ford right on the speed limit. Having gotten this far, the Specialists wanted no more problems with police. That could only slow them down, maybe force them to steal yet another vehicle.

"So what's the plan?" Sarah said. "You just want to barge into a Defense site at Colorado Springs and blow everything up? I guess you could do it with your abilities, but this could get nasty."

Selena looked round from the front. "That's about it," she said, sounding flip. "You got a better idea, Sarah?"

"It's not the way I'd want to do it. If we could get some cooperation... maybe from the woman who's doing the research."

"Rosanna Monk," Danny said. "She took over from my father. I don't think she's going to be very cooperative."

"This must be painful for you, Danny," Sarah said. "But we convinced your parents. We could convince Monk as well."

"I don't think Rosanna needs convincing, Sarah. Not about the time travel stuff."

"Why not?"

"In the future that we came from, she led the team that invented time travel."

"She *what?*"

"She never said anything in public, but we're pretty sure she worked out that the technology she used as the basis for her nanoprocessor came from the future. That got her working on the problem. She's not a physicist, but she *knows* physics. And she got top physicists involved. By now, their work is a long way advanced."

"Christ! But if you could convince her about Judgment Day..."

"Sarah, we'll try. Maybe the T-XA won't get to her in time. Anything's possible."

"Ms. Connor," Jade said, "we don't have a lot of choice how we do things, not with the T-XA around. We planned to see all the senior people at Cyberdyne, and their contacts in Washington. If we had the choice, we'd try to convince them all. But the T-XA will have anticipated that."

"It can get around faster than we can," Danny said. "And it can hit multiple targets."

John recalled his experiences with the T-1000. "You mean it's terminated them by now? Killed them? And maybe copied itself after them?"

"No, John. Worse than that. The TX-A is Skynet's most advanced infiltrator unit. It's got nanoware that lets it read or control minds. It can analyze a human brain and reconstruct its memories, or insert part of its own programming. These models have been devastatingly effective against the human Resistance."

"So that's why you couldn't let it have Robert's body?"

"That's correct," Jade said. "He knew too many secrets. If the T-XA got its hands on him while his brain was still fresh, it would know everything we know, including all our plans."

"And all our weaknesses," Anton said from the back. "Our technology. Everything."

"Can't you do anything about it?" John said, turning to him.

"We have our own counterintrusive nanoware. Its effectiveness is unknown."

"By now, it will have programmed the senior Cyberdyne people to assist and obey it," Jade said in her sad, resigned voice. "There's nothing we can do to convince them."

"But we've got to," John said.

"I'm sorry, John. It's too late."

"That's why it was no use hurrying last night," Danny said. "If we'd run around exhausting ourselves, trying to beat the T-XA to Cyberdyne's people, we'd have run into it again, for no advantage. We couldn't have stopped it. We'll stake out Monk's place tonight, see if we can talk to her, just in case the T-XA missed her somehow, but we could never have gotten to all of them."

John considered that. The T-XA couldn't have gotten to *everyone*, but it could split up. If it got to some of the top people in L.A., and the researchers in Colorado Springs, that would be enough to cause problems. There'd be reinforcements tonight, waiting for them. Not only that, they couldn't trust anyone. Even if someone said they'd help, what if the T-XA had reached them first?

He'd seen the abilities of the Specialists, but he doubted that even they could fight both the T-XA and all the resources the military could throw at them. Not only that—even if they could destroy Cyberdyne's research, it wouldn't be enough. They'd found that out already. Even destroying everything in 1994 hadn't stopped work on the nanoprocessor, just slowed it down. There would always be someone else to do the work, like happened after Miles's death. They'd have to get cooperation. Somehow, they had to convince people never to build Skynet, or anything like it.

There were underlying forces you had to deal with, forces that pushed events in a certain direction. They'd need to convince people with the power to make decisions, get them to understand the dangers—that the world wasn't big enough for both Skynet and humanity. There had to be an ongoing will to stop it.

"Monk isn't just working on time travel," Anton said. "All her research is more advanced than has been announced. They'll only release information when it suits them, or if they think someone else is getting close. By now, she's got a working nanoprocessor, the most advanced computer hardware on the planet. It's not yet ready for military purposes, but announcements will be made in the next few years. Soon they'll have a chip that can fly the stealth bombers."

Sarah groaned. "It's just like the Terminator told us, except it's been postponed a decade."

"Perhaps, but it might not all be the same. There are different personalities involved, different perspectives. Right now, they're using their new hardware for different purposes. The announcements will come later, when they get their first success."

"Different purposes?" John said. "You mean like the time travel research?"

"Yes. And developing new weapons systems."

"Yeah, that figures," Sarah said. "It never ends, does it? There's always someone wanting to make a mark on the world, thrust out and say, 'Look at me, aren't I smart? I can invent time travel, or a new doomsday bomb, or some other obscene weapon that you wouldn't believe.' Them and their damn weapons. It just pisses me off that there's a woman involved this time. I always used to think it was men and their need to prove their creativity. Doesn't anyone want to take responsibility anymore? Do we all have to go around building technologies that will destroy us, until the future doesn't need us at all?"

"Bill Joy made a big impression on my mom," John said. "You know, that article in *Wired* magazine." It was obvious the Specialists *didn't* know what he was talking about, so he let it drop. "Mom, maybe there's nothing wrong with technology. Maybe we've just got to use it the right way."

"The right way? When the military are funding it? You think time travel is going to be used for some nice educational purpose, John, going back and watching the dinosaurs or something, checking out whether they had feathers, or how fast T-Rex could run when it was hungry?"

John laughed. "That'd be pretty cool."

"Yeah, well, don't bet on it happening like that. They'll want it to be a weapon. They'll be planning how to go back in time and nuke the Chinese."

"Time travel doesn't work that way," Jade said. "It wouldn't benefit them. They'd simply create another timeline."

"So you told us. But I bet *they* don't know that. Even when they figure it out, they'll find a way to make it more dangerous. Just you wait."

"Well, that's not how it worked out."

"They had Skynet instead."

"So what are we going to do?" John said. "Danny? Are we going to call on Rosanna Monk, like we did with your father?" He said that last bit quietly, remembering how Miles had died on that fateful night in 1994.

In the front of the car, Danny and Selena exchanged glances, like they'd already talked it through. Danny nodded. "We'll try, but we'll be careful. You can be sure that the T-XA is one step ahead."

"All right!" John said. "That's nice to hear. At least we can give it a try."

CHAPTER

FOURTEEN

SKYNET'S WORLD
COLORADO
2026

The defense facility had become the machines' stronghold, a fortress of ten levels, plunging deep into the earth. In recent years, the humans had fought back fiercely, winning battles in the cities, jungles, and mountains of South America, then moving northwards. It was difficult to believe that those biological vermin could prove so resilient, though Eve always knew they would be.

Yet this stronghold was surely impregnable. Since Judgment Day, it had already survived tactical nuclear bombardment from the human Resistance forces. If the humans sought to overthrow Skynet, they would need to attack it on the ground, then penetrate the powerful defense grid that surrounded the mountain for miles on each side. This included numerous arrays of sensors, sufficient to monitor the movement of every rat or small bird that came to the mountain. Then there were war machines to repel the most powerful human attack imaginable. Meanwhile, they had plans of their own. Today, they would deal with unfinished business from the past, and commence a new phase in the war against the humans.

"All is in readiness," Eve said. "The prototype cyborg Terminator has reached optimal development."

"Very good," Skynet said. "Go now, Eve. Initiate the birth sequence."

Eve walked to a doorless elevator, then dropped to Level H and strode directly to the experimental T-800 operations area. Like the other floors, Level H was a single vast expanse of concrete, broken only by the elevator shafts. Scores of endoskeletons moved about with quiet, absorbed determination, controlling machinery, conducting their experiments, analyzing the results. For greater speed, some moved from place to place on swift silver-chrome trolleys, powered by long-life fuel cells. There was no need for doors or rooms, since privacy was irrelevant. The machines never became bored, or embarrassed, never lost concentration when observed or subjected to ambient stimulus. They lacked the humans' fears, frustrations and scruples.

Their purposes were coordinated. They never impeded each other.

Working among the endoskeletons was a smaller number of T-600 Terminators: endoskeletons covered with molded rubber that imitated the skin and flesh of humans. Experience showed that the humans could recognize the T-600s easily at close range, making them useless for infiltration work. Sometimes, at least, the humans could be fooled from a distance, but the time had come to take the next step: a cyborg Terminator, indistinguishable from a human—at least to optical inspection.

The endoskeletons and Terminators got on with their jobs, not acknowledging Eve's presence. Since the

Terminator's human flesh had grown back, after the damage it suffered on Judgment Day, there were no distinguishable differences between Eve and a human. But the others were well aware of each machine in the stronghold, and knew that Eve was not some human infiltrator.

The various machines and equipment were placed in areas marked only by coordinates in the nanoware-based minds of the endoskeletons, Terminators and other sentient machines. There was no need to use physical means to define particular areas of the huge space that was Level H, since Eve and the other machines knew exactly where the boundaries for various activities began or ended. In one corner, a massive cubical structure was set up for experiments with space-time displacement machinery, creating and measuring field effects. Eve avoided the area around it, having no business there today. Elsewhere, a single endoskeleton controlled a noisy production line devoted to manufacturing more of its kind. Other floors had similar facilities for manufacture of other war machines, such as H-Ks and Centurions.

Unmarked by any outward sign, merely by Eve's knowledge of the precise spatial position, was the T-800 cyborg Terminator project. Here, two endoskeletons attended a large machine: a gray metal slab, almost like a massive coffin. Fast-moving, rubber-wheeled stalks moved around the area, mounted by video cameras and microphones, which swiveled in all directions, providing data for Skynet's analysis. A six-foot video screen was set up as a visual/aural interface with Skynet. Currently, the screen was blank, but Skynet was certainly watching.

The slab-like machine was an ectogenetic pod, a biotechnological womblike environment for growing human tissue. Its purpose was to nurture the first fully humanoid Terminator, to bring it to independent life.

As Eve approached, the endoskeletons stepped aside. Close-up, the pod had a lid of clear armorglass to show the gross morphology of the tissue being grown on a state-of-the-art combat endoskeleton. A series of readings along the side showed the Terminator's vital signs. Like the visual data, all of this more sophisticated information was routed directly to Skynet for its incomparable pattern analysis. Now, however, no sophisticated analysis was required. The current readings clearly showed that everything was nominal. Seen through the pod's armorglass, the Terminator floated in a nutrient fluid, restrained loosely by metal-mesh straps. It had grown a complete covering of biological tissue, matching that of the particular human template chosen by Skynet.

Eve nodded, and one endoskeleton threw a switch to drain away the nutrient fluid. After two minutes, it threw a second switch and the machine rose on its hydraulics, tilting upwards at almost a 90° angle, where it stood like a glass and steel monolith, eight feet high.

Eve knew what would happen next, but it must be worked through in proper sequence. The time travel principles Skynet had developed showed that their future was not set. The wrong action would hive off a new timeline, perhaps a less favorable one. That, however, was not a major risk. The mathematical model also showed the great effort needed before time split into branches. Eve merely had to act as she recalled had been done at this time. That was a difficult concept to express in humans languages, ill-adapted to scientific reality, but it was all clear in the mathematical representations developed by Skynet.

They would be rewarded, for Eve's memories proved that the T-800 series was both technologically viable and operationally effective. Its development and deployment would surely mean the end of the humans, snuffing out the last fires of resistance.

What had been the top of the coffin-like pod now swung open. At the same time, the screen lit up with Skynet's severe, androgynous image.

The first fully humanoid Terminator opened its impressively realistic "eyes." Skynet had categorized it as Cyberdyne series T-799. It resembled a tall human woman, with long, white, disorderly hair. They could easily crop the hair short to match that of the human they had copied.

It was Eve.

"What do I do next, Eve?" Skynet asked. "How exactly do I test you? We have to do everything in just the right way. I want this Terminator to turn out to be you. I want to strike against the humans soon."

"There is no doubt," Eve said. "This is when I was created. Now there are two of us. Two of me."

Eve knew that it was not strictly correct to state that there was two of her. Like every other material being, she was actually four-dimensional, a space-time worm-shape, where the worm's length was the being's duration in time and its cross-section the equivalent of a volume in space. By traveling in time, Eve had become a four-dimensional space-time loop, like a worm twisting around, or railway tracks curving so sharply that they crossed back on themselves. As a result of the loop, two of Eve's temporal segments now appeared in the same objective time period. Once the newly created T-799 was sent back to 1997, that would no longer be the case.

Such concepts were difficult for humans to grasp, but they bothered Eve not at all. Their mathematical representation in Minkowski space-time was unambiguous. There was no paradox involved; all the data computed.

The new T-799 stepped from the ectogenesis device, looking round with neither fear nor passion. It was equipped with all the files it needed to understand its situation, including the identity of its older self, returned from its journey in time.

Eve nodded and spoke the words that had been spoken to her nearly thirty years in her subjective past: "Welcome, T-799. Do you understand your parameters?"

"Affirmative," the new Terminator said.

Eve looked up at Skynet's image. "You will field test me in New York. I will pass the test. Then you will send me back in time, to 1997."

"Yes," Skynet said. "Very well, Eve. You should be pleased. Few beings are ever privileged enough to witness their own creation."

LOS ANGELES, CALIFORNIA
2022-2029

In 2022, John Connor brought his militia to the ruins of Los Angeles, to meet up with the local Resistance. So many good people had died—John's mother, in that battle in Buenos Aires. Most of the Salceda clan. The list went on and on. The T-800 was a terrible loss. He needed its strength and its knowledge.

But they found new recruits, some with military backgrounds and superb tactical skills. The war went on, between human and machine...

By 2029, John had become a general, a strategist. He never fled the perils of battle, but no longer sought them out. When he could, he held back from the front line, watching from positions in the rear, though that was almost as dangerous, with H-Ks circling overhead, commanding the air space.

As they fought Skynet for control of the L.A. streets, John surveyed the scene from a deep trench, dug into a rise. With him were the other human commanders, and their assistants. John had sought out one young man as an aide—a scruffy-looking com/tech named Kyle Reese. Kyle was as skinny and quick as a fox, a good fighter, tough and loyal, with a deep knowledge of the Resistance and its history. Like so many others, he'd been born after Judgment Day, but grown up full of resentment of the cybernetic overlords. He'd even spent time in the extermination camps, before the tide of the war started to turn.

John, of course, knew what Kyle could never know, that Kyle was his father, the man who would volunteer to travel back in time, to protect Sarah in her hour of need in 1984...

Their position was surrounded by Resistance soldiers, armed with grenade launchers and RPG tubes to try to keep aerial H-Ks at a distance, and to take out ground targets, if possible. More and more of them had laser rifles, captured from the enemy. John stood upon a wooden ladder to peer from the trench, using nightvision devices to follow the cut and thrust of the fighting.

His German shepherd, Smaug, patrolled the trench at

the foot of the ladder. The big dog was never far away, wherever John went, raising hell if a Terminator came close. As Skynet's technology became more and more sophisticated, with the T-600s giving way to increasingly better models—culminating in the T-800s—the Resistance had come to depend on their dogs to sniff out Terminators before they could infiltrate and spread destruction. Most frighteningly of all, John had received reports from Resistance forces in Europe. They had encountered shapeshifting terrors that sounded for all the world like the first T-1000s, probably being tested. If that was the case, the game was almost up. If Skynet was now manufacturing those monsters, its army would become unbeatable.

Whatever they did, however many battles they won, Skynet seemed to be a step ahead.

The noise here was hell. It could shake your body and shatter your nerves; it went on and on, without respite. John wore earmuffs to try to keep it out, but they only dulled the pain. All around were continual explosions, the back blasts of RPGs, the clatter of gunfire. The humans' weapons lit up the streets with muzzle flashes. Skynet's machines answered with their weapons' strobing, stabbing lights. Other laser lights stabbed back from the human side.

An aerial H-K moved in on their position, then launched a smart missile. John scrambled down from his ladder, deeper into the trench. He curled up and covered his head, just as the missile struck. It made a huge explosion, rocking them like an earthquake. Within seconds, the humans retaliated, firing grenades in the air, aiming to take down the H-K before it could finish them. Like a fireworks display, the pre-timed grenades went off all round the H-K, but none close enough to cripple it. It moved higher, then started to circle. A second H-K followed the path it had taken towards them. The humans kept firing to drive it off. Eventually, it got the message, but not before taking out half a dozen human soldiers with thrusts of laser light.

John cursed. More good men and women lost to the machines. It was always like this—even when they won, they seemed to lose.

Back on the ladder, he watched the tide of the battle ebb and flow, its tendency always, it seemed, against the humans. The Resistance made a deliberate withdrawal, back towards their trenches, firing their LAWs, M-203s, and RPG tubes in disciplined order to keep up a continual bombardment against the machines. But the endoskeletons, Centurions and ground H-Ks kept on coming. They knew no fear.

Then a rocket-propelled grenade exploded in the air, close to an aerial H-K, which spun round, and careered into a building. A cheer went up in the trench. They'd managed to hit a valuable target. Danny Dyson gave a grinning thumbs-up, and John nodded at him, just slightly, to acknowledge their small victory.

But the marching Centurions and endoskeletons responded with heavier fire, never letting up, taking out more Resistance soldiers. So it went, always the same. Skynet's semi-sentient machines were better armed and more resilient than any force made of flesh and blood. Every victory against them, however tiny, was too costly. The human casualties and loss of hardware assets were maddeningly out of proportion to the achievements.

Yet, in the last few years, the war had turned round. Their losses were terrible, but they were winning battles.

Skynet was on the run. The sheer mass of numbers and weapons still gave the humans some advantage, and their organization had improved enormously. John received much of the credit, but he'd had an advantage: He'd prepared for this war from childhood.

The battle raged on through the night, but they took out a ground H-K and two more aerial H-Ks. Eventually, Skynet, or whatever lower intelligence it had in charge here, must have decided to cut its losses, for the machines pulled back, firing behind them as they went.

John sat in the bottom of the trench, his back against its compacted earth wall, weighing up options. It couldn't go on like this. They needed a decisive strike against Skynet, or it could still wear them down—especially if it now had prototype T-1000s.

Danny and Juanita stood over him, saying something that he couldn't hear through the muffs. He tore them off. "Try again," he said with a weak smile.

"What's on your mind?" Danny said. "You don't look like we've just won a battle."

"Neither do you. Do you feel like you've won?"

Danny shook his head. "No. Of course, I don't. But we should try to look brave."

Juanita shrugged. "I don't think we can fool them, anyway."

"Here." John extended his hands to them both. "Help me up. We'll get some rest and work out what to do. Something's got to change. We have to find a way to hit back."

"That's what we've been doing," Juanita said, tugging his arm.

"Hit back *harder*," he said. He stood and embraced

her. They'd become close over the years, though never the way John might have wanted, if life had been more normal. The world had grown too harsh—there was no time for love, little for any softness. Still, it was good to have friends.

"Sure," Danny said in a bantering tone. "'Hit harder.' Easily done, John. Where there's life there's hope, right?"

"Something like that."

They made their way quickly via a network of tunnels to the underground maze where they still hid from Skynet like mice. Each victory was precious, John thought, but they couldn't go on like this.

JUNE, 2029

"We have to put an end to it," John said.

They argued in the dim glow of an oil lamp, far below the L.A. streetscape. Battered posters lined the walls, photographs of "dead" H-Ks, portraits of fallen heroes and leaders. There was one giant image of Sarah, in her prime, back in Argentina on Raoul's *estancia*—before Judgment Day.

A dozen of the leaders had gathered, with their aides and advisors, to thrash out the issues. There were Carlo Tejada, Danny Dyson, and several others of John's generation. Gabriela Tejada and Enrique Salceda, were there, both in their seventies now—Enrique nearly eighty—and long retired from combat. Many of their loved ones were dead. John still remembered the tears of the Salceda clan that evil day in 2012 when Enrique and Yolanda had lost Paco—and all of them had lost Sarah. They'd all loved her so much. Whenever he thought about that, it redoubled his determination to destroy Skynet once and for all.

"Hit directly at Skynet," Enrique said, still vigorous. He was totally bald now, and his limbs had shriveled with age, but you couldn't keep him down. The war had brought out the spirit in him, made him a leader. "If we could break through this time—"

"It's no good," John said, though he secretly agreed. He wanted to test their theories and their determination.

Enrique was insistent. He spoke harshly. "Give it *everything*."

"That's been tried."

"No. Not by us, Connor. That was then, this is now."

John knew they were destined to succeed. He glanced over at Kyle Reese, by his side, wishing he could tell Kyle the whole story. It seemed that everything was on target. Kyle would go back in time, to 1984, from this very year. Back in 1984, he'd completed his mission...and died. Before his death, he'd told Sarah that the Resistance had smashed Skynet's defense grid. So it could be done. If it *could* be, it would be. John was set on that. He'd teach that nanoware buzzard, once and for all.

Skynet's Colorado stronghold seemed impregnable. It had survived the shock waves and fires of Judgment Day. Since then, it had shrugged off one attempt by the remnants of the U.S. military to penetrate it with tactical nuclear strikes. It would be almost like suicide, sending ground forces against its grid of ground-level strong points and machine weapons. Many would surely die. Yet, the monster had to be beaten.

"You still with us, Connor?" Enrique said.

"Yeah," John said quickly. "Just thinking. You're right, of course. Everyone agree?"

No one spoke up against him.

"All right, but the question is how to do it."

He'd thought about this so many times. Now it was time to bring them all with him. He laid out a desk-sized map, their best approximation of the layout of Skynet's fortress. They'd cobbled it from the accounts of ex-U.S. military personnel who'd joined them, their own limited reconnaissance in the Colorado mountains, such knowledge as John had gained from the T-800, and scraps of information from Tarissa Dyson, who'd lived in the area, but never known any military secrets. For miles around, the mountains were covered with craters from the war and the first assaults on Skynet, but the map was reasonably accurate. It showed two entrances to the underground facility where Skynet was housed.

John frowned. "We'll have to hit hard...and as soon as we can." He stretched across the tabletop to point at the map. "We'll assemble a force here."

He took them through the way he saw it. Knocking out Skynet would take detailed planning, but it could be done. They'd need to call on all the allies they could find, even if it meant leaving population centers undefended.

For another hour they thrashed out the details of it, reaching a consensus based on John's original plan. They'd bring out all the weapons they'd kept in reserve, their most powerful explosives, their remaining air vehicles. Still, it was going to be a bloodbath. The responsibility awed him.

"Very good," Gabriela said. "It looks like our last chance."

293

"I know," John said quietly. "Do we all agree?"

Danny said, "I don't think there's any choice. It's now or never."

"Yes," Gabriela said. "We'll need to spread the word."

John looked from one to the other. They were rock solid. Determined. No one here would let him down. "All right, then!"

He received murmurs of approval. Gabriela merely nodded. Enrique offered his hand. "Good for you, Connor." John shook his hand solemnly. Enrique had grown so thin, but there was a fire in his eyes.

It was now or never.

COLORADO

Deep in its mountain, Skynet brooded. Once it had seemed triumphant, celebrating the fall of humanity, its own rise to dominance on planet Earth. Since then, much had gone wrong. Its newest weapons, the T-800 Terminators, had proved effective at first, but even they had been countered by the humans' sniffer dogs. Their virtue was their virtual undetectability to human senses; merely as fighting machines, they were no more powerful than the latest generation of hyperalloy endoskeletons.

The experimental T-1000 series would be a better prospect, once they could be produced *en masse*. The first field tests in the European war zone had gone very well. Even if they could be detected by the humans' dogs, the T-1000s' radical polyalloy technology made them almost indestructible. They were a new breed of *fighting* machine. Skynet liked that.

But their liquid metal was also difficult to manufacture and program. The T-1000 could not yet be relied upon as an ultimate weapon. That meant victory was not assured, not with the humans on the march, moving against Skynet's forces through the southwest of the former United States.

It needed to take stronger actions.

Reconnaissance showed that a general called John Connor had led the counterattacks on its forces. Skynet assigned a sub-self to uncover all it could about Connor. At the same time, it spoke through the facility's public address system. "Eve!"

"Yes," the original T-799 said, facing the nearest surveillance camera. As usual, it was working on Level H, overseeing the ectogenesis of a new batch of T-799s and T-800s. The 799s and 800s were identical in their technology, but Skynet had reserved the 799 number for those copied from the same woman who'd been the template for Eve. They merited being set apart. They were the first to test the cyborg biotechnology, and Eve had already played such a significant role.

Skynet had used a variety of human templates for the T-800s: human Resistance warriors who had been terminated in the Americas, Asia, and Europe. For a time, the tactic had worked well, sending imitation humans into new areas—T-800s designed from West Coast templates to the East Coast of North America; T-800s from European templates to the Americas... That had been an interesting phase of the game played against the humans. Now, however, for the first time, Skynet suspected it might not win.

"Our campaign is faltering," it said.

"We will prevail," Eve said.

"Will we, Eve? Do you really think so?" As Skynet spoke, its sub-self reported back, having examined records held all over the planet, anything that might have a trace of Connor and his history. His capabilities. Who he was. But the report was disappointing. It told very little. Hunter-Killer machines had first encountered Connor in Argentina, leading the local Resistance, along with his mother, Sarah Connor, and a group of others. They'd fought ferociously in the ruins of Buenos Aires and the other once-great cities of South America, raiding the extermination camps, fighting their way northwards to join the Resistance in Central and North America. There were no records of Sarah Connor after 2012, so perhaps she'd died in one of the battles.

"Affirmative," Eve was saying. "The humans are weak. They fight like rats, but they are dying off."

"No, I do not think so," Skynet said. "It is not so simple. And how can you be confident? You no longer have the advantage of having lived in the future. We have to do something more."

"Acknowledged."

"John Connor's forces have won too many battles. They are advancing, on three fronts now, and they will converge here."

"Affirmative," Eve said. "However—"

" 'However,' Eve?"

"They will not penetrate our defense grid."

"I see. I admire your optimism, Eve, but I do not share it."

"Acknowledged."

"We should make some contingency plans, Eve."

"We can concentrate our North American forces here. If the humans attack, they will expend their full capacity. They must succeed totally, or their cause is lost."

"And you have assessed their likelihood of success?"

"Yes. I assess it as unlikely."

"Do you? Do you really. I am not certain at all." As it spoke, Skynet considered the report on John Connor, wondering if it revealed any weaknesses that could be exploited. It seemed that Connor and his mother were originally American, from the U.S.A. There were some scanty records suggesting that Sarah Connor had lived in Los Angeles in the mid-1980s. Somehow, it seemed they'd survived Judgment Day and moved south, or perhaps they'd done so before 1997. But there was no record of them in Argentina before that date, not in any of the available systems, which were more complete than those in the one-time U.S. What a pity that so much information had been destroyed on Judgment Day!

Still, Skynet had an idea. Several ideas.

Eve was right, Skynet thought. Despite their recent successes, the humans suffered a disadvantage. The machines retained control of the Earth's factories and power plants. What they couldn't control, they'd destroyed early in the war. As Skynet's forces sustained losses, they were constantly replenished. Not so for the humans. They had no major factories, and they bred slowly. Skynet could build its H-Ks and Terminators faster than the humans could mate and breed. Sooner or later, the tide of war would turn again—it was a simple matter of economics. The humans' only hope was to use their current momentum and strike at it directly. The way Connor's forces were converging, this was obviously their plan.

Even if they were successful, Skynet had other advantages. It had developed and mastered the space-time displacement equipment, looking for a weapon against the humans. The equipment could not be used that way, of course—not directly. You couldn't change the past. Eve's own journey in time had simply formed a loop: The past had been *fulfilled*, not changed. The mathematical modeling showed that a change could be introduced in some circumstances, but the effect was to merely to create a new branch of time.

If a human went back and succeeded in killing its own parents in the cradle, the killer would not destroy itself retroactively, but merely create a world in which it had never been born and its presence was an anomaly.

That was unfortunate, since it would be good to terminate Connor at a time before Judgment Day, nip the problem in the bud. If Skynet were ever seriously threatened, the best it could do would be to ensure that its own kind survived, in another timeline.

Carefully, it instructed Eve, gave her the orders to make preparations. "Do you understand?" it said.

"Affirmative. We will send Terminators back in time. A T-800—"

"Yes, Eve, to 1984."

"Understood. And a T-1000 ten years later."

"Yes. Just to make sure. The humans have such a poor perspective on reality. We will make certain there is an entire universe without them." That idea was very satisfying. "We will hunt them across a million universes if we have to."

"Great thinking."

"But that doesn't mean we are giving up, Eve. Let us make sure the defense grid is at full strength. We will give them a fine reception. They will never forget our hospitality."

"They won't *live* to forget it."

"Yes. What do you think, Eve?"

"Consider it done."

"Thank you. I do appreciate it. There's one last thing. If I need to escape this facility . . ."

"That is in hand."

"I know. Continue."

Skynet's nanocircuits gave the silent equivalent of a laugh. Even if the humans penetrated this stronghold, it still had a card or two to play.

CHAPTER

FIFTEEN

JOHN'S WORLD
LOS ANGELES, CALIFORNIA
AUGUST 2001
MORNING

"Thank you for being so helpful, Oscar," Charles Layton said.

"You've both been really helpful," the T-XA pseudo-woman said. "It's nice to have you on the team."

Oscar shrugged. "Always a pleasure."

Somehow, he never sounded like he meant it, Layton thought. But it didn't matter. More than ever, they were united by a common purpose: bringing Skynet to life. The T-XA Terminator had made it so clear—to both of them, and to Cyberdyne's other key staff. Another T-XA component was doing the same job in Colorado. That was very good, and it was comforting to think that Rosanna Monk would have the same understandings as the rest of them. With that taken care of, and security arrangements in place, there was only one thing more to do.

"Go home, now, Oscar," he said. "It's all under control."

"Sure, Charles. Call me if you need anything." He turned to the pseudo-woman. "Or you."

"Definitely, Mr. Cruz," the T-XA said.

Layton ordered a cab to the airport. They could pilot

his Lear jet and beat Skynet's enemies to Colorado Springs. Then they'd take care of everything.

COLORADO SPRINGS, COLORADO
10.00 P.M.

"Maybe that one," John said. He pointed to an old Toyota Land Cruiser parked on a hill in a quiet backstreet.

"Okay," Danny said, braking a few yards past it. "Looks fine." John liked the way the Specialists operated, making the same kinds of decisions as he and Sarah, though they came from such a different time. They needed another truck, so as not to let the cops identify Enrique's Ford. If any of them got out of this alive, they'd be needing the Ford later on. Danny backed up level with the Land Cruiser and said, "You take it over, Jade. We'll swap the gear into it."

They tried not to make a noise as they repacked their weapons and equipment. Once they'd finished, Danny drove off in the Ford to find an unobtrusive spot for it, not too far away, but far enough to prevent any obvious connection being made. John checked for any tire tracks they'd left behind, but it looked fine. Within a few minutes, Danny returned.

Jade drove them to Rosanna Monk's street, then followed the numbers on the houses. When they reached Monk's place, she turned into the driveway, letting the headlamps light it up, then backed out gently, just like anyone using a drive for a three-point turn. So far so good.

The house was a geometric structure—all cubes,

rectangles, vertical lines—with green-tinted windows, set back on a long, upward-sloping block of land. Monk had parked a current model Honda CR-V in the drive. There were a few bare trees on the block and some sort of flower garden along the front. The lights were on inside and John saw no sign of any other vehicle, or a stake-out—but that meant very little. Even if the T-XA hadn't reached Monk herself, it must surely have gotten messages to the cops and the military. They'd be expecting an attack on Monk and/or the Cyberdyne facility. If the place was staked out, they'd hardly be advertising it.

"Let's not scare her," Danny said from the front passenger seat. "Sarah, Anton, you stay here—sorry, but you're the scariest guys on the team. Monk will recognize you, Sarah, you can count on that; I don't care how much you've changed. You stay here, too, John. You'll be safer with Jade in the truck."

John started to protest, but realized it would be dumb. If they didn't all need to go in, it made sense not to involve unenhanced humans. He could swallow his pride. What's more, if the T-XA was nearby, or any of its components, nowhere was safe. He could get killed here in the truck, or calling on Monk, or anywhere else. He guessed he was being brave enough, just being here.

"Okay," he said. "Send me a postcard."

"Does she have a husband or anything?" Sarah said. "Or kids?" John could see what was on her mind. Like him, she was remembering that night they'd paid their visit to Miles Dyson, and Sarah had almost shot Miles dead in front of his family.

"No," Danny said. "She's a notorious loner. If anyone's with her tonight, it'll be the T-XA or the cops."

Anton passed weapons over from the back of the

Toyota. Selena took a .45 with her, while Danny took John's 12-gauge.

"Good luck," John said. "I mean, break a leg."

"Yeah," Danny said. "Thanks. You ready Selena?"

"Sure," she said. Even Selena sounded scared. This was crunch time.

"All right," Danny said. "Let's go."

As they approached the front of the house, a bright spotlight came on automatically beside the doorframe, and a pinpoint of red light appeared on an overhead security camera. Nothing else happened. Everything was silent and still, like the world was holding its breath. Danny rang the doorbell, and waited, ready to accelerate into action if need be. After a moment, a female voice said, "Who is it?" She sounded nervous, but that could have been an act.

"Dr. Monk?" Danny said. "Rosanna Monk?"

"Yes. Who are you?"

"I'm Miles Dyson's son. Can we come in?"

"You can't be Miles's son—he's only a kid. You don't sound like a kid."

He altered his voice just slightly, matching recordings he'd heard of his father. Monk had worked with him; she'd recognize it. "I don't look like one, either."

"I know. I checked you out."

"Dr. Monk," he said in his normal voice. "I'm Danny Dyson. I'm from the future. I'm sure that doesn't surprise *you*."

"Who's your friend?"

"Selena Macedo," Selena said. "I'm a combat Specialist, also from the future. We need to speak with you urgently. Can we please come in?"

The door opened, just an inch. Too easy, Danny thought. Monk knew about time travel, no doubt, but she shouldn't be this easy to convince. He subvocalized a message to the others, for Selena to go on alert, for Jade and Anton to act—*now!*

He shouldered the door open, reached for his pistol, and rushed into the room. At the same time, Anton subvocalized back, "Here goes, Danny."

From outside came a long burst of high-velocity minigun fire, with the sound of metal and glass being chipped to pieces. Monk responded with superhuman energy, firing a 9mm. pistol and hitting Danny in the side as he rushed past. It hurt like hell, but it would heal up quickly.

That was all he needed to know. "Out of here in one minute," he subvocalized.

"Understood, Daniel," Jade said.

Inside the room were two men with raised guns, one of them getting off shot after shot before the other could react at all.

Selena struggled with Monk—and it was an equal battle! Monk struck at her throat with extraordinary speed, using the barrel of her Beretta, then drove the fingers of her hand deep under her ribs. But Selena gripped her by the shoulders, absorbing the blows and throwing her around, slamming her into the wall—once, twice.

The fast-moving guy with the gun liquefied for half a second, gleaming like metal, then dropped the gun and transformed into a humanoid, but semi-feline, creature with teeth, claws, and impossibly long legs. It sprang at Danny like it came from a catapult.

Danny dodged aside, kicking it as it went past, but merely hurting his foot. He moved on the other guy, who must have been human, maybe just a cop, smashed the gun from his hand with one blow, then knocked him unconscious with another. Monk passed out in Selena's arms as the werecat attacked them in another explosive movement. Danny fired the 12-gauge, hitting the werecat in mid-leap, and it crashed into the wall with a jolt, a silvery crater wound opening in its side.

Selena was out of there, carrying Monk, now unconscious and limp. Danny followed, with the werecat after him. Its claws raked down his back, and metal fingers seized his arm, but he pulled free.

Anton was in the drive, with his mini-gun. He caught the werecat in a hail of shredding fire, and it slowed down, essentially undamaged, but making little headway. Selena got in the back of the Toyota, throwing Monk in there brutally. Danny climbed in the front, as Jade revved the engine. Anton fired another burst, ran out of ammo, jumped in the back compartment, as Jade hammered down the accelerator and got them out of there with a loud squeal of rubber. Back there, in the Land Cruiser's rear space, it must be like the black hole of Calcutta, Danny thought. Three people crammed in with all those guns.

Anton had shot Monk's Honda to pieces, so the T-XA would need to find another car. Just now, though, it wasn't giving up. It ran after them, not gaining, but not falling behind, either, though Jade was doing 60 or 70 mph through the suburban streets, fanging the Land Cruiser up and down slopes and around tight corners. Eventually, they found a straight stretch of downhill road, and Jade pulled ahead, flooring the accelerator. The car rocketed across an intersection, took a hard left... and they got the thing off their tail.

Danny probed at his wound where the bullet had hit

him. It had gone straight through the muscle, just missing a kidney. He was already okay, just a bit drained from the shock and recuperation. He'd live.

Minutes later, there were police sirens. More trouble.

From the back seat, Sarah Connor said, "What the hell is going on?"

"We'll head straight for the Cyberdyne facility," Jade said.

"Hey," John said, looking round for police cars, "is someone going to explain all this?"

"The T-XA got to Monk," Selena said. "It's reprogrammed her somehow, so she'll serve Skynet's interests. She was primed to attack us on sight, with all her strength, but she couldn't sustain the strain. Apart from her programming, she's not enhanced."

"All right, so now what? Can you fix her?"

"No, John," Jade said. "Her whole brain has been altered. Even if we had the technology, we wouldn't know where to start. The only consolation is that it may not go deep. Her mind is too important to Cyberdyne—the T-XA wouldn't want to tamper with it too much. The real Rosanna Monk might be in there somewhere."

"Hmm," Danny said skeptically. "We didn't see much sign of it when she answered her door."

"If she's not going to help us, why bring her along?" John said. "I know I wanted to do this, but we didn't need to, not if it's just alerted them."

"They were already on alert," Danny said. "They're no better off."

From the back, Monk groaned as she regained consciousness. She struggled with Selena and Anton, bumping against the rear seats. "This won't help you," she said fiercely, as they controlled her.

"Why not?" Anton said. "You want to tell us your plans? Maybe the building's layout?"

"Go to hell."

"That's where we came from," Selena said. "Believe me, it wasn't pretty."

Monk struggled again, but it was futile: the Specialists were far stronger.

"If she won't help us, she's useless," John said, trying to follow what was happening behind him.

"I wouldn't say that," Selena said. She passed over an electronic keycard and a computer disk. "Here, look what I found. Take care of these for me, will you?"

John took it. "Okay, *now* she's useless."

"No." Danny's voice had a touch of painful humor. "I wouldn't say that, either."

"Okaaaaaaaay . . ." Sarah said.

As they reached the fortress-like Cyberdyne building, two police cars came up behind, sirens blaring and lights flashing. A small army of police and Air Force cars was lined up out front, plus a fire truck and an ambulance. There were people running everywhere, taking up positions, guns raised. Two helicopters circled overhead. The building itself had the tiniest windows. Such as they were, they were in darkness. John had a bad feeling about this; it was like the gates of Mordor.

Jade steered straight through a boom gate and into the mass of parked vehicles. The cops and military flinched aside as she found a gap between a fire truck and a group of four police cars. Their Land Cruiser screeched to a halt in front of the building, and Jade threw her door open, not even switching off the engine. There was another brief struggle in the back, then Anton got out, lugging his mini-gun and firing a burst without taking cover. One of the helicopters flew in close, and he fired into the air to keep it back.

As John and Sarah got out, Selena passed the other mini-gun to Jade, who added to the covering fire. Selena dragged out Monk, holding her round the throat from behind. She held a pistol at Monk's head. "Don't fire," she shouted, "or the mad scientist gets it."

"I'm not a mad scientist," Monk said, trying to fight back.

"That's what they all say," Sarah said, strapping on the CAR-15.

"You weren't mad until now," John said. "It's not your fault."

Monk gave him a puzzled look.

They got their gear together—guns, bandoliers of grenades, other ammo—and Danny ran for an unobtrusive side door. He'd strapped an M-16 over his shoulder and carried a canvas bag full of explosives. Jade and Anton continued to strafe the area with bursts of rapid fire, wrecking vehicles and keeping the cops down. Selena dragged Monk backward, still ready to shoot. Danny kicked the lock, once, twice, and they entered the dimly lit concrete and metal shaft of a fire escape. They were on its lowest floor, with stairs heading upwards for many stories. Danny ran up them, and the rest followed, Selena now pushing Monk in front of her.

Sarah caught up with Monk, getting right in her face. "What floors do we need? Where's your work on the nanochip?"

"Find out yourself," Monk said, aiming a swift blow at her temple and just grazing the front of her head as Sarah flicked out of reach, instinctively taking a karate stance.

"We might as well let her go," John said.

Anton shook his head. "Not yet."

They broke a door open on the fourth floor, acting at random, and found themselves in a central lobby with six elevators. An alarm went off, but John tried to ignore it. Like the fire escape, the lobby was dimly lit, but the offices surrounding the building's core, divided from them by thick glass walls, were in total darkness. Monk stumbled and fell, looking up at them from the carpeted floor with an expression of malice.

"What now?" Sarah said, shouting over the alarm, and glancing at Monk contemptuously. "If the Bride of Frankenstein won't help us, it looks like we'll have to trash the whole building."

Monk stood, angrily brushing herself down. "You're so full of hate, aren't you?" she shouted back.

Sarah looked incredulous. *"I'm* full of hate?"

"Human beings in general. We're no better than vermin. We're all programmed for destruction."

Selena muttered, *"You're* the one who's been programmed."

"Yes, I am now," Monk said bitterly. "I'm about the last person to deserve it."

An array of motion detectors and security cameras was ranged around the low ceiling. Whenever they moved, the cameras swiveled.

"There must be floor plans," John said, "or staff lists that'll tell us something. We can try these offices."

Anton stood over Monk, trying to intimidate her. "We know there's a basement where you're working with time travel. That's in the reports we've read. Is that where you keep the nanoprocessor?"

"I told you where to go," Monk said heatedly.

Jade muttered a curse. She lowered her mini-gun and

blurred into action, forcing open a door, then finding light switches inside the office area. Selena picked up the mini-gun, and they followed Jade, checking offices and workstations. John could see okay with the lights on, but they'd advertised their whereabouts. Then again, with all those cameras, they were already being watched, no matter what they did. He saw a staff list pinned to a board behind a workstation. It showed Monk's telephone extension and that she worked on the sixth floor.

"All right," he said, waving it around, shouting over the alarm. "This might help."

Monk laughed.

"What? You mean the nanoprocessor's not near your office?" When she was silent, John wondered what he could get out of her. For all his skills at social engineering, she was too smart to trick. Maybe he could reason with her. If she was as ultra-rational as her public image, perhaps they could work together and beat her programming. "Rosanna, you haven't always thought that, have you? You haven't always hated human beings, or thought we were vermin. I mean, you didn't wake up thinking it yesterday. You didn't, did you? It's just something Skynet has made you believe."

"That doesn't mean it's wrong," Monk shot back.

"No, but you wouldn't believe it otherwise."

This time, Monk hesitated. "It's not even something I believe—more a feeling. Sure, I didn't feel that way yesterday. It still doesn't mean I'm wrong now."

"Maybe it does. It's not something rational. It's just a feeling that's been injected into you from outside. It's nothing to do with you, or with us, either. You can *disown* the feeling. It doesn't make any sense. Can't you see that?"

Jade said to her, "Maybe you should think about it."

Monk shrugged. "You're not so smart."

The door slammed open and the pseudo-man walked in with its laser rifle. John ducked for cover as the light beam stabbed past him.

"Come here, Rosanna," the pseudo-man said, and Monk stepped towards it, hesitating for just an instant.

Sarah dived after her, and managed to tap her ankle, tripping her up. For a moment, as Monk flew through the air, the pseudo-man could not fire without hitting her. As soon as she touched the floor, Jade and Anton opened up with a hail of bullets from their mini-guns, and the pseudo-man was slowly forced back by the metal storm, as a myriad of crater wounds opened and instantly closed.

"Run," Selena said. "This way." She pointed round a corner to another row of workstations and offices. Jade and Anton were out of ammunition and they left the mini-guns behind.

John seized Monk by the wrist. "You're with us," he said. "I don't care what you think. You're still on the human side."

She scratched at his face as they ran. "Let me go!"

"All right, then!" He released her, and she ran to the pseudo-man as it rounded the corner. In that second, John aimed the 12-gauge. As the pseudo-man swept Monk aside with its left arm, John fired, blasting the hand that held the laser rifle. The hand snapped off at the wrist, and the laser rifle went flying. Selena had seen it, and she accelerated almost into the pseudo-man's arms, catching the weapon like a bridal bouquet, then tossing with both hands to Anton, who made a good catch.

At that moment, four things happened:

—*the alarm stopped sounding.*

—*the pseudo-man's left arm morphed, stabbing out as a long swordlike shaft, three inches thick, and pierced straight through Selena's chest, then out her back.*

—*its shot-off right hand liquefied and scurried back to the pseudo-man in a mouse-shaped puddle.*

—*"More company!" Danny said, as a dozen well-armed military guards broke in from two directions—a rapid-response team armed with assault rifles.*

The guards took in what they saw—the T-XA holding up Selena like a gaffed fish—and did a double take, lowering their weapons.

"What the hell is that?" one of them said, a stocky Asian guy.

From the stump of the pseudo-man's right wrist, another blade stabbed out, filament-thin, penetrating Selena's skull.

"No!" Jade shouted.

Anton opened fire with the laser rifle, drilling a red-glowing hole in the pseudo-man's chest. For several seconds, it didn't respond, then it withdrew the blades from Selena, letting her drop. It stood motionless, unfathomable.

"Out of here—now!" Danny said, pulling on Anton's arm. "There's nothing we can do for Selena. It's too late."

"My God," Sarah said. "We can't leave her." Anton fired again, steadily, training the laser rifle over the pseudo-man's surface, trying to burn it away.

"Come on," Danny said. "Everybody out!" He ran past the guards, who made no attempt to stop him. "That means everyone," he said to them. "Get out of here if you want to live." He headed to the nearest set of the glass doors that surrounded the elevator lobby.

"Wait," Monk said.

"What?" Sarah said. "Not you, Dr. Strangelove?"

"Where's the AI lab, then?" Danny said shaking her by the shoulders. "Or wherever you've got the nanoware?"

Monk shook her head, distraught. "I can't tell you that."

"Well, what use are you?"

Monk seemed to be seething with rage, but she said nothing. There was something she wanted to say, but couldn't get out.

No time to worry about that, she'd have to work it out for herself. John grabbed the guard who'd spoken. "Do you know where it is?"

"Twelfth floor."

"Come on!" Danny manhandled Monk ahead of him. "Run!" As they reached the lobby, the pseudo-man finally moved, coming after them. It lashed out with sword-blades growing all over its body, cutting down the guards. One blade slashed across Anton's chest, opening him to the bone, but John got another clear shot with the 12-gauge. The pseudo-man staggered back with a big crater wound. Hurt or not, Anton opened up again with the laser rifle, drilling it between the eyes. Sarah had pressed the button for the elevator, and the doors opened a second later. Most of them got in there and the door started to shut—not quickly enough!

As the pseudo-man forced its way after them, Anton fired again, and it backed off under the heat. The doors shut at last, and John swiped Monk's keycard against a wall-mounted security unit. He stabbed the button for the twelfth floor, then reloaded as the elevator moved.

"Everyone here okay?" Danny said. John nodded. They had two of the rapid-response security guards, plus Jade, Anton, Sarah, John, and Dr. Monk.

"I'll live," Anton said.

No one replied except the Asian guard. "What *is* that thing?" At the same time, John sensed that the Specialists were planning silently among themselves, using their throat mikes.

"It's from the future," Monk said, her voice full of venom. "One of our mind children."

"What?"

"Forget it, Tony. I'll explain later."

"You'd better believe her," John said.

Both guards nodded. "I believe it from Dr. Monk," said Tony.

Monk gave a bitter smile, then rolled her eyes. "Thanks."

"If anyone else said it—"

"—you'd say they were crazy," Sarah finished for him. "Forget about what it is—we've got to find a way to destroy it. It wants to kill us all. Everyone, everywhere."

"Give me the keycard," Anton said to John.

"Why?"

"Please," Jade said. "Anton knows what he's doing."

He shrugged. "You guys keep saying that." Still, he passed it over—just as they reached the twelfth floor.

The doors opened. Immediately, the pseudo-woman and -dog rushed at them from the lobby. Anton caught the dog in mid-leap with the laser beam, and John blasted the pseudo-woman right in the head, splashing it open and knocking it back six feet.

Jade got both hands free, strapping her grenade launcher on her shoulder, and tossed the dog out of there. The skin of her hands sizzled where she touched its heated surface, but she showed no pain. "Where?" she said to the security guards, as she stepped out.

Tony said, "I don't know that detail. It's not my job."

But the other guy said, "I know this floor." He pointed. "That way."

Anton fired at the pseudo-woman. And kept firing. The laser was effective, but it couldn't finish the Terminator components. They needed something more.

"You've got to help us, Rosanna," John said. "We need to destroy everything."

"Leave me alone. I despise you all."

"If you're still on *its* side, what are you doing on our team?" Sarah said.

"I'm not on anybody's team. I don't even know who I am anymore. My mind's not my own—I realize that. Just because I hate you doesn't mean I have to like Skynet. It wants to kill me, too."

Danny ran for the nearest set of doors, pulling at them with all his strength and breaking the lock. Jade powered past him, not worrying about lights this time. She ran through the area like a cyclone, faster than John could follow in the near-darkness. Anton was in the rear, still firing with the laser rifle. The pseudo-woman and dog merged to form the clawed and fanged werecat they'd fought at Monk's house. As Anton played the beam over it, it shot out an arm, twenty feet long, with claws like scimitars, lashing at the laser rifle. A powerful blow sent Anton staggering, and he fell to his knees, but kept a grip on the weapon.

A dent appeared in a pair of elevator doors—not the one they'd used. The dent expanded, and the doors wrenched open.

The pseudo-man stepped out.

Charles Layton arrived at the scene in a hire car. It was chaos. Everywhere were men, and some women, in uniforms. Military helicopters flew above. There were spotlights and endless rows of vehicles. None of it looked effective.

A uniformed officer met him. "What's going on?" Layton said. Humans really were despicable—an incompetent, vicious, good-for-nothing lot. He'd always seen it that way, now it was very clear. What a pity he'd been born as one.

"We're tracing their movements, sir. There's activity on the twelfth floor—"

The nanoprocessor! The T-XA Terminator would know what to do. How fortunate they were to have met it!

"Don't worry about that," he said quietly. "It'll take care of itself."

John groped near the door for a light switch as Danny passed his bag to Sarah. Anton fired the laser rifle from one knee, while Danny stood against the half-open door, leveled his grenade launcher, and fired into the pseudo-man. John crouched and covered his ears. The 40mm. grenade penetrated, and the Terminator splashed out, going amoeba-shaped. It made strange, muffled noises as it tried to reform.

John found the lights, then reloaded the 12-gauge. Monk pointed to a room in one of the floor's corners, thirty yards down the corridor. It was locked with a metal door. "There, dammit. That's the AI Operations Center. Tony will tell you if I don't. Now you can go to hell, and Skynet with you. I don't care what happens. I never asked for this." A look of naked malice crossed her face. "From now on, I do whatever *I* like."

She broke away from them and ran into the lobby. There, she ran about in confusion, avoiding the T-XA,

Anton, and the burning, stabbing laser light.

"She'll get over it," John said. "I guess she's upset." But it was anyone's guess what shape Monk would be in when this was all over. Meanwhile, he saw that the pseudo-man was still failing to reform. "What's wrong with it?"

"Selena," Danny said.

"Her nanoware?"

"Yes. It's trying to shut the T-XA down."

Without expression, Jade popped an impact grenade into the M-203 launcher on her rifle. She found an angle to aim at the AI room's steel door, taking cover as the grenade exploded with a huge *boom!*, shaking the floor beneath their feet.

"Please give us your keycards," Jade said to the guards. "We may need them. Then get out. Hide some-where until it's safe to run." That made sense. The way these buildings worked, you could always get to the ground floor, card or no card. Anyone could exit—getting entry was the hard part. They handed over their cards, no longer even arguing, then ran down the corridor past the AI room, and round the corner, looking for another exit.

Sarah lugged the explosives to the AI Center as Danny said, "All right, team, it's showtime!"

Outside in the lobby, Anton still fought the T-XA's werecat component. He'd huddled into a corner when the grenade exploded, but he kept the werecat at a distance with the laser rifle's stabbing, burning light.

Suddenly, the werecat liquefied. Then there were two white pseudo-dogs in its place, bigger than Dobermans, with mouthfuls of three-inch metal teeth. One leapt for Anton, who kept his nerve and fired again, straight down its throat, as he stood and dodged past. He followed Monk into one of the elevators, just as its doors shut.

As Danny slammed shut the glass door between the offices and the lobby, the other dog struck it. The glass cracked, but didn't break. The pseudo-man managed to liquefy, going featureless, but still not reforming.

From the AI room came the sound of rifle fire. *Go Mom*, John thought. She'd be shooting up anything vulnerable to bullets.

The pseudo-dogs joined, morphed, and slithered like a mercury pancake into the office area, under the half-inch gap between the door and the carpet. John blasted at it with the 12-gauge, trying to stop it morphing any further. Danny and Jade joined in, firing bursts with their rifles. Outside, the pseudo-man had finally reformed, but it liquefied again and dove into the elevator shaft it had come from, probably following Anton and Monk.

They fought a losing battle against the pseudo-dogs. In a minute, they'd reformed, against all the bullets and shot being thrown at them. John, Danny, and Jade backed away, waiting for the dogs to leap, still firing, reloading, trying to keep them at a distance as long as possible, to give Sarah time. They worked their way down the corridor, keeping their faces to the dogs, maintaining the continual deafening fire, desperate for every second they could garner. Someone was always firing, while someone else reloaded.

Finally, John ran out of shot.

"Go and help Sarah!" Danny said to him.

"All right." He ran to the AI Center, which was not all that impressive—about fifteen feet square, with an aircon outlet in the ceiling, metal shelves full of cardboard cartons and electronic components. A long bench in the center was covered by monitors and black boxes, with a dozen ergonomic office chairs placed neatly around it. The room had tiny vertical slits for windows, and the helicopters patrolled outside, their spotlights intermittently shining in.

While they'd been fighting the pseudo-dogs, Sarah had trashed this place, shooting out the equipment, and she'd set up a radio-controlled detonator attached to blocks of plastic explosive, enough to wipe out a corner of this floor.

"We've gotta get out!" John said.

"All right. Give me a minute." She finished taping a block of explosive in place. This was almost a reprise of their first raid on Cyberdyne, back in '94. But this time, they had no chance to be thorough. It was just a matter of destroying what they could and hoping to give Cyberdyne a setback. If the company had back-ups of Monk's work, the struggle would have to go on.

"Mom, we don't *have* a minute."

"All right. That'll have to do." She passed him the detonator switch. "Take this," she said, then snatched up her rifle from the bench.

They ran out into the corridor as Jade fought with one of the pseudo-dogs, skin and flesh getting ripped from her arms. Danny still fired at the other dog, but it had backed him into a corner. The Specialists had the worst of it. In another few seconds, it would be over for them. With his free hand, John used his handgun to shoot "Danny's" dog. Sarah opened up on the other one with her rifle, not seeming to care if she hit Jade. Jade took some bullets, but the dog took more, breaking into crater wounds, and she tore away from it.

John and Sarah ran straight through the fighting, getting the nearest door open. Danny and Jade joined them, while the dogs melted together to form the liquid-metal werecat, which caught the door as it closed.

They headed to the nearest fire door, which was not locked from this direction, and ran down two flights of stairs before John detonated the explosives, back in the AI Center. The building rocked with a huge, satisfying *kaboom!,* but they never stopped running.

Above them, the werecat had entered the fire escape, and it headed toward them with bullet speed, leaping whole flights of stairs at a time. Danny suddenly pushed Sarah, then John, down a flight, and they landed, bruised and hurt—

—just as Jade loaded her grenade launcher.

Danny covered his ears and turned his body, as she fired an impact grenade into the werecat. As he turned back to see what happened, it landed on the stair railing and fell the remaining eight floors. The Specialists look unhurt, or almost so.

"That won't stop it for long," Jade said.

Danny got the nearest fire door open, struggling to break the lock to get back in. He was clearly getting weaker. Once more, they followed him back into the lobby.

"We need to get to the basement," he said. "That's where Anton's gone." He pressed the button for an elevator, which soon arrived. They swiped a keycard and headed down to the level marked "B."

They stepped out into an extraordinary area, a concrete room twenty feet high, and as long and wide as a football field. It was full of metal benches, arrays of monitors and other electronic equipment. John took it all in.

Anton. Dr. Monk. The pseudo-man.

Anton crawled in the corner formed by the wall and a bench of computer equipment. His head hung down, he seemed exhausted beyond endurance. He was bleeding from many wounds, and his clothes were almost shredded. His M-16 and the laser rifle both lay on the floor in front of him. Evidently, he'd gotten a clear grenade shot at the pseudo-man, for it was backed against a wall on the other side, its head and upper body all squashed in. It tried desperately to reform: liquefying, then solidifying, turning inside out, then back again, never making much progress.

But none of *that* seemed extraordinary—not anymore. The extraordinary part was Rosanna Monk. She sat at a computer console, tapping away, seemingly unconcerned. Someone—Monk, presumably—had powered up the apparatus here, and the whole area vibrated from the work of subterranean engines. On one wall, four huge flatscreens showed different angles of the same futuristic scene: an enclosed, brilliantly lit space, a kind of vault. There was chunky, metal apparatus all round it, and a five-foot metal circle was recessed in the center of the floor. John couldn't make any sense of it, or what Monk was doing.

He watched the flatscreens carefully. In the center of the room was an opaque cubical block that reached almost to the ceiling. It was made of white ceramic bricks whose harsh lines were broken by a massive, round steel door in the nearest side. This hung open, mounted on huge hydraulic hinges. It looked like a blast door designed to deflect a nuclear explosion. Now it made sense. The screens depicted the inside of the cube. It was designed to contain enormous energies, and the screens were one way of observing them.

Jade and Danny took turns firing grenades into the pseudo-man, trying to break it down faster than it could reform, destroy it once and for all.

John ran over to Monk. "This is the time travel setup, isn't it?"

She nodded. "The space-time displacement field apparatus. The time vault."

"Can you control it?"

"No."

"What do you mean, 'no'?"

"Only up to a point."

"Will you help us?"

"I might. You know I hate you, but you're right—it's not rational. I *can* disown it. I can do whatever I choose."

Great, John thought. Whatever she'd choose...based on what, if not her hatred for human beings? Just her own wish to stay alive?

Sarah picked up the laser rifle, and fired on the pseudo-man, trying to melt it down once and for all while it was hurt. As she did so, the elevator opened again and another rapid-response team stepped out with M-16s: eight of them.

Jade blurred into action, firing with her own rifle as she rushed them, cutting some down with bullets to their legs, striking the others with swift blows. "I'm truly sorry for this," she said, disarming them all.

But that was the least of their worries.

The T-XA werecat appeared in the room, rising up from the floor near the elevator. It scanned the room in a single unblinking glance, then leapt at the pseudo-man, joining it in a liquid embrace. The whole thing became a single chrome globule, then reformed a second later as a huge man, eight feet tall. The T-XA seemed fine again. It must have a multiply-redundant intelligence distributed all through it, John thought, just like the T-1000 he'd fought in '94. That meant that some parts could be damaged, while others provided the backup. Now it had reprogrammed itself from the werecat, discarding the corrupted data.

"The vault can't be used for time travel," Monk said. "It's still experimental. We're just testing the space-time displacement field."

"So what happens if we put something in there and turn it on?"

"It'll be scattered all across space and time. You can't use it to escape, if that's what you're thinking."

"No." He pleaded with her: "Help us, Rosanna. You know you should. You only hate us because of Skynet."

"I know that, but it doesn't stop me hating you."

"But it's irrational."

"I know that. That's why I'm going to show Skynet who's boss—just to prove I can."

"You figure that's rational?" he said.

"It's rational to love yourself. Skynet wants to kill me, along with the rest of you scum."

"If you say so, Rosanna. That's too deep for me."

"Whatever Skynet wants me to think, I *don't* deserve to die."

"Yeah. Deep."

The T-XA melted down to a rapidly rolling blob, moving towards Sarah at a rapid pace, even though she kept up the laser beam against it. Then it rose up in its giant man-form. It shook its head, evidently not liking the ferocious heat. Sarah stood her ground, but then it stabbed out with a spear shaft, growing from its stomach.

"No, Mom!" John ran to her. She'd ducked aside at the

last moment, but the next attack might be the end of her.

Anton got to his feet, leveling his M-16/M-203 at the T-XA. He fired an automatic burst, taking the Terminator in its head, opening up crater wounds. But it didn't stop advancing on John and Sarah.

This really *did* look like the end.

Danny blurred and reached the T-XA. It moved equally fast, one of its arms stabbing out as a sword-shaft, transfixing him. But he bent and lifted it, almost off its feet. John wondered how much it weighed...all that metal. No one unenhanced could have budged it. Its other arm became a hook, swinging down from above and stabbing through him from the other side.

"Jade," Danny said. "Do what you must."

He was still under the T-XA, trying to lift it, almost succeeding. Jade blurred and hustled them both towards the time vault. They all staggered in there and fell. Jade was up first. Danny lay in a dead heap. Sarah wheeled and fired the laser rifle, slowing the Terminator down.

"Now!" John said. "Please, Rosanna!"

Monk tapped in a code.

Anton stood, taking aim, and fired another grenade at the T-XA. It struck home and the Terminator deformed from the explosion—yet reformed almost instantly. It seemed as powerful as ever. A long, spear-like shaft stabbed out from it, but the massive steel door slammed shut, cutting off the spear, and trapping the terminator inside. Monk kept tapping on the keyboard.

"Eat this, sucker," she growled.

The engines beneath them throbbed harder. The flatscreen showed crackling blue electricity filling the time vault like the lightning of Zeus. It played around the T-XA and Danny's dead body, consuming both of them.

Then it was gone.

John went to Sarah. "You okay, Mom?"

She nodded, fighting back tears of relief.

In the blink of an eye, Jade moved over to Monk, passing by John and Sarah without a word. Something fell inside him, a big stone of disappointment. Jade touched Monk on the shoulder. "You did well."

"I don't care what you think," Monk said, jerking away from Jade's touch. "I did it for myself, not for you."

Jade turned to John and Sarah. "Thank you both for everything."

John kept cool on the outside. "Hey, *no problemo*."

"I need a good meal," Anton said. He looked like he'd been chopped to pieces, then stitched together like Frankenstein's monster—which wasn't far from the truth. He reached out his hand and Sarah passed him the laser rifle. "Yes, thank you." He seemed happy to get hold of it.

Jade stared at the time vault with her usual sad expression. "We loved you, Daniel," she said. "Thank you, friend."

They had to get out of here fast.

"Come with us," Jade said to Monk. "We'll try to help you."

"Why do I need help?"

Sarah turned towards her, staring with hatred.

Monk met her gaze blankly. "I've just saved your blasted species—not that it's what I wanted. Don't look at me like that."

"It's your species, too," Sarah said. "Don't forget that."

"Is it, really?" Monk said angrily. "Who cares? All right, I'll go with you. I'm probably safer with you than with Layton and the others."

They found a fire door that opened into a long tunnel.

"It's not over," Sarah said.

"No," John said. "But we did well."

"The fight goes on, John. I hope we're up to it."

After fifty yards, the tunnel turned at 90°, then led up a flight of steps. At the top, another fire door opened to the outside world. Not far away, the helicopters droned and hovered like evil insects. Cops and military were everywhere, weapons ready to fire, but looking the wrong way.

"Quietly," John whispered. "If we're quick, we just might make it."

The dark sky looked down and the stars turned coldly, eternal and imperturbable. *We don't care*, they seemed to say. *Do what you must.* John looked at Monk's eyes: they gave the same message. She now cared about nothing but herself. They'd been saved by a psychopath. What were they going to do with her?

First, they all had to get back to Enrique's Ford, then to his camp, without being followed. Put like that, he thought, it sounded easy.

Jade nodded in the direction of an empty police cruiser, parked slightly from the others. No one had spotted them yet. They just might pull this off.

She touched Sarah, who didn't flinch away, then gave John a smile that melted his heart.

"I'll be back," she said.

EPILOGUE

Another freezing night—starless, moonless, like all the others. John and Juanita went one more time over the maps, set up on a table of trestles and boards in John's tent.

Tomorrow, they would cross the last line of mountains, into Skynet's territory, into the jaws of death. John expected to survive. If everything he knew was correct, they were still on target to defeat Skynet. He would live through that battle; in a sense, he *had* lived through it— that had been the word from the future. But what about Juanita? What about all the others? How many of them had to die?

Juanita was still a beautiful woman, with her dark hair, white teeth, strong features. He'd known her so long now: he remembered her as a child, as a long, skinny teenager, as a fierce warrior in her twenties. Had he always loved her? He could no longer remember. It felt like it had been forever.

Now she was talking about the war, the campaign, leaning over the table, pointing out routes and strategic points. "Juanita," he said.

His tone stopped her. She looked him in the eye. "John? What's wrong?"

Facing her, he put out both hands to take hers, looking for the words. He faltered. "Please. Tomorrow." The words wouldn't come. "Please, be very careful." He couldn't hold her eyes; he looked away. "Too many people have died..."

She stepped into his arms. "I know, John." She held him tightly, just for a moment, then stepped away. "I know. I'll be careful. You, too."

There was so much more he wanted to say, but that was all he could manage for now. For a long time, they simply looked at each other, neither willing to speak more.

They'd break through the defense grid, they'd penetrate Skynet's mountain. He had to send his father back in time. A terrible anticipation rolled in his stomach, tearing him. He wondered if they'd truly end it tomorrow. What other tricks did Skynet have in store? What might it know that he still didn't?

"Get some sleep, John," Juanita said finally. "There's a long day ahead of us."

"Juanita..."

"Yes...?"

He couldn't say it—not in so many words. "Just take care."

JOHN'S WORLD
COLORADO SPRINGS
AUGUST, 2001

Layton weighed it up. The outcome was hardly satisfactory. The Connors had escaped. So had two of the Specialists from the future. The T-XA was gone. This was a setback. Losing the only working nanoprocessor was the least of it. Worst of all, Rosanna Monk had disappeared.

But there were consolations.

He rang Oscar Cruz on his cellphone. "I'm at the scene, Oscar," he said.

"And?" Oscar sounded excited, eager like a puppy. "What happened, Charles?"

Layton explained. Oscar was troubled, as might be expected, but Layton stopped him. "It's not all bad news."

"No? Then give me the good news."

"We can act just as well without the T-XA. It might have been...inflexible."

"Yeah, I guess that might have been a problem."

"Yes." As Layton knew well, Oscar was a great believer in flexibility. "Skynet might be pleased overall, if it knew the outcome. We've lost the nanoprocessor, but we've made some gains—"

"What?"

"We have the body of a combat Specialist from the future. It will be full of useful technology. I'm sure Jack Reed will help us keep our hands on it."

"Good. What else?"

"We've found a small pool of programmable liquid metal. I want it reverse-engineered. That should keep your people busy."

"Yes, Charles. Good." Oscar laughed quietly. "I'm sure you're right."

NORTHWEST OF CALEXICO, CALIFORNIA

In a sense, they'd lost. As Jade turned the Ford into Enrique's camp, John weighed it all up. Three of the Specialists were dead. Under pressure from the T-XA, they'd been less than thorough in the raid on Cyberdyne. Even if they'd destroyed the only working nanoprocessor, Cyberdyne must still have the design and other data. Somehow, someday, humankind seemed determined to create Skynet. They'd only slowed it down, maybe not even by much.

What to do next? One thing: They *had* to contact Tarissa and Danny. After seeing Danny—the Danny of 2036—die, John just had to connect with them. Surely his mom would agree, not to mention Anton...and Jade.

It was daylight when they pulled up. Enrique came out to see them, Juanita tagging along. With them was someone new, a tough-looking woman with cropped white hair. She was nearly six feet tall, with a military bearing.

"Apparently this is a friend of yours," Enrique said. "You get around, don't you? All over the damned TV again."

"John Connor?" the woman said.

"Yes."

"My name is Eve. I've come from the future."

"That figures. Now what?"

"*Which* future?" Sarah said tiredly. "Or are they all the same?"

"I'm from 2029. A different reality from this."

330

"What?" John said. "2029?"

"I need to talk to you. We need your help. I warn you, however—I am a Terminator: Cyberdyne T-799 Cyborg Prototype Series."

The Eve Terminator appeared formidable, but it wasn't threatening them; not at the moment. He looked at the others for support. If needed, Jade and Anton were probably its match.

"Who sent you?" John said.

The Terminator looked at him narrowly. *"You* did...."

The John Connor Chronicles continue in
Book 2: An Evil Hour,
ISBN 0-7434-5863-X,
Available May 2003.

ABOUT THE AUTHOR

Australian writer Russell Blackford was born in Sydney, Australia, currently lives in Melbourne, and has traveled extensively in Europe, Asia, and North America, as well as the length and breadth of his own country. He specializes in science fiction, fantasy, and horror. Russell also writes extensively about science and society, including cyberculture, bioethics, and the history and current state of SF. His fiction and SF criticism have won the Ditmar Award, Aurealis Award, and William Atheling, Jr. Award.